"Ms. Madison has penned another delightful spell that will ensnare and bewitch readers and leave them wanting more . . . This book is one that you won't want to put down until you read it from beginning to end and it will leave you craving more. This is a definite keeper . . ."

—Night Owl Romance

"Fans will enjoy this delightful paranormal romance filled with two wonderful lead characters and a strong support cast . . . Anyone who enjoys *A Taste of Magic* will appreciate this lighthearted frolic as once again, Tracy Madison provides a charming whimsical urban fantasy."

—*Midwest Book Review*

A TASTE OF MAGIC

"*A Taste of Magic* is a yummy concoction that will leave you craving more, more, more from exciting new author Tracy Madison!"

—Nationally Bestselling Author Tori Carrington

"Tracy Madison is an author to watch. *A Taste of Magic* is . . . magically delicious!"

—Annette Blair, Nationally Bestselling Author of
Never Been Witched

"*A Taste of Magic* is a magical tale of romance and revenge. Ms. Madison takes readers on an adventure in baking that's highlighted with tasty treats, sexy men, and a touch of humor."

—Darque Reviews

"This whimsical urban fantasy is a fun tale as the lead character will learn the effect of unintended consequences when she bakes her wish into a cake."

—Harriet Klausner, Genre Go Round Reviews

"[Madison] has a breezy, intimate style that's fun to read."

—*RT Book Reviews*

MAGICAL MATCHUPS: THE PROMISE

There weren't any words etched into the book's cover. A chain of trembles wove through me. I turned the book in my hands, checking the spine, but that was also blank. My shivers increased and goose bumps dotted my arms. When I opened the book, there, written on the first page in spidery handwriting, was:

All happily-ever-after endings have a beginning.
Use this journal to capture those hopes, wishes, and fantasies that are truest of heart, purest of soul.
The magic of your happily-ever-after begins here.
This is my gift to you.

Other books by Tracy Madison:

A BREATH OF MAGIC
A STROKE OF MAGIC
A TASTE OF MAGIC

TRACY MADISON

By Magic Alone

Dorchester
Publishing

DORCHESTER PUBLISHING

December 2010

Published by

Dorchester Publishing Co., Inc.
200 Madison Avenue
New York, NY 10016

ISBN 13: 978-1-4285-1113-2
E-ISBN: 978-1-4285-0980-1

The "DP" logo is the property of Dorchester Publishing Co., Inc.

Printed in the United States of America.

Visit us online at www.dorchesterpub.com.

To my editor, Christopher Keeslar, with my utmost gratitude and respect. Not only have you believed in me and my stories, but you have helped me become a stronger writer. I am continually in awe of your patience, brilliance, and your unflagging ability to make me smile. Thank you.

ACKNOWLEDGMENTS

As always, my heartfelt love and thanks to my family, friends, and critique partners for standing by my side and cheering me on. Your support means the world to me.

I'd also like to thank everyone at Dorchester Publishing for your talent and devotion to publishing fantastic books with gorgeous covers. The first time I held one of my books in my hands, I cried buckets of tears. Thank you for giving me such beautiful books to hold.

Thank you, as well, to my awesome agent, Michelle Grajkowski. I can't imagine doing any of this without you.

By Magic Alone

Chapter One

"I've given this a lot of thought, and I'm pretty sure she's a witch." Kara Lysecki—my formerly sane friend—squirmed in her chair, but her moss green eyes met mine head-on. "And yes, before you ask, I'm well aware of how crazy that sounds."

"Well, okay then. As long as you're aware of that." I sat very still, waiting for the punch line so I could laugh. But when a few seconds passed without Kara offering one, a slow dread began to build. "Tell me you're joking."

"I'm completely serious, Julia. A good witch, though. Like Glinda from *The Wizard of Oz*."

I narrowed my eyes, still looking for any sign of humor. "Uh-huh. And how many margaritas did you consume with lunch to reach this illuminating conclusion?"

Kara flipped her gaze to our other friend, Leslie Meyers, who was seated next to her in my office. "I told you she wouldn't believe us."

Leslie, who thus far had remained so quiet I'd almost forgotten she was here, had an odd expression on her face. My dread increased. "I've also thought a lot about this, and I've changed my mind, Kara. I don't think she's a witch."

Whew. For a second there, I was seriously starting to worry. "Yay for the voice of reason. Now that the fun and games portion of this meeting is over with, can we move on to business?"

Kara's cheeks flushed bright pink. "You changed your mind but couldn't be bothered to tell me? Jeez, thanks Leslie."

"I didn't have a chance! You jumped right in as soon as we sat down." Leslie sucked in a breath. "Look, I haven't completely altered my thoughts on this. I just don't think Verda is a witch. I . . . I think she's more like a fairy godmother. And we're her—"

"Cinderellas!" Kara bobbed her head so hard that her short mop of blonde curls bounced. "That's perfect, Les. Why didn't I think of that? Verda's taken us under her wing to find us our perfect love matches with her own special brand of magic." A goofy grin lit her heart-shaped face. "*Fairy* magic."

I silently counted to ten. My two best friends stared at me with stars shimmering in their eyes, as if they thought I was going to leap on board their insanity train. Not likely. I'd never been one for fairy tales.

"Only one of you can be Cinderella," I pointed out, not bothering to mask my sarcasm. "But hey, there are plenty of other Disney heroines to choose from. We have Snow White, Belle, Aurora, and . . . um . . . Little Red Riding Hood. Take your pick."

"Little Red Riding Hood is not a Disney heroine. She was also nearly eaten by a wolf." Kara shivered. "As for your other examples, neither Leslie nor I would fall for the Beast, so that leaves out Belle—"

"What's wrong with the Beast?" Leslie interjected. "He has a big heart, lives in a huge house, and is financially stable. He's a good catch! Belle could have done much, much worse."

Kara blinked. "You'd go for the Beast? Really? I'd have pegged you for Aurora."

"You're kidding, right? I am so not Aurora. You're more like Sleeping Beauty than I am. She's innocent and sweet. And I'm . . . not." Leslie frowned. "In fact, I'm not Disney-heroine material at all. Though I'm closer to Cinderella than you are."

"Anyway," Kara drawled, returning her focus to me. "*You'd* be Snow White, so she's off the table. Hm, who else is there?"

"Why am I Snow White?" I regretted asking the second the question slipped from my mouth, because why she thought I'd be a good fit with dwarves and poison apples didn't mean squat. "Never mind. Doesn't matter."

But it was too late. Counting on her fingers, Kara said, "You look like her, for one."

Again, I waited for her to laugh. Again, she didn't. I asked, "Do you see me in puffy blue and yellow dresses often?"

"No, but yellow is a good color for you. Not everyone can wear yellow, but you can." When I didn't respond, Kara added, "Besides, that wasn't what I meant. Your hair is so dark it's almost black, and you have blue eyes. You love apples, and I'm assuming that Snow White also loves them or why would she eat the poison one, you know? And if she were real, she'd be into animal rights, just like you!"

I truly had nothing to say. I should be used to these oddball conversations by now. I've known Kara almost my entire life. But somehow, they—and she—took me by surprise on a fairly regular basis.

A few minutes passed where the three of us stared at each other. Then Kara shook her head. "Sorry. I went off topic, didn't I?"

"Kind of. So let's start over, because I'm quite sure that after four weeks on the job, you have more valuable information than 'Verda is a fairy godmother.'" I breathed deeply. "You do, right? Tell me you do."

It was Leslie's turn to shake her head. "No. We really don't."

I waited for her to say more. She didn't. Swallowing another bout of sarcasm—because with the mood these two were in, we could end up off topic for hours—I worked out my anxiety by untwisting a stray paper clip. It helped until I punctured my fingertip with a pointy end.

Curling my hand around the mangled wire, I fought for steady nerves. "Come on. You can't really expect me to believe that Verda is a fairy godmother. *This* is how Magical Matchups is stealing all of my clients away? With magic?"

Leslie's cheeks puffed out and her cinnamon eyes held a light of indignation. "No. *You* come on. Aren't you overstating your predicament? You haven't lost all of your clients." She combed her fingers through her long, glossy, auburn hair as if she were a cover girl prepping for a photo shoot. "Besides which, you can't categorically state that every lost client is due to Magical Matchups. That isn't fair, and it isn't realistic."

"I *own* this business. I could *lose* this business. That's my reality, and this fairy-godmother stuff isn't helping."

"Have you considered that some of your past clients might have dropped out because you matched them up with the right person?" Leslie asked. "I call that a success."

I unclenched my fist to release the paper clip and reached for a stack of papers sitting to my right. Fanning them out across my desk, I gave a jerky nod. "These are exit interviews from the past several months, and in every one, the client—past client—states their reason for leaving Introductions is that they've decided to take their business to Magical Matchups." I shoved the papers toward Leslie. "Take a look yourself. I'm not overstating my predicament. If anything, I'm understating it."

"Oh." Leslie blew out a mouthful of air, deflating her cheeks. "Maybe you should have been clearer from the beginning, because from what I remember, you told us that Introductions was facing a 'slight decline' in business, and you wanted us to join Magical Matchups to discover what all the fuss was about." Her gaze dipped downward. In a softer tone, she said, "I didn't realize you'd lost so many clients. Is it really that bad?"

"Why didn't you tell us this to begin with, Julia?" Kara asked. "We . . . we had no idea you might lose the company."

Because the thought scared me. Because I'd barely admitted to myself how bad things were, let alone to anyone else. "Yes, things really are that bad," I said, choosing to answer Leslie over Kara. "And I don't know how to fix it."

"I remember when you first opened Introductions. Everything was great you even had testimonials from all the couples you put together. What happened?" Leslie asked.

I shrugged. "I don't know. But I haven't been that successful lately, and no one is beating down the door to write anything positive about my services." I'd given this a lot of thought, wondering if my process had gradually changed, wondering if my current struggles were a result of something I was doing different. I'd even gone through my files, looking for any clue that would help set things right. But from what I could see, my day-to-day operations were the same as they'd been since day one. To my thinking, that meant I had to look elsewhere to find the answer. "But that's not the point I'm trying to make. I paid for your memberships to my competition so you could gather information. So maybe I could pull Introductions out of the hole. You recall this agreement, right?"

Neither of them answered. The air around us filled with the heavy weight of tension and anxiety. Mostly mine, I'd wager.

Finally, they both nodded.

"Good. So you can see why this"—I swallowed away the words I wanted to say and went with—"information you've brought me is less than helpful. You know that fairy godmothers don't exist, right? And who is this Verda person, anyway? I thought the owner's name was Chloe Nichols."

"Oh! Chloe is Verda's partner, but Verda runs the place.

We've never even met Chloe," Kara explained. "And Verda is a doll. She's this really sweet elderly lady. She might be a little kooky, but she knows her stuff. You have to believe that, if nothing else."

Well, yeah. That was fairly obvious. Seeing as her start-up company was kicking my three-year-old company in the butt. "What stuff? How to fill your heads with delusions of magic and fairy godmothers?" Ouch, the snark came back when I wasn't paying attention.

"Believing in love is not delusional," Leslie said. "Most people believe in love."

"Wait! I have a better comparison," Kara interrupted. "Verda is like a fairy godmother and Pat Benatar all rolled into one."

I glanced at Leslie. She appeared as perplexed as I felt. "What are you talking about now, Kara?"

"Verda, of course. She's like Pat Benatar and that song 'Love is a Battlefield.'" Kara hummed a few bars. "She's using her magic to search the lean, mean streets of Chicago for us, taking on the battle of love herself so we don't have to!"

"That doesn't make sense, and it isn't even what the song is about." Oh, God, we were, once again, headed down a path I'd likely regret.

To give Kara credit, she took a moment to think things through. "Okay, I don't know. I'm trying to find something you can believe in, so you can believe us."

Leslie reached over and placed her hand on Kara's shoulder. "Let me try."

"If you think you can do better, then go ahead." Kara shrugged. "Everything I say seems to upset her more."

"Please don't do that." I found the paper clip and began twisting and untwisting it again. "Please don't talk as if I'm not here."

"Sorry, Julia. We're . . . well, we're really excited about

Magical Matchups and we like Verda a lot, so maybe our enthusiasm to explain has gotten the better of us," Leslie said. "Verda has this way of knowing more about what we need in a man than we do. So the process *feels* magical. With her, I believe I can find true love."

"Me too," Kara said in a hushed tone. "I *want* to fall in love. You can understand that, can't you?"

A look of deep longing crossed Kara's features. Great. She'd once again been taken in by all of the greeting cards, movies, books, and now the wily Verda, and their promises of everlasting love. My heart broke a little.

I was pissed off, too. "Of course you want to fall in love, sweetie. But that type of love isn't real. What you need is to find someone who has the same goals for the future as you, someone who likes the same things, someone with whom you can create a future based on these commonalities."

"But what about sex appeal?" Kara cried, emotion glittering in her eyes. "What about that feeling you get when you see a man and your knees go weak, and all you want to do is eat him up? Why can't I have both? I've been in love before. I want to find that again, and I want it to last."

"Uh-huh. And where did those relationships lead you? Nowhere!" Irritation at Verda and her false promises drove me onward. "You've had your heart stomped on again and again because you keep falling for the wrong type of men. You can't trust weak knees, Kara. You can't build a life on wanting to eat someone up."

How many times had I been there after a guy dumped her? Too many to count. How often had we had this exact same conversation? Tons. I was tired of seeing my friends get hurt. Especially with something that was so easy to avoid.

She blinked but kept her gaze on me. She'd yet to say anything, so I asked, "What are you thinking?"

"That I feel bad for you. That I wish, for one moment, you could feel what I'm talking about. Maybe then you wouldn't be so quick to write off love as a joke."

"Love isn't a joke. I know love is real . . . just like I know magic isn't."

"Then why are you so dead set . . . ?" Kara's voice drifted away as her eyes rounded. "Oh my God. This is about Ricky Luca, isn't it?"

"No! Ricky was forever ago. My God, Kara, you have a memory like a freaking elephant. I was what . . . ten?"

"Twelve," Kara said. "I remember because we were in seventh grade, and it was your first year at Worthington Academy." A slight smile crossed her face. "You hated the school uniform."

"Pleats," I mumbled. "I hated the pleats." Kara and I had gone to the same elementary school, but once we hit junior high, I moved on to private education.

"Anyway," Kara drawled, "you couldn't stop talking about Ricky."

"Ricky who?" Leslie interjected. "And why haven't I ever heard this story?"

"It's nothing," I said, desperate to change the topic. "Moving on—"

"We never told you about Ricky?" Kara angled her body toward Leslie. "Ricky was Julia's first crush. They used to leave each other love notes underneath the bust of Abraham Lincoln in history class."

"Stop. Please . . ." I hadn't thought about Ricky for years, and I didn't particularly want to think about him now.

But Kara was on a roll. "There was a school thing . . . what was it, a science fair or something?"

"The fall carnival," I said. "It wasn't a big deal. Ricky and I were supposed to meet there, but I got sidetracked." Actually, I'd had my fortune told. A waste of time, as I later discovered.

The heavily made-up woman gave me the exact same pretend fortune she gave every other preteen girl who strolled in. "He . . . ah . . . got tired of waiting, I guess."

"And he spent the day with Celeste Morrigan." Kara sniffed. "Your other best friend."

"She wasn't my best friend." But we were close. Close enough that her betrayal had stung more than Ricky's. "They were a better match." Something Celeste had explained when I'd confronted her. She'd pointed out all the ways that she and Ricky were similar, and all the ways that Ricky and I were not. She was right. Celeste and Ricky remained a couple all through high school. "But this has zip to do with my feelings about love." Or magic.

"I don't know," Leslie murmured. "This explains a lot."

"It does, doesn't it?" Kara whipped around to face me. "I should have seen this before."

"Seen what?" I said through pressed-together lips. "What girl hasn't had her heart broken when she was young?"

"Your mom," Kara whispered. "When she found out about Ricky . . ."

"Yes. She told me not to trust my heart. But that has *nothing* to do with any of this." I tried to think of different words for an explanation I'd given many times, but couldn't. "Our definitions of love are different, that's all. I believe that love is a slow-building process, something that can take years to happen but will last forever. You believe that love will strike you fast and hot, like a bolt of lightning. My definition will save you pain and heartbreak. Yours will keep leading you to misery, because that isn't love—it's physical stuff that has nothing to do with real emotion. Trust me on this."

"Not necessarily! Sometimes that quick flash leads to the best relationships." Leslie exhaled in frustration. "So we have different definitions. So what? That doesn't mean that either of us is wrong. Most people want both. There's nothing wrong with that."

"No, there isn't," I conceded, pleased to be off the Ricky subject. "It's just very unlikely you'll find both. It's like playing the lottery instead of methodically saving for the future." I gave Kara and Leslie a hard stare. "Would you bet your retirement on the less-than-minuscule chance of winning the lottery? No! You don't do that. You save money, you make use of your employer's 401(k) plan, and you take the proper steps to ensure your future won't be penniless! This is no different."

Kara whispered to Leslie, "She's getting all worked up again."

"Yes, I am! Don't you see? Your chances of securing a successful lifelong partnership increase substantially when you take sex appeal out of the equation." I instructed myself to calm down. "It's about brain matter, not body matter. It's about logic and fact. Not how sexy a man looks in jeans!"

Leslie snickered. "Sexy in jeans is a damn fine trait to have in a man, but that's not exactly what we're talking about here. You know that. You've delved into your sales pitch for would-be clients, and we've heard all of this before."

"Then what is it about?"

"It's that electrifying pull you sometimes feel when you look across a room and see some man you've never seen before. It's the way your skin heats up when you think about him touching you, about you touching him. Have you truly never felt this way, Julia?"

Had I? Once or twice, maybe, but that didn't prove anything. "Those feelings don't last. They're not real," I managed to say. "And they're certainly not logical. Who bets their future on a feeling?"

"I give up. You can't see outside of the box you've erected around yourself long enough to listen to any opinion different from yours." Leslie held her hands up in surrender. "You're right and I'm wrong. Hell, most of the world is wrong then, too. We should all toss away our hopes and dreams and wishes."

"So if a guy doesn't live up to your hot and sexy standards, you don't want him? I mean, that's what this really boils down to, isn't it?" I said.

Leslie reddened. "Not at all. But there should be a spark, something that pulls us together beyond the 'commonalities' you talk about."

"I see." I didn't. Not really. But this conversation had veered incredibly off the path, and this time, it was my fault. "I guess I don't understand where all of this is coming from. I thought we were mostly on the same page here."

"From a practical standpoint, you make a lot of good sense, and that's why it's always been so difficult to argue with you on this topic. But there is *nothing* practical about love. Verda has helped me see that I want it all. *She* makes us believe that love—our definition of love—is possible." Leslie exhaled another long, drawn-out sigh. "Verda's method is unique."

There it was. The lifeline I needed. "See? This is what I need to know. *How* is Verda's method unique?"

Kara and Leslie exchanged a look.

"Well?" I prompted.

"We . . . um . . . can't really tell you," Kara admitted. "So that's why—"

"We're paying your money back, so you're not out anything." Leslie reached into her purse and pulled out a check, which she slid across the desk toward me. Kara followed suit.

I glanced at the checks. Yep, both were made out to me—Julia Collins—and were in the correct amount. I didn't want them. "You two are supposed to be on my team."

"Oh, honey, we are. But we can't give you any inside

info on Magical Matchups." Leslie ran her fingers through her hair again. This time I recognized the action as a sign of her nervousness. "We . . . You see, we sort of signed a confidentiality agreement."

"You 'sort of' signed one, or you actually signed one?"

"We signed one. It was the only way—"

Every bit of my composure dissipated. "Uh-huh. Give me a second here."

I closed my eyes and counted to ten, then twenty, and hoped like hell the panic building in my chest wouldn't lead to a heart attack. My business was going downhill fast, my investors— okay, my parents—were watching the business's profit and loss statements with their eagle eyes, and everything I'd worked for was about to disintegrate between my fingers. All because of some company that had seemingly sprung up out of nowhere and had taken the singles of Chicago by storm.

"That vein in her forehead is throbbing," Kara whispered. "That can't be a good sign."

"Shh," Leslie hissed. "Julia? Do you want me to get you some tea or something?"

"No." Alcohol would have been good, though. And not some fruity umbrella drink, either. No, I wanted a shot of . . . of . . . whiskey. Something hot and wicked. Something that would burn going down and make me forget everything.

"What are you thinking?" This question came from Leslie.

"I'm wondering why you signed a confidentiality agreement when the only reason you were at Magical Matchups was for me. It would stand to reason that you'd refuse to sign something that would preclude you from living up to our agreement."

"When you put it that way, it doesn't sound that great," Kara admitted. "But we didn't think of it in exactly those terms."

I snapped my eyes open so fast that my head began to ache. "How did you think of it?"

Neither of them spoke, but I saw the wheels turning.

I rubbed my temples, trying to ease the headache before it increased. "I sort of expected this from Kara," I said. She gasped, so I tossed her a smile to lessen the sting. "But Leslie, I didn't see this coming from you."

How could I? Leslie had a practical—which I appreciated—but unrealistic way of seeking out men. They had to fall within five guidelines: handsome, honorable, charismatic, sexy, and—to Leslie, the most important of them all—rich. Leslie isn't a snob. Not really. But she was raised poor. The lucky-to-have-food-on-the-table-and-shoes-on-her-feet type of poor. Therefore, money was a huge issue.

Unfortunately, men that matched all five of these requirements weren't dropping from the sky. When you added in Leslie's age limitations—no more than two years younger or six years older—the available pool shrunk more. Over the years she'd found a couple of guys who'd hit four out of five, but as Leslie liked to say, "Close isn't good enough," so she'd done what she did best: pushed them away.

Leslie said, "Do you remember Scot Raymond?"

He was just one of the guys I'd been thinking of. My jaw dropped open. I jerked it shut and tried to smile serenely. Did I remember Scot Raymond? Tall. Gorgeous brown eyes. A husky, deep voice that made my insides tremble. And not that I'd admit it out loud, but an awesome ass that looked mighty fine in a pair of jeans. Of course I remembered him. An uncomfortable blaze of heat whipped through me. "Um . . . barely," I lied. "Why?"

"Because even though our relationship didn't last, he's the type of guy I should be with. *He* is the one I shouldn't have let get away."

"He didn't 'get away.' You pushed him away. He wasn't rich enough for you," I nearly screeched. "You cheated on him and made sure he knew it. Then he broke things off with you, which is exactly what you wanted!" Whoa. Where had that come from?

Kara gasped again, and Leslie's complexion drained of color. Both of them looked at me as if I'd lost my mind, which probably wasn't that far off base. Knowing the truth about your friends doesn't necessarily give you permission to throw it in their faces. "Oh, God. Leslie . . . I'm so sorry I said it that way. I . . ."

She sighed and a tremor rolled through her. "I'm going to let your comment slide because I know you're upset. But he . . . I regret what I did. My feelings for him scared me, so I purposely demolished the relationship before anything could come from it." Her mouth compressed in a defiant line. "I made a mistake. A huge mistake, but I've learned from it. If I could have one more chance with him, I'd grab it in a second."

This was a news flash. Leslie tended to look forward at all times. "Really? Then maybe you should call him. Why waste your time with Magical Matchups if you think this guy is *the* guy?"

Her eyes glazed over with pain. "It's too late. I need to move on, and Verda's going to help me so I don't make that mistake again. She believes in me."

"I believe in you! Don't you know that?"

"Yes. But I need someone on my side who also believes that what I want is possible. Verda can do that. I don't think you can. I'm sorry, Julia."

That hurt, like a punch in the stomach after eating a full seven-course meal. Tears sparked behind my eyes, but I shoved them away. Why was I arguing? Leslie had the right to go for what she wanted, and if—when—it backfired, I'd be here to pick up the pieces.

"If this is what you want, I support you." I looked at Kara. "You too. I will always support both of you. We don't have to agree for that to be there."

Relief slid into both of their faces and their bodies relaxed. "Thank you," Leslie said. "I'm sorry we can't be of more help, but I do have an idea that might give you the information you need."

"Um . . . Les? It was my idea," Kara rushed to say. "Remember, we talked about this last night."

Leslie arched her right eyebrow. "Fine. *We* have an idea of what you can do next."

"Not we. *Me.* It was my idea," Kara repeated. "Give credit where credit is due."

"That's not the way—" Leslie clamped her lips together and nodded. Motioning toward Kara, she said, "Go ahead and tell Julia *your* idea."

Wow. We were all stressed to the max. And while some of my friends' stress was my fault, I put most of the blame on Verda and her lovey-dovey voodoo. "Go on, Kara. I'm listening." I mentally crossed every one of my appendages that her idea was a good one.

"You need to join Magical Matchups yourself. If you're a client, you'll learn whatever it is you want to know on your own." Kara's eyes had that shimmery glow again. "Maybe we could even go on some triple dates!"

Again, both Leslie and Kara watched me expectantly. I figured they wanted me to jump in with both feet because it would dispel any of the guilt they might be experiencing for letting me down. But, "I already thought of that. And it's not a good idea."

"Why not?" Leslie asked.

"I'm not impartial. How can I go through Verda's process, whatever it is, when my beliefs are what they are? Besides which, I'm her competition. She probably already knows who I am." I shrugged my shoulders. "I don't see how it can work."

"I don't think Verda will care who you are, as long as she believes you're serious about finding love." Leslie leaned forward, so we were eye to eye. "Unless there's another reason? Are you worried that maybe, just maybe, Verda will make you a believer, too?"

"No," I said between clenched teeth. "I mean what I said."

"Well, then, I don't know what to tell you." Leslie returned to her prior position and gnawed on her lip. "So you're going to give up?"

"Of course not! That would be the same as shutting down Introductions myself." It would also require admitting to my parents that I'd failed. I winced at the thought. "No, I'm not giving up."

"Then what? Do you have any other ideas?" Kara asked.

"I'll figure something out." What, exactly, I didn't know. My two best friends bailing on me and deserting to the other side was not a possibility I'd considered. Maybe the temp agency I sometimes used had a special subterfuge and secrecy division for these types of projects? Unlikely, but I could always hope. "It'll be okay."

"Would Gregory and Susanna give you another loan?" Leslie asked. "I mean, they are your parents, and they're not exactly hurting for money."

I shuddered in reflex. Don't get me wrong, I love my parents. But there was no way they'd pull my butt out of this particular fire. "That isn't an option," I said tightly.

"Why not? Think about it, Julia. They're all about business, so if you brought this to them as an investment opportunity, they might go for it," Leslie pushed. "And another infusion of cash might be enough to get you through this rough spot."

I shook my head. "You're right. My parents *are* all about

business, and I still owe them money from the original loan. They won't see this as an investment—they'll see it as throwing more cash into a losing enterprise." Besides which, my relationship with my parents was tenuous at best. The last thing I wanted was to make things worse.

"She's right, Les," Kara said, reaching over and squeezing my hand. "We really are sorry. Can you forgive us? We hate disappointing you."

"I know," I said in a soft voice. "I appreciate the honesty." And even with everything else, I did.

"So you're feeling better?" Leslie asked.

"Absolutely," I lied. I twisted my lips into a smile that I hoped appeared real. "I'll figure this out," I said again.

They returned my smile. Theirs were as fake, but hey, points to them for pretending. That didn't stop my stomach from cramping. If my friends doubted me, then it was no wonder I'd lost so many clients.

But I'd fix it. I'd fix everything. How hard could it be? All I had to do was figure out how to plump up my company's bottom line, discover what the mysterious and "kooky" Verda had that I didn't, and bring in a bunch of new business. Piece of cake.

Right. If I had to bake that cake over an open campfire in the middle of a blizzard with my bikini on and wearing a blindfold. Easy peasy.

I gulped back a groan and smiled wider. So wide, my cheeks hurt. "Let's go grab some dinner. Somewhere that serves margaritas." I stood up. "My treat."

Kara and Leslie nodded and followed me out of my office in silence. As we walked, I tried to conceive a plan that would accomplish everything I needed. Not a whole lot of anything came to me. But deep inside, there was this teeny-tiny part of me that wished that magic and fairy godmothers were real.

Because if I could blink my eyes—or have someone else blink their eyes—and have every last thing fall into place, well, that would certainly make my life a hell of a lot easier.

"Hey, Julia?" Leslie asked as I locked the building's front door.

"Yeah?"

"You can't go out to dinner with us, can you? It's Wednesday. Don't you have your weekly dinner at your parents' house?"

"Shit." I twisted my wrist to see my watch and cursed again. "Yes. Yes, I do. And I'm going to be late." I pulled a couple of twenties from my wallet and handed them to Leslie. "Here. Have fun and drink a few margaritas for me, please. I'm going to need them."

Chapter Two

An hour or so later, I pressed the doorbell outside of my parents' mausoleum-like home and waited for the maid to let me in. Amanda had opened the door the past four Wednesdays with a smile and a proper greeting. If she lasted two more weeks, she'd beat this year's record. Four more weeks, and she'd be the three-year champion.

My family's inability to retain household help wasn't a secret. Five years ago, my mother's longtime maid and confidant Eloise retired to Florida. My normally unflappable mother hadn't handled the exodus well, and since, the Collins household had seen an ever-changing rotation of maids in a seemingly endless quest to fill Eloise's perfect shoes. Extrawide white oxfords, if I recall correctly.

My mother, Susanna Marie Kaiser-Collins—of the Philadelphia Kaisers, by the way—didn't or couldn't comprehend that her failure to find good help had more to do with how much she missed Eloise than it did actual housework and a pleasant demeanor. I'd tried to explain this emotional-connection concept to her about three years ago, but that conversation had gone downhill almost as quickly as Introductions.

These weekly dinners had become sort of a betting match between me and Mom, albeit a silent and secret one. My rules were simple: Each week that passed without my mother firing the maid—or that the maid didn't quit—I'd tuck away a five-dollar bill toward a special gift for my mother. The week following a firing or quitting, I'd present her with an item purchased with the money I'd saved. Most of these gifts were bought from one of Chicago's many dollar stores, though I'd picked up a few at thrift stores. Watching my always impeccable and socially adept mother attempt to understand the wide variety of interesting items I gave her was pretty much priceless. Strangely, she'd yet to question me on any of them, and as far as I knew hadn't connected the dots of what I was doing. Which made the game all that much more fun, because it was probably the only thing I'd ever kept from her. If the impossible ever happened and a maid lasted an entire year, I'd already promised myself that besides coming clean with Mom, I'd triple the pot and give the entire amount to the maid. Even with the present state of my business, I wasn't all that worried.

I rang the doorbell again, my hopes for Amanda fading fast. I was already considering what quirky item I might buy with the current pool of fifteen dollars when the heavy door swung open. A flustered young woman who appeared to be sweating profusely stared at me with wild eyes—the type you might expect to see on a caged and starving animal repeatedly mocked with the promise of freedom and an all-you-can-eat buffet.

Poor Amanda. I'd truly believed she'd last longer than three weeks.

I smiled at the new maid. "Hello, I'm—"

"Mr. and Mrs. Collins' daughter, yes?" the young woman said in a barely coherent rush. "Please come in."

"That's me. I'm Julia. And you're . . . ?"

"Helen. Please come in," she repeated. "Dinner is almost ready, and Mrs. Collins would like you to join them for a drink before the meal is served."

I nodded and stepped into the marble foyer. "Are they in the living room or the parlor?" Yes, my parents had a parlor.

"Living room. Please, Ms. Collins, your mother was quite insistent." Helen darted a nervous look over her shoulder. "Your coat, please. Mrs. Collins would you like you to join them posthaste."

"She's always insistent, and *posthaste* is her favorite word." I unbuttoned my coat. Helen tugged my right sleeve and then my left until the coat was ripped from my body into her arms.

I wanted to offer Helen some words of encouragement. My mother wasn't a bad person, and I knew she paid her employees a more-than-competitive wage. But working for her required a strong backbone, thick skin, and a fearless attitude. I'd learned, though, that no matter how good my intentions were, nothing I said made a lick of a difference.

I tried to help in a different way. Reaching into my purse, I pulled out a business card and handed it over. "Here. Take this in case you need it. I've done business with the owner, so if things don't work out here, give her a call. She'll help you find a better fit."

Helen accepted the card and held it up so she could read the writing in the subdued light. "Oh. They won't see me. I don't have enough experience."

"Yes, they will. Susanna Marie Kaiser-Collins hired you, and I'm referring you. Just mention my name."

"T-Thank you, Ms. Coll—"

"Julia? What is taking you so long? I don't appreciate dawdling." My mother's cultured voice entered the foyer before she did. Helen tucked the card into her apron pocket and backed away. Ack, she wasn't going to last the night, let alone the week.

"I'm right here, Mother," I said. "I'll be right in."

She flicked her blue-eyed gaze from me to the maid. "Helen. There you are. Please tell the chef to hold dinner for another thirty minutes. Julia is late."

What she didn't say but still managed to convey was the word *again*. As in "Julia is late *again*." I never planned on arriving late, but something always seemed to pop up on Wednesdays. Last week, I'd broken the heel on my right shoe and had to run home for replacement shoes. The week before, an impromptu meeting with a potential client delayed me.

"Yes, Mother. I'm running"—I checked my watch—"fifteen minutes behind schedule. I apologize."

I didn't bother to point out that fifteen minutes was more than enough time to down a drink—especially in my current mood—or that delaying dinner for another thirty minutes was fifteen more than necessary. Poking the punctuality stick at my mother simply wasn't done. Not if you wanted to keep all ten of your fingers.

"I cannot comprehend how you are always late. It's simple mathematics." Mom pursed her lips. "You know what time you have to be here, you are well aware of the traffic patterns this time of day, so therefore you should be able to deduce the proper time to leave your office. Wouldn't you agree?"

Every now and then, when I was feeling especially frisky, I'd shoot back a passive-aggressive reply. Not today. "I certainly do agree, Mother. You're absolutely correct. There is no excuse for my tardiness."

She raised her plucked-so-thin-it-was-barely-there left eyebrow and tipped her head to the side. My mother is a solid two inches shorter than my height of five foot five, weighs precisely twelve pounds less, and has the fragile and elegant appearance of fine bone china. This was a case of appearances-can-be-deceiving, because when Susanna Collins entered a room, everyone noticed. Hell, the very air rippled with her strength and purpose. Other than our shared hair and eye color, we were about as opposite as two people could be—a fact my mother disparaged at every possible moment, and one that I was forever trying to change.

I clamped my lips shut and waited for her to finish her appraisal, knowing that the harmony for the rest of the evening would likely be decided here. Another thirty seconds passed before she nodded. A ball of stress that had been touring the lower regions of my stomach eased.

"Well, come along. Your father is waiting." She pivoted sharply on her heel and headed for the living room.

I inhaled a deep, steadying breath, smoothed my skirt with my hands, and followed. Maybe tonight wouldn't be so bad. Maybe, for a change, the evening's chitchat wouldn't be filled with innuendo and barely concealed comments regarding my inadequacies.

Crossing my fingers that hell had indeed frozen over and that pigs were circling the Sears Tower, I walked quietly into the room and took my place on the antique sofa. My parents were seated across from me in matching Queen Anne chairs.

My father appeared austere and opposing, and very little like the daddy I'd adored as a child. His mostly gray-haired head was bent forward, his despised glasses were on, and he held a book in his hands, which he closed with a snap as I sat down. Removing his glasses, he nodded in my direction by way of greeting.

I nodded back. Without waiting to be asked, I leaned over and grabbed my drink—a brandy Alexander, because we'd moved solidly into fall, and my mother chose her before-dinner drinks based on the season—and took a small sip. Not my favorite, but going without alcoholic fortification in the Collins household was not recommended.

"So . . . ah . . . dinner smells terrific," I said, as I did every Wednesday. The one saving grace to these weekly dinners was the amazing food my mother's chef prepared. I'm a foodie, if of the regular variety. I tend to be just as happy wolfing down buffalo wings and French fries as I am dining at one of Chicago's finest restaurants. I'm an equal fan of Doritos— preferably salsa verde flavored—and foie gras. As long as the food is well prepared, and not lamb or potato soup, I'm not a picky eater. "What's on the menu tonight?"

"Roasted lamb shank, buttered baby peas, and herbed rice," my mother answered. "I do hope you've come with an appetite this week, Julia. You barely touched your plate last Wednesday. The chef's feelings were quite hurt."

Uh-huh. Sure they were. Rosalie's feelings didn't get hurt. She had the required thick skin, strong backbone, and fearless attitude for this place. "Sorry about that. I'd had a late lunch."

"Oh, that's right." Mom circled the rim of her glass with her index finger. "What about today, dear? Did you have a late lunch today?"

"No, Mom, I ate at the proper time."

"That's delightful news! Did you hear that, Gregory? Julia came for dinner with an appetite this week. The chef will be so pleased."

I took the bait even though I knew better. "As a matter of fact, I'm quite hungry. But I don't think that will affect how much or how little I eat."

"Oh? Why is that, darling?" God, she was good.

"I'm not a fan of lamb, Mother. Which I know you know, so I have to assume you're serving lamb because you've seen my financial statements from last month." I gulped my too-sweet drink and waited for Armageddon.

"Why would your little company's financial statements have anything to do with what we're having for dinner?" Her smile appeared real, and her eyes held just the right amount of confusion. Like I said, she was good.

"Because you're obviously unhappy with me, and rather than getting right to it, you've decided to make the entire evening awkward enough that I'll go along with whatever your newest plan is regarding my business. But it won't work." Pleased with my bravado thus far, I pushed another inch. "I am not ready to admit defeat."

My father cleared his throat. "Of course you aren't. You're a fighter. But you do realize that lamb is my favorite, don't you? The menu tonight has nothing to do with your company's struggles."

Ha. Not true. Dad liked lamb well enough, but he far preferred an old-fashioned beef roast with all the trimmings.

"If you like, I can have the chef prepare you something else. A grilled cheese sandwich, perhaps?" Mom asked. "Or maybe she could open a can of soup. Or both, if you desire. Your wish is my command."

Hm. Even for my mother, this was a little over the top. I stole a glance at her and then at my father, trying to read their body language. Neither of them gave anything away, but I'd swear the air chilled several degrees. "Is there something else going on that I'm unaware of?"

My father set his drink down, clasped his hands, and exhaled a disapproving breath. Well, I suppose it could have been a disappointed breath. I tended to mix the two up. My mother seemed to have found a sudden interest in a portrait that had hung in this room since I was a child, but she held herself in that stiff and unrelenting way that told me I'd either crossed a line I shouldn't have or hadn't done something that was expected of me.

The waistband of my skirt shrank as I sat there, contemplating the vast number of possibilities regarding their unhappiness. My shoes, which I'd worn comfortably all day, bit painfully into my ankles. Even my bra felt tighter. It was as if every article of clothing I wore had somehow become two sizes too small in the last five minutes and was now out to strangle me.

"We're concerned about you," my mother said. "We're your parents, and we only have your best interests at heart." Her voice was so calm it scared me.

"I know that, Mom."

"We—your father and I—believe that you're spending too much of your time and resources on a business that is primed for failure."

I started to object but then had second thoughts. Might as well hear her out before making the situation—whatever it was—worse. "Go on."

"What will you do when you have to close Introductions? Where will all of this time and energy you're currently expending go to then?"

My mother never, ever, got right to the point. Instead, she'd broach a different topic, usually one about which the other person cared a great deal, and then she'd steer the conversation to whatever mysterious subject she really wanted to discuss. Knowing this about my mother meant that no matter what she'd just said, this had zip to do with Introductions.

Then, all at once, I knew. This—serving lamb for dinner, my father's disapproving/disappointed breath, my mother's odd behavior—could only mean one thing. They were on the "Let's get Julia married" bandwagon again.

My parents didn't believe in romantic love any more than I did, but they only have one child—me—and they viewed my single-at-thirty-three state as a blemish on their high-society standing. Because the people they socialized with were, by and large, the same people my father did business with, my personal life had become a hot topic in recent years. It was something I mostly managed to avoid.

I let out a sigh. "This is about dating, right?"

"Did I mention dating?" My mother turned to look at my father. "Did I, Gregory?"

"Oh, just get on with it, why don't you?" My father huffed again, frustrated. He faced me. "We have supported you in your business from day one, even though both of us expressed our doubts concerning its viability. We've mentored you and offered you advice whenever you've needed it, and we've followed through with our agreement with you."

He was right. Mostly, anyway. Often, their advice wasn't asked for or required, but they'd invested in my business and had pretty much kept to the hands-off policy I'd insisted on.

"Then why is it that you cannot follow through on your agreements to us?"

My head spun. Was this about Introductions or not? The only agreement I could think of was my promise to go work for Dad if Introductions failed. But as bad as things were, we were not there yet. Were we? My skirt shrank another size.

"I'm at a total loss here. What agreement?"

He did his disapproving/disappointed exhalation again. "My clients are critical to my business, Julia. You run a company, so I assume you understand that keeping your clients happy is essential. Am I mistaken in this assumption?"

My father worked as a headhunter. Most of his business dealt with finding the best of the best for financial institutions, top-tier law firms, tech companies, and the like. He was good at it. He had this uncanny ability of being able to sense a person's worth within seconds of meeting them, regardless of their schooling, experience, or the amount of their prior paycheck. Due to this, his services were in high demand, and he commanded a hefty commission from both sides of the equation.

"You are not mistaken," I said. "But what does—?"

"William Parkington and I have done business with each other for a long while. Successful business, if I do say so myself. We've known each other for going on twenty years now, isn't that right, Susanna?"

"Yes, Gregory, that's right. His wife Delia and I see each other often, as well." My mother tilted her chin up just enough so that I could see the glint of battle in her eyes. "We are very fond of the Parkingtons and would hate to upset them in any way."

Parkington? The confusion cleared. Dear God, I'd managed to enter the fray without even realizing I had. "I didn't know . . . didn't realize that you wanted me to—"

"I believe you know William and Delia's son." My father leaned forward, his gaze level with mine. "Jameson is a fine young man, full of potential. He's doing wonderfully in William's firm. He phoned you this week, didn't he?"

I gave the innocent routine a try. It rarely worked, but this was not looking so good. "William? Why would William call me? As far as I know, I'm not in need of an attorney. What's his specialty again?"

"That's neither here nor there. You know very well we're talking about Jameson." My mother stood and walked over to the drink cart. "We spoke with you about this last week. Why would you reject that poor boy's proposal?"

"He didn't have a ring," I quipped in a continued effort to divert their attention. "You cannot expect me to marry a man who doesn't offer me a ring." I waved my naked left hand in the air. "Why, that's downright rude."

"Stop this nonsense," my father growled. Wow, he was really bugged by this. "The proposal your mother speaks of is the Parkingtons' annual preholiday party." Dad pulled his glasses from his front pocket and slipped them on. "William and I met for lunch a few weeks back and, among other things, discussed you and Jameson."

"We explained all of this to her last Wednesday," my mother said in an aside, mixing herself another drink. "And she agreed to attend a few of our social functions."

"Yes, I did," I agreed. "But I didn't realize you were going to start fixing me up again." I mentally replayed the conversation and shook my head. "No. You did not mention you wanted me to date Jameson." God, I didn't think they had, anyway. "You did mention that he's single and might be interested in the services Introductions offers. So when he phoned, I assumed there was a miscommunication."

"And that's why you turned him down?" my mother said.

"Yes. But we set up an appointment for him to come into the office to go over his profile. He's probably filling it out now! And he wasn't upset in the slightest, so I don't understand why you two are."

"Because William and Delia are upset. They have it in their heads that you believe you are somehow better than their son. This isn't a good situation for any of us," Mom said. "If you didn't want to date Jameson, it would have been far easier if you told us that last week. When we would have been able to do some damage control."

Oh, God. I couldn't argue with her. One: chances were low I'd win. Two: well, sometimes I spaced out during these dinners. As much as I hated to admit it, the possibility existed that I had agreed to this, even if I didn't remember. "So, what do you want me to do?"

My mother swooped in and sat next to me on the sofa. "Perhaps you could phone Jameson tomorrow and apologize."

"Sure. That's easy enough." He'd probably think I was a freak, but so what?

Squeezing my hand tightly, she smiled. "And?"

Yep. I'd have to go out on at least one date. "Yes, Mother. I'll accept his invitation."

"Thank you, Julia," my father said as Mom drew me into one of her stiff hugs. "This will help ease the awkwardness."

"Now, about your business," my mother said, backing out of the embrace. "Didn't you say last week that you had a plan you were putting into motion?"

I nodded. Hopefully, she wouldn't ask about the plan.

"Good! We can put off any further business discussion for another month or so. We'll give this plan of yours a chance to work." Mom pulled herself upright. "Let's eat. You'll be pleased to know I instructed the chef to prepare a second main course tonight."

Ha. I knew the lamb was a bad sign. If I'd refused to call Jameson Parkington, the second main course wouldn't have made an appearance, and Introductions definitely would have been in the line of fire for the next couple of hours. So yeah, as much as I didn't relish the thought of dating anyone right now, going out with Jameson was well worth the effort.

Hey, I had to find the silver lining wherever I could. That's just the way it was on Wednesdays.

I pulled my ten-year-old Volvo—a college graduation gift from my parents—to a stop and turned the ignition off. The rest of dinner had been filled with nonconfrontational chatter, for which I was grateful. But by the time the maid cleared the last dish, I was less than perky. All I wanted was to go home and take a long, hot bubble bath.

But I hadn't gone home. Instead, I found myself driving aimlessly, somehow ending up on the street in front of Magical Matchups. I knew where the business was, of course, as my curiosity had gotten the better of me and I'd done several drive-bys over the last month, but I hadn't planned on swinging by tonight.

I stared at the darkened windows, wondering again what went on inside that compelled my friends to believe they could find romance-novel love. From the exterior, it appeared a normal business. There were no sparkles, flashing lights, or magic wands anywhere in sight. Truth be told, it looked fairly basic. There weren't any signs on the windows that boasted false promises of a Disney fairy-tale ending if you walked in and signed on the dotted line. Heck, there weren't any large signs at all. Just a simple storefront with the name of the business printed on a tiny placard above the door.

Yet beyond that door existed some ingredient that my business didn't have. I needed to know what it was. I needed to understand how this company that hadn't even existed five months ago was beating my veteran company into the ground.

It shouldn't have been possible. From the day I opened Introductions, I'd done everything by the book. I hadn't waded in without weighing the odds, and I hadn't spent one cent of my money or my parents' without knowing the risks. My business plan was solid. The first year, I hadn't expected to make a profit—and I was right. But I hadn't lost money, either. The second year brought increased publicity, more clients, and the slight profit I'd predicted. But now, it didn't seem to matter how many hours I worked or how solid my business plan was. Even my success with matching couples had waned, but I couldn't put my finger on why. Failure loomed.

I grasped the steering wheel tightly with both hands and tried to do what I always did: ignore the dread climbing through me. Only it didn't work. The truth I'd been avoiding washed in: I didn't have one iota of a clue of how to fix this. Even worse, I was beginning to believe that I couldn't.

My gaze fell on Magical Matchups again, and the urge

to discover its secrets had me unclasping my seat belt and stepping from the car before I fully realized what I was doing. The chilly November night air touched my cheek, whispered down my neck, made me shiver as I crossed the street.

My steps faltered as I neared the door. This was nuts! What did I think I was going to do—play MacGyver, use a bobby pin to break in and rummage through Verda's desk? Okay, if I even knew how to open a locked door using a hairpin, then that might have been a course of action worth considering, but not without proper planning, and certainly not without a lookout.

Panicked laughter gurgled from my throat. As if the properly raised daughter of Gregory and Susanna would ever break the law. Though on second thought, the look on my mother's face might be worth jail time. If nothing else, it would give her socialite friends something to talk about.

My heart started fluttering like crazy. The portion of my brain that remained clear thinking and sane urged me to retreat to my car. I gulped in a lungful of air, because it seemed I couldn't get enough oxygen into my body, and then slowly walked by the store. When I reached the shop next to Magical Matchups, I paused as if I'd gotten lost, turned around, and retraced my steps.

I probably did this a half dozen times before I found the courage to do what I really wanted. Stopping just to the right of the front door, I glanced over my shoulder to be sure I didn't have an audience, and then I framed my eyes with my hands and peered in.

My breath caught. Tendrils of a soft, whispery light gave the business a strange, ethereal glow that made me shiver again. Large, darkened shadows stretched across the floor, accentuating the furnishings in such a way that they almost appeared to be living and breathing entities. It was as if . . . I shook my head, annoyed by the image that had burst into my mind: one of a little girl stepping into a wardrobe and exiting into an entirely new world.

I blamed Kara and Leslie and all the talk of fairy tales, but even so, the image persisted. Craning my neck to the right, I tried to make out what actual objects were, so I could lessen the otherworldly feeling I had going on. One by one, I mentally attached names to the furnishings—couch, chair, desk, table, more chairs—until finally, the strange, tingling sensation lightened. But it didn't go away completely, and the urge to escape to my car crawled over me once again.

I almost let the urge control me, but I focused harder on the room and on the details I could see. Leaving now, even though there was nothing I could do here, would be paramount to admitting that Magical Matchups had some sort of hold over me, that this place was stronger and better than Introductions. Yeah, I know. My thought process made zero sense and wasn't rational in the slightest. But somehow, at that moment, holding my ground seemed of upmost importance.

"See? Just a normal room with normal stuff. Certainly nothing to get all worked up over. There are no boogeymen, talking lions, or anything else that is out of the ordinary," I whispered. Just as I used to do when I was a child and believed there were ghosts and monsters lurking in my closet. Unfortunately, my self-assurances didn't work any better now than they had then.

Exasperated with myself and with this stupid game I was playing—I mean, what was I trying to prove, exactly?—I dropped my hands and backed away from the window. I glanced down the street again, noting that a few pedestrians were ambling my way. Without processing why, I grabbed the door handle, twisted, and pushed. The door creaked, as if the hinges were rusty and old, and slid open.

Open? Was someone in there?

I waited for a voice to call out, for an alarm to go off, something that would announce my unlawful action, but everything remained eerily quiet. Tipping my head to the left, I gauged the distance between me and the pedestrians. They were nearly to me, and while they had no clue that I wasn't supposed to be doing what I was doing, I had the irrational fear that they *did* know. My skin itched with the desire to enter, to leave this world for the one on the other side of the wardrobe. How dumb was that?

"Hello?" I called into the darkened room. "Is anyone there?"

Nothing but silence came back to me, so I . . . well, I acted completely out of character. I stepped into the lobby of Magical Matchups.

Chapter Three

The door swung shut with a soft thud. Blood rushed through my body, echoing in my ears like crashing waves. I shivered. The faint scent of flowers prickled my nose. Roses, perhaps, but I couldn't be sure. I took one step forward, and then another. Was I truly alone?

It seemed I was, but you get a certain sense when someone else is sharing space with you. I had that sense. Anticipation mixed with nerves tiptoed down my spine, leaving a trail of icy goose bumps on my skin. Knowing my luck, a burglar had broken in minutes before I'd arrived and was now hanging out in back, waiting with a tire iron in his hands.

But that . . . Well, it didn't *feel* right. I didn't feel alone, but I didn't feel anything malevolent, either. I took another hesitant step and called out again. "Hello?"

Silence.

Who left their business empty and unlocked? A slight tightening in the back of my throat forced a swallow. If this were my place and I had this feeling, I'd hightail out of there fast and have the police do a walk-through. But this wasn't my place. I wasn't supposed to be here. And that left me with two choices: leave and possibly save myself from injury, death, or at the very least arrest; or pray that I was as alone as it seemed and sate my desire for information.

I knew I *should* leave. That was the right, the legal, thing to do. But something compelled me to stay. And hey, I'd already walked through the freaking wardrobe, right? Why not look around Narnia a little? Maybe, if nothing else, I would find an introduction packet to the matchmaking company's services. Even that would be more than I had now. It might be enough to help save my business.

The thought pushed me forward. I took another step and then stopped so I could gather my bearings. A large, ornately styled desk stood sentry against the back wall. If Verda ran Magical Matchups in any sort of a predictable manner, that desk would have brochures, price lists, and other basic information for folks who walked in without an appointment. That desk was my target.

I moved toward it silently, pretending I was on a covert mission. The flutter of butterflies in my chest swirled and bobbed and my stomach dipped. Not so much out of fear as incredulity that I hadn't yet succumbed to the voice of reason, the one that sounded a hell of a lot like my mother commanding me to leave.

I rounded the desk to the other side. Again, the sensation of not being alone pressed around me, stronger than before. Sweat beaded on my forehead and the tightening in my throat worsened. I glanced across the dark room, expecting to see someone staring back at me, but other than shadows, furniture, and that weird, whispery light, nothing met my eyes.

Inhaling a long, slow breath to ease my nervous shudders, I focused on the surface of the desk. There was a telephone, one of those all-in-one computers with a massive monitor, a memo pad opened to a blank page, a stapler, and one lone pen. I cursed in frustration. Of course Verda would be a neat freak. Of course she wouldn't leave anything telling out in the open.

I gave serious consideration to powering up the PC but decided against it. For one, the computer was likely password protected. For two, e-rifling would take far too long. Besides which, taking that step, as idiotic as it might sound, seemed one too many toward the dark side.

"Think, Julia," I said. "Find the intro pack and get out of here."

A hip-high wooden file cabinet abutted the desk. I tugged on the top drawer. Locked, naturally. Going on instinct, I shoved the chair out of the way and pulled open the middle desk drawer. Maybe the file-cabinet key was stored there. Clear-wrapped candies, various pens and pencils, and a few other odds and ends rolled to the front, the sound erupting into the silent room as if a zillion and one miniexplosives had gone off.

I paused and held my breath, ready to run. But the next minute ticked by without anyone confronting me, so I exhaled a sigh and tried to shake off my creepy-crawlies.

What in the hell was I doing? Who did this sort of crap? If all I was after was something that Magical Matchups probably gave to anyone who walked in off the street, that was easy enough to get my hands on. I'd come back during normal business hours and pretend to be a potential, nameless client. It wouldn't be hard at all.

Decision made, if praying I wouldn't regret it later, I turned to leave. I was ready—more than—to reenter the normal world. The heady aroma of a garden wove in then, soaking the air with such weight, such volume, that I would've sworn bouquets of full-on blossoming flowers surrounded me. Roses, actually. I was sure of that now.

My nose twitched, itched, and I sneezed. My eyes watered from the now-overpowering scent. Prickles of awareness cascaded over my skin. The feeling of another presence became more potent than ever. My heart rate doubled then tripled in a matter of seconds. I tried to force my legs to move, but they refused to cooperate.

"Hello?" I said in a shaky voice. "I found the door unlocked. I—I'm sorry. I shouldn't have come in."

Soft laughter, reminiscent of Sunday church bells, danced through the room, followed by a faint stirring of air that touched my cheeks, ruffled my hair. I'd been afraid before. Who hasn't? But I'd never truly, to the depths of my soul, been as scared as this.

I tried to run again, but found that my legs remained frozen. Probably by fear. Maybe by something else. I reached into my purse, grappling for my cell phone, intending to call for help before . . . before what? Roses and a church-bell laugh did me in?

Um. Yeah. Hell yeah, even. Where was the damn phone?

Giving up my search, I gathered every bit of strength I had and surged my body forward. My legs came unglued. I rushed toward the door. My heart galloped and sweat poured down my face. Out, I thought, get out. *Now.* My body complied—hell, I'd probably never moved so fast in my life. But I rammed smack into the arm of the sofa, my legs buckled, and I fell face-first over the edge onto the cushions in an ungainly heap.

Before I pulled myself up, a gentle, warm breeze floated around me, filling me with a surge of calmness that somehow, in some way, knocked my fear down a notch. But that didn't mean I wanted to stay. Uh-uh. I struggled to my feet and thrust myself toward the door.

No one tried to stop me, a voice didn't holler out from behind, but the scent of roses remained just as strong, just as overwhelming. I made it to the door, saw my car through the window, and my panic dropped another level. But wow, was I happy to be leaving. I grasped the doorknob and pulled.

The door didn't budge. I twisted the lock to the right and then the left, thinking that maybe the door had locked automatically behind me when I'd entered. That didn't work either.

"What the hell?" I pulled, twisted, and then—as a last desperate move—pushed with all of my might. Nothing. Had the lock somehow gotten jammed? Maybe. Probably. A fresh bout of panic clouded my thinking. This . . . this was bad. Really, really bad.

I paced the area in front of the door, eyeing my car across the street as if it were an oasis in the middle of a desert, trying to figure out how I was going to get out of this mess.

"Calm down. There is always a way," I said. "Think this through." The sound of my voice brought one rational thought: maybe there was a back exit? Yes! Of course there was. Fire laws and all that stuff. I took off across the room and down the hall. It took all of two minutes to discover that if another exit existed, it was behind one of the locked doors off of the hallway. The only door I'd been able to open was the one to the restroom. Lucky me and my bladder.

"Suck it up, Julia. Time to call for reinforcements." I rummaged through my purse until I found my cell phone. I hated the thought of calling the police, but I didn't see how anyone else would be able to get me out of here. It wasn't as if I even knew Verda's home number, let alone had it on speed dial. Though maybe Kara and Leslie did.

Relieved I might have an out, even if it was embarrassing, I dialed Leslie's cell number and hit the send button. The call didn't go through.

I tried Kara's. That call didn't connect, either. Fear returned as I tried dialing my parents, and then Leslie and Kara again. Still nothing. I stared at the backlit display, proof that the battery had power, and gave it one more go without success. Maybe it was broken. Maybe Magical Matchups was somehow located in a dead zone. Regardless, the phone was not going to be my salvation.

"Great. Just friggin' great," I said, shoving it back into my purse.

More annoyed than wigged-out now, I tried to use the Magical Matchups phone. But there wasn't—surprise, surprise—a dial tone. Another light breeze wafted through the room, redolent of roses. I clutched the edge of the desk as a series of tremors whipped through me. The ridiculous notion that I was *supposed* to be here overtook all other thoughts, followed by the feeling that I was meant to experience whatever the hell was going on, and that I was not going to be able to leave until . . . well, until *what*, I didn't know.

My legs weakened and I sank to the floor. I pulled my knees to my chest and wrapped my arms around them. It seemed I really had walked through the wardrobe. I just wish I'd known it was a one-way trip.

The first two hours of my unexpected lockup passed in a smog of panic-induced activity. Every thirty minutes, I'd try my cell again. When that didn't work—because it never did—I'd check the business phone for the always-nonexistent dial tone. After that, I'd return to the front door and give it a few hearty yanks. I even attempted cajoling the lock open with a straightened paper clip. Where was MacGyver when I needed him?

Somewhere in the third hour, I considered heaving the desk chair through the front window and making a break for freedom by crawling over shards of jagged glass. I got as far as rolling the chair across the room before changing my mind. No one had pushed me into entering Magical Matchups. It felt wrong—so wrong—to damage someone's property because I'd decided to do a foolhardy thing.

I sat on the edge of the sofa with my arms crossed

defensively over my chest. Likely, I'd gotten worked up for no real reason. What I'd experienced *had* to be nothing more than an adrenaline-based reaction to behaving out of character. All of this made sense, so I did my best to ignore my panic, to forget about my earlier fear, but remnants of both remained strong enough that I couldn't relax. Probably not a bad thing, as it seemed far smarter and safer to be awake and alert when morning came.

But somehow, as the hours progressed, my eyelids grew heavier and heavier, and my fixation with unexplained breezes, scents, and church-bell-like laughs drifted away. I closed my eyes with the promise that I'd sleep for only an hour. Maybe two.

Waking up *hurt*.

Pinpricks stabbed my neck from sleeping at an awkward angle, the achy soreness in my jaw told me I'd clenched it throughout the night, and the rest of my muscles were tight and tender. I stretched my legs out, lost in the disorientation of those initial seconds of wakefulness, unable to comprehend the warning signals my sluggish brain was firing off.

My first conscious thought was that I'd fallen asleep in my living room. My second was that I smelled coffee. My third was how odd that was, because the timer on my coffeemaker had stopped functioning months ago and I'd yet to get around to replacing it. Had Kara or Leslie popped in while I slept?

Maybe. They shared the apartment across the hall from mine, and we had copies of each other's keys. I cracked one eye open and then the next. Sunlight streamed in the window, bouncing off the polished hardwood floor so that it shone in a glittery, gleaming way. Almost reminiscent of the surface of a lake on a hot, steamy day.

My hazy brain latched onto that, and then a rush of images,

sounds, scents, and feelings flooded in. My heart picked up speed, thumping wildly beneath my breastbone, waking me up as completely as if I stood beneath the full-stream blast of an icy-cold shower.

I jumped up—fast—and pivoted, taking note of the coat slung over the desk chair. Someone else was here with me, but they . . . what? *Hadn't* noticed me sleeping in the center of the room on their sofa? *Had* noticed but decided to let me get my beauty sleep while they brewed a pot of joe? I felt as if I had simultaneously become Goldilocks *and* the three bears.

My gaze skittered to the front door. Every instinct screamed to rush out, get in my car, and drive away without a backward glance. But my legs defied my instincts and carried me across the floor, down the hallway, to an open door on the right. I was curious. Curious enough that it pushed me forward, outweighed my desire to run.

I peered in and saw an empty break room that looked to be a miniature replica of a country kitchen. Fruit-laden wallpaper covered all four walls, a colorful backdrop to the bright red-checked dish towels folded neatly on the small, round table and the equally red coffeemaker, toaster, and small microwave perching on the butcher-block counter. I retreated a step. Acid sloshed in my stomach at the absurdity of the situation. I should've been awakened by a cop hauling me to my feet or, at the very least, a scream of surprise. But this was weird. Bordering on *Twilight Zone* weird.

"There you are!" A way-too-chipper voice came from the other side of me, farther down the hall. "I was just on my way out to check on you. Ready for some coffee, dear? Oh, and I might have a few day-old pastries left in the cupboard, if you're feeling hungry."

A petite elderly woman—most likely the mysterious Verda—slipped around me and entered the break room. She wore a dress of varying shades of purple so vivid that my eyes watered in defense, and her short, curly hair was the hue of a pale lemon. She stopped in the middle of the room and stared at me inquisitively with light blue eyes. "Coffee?"

I ignored the impulse to wrap my arms around myself and returned her stare. In most scenarios, one could expect a specific type of response from another person. We were in a ridiculously peculiar situation, and this woman was not behaving in any sort of a predictable manner. It threw me, confused me, and sent another wave of apprehension through my body.

Perhaps that was her intent? Maybe her goal was to delay me until I was cuffed and tossed in the back of some cop car? I couldn't rule it out.

Keeping my voice steady, I asked, "Are the police on their way?"

Her frail shoulders lifted in a tiny shrug, as if amused by my question. She opened a cupboard door, bringing out a white rectangular box labeled with the name A TASTE OF MAGIC. "Ah, yes. Here they are," she said. She lifted the lid before setting the box on the table. "There are several left. My granddaughter, Elizabeth, owns a lovely little bakery in Highland Park."

"I'm not hungry." I took a few more backward steps and measured the distance between me and the front door. Was it open? Even more to the point: could I make it?

"Oh, dear. Listen to me! I haven't even introduced myself." She approached me with a lopsided smile and twinkling eyes. Holding out her hand she said, "I'm Verda."

Without thinking, I placed my hand in hers. "I'm Julia," I said, and instantly wished I'd made up a name. Or given her my middle name. Or my mother's. Yeah, definitely my mother's.

Tipping her head to the right, Verda appraised me. "Yes, you look like a Julia. Let's sit down and get acquainted. I'm so very excited you're here!"

What? "Excited?"

"Well, of course I am! I've been waiting months for you to show. When Miranda told me this morning—" Verda shook her head. "Never mind that for now. Why don't you help yourself to some coffee and a pastry while I get my tea started?"

Okay, I didn't know which question to ask first. Why was Verda excited to meet me? Why had she been waiting for me? Who was Miranda, and what did she have to do with my being here? See? Way too many questions. And why wasn't Verda asking me any? Deciding again that this was too weird to deal with—especially in yesterday's clothes—I went with "I should probably leave. I . . . I have to get to work."

All good humor left Verda's face. She wrinkled her nose. "Nonsense. It's not every day I find a strange woman sleeping on my couch." She leveraged her hands on her hips. "You can spend a few minutes talking with me, or I can contact the authorities. What will it be?"

Ha. I figured she meant to scare me into staying, but her words had the opposite effect. I understood this response. I liked the *logic* of this response. And that bolstered my sagging comfort level. After all, I knew how to behave when logic ruled.

"Coffee it is," I said. "But I need to make a phone call first. And if you don't mind, I'd like to freshen up."

The tension eased. Verda gave me another once-over and, apparently deciding I'd spoken the truth, smiled. "The restroom is across the hall. Do what you need to do, dear. I'll be right here."

In the ten minutes that followed, I washed my face and brushed my hair. I checked my cell phone and found it functioning—how odd was that?—and called Introductions. It was Thursday, which meant my part-time assistant would be in shortly. I left her a message that I'd be delayed a few hours. Now, I was seated across from Verda at her itty-bitty table with a cup of coffee. And a pastry. She'd insisted.

Verda sipped her tea while she watched me. I had the nagging suspicion that she was sizing me up and determining my worth. That was okay. I was doing the same with her. Besides, if sitting here kept her from calling the cops, I'd sit all day. A long minute passed, maybe two. She set her cup down hard enough that tea splashed over the edge.

"Why did you come here?" she asked.

"I . . . um . . . Two of my friends are clients of yours. They've said a lot of positive things about you. And about Magical Matchups." So far so good. "I came by last night to see what all the fuss was about. The door was open and I came in, but no one was here. When I tried to leave, I couldn't open the door." Wow, I hadn't lied. Kudos to me.

I assumed Verda would press for more details, but she didn't. Instead, a pleased expression flashed over her. "Did anything else occur that might be considered odd?"

I wasn't about to mention the laugh, the breeze, or the aroma of an invisible rose garden. In the bright light of day, I was more than willing to chalk the prior night's episodes up to nothing more than panic. "Like what?"

"Oh, I don't know." An all-knowing glimmer brightened her eyes. "You must have been frightened. Why didn't you phone for help?"

"Um . . . my cell wasn't getting a signal last night."

"You should have used my phone."

"I tried." I chuckled humorlessly. "Your phone didn't work, either."

"Ah, I see." Verda leaned forward and clasped my hand with

one of hers. Normally, I don't like being touched by people I don't know that well, but for some reason this didn't bother me. "That's an odd occurrence, wouldn't you say?"

I refused to give any additional credence to my wild imagination or the spaz attack that followed. I wanted to understand why Verda seemed pleased to see me, and what in the hell she'd meant about waiting for me to show. "It was just one of those things," I said. "But you didn't seem surprised to find me here."

"I wasn't. As I said, I've been expecting you."

"Did Kara and Leslie tell you about me?" That made sense. Either that, or—just as I'd predicted—Verda had done her research and knew exactly who I was: her competition.

"No, Julia." She sighed in a dramatic manner. "I opened this business *because* of you."

"Wh-What?" I wagged my head to the side. "You did what?"

"You heard me correctly. I opened Magical Matchups because of you." Verda's chin gave a slight tremble. "Well, I didn't know your name and I didn't know what you looked like, but I knew that I needed Magical Matchups to find you." She clapped her hands together. "And here you are!"

"Yes . . . here I am. But, I'm sorry, do I know you? Do you know my parents?" The absurd thought that maybe they were behind this, that they were somehow in cahoots with Verda, had me sitting up straighter. Was this their way of pushing Introductions toward failure, so I'd have no choice but to go work for my father? The calmness I'd been hanging on to for dear life whipped away in a burst of annoyance. "Did my parents set this up?"

Verda blinked several times. "Now, there's no need to look so jumpy. I don't know your parents. I opened Magical Matchups because you are the ideal mate for my grandson. It is critical that I bring you two together."

Okay, this woman? Certifiably nuts. What Kara and Leslie pegged for magical was actually insanity. I stood. "I've heard enough. I shouldn't have walked in here last night. I'm sorry I did. But—"

A male voice, one that made my skin itch with something I couldn't identify, came from the front room. "Grandma? Where are you? I came as soon as you called."

"Oh, goodie, he's here! I've been waiting for this for so long." Verda pushed her chair away from the table and pulled herself up. "We're back here. Come join us!"

"Who's here?" I asked, even as my intuition told me to keep my mouth shut.

"Why, your soul mate, of course."

My soul mate? I ranked the possibility of soul mates at about the same place I ranked romantic love—down there at the bottom. I opened my mouth to put a stop to this nonsense, but snapped it shut when a man sauntered into the break room. Not just any man, though. No, I couldn't be that lucky. It was Scot. *Leslie's* Scot. Well, her ex.

He looked just as delicious as I remembered. Around six one, maybe six two, he had the athletic body of a man who'd earned his muscles the old-fashioned way: playing and working hard. His short, almost black hair tousled around his strong, boldly angled face held the barest hint of a wave. He wore dark blue work denim, a thick flannel shirt, and heavy boots. Every ounce of Scot Raymond, from head to toe, screamed tough, sexy, masculine.

I wheezed out a breath and stared in shocked silence. Verda thought Scot was my soul mate? Impossible. I started to say so, but she spoke first.

"Julia, I'd like you to meet my grandson, Mr. Scot Raymond." Verda beamed at the two of us as if we'd just announced she'd won the lottery. "Scot, this is the woman you're going to marry. Isn't she lovely?"

Scot leaned against the wall. He looked at me in an appraising way that sent chills trickling over my skin. "Is that so?"

"Yes! Isn't this exciting?" Verda stood on her tiptoes to give her grandson a kiss on his cheek. "I told you I would find her, and here she is!"

Scot wrapped his arm around Verda's shoulders and pulled her close for a hug. She couldn't see his face, but I could. Irritation sparked in his dark brown eyes. He was mad? At me? What the hell for?

"How did you two find each other?" he asked, his voice calm.

"Oh, Julia found me. She was asleep on the couch this morning when I arrived." Verda stepped out of his embrace. "Should I leave you two alone so you can get to know each other a bit better?" She winked. "In private?"

"No! That's not necessary!" I nearly screeched. But hey, at least I'd found my voice. "I really should be going."

"Actually, I think a few minutes to talk in private is a great idea," Scot said, easily overriding me. "Thanks, Grandma."

Verda clapped her hands. "This is so wonderful! I'll be in the other room. Let me know when you're done."

She slipped out the door. The second she was gone, Scot's body language changed. Tension rippled through him, heavy and fierce. "I don't know what game you're playing, but you need to stop. Now."

"Game?" Confusion seeped in. "I'm not playing a game, Scot. I have no idea why your grandmother thinks—"

"I'm going to say this once and only once. Leave her alone, Julia."

He stepped forward, allowing his gaze to slip along the length of my body before resting on my face. His intensity shook me. And his scent . . . dear God, how had I forgotten the smell of Scot Raymond? Sunshine and trees. Autumn leaves and winter snow. It was as if Mother Nature had kissed Scot's skin, and I had the sudden craving to bury my nose in his neck.

A craving which I, of course, ignored. "Wh-What?"

Tiny crinkles around his eyes deepened. For a brief second, a flash of something flickered over him. Interest? Hunger? His face went passive before I could define it. "Whatever you did to put these romantic ideas about us in her head, you need to get them out."

I gripped my hands into fists. You know, so I wouldn't smack him. "You think I want to date you, so I came here and convinced your grandmother—when I didn't even know she was your grandmother—that we're soul mates? If you knew me at all, you'd know—"

"I know you well enough."

"Well enough for what?" I fired back, at a complete loss. I mean, did he really think I was so hot for him I'd waltz in here with some story about us being soul mates? And manipulate Verda? "I have no desire to date you, Scot." I lifted my chin. "None at all."

My statement took him by surprise. He stepped backward, blinked, and said, "Good. Then we're on the same page, because you're the last woman I'd want to become involved with." His eyes narrowed. "She's coming back. We need to fix this."

"Fix what? Just tell your grandmother—"

Verda stuck her head in. "Instead of getting to know each other here, why don't you two go out for breakfast?"

Scot, who was now standing behind Verda, shook his head and mouthed, "Fix this."

I glared at him. "You've been so sweet, Verda, but there's no need for that. Scot and I aren't . . . right for each other. There's no spark!" Lie. Huge, fat lie. "So, thanks for everything, but I need to take off."

The light in Verda's eyes dimmed. "Why, you've barely just met. Don't be so hasty, dear. I'm very sure that you two are meant to have a future."

Scot coughed. Oh, was he going to help? Nice of him.

"Julia's right, Grandma," he said quietly. "I love you, and I know we have a . . . deal, but in this instance I think your instincts are off. Trust me on this. And I'd love to stay and explain more, but I'm late for a job. We'll have to talk about this later."

With that, he gave her a quick, tight hug, turned on his heel, and left me alone with his grandmother. The rat! Who did he think he was? If I ever saw him again, I was so going to kill him. Well, if his scent didn't do me in first.

Even so, the second he disappeared, my heart grew a little heavier. There was a minute there, just one, where the thought of being cosmically connected to Scot hadn't seemed so out-there. I know, dumb. But it was a damn good thing I didn't believe in romantic love, fairy tales, or sex appeal leading to anything more than a night of toe-curling sex, or I might have been disappointed.

Hell, I might even have been devastated.

Chapter Four

Verda squinted at the space her grandson had just vacated, confusion paling her rosy pink complexion to a pasty white. She jiggled her head and wispy strands of lemon yellow hair tousled forward. I wanted to leave. I also wanted to offer comfort.

Which was nuts. Sure, Verda seemed like a nice enough lady, but come on. I needed a shower. I needed to brush my teeth. I needed to get to work. More than anything, though, I yearned to be alone. I didn't know Scot all that well, so his comments and behavior were highly uncalled-for. They also hurt and more than made sense. Far more than I cared to admit.

"Look, I don't know what's going on here, but I really have to get going." I winced at my harsher-than-intended tone. Softening it, I said, "Thanks for everything, but I—"

"This isn't supposed to happen this way," Verda said, her voice one notch above a whisper. Her lips screwed into a pucker and she twisted her fingers together. "I've been planning this for months. I wrote everything down, every little detail, just so . . ."

"Okay. Well." I edged closer to the hallway. "Thank you for not having me arrested. And for the coffee. Oh, and for . . . um . . . trying to fix me up with Scot. I don't understand why. We have nothing in common, but thanks."

This snagged Verda's attention. Focusing on me, she frowned. "Do you know my grandson?"

Oh. Why'd I open my big mouth? "Sort of. He dated a friend for a while." And because Leslie always shared pretty much everything about the men she went out with, I had zero doubts about my lack of compatibility with Scot. "We've met a few times."

Myriad tiny lines in Verda's forehead deepened. "Is this one of the friends you mentioned earlier?"

"Leslie Meyers," I confirmed, happy to pass on any information that might divert Verda's concentration from me. "She and Kara Lysecki are clients of yours." I backed up another step. Maybe I could slip away without Verda noticing?

No. Fate wasn't going to be so kind. "*This* is the man whom Leslie wishes she'd handled things differently with?" Verda asked. "*My* grandson?"

I nodded. "But this isn't really my business. You should talk to Leslie about it." Maybe, with Verda's help, Leslie would get her second chance with Scot. My heart skipped a beat at that thought. Out of happiness for Leslie, of course.

"Was I wrong?" Verda's shoulders slumped. "I was so sure you were the one."

"Why?" I demanded. I shouldn't have asked. I mean, Verda believed in soul mates. I didn't. What else was there? "Why were you so sure? You've never met me before today!"

"I suppose it's possible I misinterpreted the signs," she said, mostly to herself. Then she shook herself, as if waking up from a dream. "But you said the front door was unlocked last night, and when you tried to leave, it wouldn't open."

I reined in my frustration. "Yes. I don't know why the door was open, but I figured the lock broke. But that doesn't seem to be the case." Since, you know, Scot breezed in and out in under ten minutes flat. Ugh. Why did that hurt? I *hated* that it hurt. Verda's question replayed in my mind, and suddenly, I understood her madness. Or I thought I did. "Wait a minute.

You thought because I was stuck here, that was some sort of a sign?"

Verda huffed out a tiny breath. "I believe in signs, Julia. I believe in a lot of things."

"But that doesn't mean—"

"I didn't fib to you earlier, young lady. I opened Magical Matchups with the primary purpose of finding Scot's soul mate. When I discovered you here this morning, on the heels of Miranda insisting I get here quickly, I believed you were that woman."

"Uh-uh. Not me. Sorry." Could crazy be compelling? Because I had to admit, Verda talked a little—okay, a lot—loony, but somehow I was also weirdly drawn to her. "Listen. Last night wasn't a sign. Sometimes, things that seemingly don't make any sense just happen. An unusual conglomeration of coincidences. That's all last night was."

"Hm. Maybe. Maybe not. I'll have to give this . . . predicament . . . more thought." Verda collapsed into her seat. Wrapping her hands around her teacup, she asked, "But neither your phone nor mine worked?"

I sighed but kept my voice even. "Correct. May I leave now?" Okay, technically I didn't have to ask for Verda's permission to leave, but she looked shaken and wasn't exactly young. Every good manner I'd ever learned prevented me from walking away.

"Please humor an old lady for a few more minutes. I'm feeling a bit . . ." She blinked several times and fanned her face. "Faint."

I narrowed my eyes. She'd grinned for a split second. I was sure of it. Mostly sure, anyway, but what if I was wrong? "A few more minutes," I agreed, joining her at the table. "Do you need anything? Can I call someone for you? This Miranda person you keep mentioning, perhaps?"

"Call Miranda? What a delightful idea." Verda chuckled, more amused than seemed warranted. "No, dear. Thank you for the offer, but I'll be fine shortly."

Patience is not a strong suit of mine, but I tried. I really did. I picked at a raspberry and chocolate pastry while waiting for Verda to give some type of indication that she was feeling better, so I could escape and carry on with my day. After a while, though—probably no more than ten minutes—the quiet unnerved me. "Um . . . what time do you normally open for business?"

My voice startled her enough that she flinched. "Oh, I operate by appointment only. I don't have anyone coming in today until early afternoon."

"That's . . . nice." Wow. Walk-ins were a large part of my business. How could she be so successful with an appointment-only process? I so wanted to pick her brain, but doing so would open up questions I'd rather avoid. Like, why was I so interested?

Verda sipped more of her tea, her expression vacant, already lost in thought. I fidgeted, looked at my watch, and fidgeted some more. A shiver skittered down my spine at the same instant something pulled Verda out of her haze. Her blue eyes darkened a shade. A rush of pink returned to her cheeks. Angling her neck, she centered her gaze to the right of me and nodded. The corners of her mouth bowed upward in a slight smile—but I'd have bet every dollar in my bank account that she wasn't smiling at me.

I swiveled in my seat, my heart in my mouth, somehow thinking that I'd find someone standing behind me. Scot, maybe. Why that thought was so appealing, I didn't know. But no. Verda and I were still alone. The faintest whiff of a fragrance floated by. Roses. Again.

"What is that?" I asked Verda, immediately reminded of last

night's bone-chilling, inexplicable fear. "What is that smell? Do you have one of those scented furnace filters or something?" Please, please let that be the case.

"Wh-What?" Verda asked, nearly spilling tea in her shock. "What's that, dear?"

"The roses, Verda. I noticed the scent last night, and again just now, but I haven't seen flowers anywhere." I came off like an idiot. I knew it, but so what? "What is it from?"

"Oh, the roses?" Excitement pitched Verda's voice higher. "You can smell them?"

"Yes! How could I not?"

Verda exhaled a breath—if I hadn't known better, I'd have sworn in relief. She jiggled in her seat and mirth danced in her eyes. "Well, that's something, isn't it? You can smell the flowers!" Leaping to her feet, she grabbed my hands and squeezed. "Isn't this wonderful?"

I wouldn't go quite that far. "Um. Sure. I suppose." I pulled out of her grip. "But where *are* the roses?"

"Oh, they're not real." Calmer now, she stared at me a few seconds longer. Her lips did that twitchy, almost-a-grin-but-not-quite thing. "Exactly as you said. Special furnace filters. We started using them to . . . ah . . . cover the nasty odor of exhaust fumes that come in from the street." She winked. "Forgive my excitement, Julia. I wasn't sure if they were working."

There it was. The perfectly sane and reasonable explanation I wanted to hear. So why didn't I believe her? "I see. Well, that's good. That they're doing the trick, I mean."

She cleared her throat. "You've been so sweet to stay here with me, but I'm feeling so much better now."

Yay! Escape. "Oh, it was nothing." I pushed away from the table. "Glad to help."

She gestured for me to follow and then scurried out of the

break room. She moved fast. When I caught up with her, she was already dragging documents out of the file cabinet in the lobby.

"As an apology for delaying you for so long, and to make up for your . . . um . . . inability to leave, I'm offering you a free membership to my services," she said, continuing to stack papers at an alarming rate. "I'm very good at what I do. We'll find you your soul mate, mark my words."

"No! That is so not necessary," my voice rang out—too loudly, so I lowered it. "I'm fine, and—no offense—but I consider soul mates to be nothing more than a fairy tale. I don't believe in either, so really—"

She waved away my arguments. "It doesn't matter what you believe. Besides, we'll cover all of this later, after you've filled everything out."

"Um, excuse me? It does so matter what I believe."

Verda's shoulders quaked in silent laughter. Tilting her chin up, she looked directly at me. "But don't you see? You came to me. I didn't come to you. That's reason enough for me to help you." Whisking the many papers together, she shoved them in a manila envelope, along with a book of some sort. "You are a special girl, Julia. You deserve a special partner. Let me use my abilities and Magical Matchups to find that partner for you. What do you say?"

I hesitated. This was difficult to pass up. Here she was, offering me everything that had led me here to begin with. But after spending the morning with her, that inner moral voice of mine screamed louder than ever. Finally, I shrugged. "I—I don't know."

Razor-sharp eyes bored into me. "I don't take 'no' easily. All of this will be much easier on you if nod your head and agree."

And this was the point I should have walked—no, run—

away. But in her hands was the information that might help me save my company. I *had* been stuck here for hours and scared out of my wits. Right? Besides which, I had the sinking feeling that no matter what I said, she'd find a way to convince me otherwise. Or maybe I was using that as an excuse. Regardless, I found myself nodding in agreement. "If you insist."

"Oh, I do!" She passed me the thick envelope and then patted my cheek. "I know you're late for work, dear. So why don't we plan on getting together after you have time to go through all of this?"

Was it my imagination, or was she making this really, really easy? "Yeah. That would be terrific."

Verda beamed. Her smile virtually sparkled. "Do you think you'll be ready by tomorrow evening? I'd like to get moving as soon as we can, but the paperwork is quite extensive, so if you need a bit more time, then I suppose next week will have to do."

I swallowed. Chances were high that I wouldn't be returning, but she didn't have to know that quite yet. I'd call her tomorrow, tell her I'd changed my mind, and that would be that.

"Absolutely," I said, matching Verda's enthusiasm with my own, albeit fake, version. "Tomorrow evening is ideal."

Two mad-dash drives later—one to my apartment for a quickie shower and a fresh change of clothes, and the other from my place to work—found me at my desk slightly before eleven o'clock. Not so bad, if I did say so myself.

I'd purposely left Verda's envelope at home, so I wouldn't be tempted to go through her client paperwork immediately. Right now, I needed to focus on my one and only appointment for the day. Normally, my prep time extended well beyond an hour. I was very careful in putting together my recommendations, and that began with understanding as much as possible about the client, or prospective client, before we ever met face-to-face.

Not only did I read their responses from their profile questionnaire, but I read between the lines to develop a fuller picture of their needs versus their wants. This was easier with women. Partially because I understood women more, but also because women tended to give complete, detailed responses.

Men, on the other hand, at least the men I'd come across at Introductions, were very spare in detail. Though they had one thing going for them: honesty. They rarely tried to cover anything up. Maybe it was because they were generally more confident than women, or maybe they didn't view their weaknesses as weaknesses, or perhaps it simply didn't occur to them to care. Or, you know, that whole "Man is King" attitude.

These one-on-one interviews were essential in digging out the rest of the picture. I had a lot of faith in my compatibility program, which was based on a series of yes/no and true/false questions, but relying on it completely would be foolhardy.

Today's appointment was with a man who'd electronically sent his profile information in the day before and had immediately set an appointment. That gave me hope he was serious. But I only had about fifteen minutes to get everything together.

I hurriedly clicked on the link my assistant Diane had embedded in my e-calendar and waited for his profile to open on my screen. Diane had worked as a temporary employee off and on my first year. I'd hired her permanently the second year as a part-time employee. My hope had been to make her full-time this year, but unless things picked up, I'd have to let her go. I *hated* that thought. I needed this appointment to go well.

I ran the man's compatibility numbers and printed off the

profiles of the three highest probable matches. All were in the mid–60 percent range. Not great. Not by a long shot. But I didn't have time to go over them in depth, so I tucked them into a folder and moved on. Next, I skimmed through the questions he'd answered, searching for anything that might jump out as unique, especially interesting, or flat-out weird. Interesting was good. Weird was not.

I'd barely started my perusal when Diane knocked on the door and stuck her head in. "Your eleven fifteen is here, Julia." She pursed her lips in a silent whistle. "I might be willing to date this one. He's a doll."

"That's good to know, though your husband might not be so pleased," I joked.

"I'm allowed to look. So, are you ready for him?"

"Not even close, but send him in anyway." I'd have to wing it. I drank some water to moisten my mouth before putting on my most professional smile.

A man in his midthirties entered my office. He looked vaguely familiar, but I couldn't place him. Probably, he just had one of those faces. His top-of-the-line charcoal suit fit him in a way that bespoke a professional tailor. Which meant money. He stood average height, around five foot ten, and his dark hair had the tiniest amount of salt dotting his temples. His chin was more soft than hard, but not enough to detract from his appeal, and he had the greenest eyes I'd ever seen. So green, my guess was on colored contacts.

That, and the fact he wore a matching green tie to show off those emerald peepers, told me he put a lot of stock in appearances. Diane was right, though. *Doll* described him well.

I held out my hand and he shook it with a firm grip. I liked that. Glancing at my monitor, I said, "Nice to meet you Mr. Johnson. I'm Julia Collins, the owner of Introductions."

I nodded toward the twin chairs in front of my desk. "Please take a seat."

"Thanks. I'm happy to be here." Settling himself, he tossed me a grin that turned him from doll to debonair. Wow.

"May I get you some coffee, water, tea?" I asked, slipping into flight-attendant mode.

"Nope. I'd rather get right to it." He had this slow, lazy way of talking that oozed charm. I wondered how many hours he'd spent practicing to get the perfect cadence. My guess was most of his twenties. "I'm rather anxious to get started."

Just what I wanted to hear. "Why don't we start informally? In your own words, what brought you to Introductions?"

"I'm tired of the dating scene. It gets old, especially when you're as busy as I am." He steepled long, tapered fingers under his chin. "Saw one of your ads, I don't recall where at the moment, but figured, why not? Created an account, filled everything out, and here I am."

A quick decision maker. Something else I liked. I filed that away for future reference. "I was hoping we could go through your profile together. That way, I can ask questions as we go along to deepen my understanding of the type of woman you're looking for."

"So you don't prescreen before meetings?"

Of course he'd ask that. "Normally, I do. But your profile just came in yesterday and I was running late today. I'm sure we can get through everything relatively quickly."

I expected him to be annoyed. This wasn't the most professional way to run a first-time meeting, and this guy hadn't fallen off the turnip truck. Instead, though, a pleased expression darted over him. He rubbed his hands together. "Perfect. Let's get started."

I gotta say that I was feeling really positive about this guy. If the rest of the appointment went well, I'd have a check in my hand and a match for him in no time. Turning my attention to the computer screen, I read, "You're thirty-five, have lived in Chicago your entire life, you're a . . . monster-truck driver?" Okay, I'd never met one of those before. I sifted this new information in with what I'd already gathered. "Is that your only line of work?"

"Oh, no. It's not even my most exciting line of work, but it gets my adrenaline going. Really more of a pastime." Leaning forward, he squared his elbows on my desk. "I think . . . yes, go down a few more questions."

My gaze traveled down. "Oh. You . . . recycle cans and bottles to earn money? And . . . make 'special' videos?" My voice squeaked. Seriously? "What kind of videos, Mr. Johnson?"

"All types of videos. You wouldn't believe the market for a camera guy who will shoot just about anything."

"Weddings? Graduations? Things like that?" Oh, God, let him say yes. "Birthdays and anniversaries?"

"Um. Sure. Those, too."

I swiveled in my seat, facing him. "What else, Mr. Johnson?"

"Bar Mitzvahs. Bat Mitzvahs." Waggling his eyebrows, he said, "All-girl slumber parties. Pillow fights. You know, almost anything."

"Uh-huh." I forced a swallow past the lump in my throat. Typically, my instincts about other people were solid. Typically, my first impressions about someone stuck. "Let's move on."

"It might be best if we skip to the end. Those are the important questions." Humor slid into his voice. "You know, the ones about the type of women I'd like you to find for me?"

"Yes. Of course." I needed new clients, a new infusion of cash, so I was willing to give this guy the benefit of the doubt. For now, anyway. Clicking through the next group of pages, I found the questions he wanted.

Clearing my throat, I said, "You'd like to find someone who is adventurous and isn't afraid to try new things." A little redundant, but I didn't point that out. "And someone who is talented in—" I stared at the words so long that my eyes began to water. Blinking, I read them again. And then again. "Talented in . . . Are you serious, Mr. Johnson?"

"Very. Basically, I'm hoping for a vacuum," he supplied. "And the next question? The one about my goals matching my prospective mate's goals? Those are a deal breaker. Just so you're aware of my feelings about that up front."

Distaste churned in my gut as I continued to read, "Household objects . . . without fear of injury? Foursomes? Oh. Really?" I shook my head and closed my eyes, not able to read anymore. I'm not a prude, but this went beyond having a little fun in the bedroom. "I believe you are mistaken about the services I offer. Introductions is not a brothel. My clients are not interested in"—I glanced again at the screen and nearly choked—"playing 'fun and innovative games with farm animals.'"

"Do you know that for sure?" he asked. "Have you ever actually asked anyone? People can surprise you. Especially fine and upstanding men like myself. We're not always what we appear to be."

"I'm sure," I said coolly. "And I am not a madam, and I do not cater to the clientele you are apparently seeking." I almost wanted to send him to Magical Matchups and turn Verda loose on him. She'd set him straight. Of course, I wouldn't do that, even if I figured she'd be able to handle this jerk better than I could.

"Again, I have to ask. Are you sure?" Now, rather than charm, I heard slimy smugness.

"Oh yes, Mr. Johnson, I am one hundred percent sure." Yes, I needed clients. But not this badly. Hell, there wasn't a woman alive I'd set this piece of work up with. At least not a woman I'd yet met. I aimed my gaze toward the door. "This meeting is over."

"Oh, calm down. Surely you've seen worse." Smoothing his hair back at the temples, he continued, "So I have a few fantasies. Most men do."

My seething emotions didn't allow a response.

"I'm also interested in having a true partner. Maybe a gal who could help me run my film business. Go out and collect cans and bottles when I'm busy with other things."

"Please leave, Mr. Johnson." *I will remain calm,* I chanted to myself. *I. Will. Remain. Calm.* I cared about my clients. Their well-being was important to me. And this . . . this creep thought I'd set him and his household appliances up with one of my girls?

Screw calm.

I turned on him, fire in my blood, ready to lash out with every ill thought I had. But his chest quivered in quiet laughter. Instead of catching this, my rage grew. "You think this is funny, Mr. Johnson?"

"Hilarious. Please call me by my first name, though. Harold." He paused, his lips quirked, and the muscles in his cheeks flinched. "Or, rather, Harry."

"Fine. Harry, your profile tells me that you're a sick—" I stopped. I breathed. I added everything up and then I slumped in my chair. Wow. I was losing my touch. How had I not seen this earlier? I mentally went through everything again, and when I was sure, said, "I don't appreciate these types of jokes. You might think this is funny, but I do not."

Blinking, as if confused, he said, "Joke?"

Any remaining doubt fled. "Harry Johnson is not your name. And this"—I pointed to the computer screen—"is not your profile. I don't know why you thought it would be funny to—"

"Maybe they are. How do you know?" he shot back. "As I said, people can surprise you."

"Yes, but I have excellent instincts." People rarely surprised me. Though this guy had.

"Do you?" he asked with a wink. "Explain, please."

"I pegged you as a well-off businessman the second you walked in. You probably come from money. You were courteous and respectful." I pushed out a breath, trying to keep my temper at bay. "And while you care deeply for appearances, you did not set off my slime alarm."

"Go on," he prodded. "This is fascinating."

"But as soon as we delved into your . . . abnormal responses, you were unable to keep a straight face. Then, right there at the end, your muscles tensed, your voice pitched, and your eyes. They're a dead giveaway." If my temper hadn't climbed so high, I would've caught on sooner. I couldn't believe I hadn't caught on sooner. I blamed my lack of comprehension on the past twenty-four hours. "Why would you do this? My time is valuable to me, Mr. Whoever-you-are, and I don't appreciate it being wasted."

He had the nerve to whistle. "You are good. Your dad said you were, but I had to see for myself."

"My father?" All at once, the rest of the pieces came together. I squinted my eyes, merging the face I remembered with the face in front of me. "Jameson Parkington?"

"There you go. Can't believe you didn't catch on right away." Warmth flooded his features, reminding me of how much I'd liked him when he walked in my door. "It was a bet of sorts. I had no idea you'd get so upset."

I counted to ten, but no way was that going to be enough, and I didn't relish the thought of counting to one hundred. Instead, I asked, "Bet? With my father?"

"He said I wouldn't be able to put one over on you. For

some reason it was important to him that I try. And what's important to your dad is important to mine." Jameson shrugged in a careless manner. "But when you became so angry, so protective of your clients, it didn't seem as funny."

"Wait. Why would my father *want* you to do this?"

"Something about proving you were a chip off the old block." Jameson schooled his expression so I couldn't read it. "Maybe he has plans for you at his firm?"

Even as I accepted that as the truth, it brought a new bout of aggravation. This sounded exactly like something Gregory Collins would do to a prospect. In truth, I'd always thought his methods were inventive and sort of cool. Being the target was a different story.

"There was a second there, right when I got here, that I was sure you'd recognized me," Jameson said. "I'm surprised you didn't."

I wasn't. I hadn't seen Jameson since my college-graduation party. He'd had long hair, thick-rimmed glasses, and we'd said maybe three words to each other. Actually, it was a shocker I'd recognized him at all. "Does my father know *how* you were going to pull this off?" Because try as I might, I couldn't see my dad putting his stamp of approval on any of this.

"That would be a no. It's probably best if we don't tell him, either."

The faintest flicker of humor came alive. Oh, don't get me wrong. I was still ticked, but I'd be hard pressed not to admit the joke had been clever. Disgusting, yes. Annoying, hell yes. But clever. I rubbed my hands over my face and groaned. "Really, Jameson? Household objects? Farm animals? It worries me that you thought of those at all, even as a joke."

"Nah," he said easily. "Wasn't my demented brain that came up with that stuff. I called an acquaintance of mine. He . . . ah . . . ran several *specialty* Web sites for years. He supplied the down and dirty answers." Jameson pointed at the monitor. "But somewhere in Chicago, a guy with that name is sure to exist. You might want to delete the profile."

"Oh, I will." Like the second he exited my office. God. I still wanted to throttle him. "I thought you were coming in Monday, anyway. Your little joke couldn't have waited until then?"

"I thought of that," he confessed. "But decided not to. My plan was to leave today with you thinking I was Mr. Johnson. Which would've made Monday a lot of fun. But you were too upset for me to keep going," he added sheepishly.

He angled his left leg over his right, the tension in his slacks pulling them up at the hem. I chewed on the inside of my lips to stop a grin from emerging. He wore socks emblazoned with cartoon characters. My *favorite* cartoon characters: Wile E. Coyote and Road Runner.

In the snap of a finger, the rest of my annoyance evaporated. Here he was, dressed in a suit that cost more than most people earned in a month, and he'd teamed it up with quirky socks. Yeah. I liked that.

"It's funny you showed up. I . . . um . . . was going to call you today, anyway."

His brow raised in question. "About?"

"That preholiday shindig you invited me to. If the offer is still open, I'd love to go." There, I'd said it. And the words didn't kill me, either. How about that?

"Admit it. I bowled you over with my creativity, didn't I?"

"That's one way to put it." I laughed in spite of myself. "Well? No fair to keep a girl waiting."

"I'd love to escort you to my family's 'shindig.' But why don't we get together this weekend, too? Say Sunday for lunch? Brunch?"

"Um . . . sure, that sounds okay." If he were really interested, he'd have gone for a Friday or Saturday evening. Sunday lunch/brunch was saved for current girlfriends, not would-be girlfriends. But I was okay with that. More than okay, actually. "About one?"

"One it is." He rose to a stand. "I am sorry for upsetting you. I like jokes, and I remembered you were always the serious sort. When Gregory broached the idea of testing you, I thought it might be fun to shock you."

"You were successful, Jameson." I rounded the desk to show him out. "About Monday. Are you still coming in?"

He stared at me in an intense way that brought about inane thoughts of hearts and flowers and chocolates. "Well, why not? My profile's already loaded and ready to go." Tipping an imaginary hat, he said, "It's been a pleasure, Julia."

I nodded and watched him leave. The instant he disappeared, I beelined it for my PC. With a few taps of my fingers, I had Jameson Parkington's real profile up. With a few more taps, I had the women he was most compatible with.

"Well, isn't that interesting," I mused, staring at the results.

Ninety-four percent compatibility. One of the highest I'd seen. And the lucky woman was none other than myself. Yep. Definitely interesting. And slightly off-putting to see that my parents were, once again, right on the money.

Chapter Five

"Why is there never anything to eat when I'm starving?" I grumbled, searching the freezer for something other than one of the many low-calorie, low-fat, and low-flavor frozen meals I'd bought. Hey, they were on sale: two for one. I figured they'd be edible.

Wrong.

Frustrated and ravenous, I gave up and grabbed the box that claimed to be spaghetti. Nights like this almost made me yearn for Wednesdays. My parents might drive me crazy, but Rosalie was an excellent cook. Well, when lamb wasn't on the menu.

Some of my best childhood memories were of Rosalie teaching me to cook. I was good at it, too. But who had the time? Not me.

I ripped open the packaging, air-vented the plastic coating, and set the meal to rotate through radio waves that would cook it by exciting the food's water and fat molecules. Yes, I am well aware of how geeky it is to understand the basic science of microwave cooking. I like to think that's part of what makes me special.

After my long night at Magical Matchups, my morning with Verda, and the weirdness of Jameson, aka Harold, I was ecstatic to be home. Even better, I'd decided to play hooky the following day in order to go through Verda's paperwork. I rarely skipped, but Friday was the only day of the week that Diane put in a full eight hours, so the timing couldn't have been better. Especially with zero appointments scheduled. Well, that wasn't exactly good news, but it made taking the day off easier. Tonight, however, was me, the couch, and as much of the first season of *Seinfeld* that I could fit in before falling asleep.

While the faux spaghetti did its thing, I stripped off my skirt and blouse in my bedroom. The panty hose came next. I sighed in relief as I slid on my oldest, comfiest, I-wouldn't-be-caught-dead-in-these-in-public pajamas. I washed my face, removed my hair from its clip, and was about to grab the DVD when someone knocked on my door. Unless Kara and Leslie had changed their minds about the horror movie they'd suggested, it wasn't them. Besides, they almost always let themselves in.

Returning to the living room, I slid the chain onto the door before opening it a crack—just in case—and peered through. My gaze landed on the last man on earth I expected to see. Seriously. I'd have been less shocked to find Elvis Presley.

"Why?" I sputtered, instantly caught somewhere between pleasure, confusion, and defensiveness. "What are you doing here?"

"Open up, Julia. We need to talk," Scot—yes, *that* Scot—said.

"I don't know why you're here, but I'm not interested. Go away, Scot."

"This is important. You can let me in or I can make a nuisance of myself out here." Raising his voice to just this side of a shout, he added, "In the hearing of all your neighbors!"

"Go ahead and shout! I don't care if my neighbors hear you," I replied. He probably meant Leslie, who wasn't home. He could make all the noise he wanted.

"This is silly. We can stand here and go on and on, or you can let me in, we can talk, and then I'll be more than happy to take off."

My confusion increased. "But why are you here? What could you possibly have to say to me after this morning?"

"If I told you now, there'd be no reason for me to come in, would there?" His voice dropped to a husky whisper. "Let me in."

A shiver rolled out from the pit of my stomach. I bit my lower lip and pretended to consider his request. "I don't want you here. Go away," I said again.

He sighed. "Okay, look. I know this seems odd, and I don't want to be an ass and create a scene, but for something this important, I will." He blinked long, thick lashes at me. Lashes that deserved to frame a woman's eyes. "Just give me a chance to explain."

Important? What was he going on about? "Or what? You'll huff and puff and blow my apartment down? As strong and manly as you are, you can't have that much hot air."

"Are you flirting?" he asked, suddenly grinning. "I didn't expect that."

"No! I am not—" The microwave beeped in the kitchen, saving me from saying something else stupid. "My dinner's done. Closing the door. See ya."

Scot stuck one foot into the opening, effectively halting the slam. "I come bearing gifts." He brought a large box into view. "Pizza. And not just any pizza, but Vito's. Pepperoni and mushroom. Your favorite, isn't it?"

Oh, dear God. I could smell it. My mouth watered. My stomach growled. I'm not ashamed to admit that there is very little I wouldn't do for a Vito's pepperoni and mushroom pizza. I scowled and shored up my willpower. "I have dinner. Take your pizza and go."

Lifting the lid, he tilted the box forward. "Come on, Julia," he said. "Thirty minutes of conversation for half of this pizza. What do you say?"

Hell. I could let him in, eat a decent dinner, hear what he had to say, and then go on with my evening. "I'm pretty sure

I hate you right now," I said, though my eyes fastened on the pizza. My stomach growled again, louder, and a silent moan gurgled in my throat, begging to be released. "But you win."

"Good. I'm glad you see it my way."

I kicked at his foot with mine, trying to convince myself that this wouldn't be so bad. I mean, I had a few questions for him, anyway. He pulled his foot back; I closed the door to remove the chain and then opened up again. Sighed. "Come on in."

He sauntered inside as if he belonged there, all long legs and cocky attitude. I didn't shut the door right away, just stood there like an idiot and stared. He sort of reminded me of James Dean, with the leather jacket, tousled chestnut hair, and a hint of danger in those chocolate eyes. Or maybe Johnny Depp.

Okay, I know—very different guys with very different looks, but somehow, Scot reminded me of both. A realization that did nothing to calm my whipped-up nerves.

"Cute pajamas," he said, taking in my appearance. "Are those baby sheep?"

Heat flushed through me. "Yes. They were a gift from a friend." Hell, why was I explaining? "I wasn't exactly expecting company." I resisted the urge to run to my bedroom and change. "Now, why are you here?"

"Close the door," he commanded. Firm, sensual lips curved into a stiff smile. Again, I had the nonsensical want to bury my nose in his neck and breathe in. No man has the right to smell that freaking fantastic. Balancing the pizza box with one hand and then the other, Scot unzipped his jacket and shrugged it off. His movements were fluid, graceful, and for some reason, surprising. My mouth went dry, and suddenly the last thing on my mind was dinner. "Come on. Close the door and we'll eat," he said. "And then we'll talk."

Why was he being so nice? I tried to pull myself out of

my daze, tried to make sense of what he was up to. Maybe he wanted to apologize? He'd brought food. Which, for me, was way better than flowers. His body was relaxed, and he'd actually smiled.

"I'm not sure what we have to discuss, but whatever." My voice wobbled, which annoyed me, but I shoved the door so it slammed shut. Straightening my spine, I said, "How'd you know what type of pizza to bring?"

He held out the box. "I called Leslie. She said it would do the trick."

His words bounced around my brain but refused to stick. "You called Leslie?"

"Yup. Why? Is that a problem?"

Hell, yes, that was a problem. See, I hadn't exactly gotten around to telling Leslie about my night at Magical Matchups, or that Scot was Verda's grandson. I hadn't mentioned the soulmate thing, either. I'd planned to. I would've. Probably over the weekend. But as worried as I was about all of that, I was more concerned for Leslie. "Are you insane?"

"Not that I know of," he said.

"Quit being so dense! Is Leslie okay with you being here?"

Scot stared at me, unblinking. "Is there a reason why she shouldn't be?"

I stared back, trying to read him, but came up blank. Yanking the pizza box from his hands, I said, "Oh, I don't know. Maybe that you two dated? Maybe that I'm her best friend? Maybe that she might feel strange because of everything that went on between you two? Or possibly because she's been going to Magical Matchups and confiding her romantic dreams to Verda without knowing your connection?" I puffed out an infuriated breath. "Or maybe, just maybe, all of the above? I can't believe you called her!"

The easy, relaxed demeanor fled. Scot's eyes darkened and

his mouth tightened. "Leslie and I are over. She knows that. You and I are nothing. She knows that, too. And I didn't tell her about my grandmother." Tossing his jacket over the back of my sofa, he said, "So, again, I'll ask: is there a reason Leslie shouldn't be okay with my being here?"

"What did you tell her?"

"The truth. That there's something important I need to discuss with you, and I wanted to know the easiest way to get you to agree. She said Vito's."

Oh, no. Leslie, with her new romantic fantasies, likely assumed Scot wanted to talk about *her*. My cheeks heated with emotion. Anger at Scot, perhaps? But also something else. A craving for something I didn't begin to understand.

"Clueless," I mumbled, no longer sure if I meant him or me. "And if you're here to apologize, you're not doing so hot. Should work that into your skill set, Scot. Contrition might come in handy." I strode to the kitchen without giving him a chance to respond.

Scot Raymond. In my home. With Leslie's approval. The complexity of that boggled my mind, so I shoved it away for now. I kept my breathing even and busied myself with gathering plates, napkins, and sodas, all the while ignoring the telltale tremble in my muscles.

"You have a nice place here," Scot said, coming in behind me.

"Thanks," I said grudgingly.

My place *was* nice. The front room was large and airy, with wide windows and hardwood floors. My desk divided the living room and the dining room. A door to the left led to the kitchen, and farther down, a T-shaped hallway with my bedroom at the end. The bathroom had two doors, one off the hallway and one off of my bedroom.

"But it should look familiar. Kara and Leslie's place is the same setup, only they have two bedrooms." I sprinkled an obscene amount of Parmesan cheese on my slices. "Help yourself," I said when I finished preparing my plate. Then, without so much as a glance in his direction, I left him there alone and retreated to the living room.

I slid the first DVD in and started the pilot episode before Scot appeared. Hey, I said I'd give him thirty minutes to chat, but damn if I wasn't going to eat my food and watch my show first. Dumb, maybe, but I desperately needed to find a measure of control, and this seemed as good a way as any to get it. Besides, who doesn't like *Seinfeld*?

Scot plopped down next to me on the sofa and balanced his plate on his thighs. Every muscle in my body tightened at his closeness. Dampness dotted the back of my neck. I scooted to the other side, but even that was too close, so I moved to the chair. Sticking to my plan to ignore him until I had no other choice, I fixated on the television.

The TV flicked off. "Turn it back on," I said.

"Nope. I can't stand this show."

Told you. Zero compatibility. "How can you not like *Seinfeld*?"

"I find it annoying," he said. "And I didn't come here to watch TV."

Whatever. "Turn it on or give me the remote."

"Nope," he repeated. "Let's just eat and get this over with."

"Sure," I agreed. "Say you're sorry. I'll pretend to forgive you, and then you can go about your merry way and leave me alone." I chewed a bite of pizza and swallowed it down with some soda. "Here, I'll help you. Just say, 'Julia, I'm sorry I was a total ass hat this morning. You didn't deserve that response and I feel really badly about it.'"

Deep, rolling laughter hit my ears. Setting my plate down,

I pushed myself up and glared down at Scot. My temper continued to rise the longer he laughed. "What is so funny?"

"Ass hat? Your Ivy League education teach you that?" He snickered again. "I am not here to apologize. Whatever gave you that idea?"

"Gee, Scot. Let me think." I touched my temple with my finger. "Oh, yeah, that's it. I remember now. You were rude! You acted as if I'd set everything up with Verda. Which is ridiculous on every level imaginable. And then, before I could even react, you conveniently took off!"

"You got all of that from the short time I was there? Huh." Scot deposited his plate next to mine. "And just for the record, the idea of soul mates is not ridiculous. My grandmother—"

"Is a very sweet lady, but a little off her rocker. Was she serious? Or is this some whacked-out game she plays to get new clients?" Ouch. I didn't mean that. Not really.

Scot's eyes iced over. "My grandmother is far from delusional."

"I didn't say she was delusional. I *like* her. But you can't tell me that you agree with her. You made that quite clear this morning." I sucked in a deep breath. "Unless you've changed your mind? Is that why you're here?"

His jaw hardened, so much I probably could've cracked an egg against it. "I am not here because I believe you are my soul mate." He laughed again, but the sound held no mirth. "In fact, I'd be willing to bet that there isn't a man alive who's right for you."

My chest constricted and I bit back shock. "What is your problem?"

"That's the same question I asked myself when I found you cozying up to my grandmother this morning." Scot narrowed his gaze. I felt the burn of it to the tips of my toes. "Maybe

I was rude. I'll give you that. And I probably do owe you an apology, but this"—he nodded toward the pizza—"wasn't about that. I just needed you to hear me out."

"And you thought the best way to do that was to come into my home and insult me?" To give him credit, he looked chagrined. But he remained quiet, so I said, "You'd actually bet money that there isn't a man anywhere in this world who is right for me? Wow, Scot, I had no idea you knew me so well."

"I know enough."

A host of stupid, messy, nonsensical emotions swarmed me. It was a first, and I reacted completely on instinct. I lunged forward, grabbed his arm and tugged with every ounce of strength in my five-foot-five, one-hundred-and-twenty-and-a-half-pound frame. His six feet plus of who-knows-how-many pounds didn't budge.

That didn't stop me from tugging harder. "Get out. This conversation is over."

His free hand clasped my wrist, the touch of his fingers searing my skin, sending a jolt of electricity through me. With one quick yank, I toppled over, and just that fast I was in his lap. His arms closed in, capturing me.

"We can sit like this and talk or you can go back to your chair. I haven't said what I came to say, and I'm not leaving until we're finished." Hot breath tickled my cheek. His scent, woodsy and warm, assailed my senses. "Your choice, Julia."

"Let go of me," I said, my voice strangled. "You are in *my* home. I call the shots here." Okay, it was rather a ridiculous statement when I couldn't even move, but that didn't make my point less valid. Still, he didn't so much as twitch, just continued to hold me tight.

A sob crawled into my throat, but I choked it down. "You said I was the last woman you'd want to date. Really? The *last* woman?"

Something about the tone of my voice must have gotten to him, because he dropped his arms. I nearly vaulted over the coffee table to escape. Right at that minute, I wished I knew karate or jujitsu or some other type of dangerous but cool-looking martial art. I'd send a flying kick his way so fast he wouldn't see it coming. Just to get his body closer to the door, mind you. Not because my feelings were so awfully hurt.

"You don't like me. I get that," I said. "But I don't get why. Why, Scot?" Maybe if I understood that part of the equation, everything else would slide into focus.

He ran his hands over his eyes, his face incredibly drawn. "Leslie, for one," he admitted. "But I'm not here to go into that."

"What does Leslie have to do with this? I mean, she didn't cheat on you with me. I was an innocent bystander." Oh. Maybe I shouldn't have mentioned the whole cheating thing. "I'm sorry. I shouldn't have said that."

He didn't seem to hear. "Innocent? You preached to her constantly about the unreliability of feelings. That her feelings for me couldn't be counted on. My feelings for *her*, either. Our relationship consisted of three people: me, Leslie, and *you*."

"What? No! I never did that! I never told her that stuff in regard to you." Had Leslie blamed me for her mistakes with Scot? I couldn't believe she'd do that. "Scot, she talked about you a lot, sure. But I never gave her advice on your relationship."

"You never mentioned how you think love is for suckers and that she shouldn't trust her heart over her brain?"

Oh. *That.* "Um. Maybe I said that stuff to her. But it wasn't specifically about you. We've had these conversations for almost as long as we've known each other." I fought to find clarity. "And you can't fault me for her behavior. That isn't fair."

"I don't," he said in a pained, quiet voice. "She made her choice. But your opinion weighs heavy with Leslie, and I bet if you go across the hall and ask her, she'll tell you the same."

"So you're upset because I've shared my thoughts over the years with a woman whom you happened to date? That's . . . well, it's nonsense," I whispered, hoping he'd see my point. "I knew Leslie long before you. Friends talk . . . they share opinions. It's hardly fair to blame me for your failed relationship."

"You're right, and I didn't. Not really." Resting his forearms on his knees, Scot bent forward, saying, "Until I walked into my grandmother's business this morning and saw you sitting there. That reminded me of everything Leslie ever said about you and your beliefs. And honestly, it struck me as the action of a cold, heartless woman. So yeah, I reacted."

"I see. I'm heartless. Yep, you've figured me out, all right." Pressure against my eyes told me tears were building, but this guy was not going to see me cry. "You have no idea what happened this morning. I got stuck there . . ." I clamped my lips shut. Really, why bother? His opinion was set. And what he thought meant nothing. Less than nothing. Negative one million degrees nothing.

Maybe if I repeated that one million times, I'd actually believe it.

"I protect my family," Scot said quietly. "And my grandmother is a very important person in my family. I won't let you use her."

I opened my eyes wider, resisting the urge to blink, not able to comprehend anything other than my desire to be alone. "I doubt you'll believe anything I say." Somehow, I managed to keep my voice level. "So we're done here."

His face crumpled into a beaten expression. He started to stand, but then shook his head and resettled himself. "I can't leave. You've put me in an awkward situation with my grandmother. I need your help to fix it."

"Fix what? I'm at a loss here."

"Introductions, Julia. I know what you do for a living, and I'm not some dumb guy who can't piece together the reason you were at Magical Matchups."

My stomach lurched. Oh. Wow. I should've seen this coming, but I hadn't. I'd focused too much on Leslie and the soul-mate garbage. His cold attitude suddenly made a heck of a lot more sense.

I shrugged, trying to act the part of a heartless woman. "What do you want me to say?"

In the snap of a finger, his entire demeanor changed. Hope washed into his expression, lightened his eyes. "Tell me I'm wrong. Tell me that you didn't go to Magical Matchups under false pretenses. Tell me that you're not out to hurt my grandmother."

I wanted to. More than I can say. But the only thing I *could* say with complete honesty was "I'm not out to hurt Verda. I like her, Scot. More than I expected to."

"And the rest of it?" he demanded.

I shrugged again, not wanting to lie, but not wanting to admit the truth, either. "This is pointless."

Disappointment cascaded over him. "That's what I thought. My grandmother believes we're supposed to be together, and she's a woman who cannot be deterred when she sets her sights on something. I promised her months ago that I'd date one woman—only one—of her choosing. She's chosen you, and I don't break promises. It's madness," he half muttered to himself. "But as long as she believes you and I are fated, then we're going to have to play along."

I stared at my pizza. He couldn't mean what I thought. "And that means what?"

"It means that, starting now, we'll date. It'll be a charade, so don't go all woozy and weird on me. We'll do this to appease my grandmother until I can convince her that she's mistaken."

"Um. No. I'm not doing that." Leslie would kill me for sure. Beyond that, hanging out with someone who seemed to loathe me? Not high on my agenda. "Have you even talked to your grandmother since this morning? After you left, she didn't seem as set on this you-and-I-are-soul-mates thing. She . . ." I slammed my mouth shut. I'd nearly told him about my free membership to Verda's services. Somehow, I didn't think he'd take the news well. "Maybe you're upset about nothing," I finished.

"She called me the second you left. I've spent the majority of the day explaining to her the reasons why you and I are not the match she believes we are." A rough and ragged sigh pushed out of his lungs. "If you hadn't gone to Magical Matchups, we wouldn't be in this position. But you did, so now we have to deal with the result of that action."

He might as well have been talking in Latin. "Just tell her I said no. That's easy enough to do, isn't it? It's not your fault if I say no."

"You can't say no. Hell, I realize how crazy this is. But trust me when I tell you that this charade is the easiest way out of this mess."

Yep. Latin. "I have no idea what you're going on about. If this is so important, then lie to her. Tell her we're going out, make up some stories, and then after a few weeks we can break up."

"With *my* family?" The line of his shoulders tightened and the cords in his neck rippled. "They'll know. Every last one of them."

"Them?" I squeaked. This was getting worse by the second. "What do you mean *them?*"

"My grandmother. My sisters. My cousin. Trust me, you don't want them combining their . . . ah . . . *wills* to turn us into a couple. And they will, Julia, if they think I'm not living up to my promise. If they think we're meant to be—"

"What can they do?" I wanted to laugh. If I dealt with my manipulative, controlling family, why couldn't he deal with his?

"You don't understand," he said, musing to himself. "You couldn't. Elizabeth and Grandma are the ones to watch. Alice . . . well, I might be able to convince her to leave it alone. Chloe can't do a lot, at least not about this, but she's tight with Grandma." He shook his head, glanced over at me. "Even if I managed to convince everyone else to turn a blind eye, Grandma won't. You got us into this mess by going to Magical Matchups. I need your help to clean it up."

"Oh, come on. You're a big, strong guy. Are you seriously telling me you're afraid of your female relatives?" A laugh did bubble out now, which surprised me. But I couldn't imagine Scot being afraid of anyone, let alone a quartet of women.

"Trust me. You have no idea what's going on here."

"Then tell me." I faked a yawn and fidgeted, ready to be alone. Ready to put this and Scot behind me. I wasn't going to do this fake-dating thing, regardless of what he said, but curiosity made me ask, "Why is this such a huge deal?"

"You, of all people, wouldn't believe me if I tried to explain." He closed his eyes as if trying to find the words that would convince me to agree. Opening them, he said, "The women in my family believe in fated relationships. If they want to, they will invade our lives in . . . well, in ways I can't really articulate. I've given this a lot of thought, and the only way I can see us avoiding their interference is to . . . put on a show. It's ridiculous, but necessary."

Honesty glittered in his voice, in his eyes. Even if I didn't understand exactly what he meant, I believed he was speaking the truth. I was almost ready to say yes, but curiosity made me ask "And if I say no?"

His gaze found the envelope from Verda on the other side of the coffee table. While nondescript, the envelope boasted a rather large sticker with the Magical Matchups logo in the upper left-hand corner. I had no idea if he'd just noticed it, or if he'd seen the envelope when he first sat down and waited for the perfect moment to throw it in my face, but his eyebrows bunched together at the evidence of my cold-hearted witchery. Swinging his attention back to me, Scot said, "Looking for a mate?"

"Maybe. Is that so hard to believe?"

He ignored my answer. "Really? *You're* looking to fall in love?"

"Maybe I am," I snapped. "Maybe I'm lonely. Maybe I'm ready to combine my life with another person's. Maybe I think Verda can help me do that. Have you ever thought of that, Mr. Know-it-all?"

Scot scratched his jaw in an effort to appear nonchalant, but his entire body angled forward. "This would make an excellent promotional opportunity for Magical Matchups, don't you think?" He leaned back, bracing his head with his hands, letting his question simmer in the air. "Yep. I can see it now: a full page, full-color ad in the paper with the proof that my grandmother's dating service is the best in Chicago. Hell, who's going to argue when the owner of Introductions is a client?"

I gasped. "You wouldn't!"

"Wouldn't I?" he demanded. "Are you sure of that?"

I didn't respond. I couldn't. I was too busy envisioning closing the doors to Introductions and punching the clock at my father's firm.

"The way I see this is fairly simple," he said. "You agree

to handle this my way, you don't do anything to hurt my grandmother, and I won't tell her a thing. We'll keep all of this"—he gestured to the envelope—"our little secret. It won't be that bad. A few weeks, maybe a month, and it will all be over." Looking into his eyes, I knew without a shadow of a doubt that he meant every blasted word.

"I'm not Snow White," I muttered, taken back to my conversation with Kara about Disney heroines. "I'm Little Red Riding Hood. And you, Scot Raymond, are most definitely not a prince." He was the wolf. The big, bad, blustery wolf.

My statement, which should have perplexed him, squeezed out a laugh. "You're mixing up your fables," he said. "How about a straight answer?"

"Yeah. Fine. Whatever." I batted my eyelashes. "We'll date. I can hardly wait to get started."

The words of agreement were no sooner out of my mouth than Scot was at the door. "You're supposed to see my grandmother tomorrow evening. I expect you'll make that appointment and share with her how excited you are."

"Yeah," I mumbled. "Excited. So very excited." God. There wasn't any way Leslie was going to understand. How could she, when I didn't?

"Good. Don't give her a reason to doubt you, Julia. This is as much for your well-being as it is for mine and hers." Pulling the door open, he said, "And I'll pick you up Saturday around seven. Casual." And with that, he was gone.

I could barely breathe, let alone process the events of the evening. For a girl who never dated, I suddenly had a booked weekend. Unfortunately—or fortunately, depending on your point of view—neither guy was all that interested in me.

No longer in the mood for pizza or *Seinfeld*, I spent a few minutes putting everything away. On the path to my bedroom, I saw that Scot had forgotten his jacket. I went to it, touched the soft leather with one hand, and then, in a moment I would never admit to another living soul, bent over and breathed in deeply.

Scot's scent was there, swirling within the pungent aroma of the leather. A delicious curl of heat wove in, startling and scaring me. I stepped back and let go of the jacket as if it were on fire. The next several weeks were going to be hell.

Chapter Six

I woke Friday morning in a state of groggy, thick-headed awareness. The weight of another person on my bed clued me in before I even opened my eyes. When I did, it was with little surprise to find Leslie's catlike gaze directly on me. She'd perched herself on the edge of the mattress but sat with her body slanted toward me. She held a Venti-sized cappuccino cup in her right hand, which she took great pleasure in waving in front of my nose.

"Come on, sleepyhead," she said. "Time to get up and face the day."

"What time would that be?" I struggled to a half-sitting position despite the strong compulsion to curl into a ball and return to sleep, and reached for the takeout cup. Leslie pulled it away and took an exaggerated sip. "That's just mean," I whined.

"This one is mine. Yours is in the kitchen, so get out of bed and meet me there."

I knew we needed to talk. Heck, I *wanted* to talk. But after the many hours I'd stayed awake the night before, I wasn't so sure how coherent I'd be. "What kind?" I asked.

"This one is a soy, sugar-free vanilla with an extra shot and no whip." Seeing my scowl she said, "Yours is full fat, full sugar, real dairy, and I had them load it with extra whipped cream."

"Nice, but—"

"Caramel. Two extra shots, so it's high-voltage." She headed for my door. "Oh, and a doughnut. Cream filled."

"White or Bavarian?"

"White." Her lips twitched, and when I swung my legs off the bed, she grinned. "Yep, figured that would do the trick. Hurry up, though. It's already seven thirty and I'm normally at work by now. So are you, for that matter."

"Day off," I murmured.

Leslie's eyebrows arched in surprise. "Really?" At my nod, she said. "Well, we can't all have days off, so get a move on. Or I take the doughnut and coffee with me."

I nodded and stumbled to the bathroom. As a paralegal, Leslie had a job that was always crazy and, more often than not, long. Depending on the complexity of the cases she was assigned, and sometimes the publicity level, she could be in the office at five in the morning and not home again until eight or nine at night. Sometimes later. She loved what she did, though, so that made the hours easier to bear. So she said.

I splashed cold water on my face in an effort to jar myself awake. It helped, but a shower would've been better. It wasn't until I ran a brush through my hair that Leslie's grin fully registered. The expression seemed to reinforce my earlier guess: Leslie believed Scot wanted to talk to me about her. Yeah. That would explain the coffee and doughnut, too. Which meant it was up to me to go out there and give her the bad news.

Ugh. Double ugh. Returning to bed was becoming more appealing by the second. I hadn't even begun to consider how to cover this particular topic with Leslie, let alone any of the others. Scot was right: this whole situation was a mess. It had the potential of ruining my friendship with Leslie and even harming my relationship with Kara, whom I'd known longer. Their friendship meant the world to me.

Bracing my hands on the sink, I tried to think of the right words to say. Nothing came to me.

Leslie's voice filtered through the closed door. "Two more minutes and I'm coming in to get you."

I sighed. "No reason to. I'm on my way out." But I couldn't see how this was going to have a happy ending.

When I entered the kitchen, Leslie was pulling the petrified dish of spaghetti from the microwave. Wrinkling her nose, she tossed it in the trash. "Okay, this is disgusting. How long has this been in here?"

"Just since last night. I . . . ah . . . sort of forgot about it." I gulped. "You know. With Scot showing up here and all."

Guarded hope swirled into her tawny eyes. "Wait. Don't say anything until I'm ready. I want to hear everything, but let me heat up your coffee first."

Because two more minutes of waiting meant two additional minutes of guaranteed friendship, I nodded. I could always tell how good a mood Leslie was in by the care she took with her clothes and makeup. Oh, don't get me wrong, Leslie always looked good. But some days she looked spectacular. This was one of those days.

She wore her hair in an extravagant twist, with soft tendrils framing her face, drawing attention to her high, aristocratic cheekbones. Her cosmetics were applied lightly but with an expert hand, and she had on what she called her lucky suit. An Armani knockoff, it was still excellent and very well constructed. Pale pink, the soft, crepelike fabric swirled just above her knees, showing off her long legs. The fitted jacket cinched at her waistline, accentuating her curves, all but screaming "I am woman, hear me roar."

In other words, she looked like a million bucks. She knew it, too.

I stifled a gasp. Oh, no. I'd worried about telling Leslie about Scot because of her regrets. Because of the friend code. But this was so much worse. That fact she'd worn that suit today said everything I needed to know: she still wanted Scot back.

My two minutes were up. Leslie handed over my coffee and doughnut, plopped into one of the kitchen chairs, and motioned to the one next to her. She has long arms, so I chose the seat across the table and scooted back a little. Just in case.

My friend sighed, a soft and breathy whisper of a sound that made my heart crack. "Here's what I know: Scot called me yesterday and said he really needed to talk to you. He wouldn't tell me what it was about, just that you probably wouldn't want to see him. I didn't understand that, but told him about your weakness for Vito's. What'd he want?"

I sipped my coffee before answering—mostly because once we started down this path, there would be no turning back. To give Leslie credit, she didn't squirm once while waiting. "Yeah, he mentioned that. He . . . wanted to discuss his grandmother."

I watched Leslie carefully, waiting for her to absorb that information before I moved forward. The expectation in her eyes dimmed but didn't completely disappear. "His grandmother? Why would he want to talk to you about his grandmother?"

I twisted my fingers, wishing I had a paper clip. "She's Verda."

"What?" Incomprehension colored Leslie's tone as if I'd suddenly started speaking in French. Or Swahili. "That can't be right."

"It is. *She* is, I mean. Verda is Scot's grandmother."

"My Verda—I mean, Verda from Magical Matchups?" Leslie's eyebrows rose. "Are you positive?"

"Yeah." I pushed out a smothered laugh. "Small world, right? Who'd have guessed that in a city this large, my greatest competitor is none other than your ex's grandmother."

"Wow. I wasn't expecting—" Leslie's hold on her cup tightened enough that the lid popped off on one edge. "Why would Scot want to talk to you about Verda? You two don't even know each other."

"Well, you see, that's not completely true. Not anymore." I licked my suddenly dry lips. "I visited Magical Matchups the other night, after dinner with my parents, and . . ." The words got stuck in my throat. I swallowed another mouthful of coffee, but it didn't help.

"You're nervous," Leslie said, stating the obvious. "Why? I think it's awesome that you went to Magical Matchups. That was my—Kara's—idea in the first place, remember?"

"Yeah. Well . . ." I told myself to just get on with it. "There's more to it, Les."

Puzzlement and unease flickered over my friend's face. "I'm listening. You met Verda . . . ?"

"Yes. And we talked. And then Scot walked in." I babbled out the rest of the story in a rush of blurred-together syllables. Most of the story, anyway. Let's just say I hit the high points and hoped those would be enough. Through it all, Leslie stayed silent and played with her coffee cup, flipping the lid off and then snapping it back on. I found myself focusing on the sound rather than my own voice. Which actually helped in a strange way. After what felt like forever, I finished by saying, "And . . . um . . . that's about everything."

Leslie slid backward in her chair. "So to wrap up, Verda believes you and Scot are destined for each other, Scot doesn't want to break a promise to her, and you have agreed to date him for a few weeks." She tapped her long, manicured, pink-painted nails on the table. "Maybe a month. Because if you don't, he'll rat you out and tell all of Chicago that you're a client of Magical Matchups. Is that everything?"

I coughed. "Pretty much, yes."

"I see."

Bracing myself for an explosion, I drained the rest of my coffee in one large swallow. She continued to click her nails and stare off into the distance.

"Are you okay?" I asked.

"Hm? Yep, I'm fine. Just piecing all of this together."

Huh. She didn't look mad. Or hurt. In actuality, she appeared composed and calm. How odd was that? "So, this doesn't upset you?"

She blinked long, mascara-coated lashes. "Why would it?"

"He's your ex," I pointed out. Never mind the fact that she wanted him back. "Isn't that, like, friendship rule number one? Never date your best friend's past boyfriends?"

"But you're not."

"But I am." Combing my fingers through my hair, I sighed. "That's what this conversation is about."

"Are you trying to upset me?" she asked.

"No . . . ?"

"Are you dating Scot because you *want* to date Scot?"

She'd worded the question calmly enough, but a thread of anxiety existed beneath the calm. I heard it plain as day. "No. I already told you—"

"Are you interested in having a relationship with Scot?"

"Hell, no." That much I was sure of.

"Do you want to roll around in bed with him and do naughty things?"

Um. Yes? No? Honestly, I hadn't quite decided on that, so I evaded the question with another truth. "Yeah, right. We could barely handle being in the same room together last night. And we were clothed."

She expelled a loud sigh of relief. "Then why should I be upset?"

All of that and we were right back to square one. I figured

I should be as honest as I could. "Perhaps because Verda has decided that Scot and I are a match."

"Verda's wrong." Leslie crushed her now-empty cup between her hands. "She has to be wrong, because you and Scot might as well exist on different planets." She screwed her mouth into a misshapen grin. "And I am not referring to Venus and Mars."

"Okay, then, Leslie. I don't know. I'm tired and cranky and I've been really worried about telling you all of this. I figured you'd be mad at me."

A real smile wreathed her face. "I was shocked at first. But now that the idea has set for a few minutes, I really am okay with it."

The ball of stress that had been weighing me down evaporated. "You have no idea how happy I am to hear that. I swear, I'll get out of this arrangement as soon as I can. I promise! Hopefully, I won't have to go out with him more than a few times."

Leslie sucked her bottom lip into her mouth, effectively removing a layer of her lipstick in the process. "I don't want you to try to get out of the arrangement, Julia. Don't you see? This is perfect. If he's dating you, I don't have to worry about him falling for someone else, and while you're dating him, you can try to convince him to give me—*us*—another chance."

Her request jarred me like a physical blow. "Exactly how am I supposed to accomplish that?"

"Just . . . well, let him know that I've changed. That I'm not afraid of my feelings anymore, that my relationship philosophy isn't the same as yours. Oh! And Verda! I'll talk to her. And you can too! To try to convince her that I'm the better match for Scot." Leslie's guarded hope returned, shiny as a brand-new penny. "It could work."

"I don't know. This doesn't feel like a good idea," I managed to say. "Scot . . . Well—"

"What?" Leslie demanded. "Did he say something about me last night?"

Oh, no. I didn't want to tell her this. But averting my gaze, I nodded. What if her hope of getting back together with him was entirely impossible?

"What did he say?"

Chicken that I was, I tried the one maneuver that usually did the trick with Leslie. "Don't you have to get to work?"

"Yes, I do," she said. "So the quicker you spit it out, the less late I'll be."

I opened my mouth but closed it just as fast. Then I steadied myself and said, "Sweetie, he said that you two are over. That you *know* you're over. He . . . ah . . . seemed pretty absolute."

She turned away. "Yeah. I know that. I haven't shared this with you, but I contacted him a few weeks ago. Told him how sorry I was and that I'd like to give us another try. He shot me down, Julia." Leslie shivered and wrapped her arms around herself. "He said he forgave me, which is great and all, but . . . he also gave me the friend speech."

I took this new information in, and while I didn't—couldn't—comprehend the level of misery my friend was going through, it cut me to the quick just the same. "And you still want me to do this? Talk to him and try to convince him to give your relationship another go? Even knowing how he feels?"

She swallowed. "It's probably a stupid idea. We only dated for a few months, and we haven't seen each other for longer than that, but . . . I guess I'm not ready to give up on him after all. Not yet. So this—you pretending to date him—might help."

Her voice wavered, and that was what made my mind up. Leslie rarely broke down.

"It might not make a difference," I said. "He might not want to hear it, or maybe he really has moved past you, but if this is really this important to you, then—"

Leslie bounded from her chair and squashed me in a tight hug. "Thank you! Thank you so much. I know it's a long shot, and I won't blame you if nothing changes."

Semi-uncomfortable, I patted Leslie on the back, trying to reconcile myself with what I'd just agreed. Was I nuts? Probably. Extracting myself from my friend's grip I said, "There's something else, though, Les. Scot doesn't like me a heck of a lot, so anything I say might have the opposite effect."

"Take it slowly," she suggested. "But really, Julia, if this doesn't pan out, it's okay. At least there's now a chance, which is something I didn't have yesterday." Suddenly realizing the time, she gathered up her belongings and fluttered her fingers in a good-bye wave. "Now I really have to leave. Thank you so much!"

I stayed at the table, staring at my untouched doughnut, for quite a while. Leslie's parting statement should have put my fears to rest. I mean, as long as she understood that I wasn't a miracle worker, there was no harm in going along with her plan. But I feared the light in her eyes and the spring in her step spelled disaster.

Two hours later found me glaring at Verda's envelope as if it were about to eat me alive. I didn't know what to do: open it and go through everything to prove to Scot that I was the coldhearted bitch he thought but possibly save my company, or throw the dang thing away, forget I ever had it, and continue along at Introductions left to my own devices until the business either sank or swam. Sure, Verda was expecting me later today, but seeing as I'd agreed to date her grandson, I sort of figured she wouldn't care whether or not I filled out the paperwork.

Verda was an odd duck, though, so the possibility existed that I was wrong and she'd somehow be upset. That was one of my reasons for dragging my heels. But not the only reason. Not even close. The larger part of my reluctance rested with Scot and the picture he'd drawn of me. Try as I might, I couldn't deny the validity of that picture. Or at least the validity of a small portion of it. So now the mere thought of going through Verda's paperwork gave me an odd, achy sensation deep inside.

Somehow, though, the compulsion to follow through remained strong. Pressing, even. Which was the crux of my dilemma.

I clicked the button of the pen I held. Once. Twice. I reached a hand out toward the envelope and then yanked it back. Slid the envelope closer and fingered the flap. Yes? No? Oh, hell. I didn't have a clue. I picked the envelope up, felt the weight of it in my hands, and cursed again. "Make a decision, Julia," I muttered.

Closing my eyes, I fought to find some balance, a little distance. I weighed the pros and cons along with the possible positive and negative results of whatever action I took. What finally pushed me forward was a combination of three things: my strong curiosity, Leslie . . . and strangely the same thing that had originally held me back. Scot.

He already believed ice ran through my veins. He already saw me in a way that would likely never change, and I was going to have to pretend to date him, to ignore my stupid, irrational desire for him and try to work some matchmaking magic for Leslie. That was a lot. It involved dealing with other people's emotions, something I wasn't particularly good at.

Besides, if I was going to change Verda's mind about me and Scot, convince her that Leslie was the better match, wouldn't it help to know how Verda did things? And if the process somehow helped me with Introductions . . . well, that was incidental.

I unfastened the flap of the envelope. Tipping the package carefully to the side, I spilled the contents—a thick stack of papers and a book of some sort—out onto the glass surface of the coffee table. A breath wheezed out of my chest and I sniffed, not surprised to smell the lingering aroma of roses, but a whisper of apprehension trickled down my spine and caused me to let go of the envelope so that it fluttered to the floor.

Weird, really, how one experience can forever change your tastes. Before the other night, roses were just another flower; I neither liked nor disliked them. Now they were akin to food I'd eaten right before coming down with the flu. To this day, I cannot stomach even a spoonful of cream of potato soup. I had a sneaking suspicion that I'd also never look at a rose the same way again.

Scooting forward from my spot on the sofa, I grabbed the sheaf of papers and moved them closer, ignoring the book for now. I'd start at page one and work my way though, one sentence, one question at a time.

The initial page was a basic introduction letter, welcoming the client to Magical Matchups and explaining the importance of fully answering every question within the packet. I had a similar letter, both on my company Web site and in our welcome folder, so I only gave this a passing perusal. So far so good.

The remaining pages were partitioned off into six separate sections with binder clips. Each segment was printed on a different color paper. Probably for no other reason than to signify a change of focus to the client, but I had to admit it was a smart, if simple, idea. This first page, the section printed on light green paper, began with basic questions such as name, birth date, address, phone number, and the like. I entered in the appropriate information and flipped to the next.

Education. This was a piece of cake, too. But my pen stalled at the career questions. Hm. No way was I putting down that I owned a dating service. But I didn't want to completely lie either. I scrawled in "Customer service rep" and continued. Hey, I dealt with people and tried to solve their problems. Relationship problems. Close enough, thank you very much.

Next came a series of inquiries related to my career, covering everything from how well I liked what I did to my favorite and least favorite aspects of my job. A medical questionnaire followed, one that reminded me of new-patient registration forms at a doctor's office. Kind of odd, and not something I included in my client workup at Introductions, but I supposed I understood the reasoning.

With the green section completed, I moved on to the lilac pages. These questions reminded me of the Myers-Briggs personality assessment, but with a broader scope. The personality-focused questions I understood, and I used something comparable at Introductions, but why Verda deemed it important to know if I liked dogs, preferred one make/model car over another, was a morning person, or listened to music in my car was beyond me. I rushed through, circled the appropriate responses, and moved to section three.

One glance at the sky blue paper forced a groan. In front of me were short essays depicting a specific scenario that at the end asked "What would you do?" Ugh. My reactions to any given situation weren't set in stone. Nor, in my opinion, were other people's. Still, I powered through, and in nearly every case, gave whatever response floated first into my brain.

The next bunch of papers—pink, by the way—was the

thickest of the entire group. Ah! *These* were the relationship questions. These were the ones that would likely give the real scoop on how Verda matched her clientele.

I read. Then I shook my head, turned the page, and read more. I did the same with the next two before flicking back to the beginning.

"Okay, then," I whispered.

Initially there were three pages asking questions about my last few relationships. Twenty questions per relationship, per page. This isn't what bewildered me. After all, good logic states that folks tend to choose the same type of person from one relationship to another. Introductions also delved into its clients' dating histories, just not this deeply. But what did shock me was her rating system for men. Depending on how I answered each of the relationship questions, there was a handy little key that ranked my exes by fruit.

Seriously, fruit.

Verda's highest-ranking fruit—er, man—was a pomegranate, followed by kiwi, going all the way down to—naturally?—a lemon. An average man was described as an apple, while the fellow who ranked just above average was an orange. Just below? A pear. In between pear and lemon we had the plum. Which, if you followed along with Verda's concept, made a weird sort of sense. You know, plums become prunes.

But, come on. Fruits? Really? I reread the key and the descriptions, trying to work this bizarre revelation in with the whole magic/fairy-godmother thing. Honestly, it flat-out didn't compute. But then, not that I'd admit it out loud, my curiosity got the better of me and I whipped through the questions with superhuman speed.

I'd only had two serious relationships over the past ten years. One of them had lasted almost two years, and the other just over one. But I'd also dated a guy in college, so I added him to the mix to give me the total of three past relationships Verda asked for. I resisted checking the key until I was completely finished. Once the totals were tallied, I discovered that my dating habits—if Verda was to be believed, of course—were all over the place.

My college boyfriend was an orange, which apparently meant he fell in line slightly ahead of those average apples, often making good marriage material but sometimes becoming too preoccupied with themselves and backsliding easily. And not just to the average level, but all the way down to a lemon. Ouch.

The two-year guy was a pear, so not only hadn't I learned anything with Mr. Orange, but I then went on to choose a guy who was two levels *beneath* the orange, going by Verda's scale. Lovely. Just lovely.

Finally, the most recent man in my life was described as . . . oh, wow . . . a kiwi? Second to the top, kiwis were described as self-starters and high achievers. They were also— supposedly—caring and attentive lovers with the right partner. Kiwis, it seemed, were keepers. Only, for a reason I couldn't quite remember, I'd let my kiwi go. A kiwi my parents had hooked me up with, by the way.

Jameson wove his way into my brain then. He was probably a freaking pomegranate.

I shoved that thought away. Fast.

The rest of the pink section was a series of intense questions that pretty much encompassed every relationship in my entire life. There were questions about my father and mother, siblings (if applicable), friends, pets, and on and on it went. I was sweating by the time I finished. But I wasn't done. The red segment was next: pages and pages devoted to my romantic wishes, hopes, and fantasies.

Yay, right? Not so much. Especially because there were a dozen or so fairy-tale questions tossed in, like "What was your favorite fairy tale as a child?" My answer: none. "Which fairy-tale heroine do you most identify with?" My answer: none. "If you could become any fairy-tale heroine, who would you be?" My answer: yep, you got it, none. This was obviously where Kara and Leslie came up with all the talk about Snow White, Aurora, and Belle the other day, but that didn't mean I wanted to dip into their madness. I was Julia Collins, not a fairy-tale princess, period and end of story.

The last bit of paperwork centered on my relationship goals for the future. Huh. What *were* my relationship goals? I posed this same question to every one of my clients, but I'd never answered it for myself. I supposed that someday, settling down with an appropriate man wouldn't be a horrible thing. I wasn't opposed to the idea of children or a white picket fence or a dog or two. But not now. Not for a while.

My fingers tightened around the pen. What should I write? Finally, I gave up and put a huge, fat question mark as my answer, then moved on.

The final page was the confidentiality agreement Leslie and Kara had spoken of. Hm, she should have had me sign this before handing everything over. Really, I was within my rights not to sign, but there was no reason not to, so I did.

Done! Good grief, was Verda thorough. I'd always worried that my entry process at Introductions was too long. Now I worried it wasn't detailed enough. Fruity men aside, was this Verda's secret? There's a lot to say about digging beneath the surface to draw a person out. She'd dug all the way to China and back. Twice.

My head ached from the intense concentration, and a solid state of bemusement settled in, mucking everything up. Also, though, a hint of frustration existed below the surface. Because as crazy as this process was, I'd expected more. A lot more. I'd expected . . . magic.

Oh, not the wand-waving, spell-casting, fantastical type of magic. But something that felt like magic, especially given my friends' raves. I wanted something that would clearly distinguish her business from mine. I should've been pleased. Our methods at this stage, while they varied hugely in complexity, were similar enough at their core to not raise any major red flags. But the disappointment hung on.

Gathering the papers together, I shoved them back in the envelope. My gaze landed on the book I'd ignored earlier. What was it? A volume of love poetry, perhaps? Knowing Verda and the questions I'd just gone through, I figured that was likely the case. Or maybe a collection of fairy tales. My hand slid across the top of the book, the leather binding soft as if it had been rubbed with lotion.

There weren't any words etched onto the cover. As I picked up the book, something—call it a hunch—sped my pulse and sent a chain of trembles through my body. I turned the book in my hands, checking the spine, but that was also blank. My shivers increased and goose bumps dotted my arms. When I opened the book, there, written on the first page in spidery handwriting, was

All happily-ever-after endings have a beginning.
Use this journal to capture those hopes, wishes, and fantasies
that are truest of heart, purest of soul.
The magic of your happily-ever-after begins here.
This is my gift to you,
                                        —Verda

I stared at the message for so long that my eyes stung, and the writing itself seemed to glitter and twinkle as if made up of millions of tiny diamonds. Ridiculous! I squeezed my eyes shut, held them that way for a minute, and then opened them again. The weird sparkle I thought I'd seen was gone, but the urge to touch the words pressed into my consciousness, overshadowing all else.

My fingers hesitated above the script. The compulsion grew stronger, and a strange sensation overtook me. It was as if another hand covered mine, guiding it, and without conscious thought, my fingers brushed the writing. The page, which should have felt cool and smooth, warmed beneath my touch. My hand moved across the message, and each letter, word, and sentence seemed to take physical form and melt into my fingertips.

Electricity sizzled at my toes and wove its way up me until my entire body vibrated with energy. The beat of my heart echoed in my ears, and the writing once again began to glow. Heat, like the sun of a hot summer day, radiated through every muscle until my skin flushed with warmth. In one fast, jerky movement, I removed my hand, dropped the book, and jumped away from the sofa.

I stared at the journal, now closed and lying on the floor, trying to find a rational, practical, not-freaky explanation for what had just occurred. The energy within me flashed once, twice, three times before draining away. My breathing erupted in raspy, short gasps of air that had me backing up another step.

"What the hell was that?" I shrieked.

Naturally, there was no response. I was alone, after all. But my throat tightened as the scent of roses infused my awareness.

I'd been wrong. I hadn't walked through the wardrobe. No, I'd fallen down the freaking rabbit hole.

Chapter Seven

I arrived at Magical Matchups exactly on time for my meeting with Verda. After the out-and-out weirdness in my living room, I'd given serious consideration to canceling the appointment, burning the journal, and wiping my hands of the entire mess once and for all. In the end, though, I couldn't.

Not because of Scot's threat or my difficulties with Introductions. Nope. My reasoning had very little to do with those and a lot more to do with Leslie. While I sincerely doubted my ability to alter anything with Scot, I had to try. For her sake.

As for me . . . well, I had a few choice questions for Verda. Namely, what the hell was up with the sparkly writing in the journal, and why had I felt as if I'd been zapped with lightning after touching it? I really, really hoped she'd offer up some good answers. Ones I could believe. Otherwise, I'd be dialing the nearest mental-health professional for an appointment and a straitjacket fitting.

Verda met me at the door with a gleam of anticipation in her faded blue eyes. "There you are!" she said, gesturing for me to come in. "Right on time. Punctuality is an excellent trait, Julia."

Nodding because I agreed with her—I hated being late for anything, even Wednesday dinners—I followed her inside.

Despite my distress, my lips twitched in amusement. Verda wore stretchy—not quite spandex but a close cousin—orange leggings and a bright yellow and orange polka-dotted tunic that fell an inch or so above her knee. Yellow beaded necklaces in varying lengths, along with white high-top sneakers laced in tangerine loopy bows, completed her ensemble. A touch of youthful pink dotted her cheeks.

Evidently, Verda wasn't afraid of color. I was oddly jealous and instantly promised myself I'd pick up a few upbeat outfits for work. Oh, nothing in her psychedelic-rainbow range of upbeat. But perhaps I could extend beyond my standard black, brown, and blue.

She locked the door behind us and led me to a room I'd yet to see. A tiny amount of stress vanished when the only scent in the air was that of Verda's perfume. Which, thankfully, held more fruity tones than floral. I'd had quite enough of roses.

The space was far more a sitting room than an office, but it was lovely. A sofa upholstered with flowered fabric—cabbage roses, naturally—rested like a queen in the middle of the room. Two chairs covered in the same fabric angled on either side, giving the impression of cozy comfort, like you might find at a bed-and-breakfast. What really caught my attention, though, was the large framed painting on the back wall. The scene was that of a window, looking out into a very realistic flower garden. It was painted with such intricacy, such attention to detail, that I couldn't help but stare.

"What a gorgeous painting," I murmured, entranced enough that I stepped in for a closer look. "I can nearly believe that's a real window with a real garden just beyond."

"My granddaughter is an artist. She painted that specifically for me." Verda's voice held pride laced with melancholy. "That was the view outside of my bedroom window when I was growing up. Alice captured every detail perfectly."

I'd seen window paintings before, but nothing so vivid or realistic. Certainly nothing so beautiful. "Did she have a photo to work from?"

"No, dear," Verda said, a twinge of sadness evident. "I don't have many photographs left from my childhood."

"Oh. That's . . . I'm sorry." Maybe my parents and I weren't always on the same wavelength, but they'd photographed nearly every aspect of my life. Too much so, maybe. "So . . . um . . . Alice painted this from what? Your description? That's amazing."

"Well, Alice is quite talented. She has a gift, you see." Verda walked over to the painting and laid her hand on its surface. More of a caress than a simple touch. "This is the view I saw every morning when I woke, from the time I was a little girl to the day I married. Sometimes when I stand this way and stare, I can feel that girl. She's still here, you know. Buried underneath all of these wrinkles."

For an eerie half second I could almost imagine the girl of whom Verda spoke—a much younger version of the woman who now stood in front of me, with light blue eyes and smooth ivory skin and the vitality of youth. One blink and the image vanished, but Verda stayed lost in the picture, in her memories.

My burning need to ask questions about the journal faded into the background. I couldn't—wouldn't—interrupt this moment, so I retreated to the sofa to wait her out.

Not quite a minute passed before she faced me with a smile, though her cheeks were pale and her recollections of the past misted over her features like a fine fog. "I'm glad you're here, Julia." Circling the sofa, she patted my shoulder. "Do you drink tea?"

"I do, but I'm fine. I can wait if you'd like to get some for yourself, though."

"No, no. If you're all set, we can get right to business." The eye twinkle returned. Maybe not quite as brilliant as before, but I was happy to see it. "Did you bring the paperwork?"

"Yes." I handed her the envelope and continued to swallow my questions. My curiosity was unabated. My concern for my sanity, too. But for now I'd let Verda take control of the conversation so she could regain her momentum.

"Perfect!" She accepted the package and perched herself on one of the chairs. Her movements were quick and birdlike; I doubted she ever sat still for very long. So unlike me. I could curl up like a slug for days, if time allowed. Which it never did. So maybe not so unlike me, after all. "I only need a few minutes to look these over."

Scot, I was sure, had already spoken with Verda. Likely she knew full well that I'd agreed to date her grandson. So her perusal of my responses probably had more to do with proving to herself that Scot and I were, in her words, soul mates. That was fine by me. Scot and I weren't compatible, and I had no true need for Verda to hook me up with anyone else.

In three seconds flat, she had the bundle of papers out of the envelope and in her grip. Nimble fingers flipped through them page by page, her eyes moving as she read to herself. I totally expected her to engage me in conversation, to ask for clarification here or to express her opinion there, but she didn't.

Every now and then, Verda would mutter an *ah*, or an *ooh*. Her mouth curved into a tiny smile one second, a frown the next, and back to a grin a second later. I wondered why. What did she see that made her happy or unhappy? I gnawed on my bottom lip. I crossed my legs, counted to ten, then to twenty, then to thirty, and uncrossed them.

She murmured something incomprehensible, and that pushed my impatience and my curiosity to another extreme. It seemed Scot wasn't the only person I couldn't read. That, along with her continued appraisal of the inner workings of my mind, created a sense of uncomfortable limbo. I suddenly had a greater respect for every client who had the guts to enter my business and put their trust in me to find them an appropriate partner.

I started to interrupt her but stopped. I wiggled and jiggled in my seat, feeling very much like a child at the dinner table impatiently waiting for the adults to finish so I could be set free.

Countless minutes later, she finished reading the last page—the one I'd marked with a question mark—and set the papers on her lap. "How did you find the questions, dear? Were they easy for you to answer, or did you struggle with any of them?"

"Um . . . they were fine." At Verda's pointed and quizzical glance, I amended my statement. "Okay, I found some of the questions a little unusual. And I didn't understand the whole fruit thing at all. And the journal—"

"We'll get to the journal later." I recognized the edge in her voice. It was my mother's don't-argue-with-me tone. My mother had trained me well, so I didn't even consider arguing. "I noticed that your last three relationships were an orange, a pear, and a kiwi. That's a little curious, you know."

"Maybe for men," I deadpanned. "But it would make a tasty fruit salad."

A delighted laugh bubbled out. "Yes," she said. "You'll fit in quite well."

Geez, this woman confused me. "Fit in well where? How? With whom?"

"Let's stay focused for now, shall we?" Verda nodded at the papers she still held. "Normally, I don't see variances this large in my clients' past relationships. Maybe two apples and an orange. Or even two kiwis and a lemon, because most of us have at least one lemon in our past. But I don't often see a kiwi, an orange, and a pear."

"And that means what?" I asked.

Verda let out a small sigh. "If I weren't so sure about you and Scot, we'd have a lot more work on our hands before I'd feel confident in setting you up with someone else."

I fought very hard not to scowl. "If you're so sure about Scot, then why did I fill all of that out? Why tell me you want to fix me up with someone else?"

"I had to. Otherwise, why would you have returned? But, dear, you have a lot of . . . barriers holding you back from understanding what you really need in a man. Preconceived notions are getting in your way." She paused, as if weighing her words. "You're quite an interesting woman. Even more so than I'd imagined."

My curiosity fired up, overriding my frustration. "You got this from *fruit*? And 'interesting' how?" Because heaven knew I'd used that term as a blanket expression for many, many different definitions. Most of them not very nice.

"Oh, not only your past relationships, but from every answer you put down. Even the question mark is telling."

I *knew* the question mark had been a bad idea. "In what way?"

She gave me a you-asked-for-it look. "You've lived a sheltered life. Now, there's nothing wrong with that. It's just the way it was for you. Your parents are probably set in their ways and traditions. In all likelihood, they've passed that tendency on to you. I doubt you've ever acted in a frivolous manner. Or if you have, you likely regretted doing so. Every step you take is with considerable thought and great caution. You are methodical, slow to adapt to change, and prefer to call the shots." Tilting her head to the side, she asked, "How am I doing?"

I was so surprised I couldn't even nod. She had just done to me what I did to other people: figured me out. As her words replayed in my mind, I was numb with disbelief. I squeezed my hands together so tightly, my knuckles turned white.

Verda noticed my reaction. "You've also purposely kept romance and love out of your life. You're afraid, aren't you, Julia? That's no way to live, young lady! Emotions and connections to other people are what make us who we are. But emotions are the one thing you cannot control, so you steer away from them at every turn."

How in the hell did she get *that* from that stack of papers? Maybe Kara and Leslie were right in the first place. Maybe Verda *was* a witch? "I'm actually kind of okay with my life," I admitted. "I have friends. And not everyone needs the same things to be happy."

"But Julia," she said in a soft, whispery voice. "You can't barricade yourself away from love. Something brought you here to me. And whether you're ready to believe or not, you *are* my grandson's soul mate."

"I know you think this, but it's impossible. Scot doesn't even like me." Ack. I was supposed to be excited about Scot, not argumentative. But I couldn't help it. I was right about this, not her. Besides, I'd visited Magical Matchups because of business, not love. "We're not a match. With everything else you've determined, you surely have seen that too. Haven't you?"

"You two are perfect for each other." Verda spoke with complete conviction. "You might need a little push to see it for yourself, but I have no doubts on this front."

"I don't need a push! I don't even believe in the *possibility* of soul mates." I instructed myself to calm down. "It's cool that you do. But—"

"You don't have to." Verda aimed her gaze toward the clock and then back to me. "They exist, whether you believe so or not. And yours is my grandson."

"Please quit saying that. Please." My voice cracked. I was drowning. Fast. So I searched for a life preserver—something to pull me to the surface. And then it came to me. Or rather, Leslie came to mind. "Scot and Leslie are a much better match than he and I are. Why . . . I was talking to Leslie this morning and—"

Verda hushed me. "You're getting all worked up, dear. Take a deep breath and calm yourself. And if you really feel so strongly about Leslie, why would you allow Scot to court you?"

"I *am* perfectly calm," I grumbled. "Yes, I'm allowing Scot to court . . . date . . ." I stopped, gathered my thoughts, and started again. "We are going to go on a date, yes. But only to humor—I mean, to see if you . . . um . . . might be right. While Leslie—"

"Leslie is a lovely girl, but she isn't right for my grandson." Verda's nose twitched. You know, like Samantha from *Bewitched*. Given what my friends had said, I almost wondered if she'd cast a spell. "You are. And I have faith that everything will work out exactly as it is supposed to."

She reached over and patted my knee to comfort me, but that so wasn't happening. "Give it a chance. Open your heart to the possibility."

Comprehension that I wouldn't change Verda's mind stopped me from pushing the argument further. She was as set in her decision as I was in mine. Besides, as far as verbal battles go, Verda was a formidable foe. Hell, I kind of thought she would be able to take my mother down in a match of wills.

Hm. I actually enjoyed that image. I might have to introduce them.

Okay, then. I'd move on to another subject. The one that would either send me screaming or to the loony bin. Or potentially both. "What about the journal?"

"What about it?"

She wasn't going to make this easy. "Have other clients asked you about *their* journals?"

Verda gave her head a quick shake. "There is only one journal for one client. You! I had it ready and waiting for the day you showed."

"So . . . Leslie and Kara don't have one?"

"They do not. And it's best if you keep this to yourself." Verda's smile vanished. "Promise me you won't say a word about the journal to either of them."

"Sure. I promise," I said instantly. Hey, the fewer people who knew about my out-there episode, the better. "Now, will you tell me what's going on with it? And please don't say we'll get to it later. Something happened, and I need to understand what."

Verda grabbed my hands with both of hers and squeezed. "Have you written in it yet?"

"No." And I didn't plan on doing so. Ever. I wasn't sure if I'd even be able to touch it again. "But this bizarre thing happened . . ." I stopped. Tried to work out the best, noncrazy way to explain. Unfortunately, my mind blanked out, so I went with "There was this—let's call it a buzz of electricity—and the letters in your message glowed. And roses. My building doesn't have a rose-scented furnace filter, so . . ." I shook my head, annoyed with my disjointed explanation. "Look, I sound like a loon. This is ridiculous. But something weird occurred, and you need to tell me what it was."

"Magic, Julia," Verda said, as if that explained everything. "You experienced magic."

Yep. There was a straitjacket at the mental hospital with my name on it. "Let me try this again. I would so appreciate if you would tell me what happened in a rational, plausible, believable, and entirely practical way. Okay? Please?"

"Julia! Stop trying to make sense of every last thing. Not every detail in life can be boiled down to the rational. Expand your mind, dear. What do you want more than anything else in the entire world?" Verda asked in a mesmerizing voice. "Any wish in the world, if you were sure it would come true. What would that wish be?"

Nothing came to me. Not. One. Thing. How sad was that? "World peace!" I said, pleased something had finally popped into my head. "Or . . . um . . . a cure for cancer. Both?"

"Very admirable wishes, but what about something personal. Something selfish, even? Something for you?"

"Um . . ." The totally selfish wish would have to be Introductions. But I couldn't say that, and before I'd thought up a different response, a loud series of pounding knocks came from the front door. Another appointment?

Verda dashed to her feet so quickly, she nearly pulled me with her. "Oh! Look at the time. My ride is here." She winked, her blue eyes alight with mischief. "And your date for the evening. We need to go."

All thoughts of wishes and magic evaporated. "My what? Verda, wait! What are you talking about?" My God, this woman was tricky. "What date?"

"You and Scot both agreed to give this coupling a chance. Correct?" Verda tugged her coat on. At my hesitant nod, she said, "Then yes, you're going to join us. We're having dinner at Alice's tonight."

I quickly added two and two. Alice was Verda's artist granddaughter, one of Scot's sisters. "A *family* dinner? Does Scot know about this?" If he did, I was so going to kill him for not giving me fair warning.

"Of course not. I wasn't up for arguments from either of you. But you're here. He's here. And we have dinner in thirty minutes." She huffed out an exasperated breath and situated her hands on her hips. "Are you going to argue with me, Julia?"

Oh, good God. I hadn't learned a damn thing about the

freaky journal. I'd barely mentioned Leslie. I understood pretty much nothing about Verda's process. Basically, as far as this meeting went, the score was Verda 3, Me 0. So you'd think continuing the evening would be an okay idea. So I could gather more information and plant the appropriate seeds. But in reality, not so much. A family gathering for my first pretend date with Scot did not, in any circumstance, sound like a plan worth considering.

"I don't know—"

Grasping my arm, she pulled me out of her office. "Everyone will love you. And you might as well meet the family now, so you know what you're getting into."

I let her drag me along. For such a frail-appearing woman, she was strong. "Look, if Scot wants me to go, then I'm game." Maybe I was cheating, but I didn't care. Scot wasn't going to agree. Heck, the last thing he wanted, based on his earlier comments, was for me to meet his sisters. "We'll leave it up to him."

"That's a wonderful idea!" Verda said with far more enthusiasm than made sense. At the door, she twisted the lock and opened up. "Look who's here, Scot! Our appointment ran over, so Julia is going to join us for dinner at Alice's. Just think. Years from now when you have children, you can tell them how your first date was surrounded by family. It will make such a lovely story."

Scot stepped in. He wrapped his arm around Verda's shoulders and pulled her in for a hug. His eyes met mine. I sent a zillion poison mental daggers at him, shook my head no, mouthed the word *no*, and silently begged him to say something—anything—that would get me out of spending the evening with his family.

"That *would* make a lovely story, Grandma," Scot concurred. "And I think Julia coming to dinner with us is a fantastic plan.

Why, I can't wait for everyone to meet her." Leaning over, he kissed Verda on the top of her head. "She'll make quite an impression, I'm sure."

His implication came through loud and clear to me. The rat was so sure of his lousy opinion, he assumed that everyone else would see the same person he did. "Ass hat," I hissed.

A wicked grin spread across his face, while at the same time Verda glanced up. "What was that, Julia? Did you say 'ass hat'?"

"No! Why would I say that? That's rude." I glared at Scot, who continued to grin.

"I don't know, Grandma. I heard 'ass hat,' too." Scot reached over and chucked my chin. As if I were a child. "What *did* you say, Julia?"

Crap! What rhymed with ass hat? Brass cat, grass bat, gas splat . . . "Class act! I was saying what a class act your grandson is."

Verda patted my arm. "You're a class act yourself, Julia."

"Yes, well. It takes one to know one, doesn't it?" Scot uttered the faux compliment in an even enough tone, but I heard the undercurrent of challenge lurking beneath every freaking syllable.

Hell. Any old excuse would've done. He could've said that he wanted our first date to be just us, and romantic. Or he'd rather get to know me better before introducing me to the rest of the family. Instead, this. He thought I was going to bomb out with his family. Well, ha. I'd create an impression, all right. One that Scot Raymond would never, ever forget for as long as he lived. Nor would the members of his family. Because, yep, they were going to adore me. And when Scot and I didn't work out, they'd bug him forever about the girl he let get away.

I channeled Mary Tyler Moore and spoke in the brightest, happy-go-luckiest, world-is-my-oyster way I could dredge up.

"Aren't you the sweetest man alive? What are we waiting for? I'm starving."

Scot, sensing a change in the air, raised his eyebrow in question. I stood up on my tiptoes and gave him a light smooch on his cheek. Just to make Verda happy, of course. And if my blood heated up a tiny amount—minuscule, really—when my lips grazed against Scot's rough-shaven skin, well . . . that didn't mean a damn thing. Really.

Verda had insisted that I leave my car at Magical Matchups and drive with her and Scot to her granddaughter's home in his SUV. While I'd have preferred my own ride, I decided to go with the flow. Especially because Scot had hinted all over the place that I might want to leave before he did, so I should take my car. At this point, I was operating under the "If it bothers Scot, that's what I'm doing" mentality. Wrong, perhaps, but also hugely satisfying.

Verda commanded me to sit in the front seat with her grandson. Scot wanted me to sit in the back. I chose the front, which earned me a scowl from Scot but a huge smile of approval from Verda. Then I proceeded to chat throughout the ride, asking Scot one question after another. He embodied the strong but silent type well, as most of what I got out of him were short, clipped responses. I loved every one, though, because they proved I was getting to him.

Hey, I was only doing what he'd asked: making his grandmother happy. He had zero reason to complain. Who knew pushing some guy's buttons could be so freaking fun? Verda piped in every now and then but mostly stayed quiet. I kind of thought she was sitting back and enjoying the show.

By the time we turned into the driveway of Alice's bungalow-style house, Scot's shoulders were tense and he kept tapping his thumb against the steering wheel. Verda was out the door the second the ignition turned off. She stuck her head into the backseat long enough to say, "You two should take a minute to be alone before coming in. Everyone will understand."

Scot drew in a long, slow breath and angled himself toward me. "Maybe this wasn't such a hot idea, but you're here now, so you should be prepared."

"I know how to eat dinner, Scot. I even know which fork to use when."

"Well, that's good, because I probably don't." There went his thumb again: tap, tap, tap. "The thing is, you're going to have to converse with my family."

"You think I'm incapable of conducting myself properly in polite company?" I inhaled a mouthful of air to combat my irritation. "Trust me. I'll be on my *best* behavior."

He raked his fingers through his hair, a jerky motion that struck me as nervous. What did *he* have to be nervous about? "I'm not all that worried about you," he admitted in a tight voice. "My family is nosy. They're going to ask a lot of questions."

I let out a shaky laugh. "I know how to handle nosy. I've had plenty of practice with nosy. I'll be fine, Scot." I undid my seat belt and reached for the door handle.

His hand enfolded my other wrist in a gentle grip. "Wait, Julia. See . . . they're not only nosy. They're—" He coughed, as if something scratchy was stuck in his throat. "Unique. And loud. They're often loud. Not my dad so much, but the rest of them . . ."

Wow. Anxiety pooled in his body language, in the cadence of his speech. This guy was seriously stressed about my meeting his family. But why? Out of nowhere, an irrational urge to comfort him came to life. "Listen. It will be fine. I grew up going to one social function after another, and I've met about every type of person there is. And hey, you've brought dates home before. Right? If they managed your family, I'm sure I can. Stop worrying."

The following silence was deafening. Scot returned to tapping his thumb on the steering wheel. My heart fluttered like a thousand and one butterflies trapped in a cage.

An impossible thought flared up, but I couldn't be right. Could I? "You *have* brought women home before. Haven't you?"

Shifting, he unbuckled his seat belt. "A few. But not for a while."

"Exactly how long is a while?"

He responded in a low growl of nearly incomprehensible syllables.

Oh. My. God. "*Ten* years?" I blinked. "You haven't brought a girl home to meet your folks for ten years?"

The thumb tapping commenced again. "I keep my private life private."

"Still . . . that's a long time. Hasn't your family been curious about the women you've dated?" My parents wouldn't let more than a month go by without being properly introduced to any man in my life. Which was a damn good reason for not dating. "Haven't you—?"

"Leslie. She . . . we'd set up a brunch thing," Scot said, expertly avoiding looking in my direction. "We had to cancel. But you know how that story ends."

Oh. God. I wanted, for maybe the first time ever, to shake Leslie. Had she not known what a big deal it was for Scot to want to introduce her to his parents, his sisters, Verda? "I'm sorry," I whispered. "That must have been tough to explain."

"Yeah, well, the past is history. But they"—he aimed his vision toward the front of the house—"are going to be very curious about you."

"It will be okay. I'll be courteous." My earlier plan took an immediate nosedive out the window. Now that I understood the root of Scot's nervousness, and how the simple act of meeting me would set up a whole host of familial expectations, I couldn't—wouldn't—do anything to increase them. "Seriously. I'll smile, answer when questioned, and make polite conversation. But I won't add fuel to the fire."

"Thank you." The thinnest layer of surprised gratitude nuanced his otherwise-gruff baritone. It seemed he didn't know me as well as he'd thought. I hoped he'd caught on to that little fact.

"You're welcome," I murmured, somehow finding this quiet moment so much more uncomfortable than the fireworks of last night. The man sitting next to me was an enigma. Big, tough, *fierce* on the outside, but those traits were only the frame of who he was, not the entire picture. Not even close. But no matter how hard I tried, I couldn't see the rest of him.

It was at that second that something soft and warm and *gushy* opened inside of me. A person of a romantic, poetic disposition might have described the sensation as a flower unfurling its petals toward the sun. Or maybe the slow drip of a melting icicle. But for me, practical-to-the-core Julia Collins, I didn't know what to make of it.

Scot resituated himself and leaned in close. Really close. So close that the scent of him, that same clean, earthy, *intoxicating* fragrance that lingered on his jacket coated the air and invaded my space. My breathing hitched. I had the wild notion that his lips were going to keep coming closer until they touched mine. My chin tilted up on its own accord. Okay, impossible, but I swear that was how it seemed.

But instead of his mouth meeting mine, his hand grazed along the side of my head. His fingers stroked my hair, his thumb on my cheek. My heart picked up speed, galloping away in my chest like a racehorse bent on winning the Kentucky Derby.

"Wh-What are you doing?" My voice held a quality I hadn't heard before—not without having a cold or a hangover. It was husky, throaty, and very unlike me. Scot's fingers fished around at the back of my head, his touches now feeling more like an examination than an act of seduction. "What are you doing?" I repeated.

His breath tickled my ear. "Your hair. Why do you insist on scraping it away from your face?"

"It—it's easier to manage."

He found the clip and gave it a good, hard tug. It unclasped and my hair fell down to my shoulders in a loose, messy pile. "That's better. You have beautiful hair. You shouldn't work so hard to hide it."

I hid it for a reason. My hair was thick and unmanageable and left to its own devices tended to increase in volume throughout the day. Knowing I probably looked as if I'd just crawled out of bed, I smoothed the sides down. Well, I attempted to. But all of that didn't stop the softness, the unfurling, the freaking melting from continuing to take place. Scot Raymond had just said something nice. To me.

"Okay. Well . . . um . . . thank you."

Realizing he'd actually given me—the icy, cunning witch of the west—a compliment, he yanked his body back to his seat. His gaze slid to the side of me. "We better get in there. They're all staring out the window now."

"What?" I swiveled my neck so fast my vision swam. But he was right. A bunch of faces were pressed against the glass of what I assumed was the living-room window. "Wow. Maybe I haven't dealt with this level of nosiness before."

"I warned you." Scot tucked his keys into the pocket of his jeans. "Let's go."

With a nod, I stepped from the SUV and pulled my spine ramrod straight. I hadn't lied. I'd attended more social functions by the age of ten than most people did in their entire lifetimes. There was no reason why a simple dinner shouldn't be a piece of cake.

But when Scot and I ambled up the stone walkway, I have to admit that I sort of felt like I was traipsing off the edge of a diving board. Or maybe the plank on a pirate's ship. Regardless, the destination was the same: lots and lots of water. And I hadn't brought my life preserver.

Chapter Eight

We entered a small, empty, wood-floored foyer. Grateful that his family, even if they were nosy, was allowing us to come to them and hadn't greeted us at the door, I shrugged off my coat. Scot hung it in the closet and proceeded to tug his toffee-and-cream-hued sweater over his head. Apparently he only had one jacket, which was currently flung over the back of my couch. And nope, I hadn't touched or sniffed it again.

His movement caused the shirt he wore beneath the sweater—a dark brown, long-sleeved button-down—to drift up at his waist. His stomach, while not quite washboard defined, was flat, firm, and sexy as all get-out. And he had a darling set of freckles that greatly resembled a smiley face beside his belly button—an inny, by the way. My tongue seemed to expand three sizes, resulting in a sudden inability to swallow.

Why? Why did *this* man have to turn me on? In my line of work, I met a lot of eligible bachelors. Many of them were excellent examples of the XY combination of chromosomes. Handsome. Hot. Heck, some of these guys had even hit on me. But no. I had to hunger for Scot. Looking at him, *smelling* him, made me ache for his touch—for his kiss.

"See something you like, Julia?" Scot asked, observing my fixation but acting with boyish charm and innocence. My ass.

I wrinkled my nose in pretend distaste. "Actually, Scot, I noticed those moles next to your belly button. You might want to get them examined by a dermatologist. You never know when those things can go wrong."

"Maybe you'd like to check them out later." He wrapped his arm around my waist and drew me to him. "I'm game if you are."

My cheeks burned at the teasing insinuation, at the nearness of his body. Flattening my palms on his chest, I shoved myself backward. "Not likely. Maybe they're not moles. They could be a rash. Have you had any questionable sleepovers lately? You might be contagious."

Deep laughter barreled out of his chest, but he stared intently at my face. The fire in my cheeks spread to my neck and continued to mosey on downward to my . . . er . . . womanly areas.

"Why, Julia. I had no idea you were the blushing sort," he said. "Or are you feverish? Coming down with something?"

"It's hot in here. Isn't your family waiting for us?" 'Cause at that instant, I wanted a ton of people around. For safety reasons.

"Yup." But he didn't move, just continued his intense appraisal. "They'll be out here in a minute."

"Then we should go to them."

Too late. "What are you two doing out here for so long?" Verda asked, leading the pack of wolves right to us. "We aren't interrupting anything, are we?"

"Uh-uh. Scot and I were just about to join you." I tried to find my inner Mary Tyler Moore again, but she'd apparently flown the coop. I couldn't say I blamed her. "Sorry for the delay. We . . . ah . . . were talking."

"Scot, aren't you going to introduce us?" This question came from a woman whom I pegged as Scot's mother. He had her coloring, and I put her at an age that would make it unlikely she was his sister. "I raised you better than that," she chided.

Aha! I was right.

"Julia, this is my mother, Isobel." Scot then nodded toward

the blond, blue-eyed man standing next to her. "And this is my dad, Marty."

He introduced his sister Elizabeth and her husband Nate. Then came his other sister, Alice, her husband Ethan, and their one-year-old daughter, Rose. What was with this family and that flower, anyway? Alice and Elizabeth had Scot's coloring, the same dark hair and eyes. But where Alice was tall and on the angular side, Elizabeth was closer to my height, with a curvier figure. Oh, and the sisters were pale, where Scot's skin held the slightest kiss of bronze.

The two husbands, Ethan and Nate, were equally handsome, but in different ways. Ethan reminded me of a young Pierce Brosnan, but with a strong Irish lilt. Nate was more the guy next door. Easygoing and relaxed but strong. Protective. I wasn't surprised to learn he was a cop. Then, I met Scot's cousin, Chloe.

Ah. Verda's silent partner at Magical Matchups, Chloe radiated a vibrancy that went beyond her vivid red hair. I wanted to hate her on sight because she was freaking tiny, a mix of Thumbelina and Lucille Ball. Her fiancé, Ben, was also in attendance, a blond bombshell of a man who had a body that must have taken some serious man-hours at the gym to achieve.

Finally, I was introduced to the last two men standing: Scot's younger brother, Joe—who looked just like his father, without the receding hairline—and Verda's live-in beau, Vinny. He had the elegant, refined appearance of an old-fashioned gentleman. Gray hair and mustache, bright eyes that defied his age, and a quiet demeanor I appreciated.

"Wow," I said. "It's very nice to meet you all, but I might forget a name or two."

"You'll figure us out soon enough." Elizabeth smiled. "We're all pretty harmless."

This, for whatever reason, caused every man to burst out in laughter. The women, all but Isobel and myself, followed suit. Even Rose giggled. Huh. Curiouser and curiouser.

Centering my attention on Alice and Ethan, I said, "Thank you for allowing me to join in at the last minute. I . . . It was rather a sudden decision."

"Any friend of Scot's is welcome in our home," Ethan said warmly. His hand grazed his wife's shoulder in a barely perceptible squeeze. "We're happy to have you."

Alice nodded but didn't echo her husband's statement. She held her daughter on her hip, so maybe that was why. I didn't think so, though. Not with the chilly breeze that blew from her to me.

I cleared my throat. "Is there anything I can help with?"

My offer paled Alice's complexion a good two shades. I tensed, ready for her refusal, but it was Verda who chimed in. "Don't be silly, Julia! You are our guest. Why don't you and Scot relax in the living room? I'll help Alice finish up in the kitchen."

Rose grabbed a chunk of Alice's hair and tugged. "Down!" she demanded. "Down now."

Alice shifted the child from her arms to Ethan's. He, in one of those strange spousal telepathy things, nodded and proceeded to whisk their daughter to another part of the house. A scant few seconds later, Vinny, Isobel, Marty, Joe, Nate, and Ben followed. Whew. Talk about a huge amount of relief! Fewer people eased the tight knot of stress in my shoulders.

Fastening her gaze on me, Alice tried to pull off a smile, but her eyes remained cool. She answered my question for herself. "Thank you, Julia. But between Grandma, Chloe, and Elizabeth, there are already too many cooks in the kitchen."

"Well, if you change your mind, I'm happy to lend a hand." I shifted from one foot to the other, waiting for someone to step in and smooth the awkwardness. No one did. Maybe it was all in my mind? I glanced at Scot, who had a mile-wide grin stretched across his face—a grin filled with approval and smug satisfaction all rolled into one. And it was directed at Alice.

Acid flew up from my stomach, burning my esophagus. He was pleased his sister didn't like me? Anxiety gave way to a quick burst of anger. Screw this. I wasn't going to sit around and be miserable for the next who-knew-how-many hours.

"You know what?" I said in a low, evenly modulated tone. "If this is too last-minute, or if there isn't enough food, or whatever, I can call a cab to take me back to my car." It would cost a fortune, but some things—like my self-respect—were worth a hell of a lot more than money.

Alice's eyes softened a tiny amount. "Absolutely not. We have plenty of food. It's silly for you to leave now." She expelled a sigh. "Ethan's right. Any friend of Scot's is welcome here."

Well. I didn't believe her for a second, but I appreciated the effort.

"Come on. We're holding them up," Scot said, resting his hand on the small of my back. "We'll go play with my niece."

I hesitated for a millisecond. Scot's you-go-girl smile had ticked me off. And yeah, it shouldn't have. Scot's whole point of asking me to date was to fend off his supposedly manipulative relatives. But for a reason I refused to contemplate, I *wanted* his family to like me.

Pride. That's all it was.

"Julia? Are you staying or leaving?" Scot's voice filtered through my haze. He applied the teeniest bit of pressure to my back. "If you're leaving, let me grab you a newspaper to read while you wait for that taxi. I hear there are some terrific ads in today's edition."

Being the intelligent woman I am, reading between those lines wasn't difficult at all. That was all it took to regain my footing. I was here for a purpose that had nothing to do with Scot's family liking me.

"Staying, of course," I said in a voice dripping with enough honey I should've had bumblebees buzzing around my tongue. I stepped away from his hand but crooked my arm through his. "Lead on, handsome."

A wheezy sound emerged from Alice. Maybe a sigh. Maybe a gasp. Maybe smothered laughter. I didn't know her well enough to speculate. But Chloe and Elizabeth both dipped their chins in slight nods. Of approval? Perhaps.

Verda's mouth quirked in humor. She gave me a wink. I returned it and tugged on Scot's arm. "Well, what are we waiting for? I thought we were holding them up."

He grumbled under his breath, but guided me down the hallway and into the living room. There, folks were sprawled in various positions: Ethan, Joe, and Nate were on the floor with Rose, playing with bright-colored blocks. Ben and Vinny were seated on the leather sofa, engaged in a conversation about the stock market. Marty was reading the paper—ha, Scot would've had to steal it from his dad—and Isobel was off to the side, watching her family with a contented expression.

Scot dropped my arm and joined the group on the floor. He expected me to follow, I'm sure, but I stood still, transfixed by the scene in front of me.

I had family. Not only my parents, but grandparents and a few cousins. I'd been to many a family occasion over the years. Who hasn't? But my family events tended to be stiff, formal affairs always focused more on social protocol than simply enjoying each other's company. These people, this scene, reminded me of television—those made-up families who, while they had their ongoing struggles that were neatly resolved in a thirty-to-sixty-minute episode, truly loved to be together. I blinked my heavy eyelids. I'd heard of families like this, naturally. But I'd heard of Santa Claus, too. Didn't mean either actually existed.

"Up!" A little hand grabbed my knee, waking me from my trance. I looked down and saw Rose. Her dark brown eyes were lit with excitement. Chubby arms rose toward the sky. "Up, up, up!"

"My daughter likes you, Julia," Ethan said from across the room. "She doesn't normally take to new people so quickly."

"Oh . . . I don't have a lot of experience with kids." I knelt down so I was roughly the same height as Rose. "Hello," I said. "I'm Julia."

Smooth, baby-soft hands touched my cheeks before moving to my hair. "Up!"

"She wants you to pick her up." Scot offered the information easily enough, but I had the suspicion that he didn't like the idea all that well. I wasn't so sure I did, either. Kids scared the crap out of me. At least kids this small.

But going back to the "If it irritates Scot, I'm going to do it" plan, I pushed my misgivings aside and pulled Rose into my arms. Standing, I tried to hold her on my hip the same way Alice had. But Rose wasn't having any of that. She twisted her entire body toward me, and I had to work really fast to alter my hold so she didn't go crashing to the floor.

Her hands found my cheeks again. She patted them twice, gave a hearty eye-stinging yank to my hair, and then nestled her head against my chest with a satisfied sigh. I am not a corny person. I do not cry at movies, no matter how sad. But this—the simple trust that this little girl placed in me—wrapped a thick, fuzzy blanket around my heart.

I settled my chin on top of her head. "Aren't you sweet," I whispered.

"Sweet," Rose burbled, as if in agreement.

I made the mistake of looking at Scot. He had the hard-edged, egg-cracking jaw thing going on again. His eyes, though, weren't hard. Or cold. Or condescending. They were soft. Misty, even. As if he was seeing me for the first time in his life. And—here's the real kicker—as if he liked what he saw.

Oh, bloody hell.

I grimaced at the bowl set before me. "Potato soup?"

"*Irish* potato soup," Verda clarified. "Alice used Ethan's grandmother's recipe. In fact, tonight's entire dinner is Irish. Isn't that marvelous?"

"Oh, yes," I murmured even as my stomach cramped. "Marvelous."

"Something wrong?" Scot shoveled a spoonful of flu-inducing soup in his mouth. Okay, that wasn't fair. But damn, of all the soups in the world to be served, Alice had chosen the only one that made me sick. If I believed in signs, I'd take this as a bad one.

"No. Nothing wrong at all." I sat between Scot and Joe at an incredibly large mahogany dining room table. Antique, probably old English. With both leaves inserted, the thing was easily fourteen feet long. While it held all of us, there wasn't much elbow room. "Smells delicious!" I lied.

The chatter in the room died as folks got to the business of eating. I tried on three separate occasions to take a bite, but my gag reflex kicked in before the spoon even got close to my lips. Deciding it was far better to appear rude than to spurt a mouthful of soup out on the table, I eventually gave up and waited for the next course.

Joe tapped my shoulder. "If you're saving room for the rest of dinner, I'll finish that off for you." He tossed me a lopsided grin and winked conspiratorially.

Wow. I wouldn't have been more relieved if a real, honest-to-God prince in shining armor had swept in to save me from the growling, hungry dragon. "Oh! Sure, Joe," I said, pushing my bowl over. "That's exactly what I'm doing."

"Figured." His blue-eyed gaze held a twinkle that reminded me of Verda.

"So, Julia, tell us a little about yourself." This came from Isobel, who was seated across from me. Uh-oh. For a while, I'd thought that maybe I was going to get off without being peppered with questions. Apparently not.

"Um. Not much to tell. I work, have dinner with my parents every Wednesday, and hang out with my friends. That's about it."

"You meet your parents for dinner every week?" Isobel asked.

Scot squeezed my knee. I brushed his hand away. "Uh-huh. It's a long standing tradition." Ha. More like a long standing order. Well, I suppose that's a sort of tradition.

"What a wonderful daughter you are! I wish I could have a weekly dinner with my children." Isobel sent The Look to each of her kids. Anyone who has a mother knows this look. "But they never seem to have the time."

Elizabeth, rather than responding to her mother's guilt tactic, asked, "What line of work are you in, Julia?"

"Customer service," I responded. Thank goodness I'd gone through Verda's paperwork. "I . . . ah . . . help people figure things out."

"Just think, dinner once a week with the kids. Wouldn't that be nice, Marty?" Isobel asked her husband, obviously determined not to be diverted. "Wednesdays won't work, but Tuesdays or Thursdays would."

Alice's laughter drifted down the table. "Mom! You're becoming more like Grandma Verda every day. If you want to see us more often, just say so. You don't have to beat around the bush and trick us into anything."

"But once a week might be asking a bit much of the kids, Isobel. They have busy lives." Marty patted his wife's hand. "And Tuesdays are not good."

"Oh, hush. You just don't want anything to interfere with your shows." Isobel squared her shoulders. "All I'm saying is how nice it is that Julia cares enough about her family to make an effort to fit them into *her* busy life."

"She's not that busy." Scot squeezed my knee again. This time I kicked his shin.

"I have a very full life!" Endless nights of watching television and reading magazines. Hm. "I think family is very, very important." Hey, I did. Otherwise, I'd simply ignore my parents' orders.

Isobel sighed. "Yes, your parents are very lucky."

Scot, with his freaking hand on my knee again, squeezed even harder. "Julia, tell us more about your job," he said. "What do you do all day?"

When I got him alone, he was so in trouble. "I suppose you could say I'm sort of a counselor, even though that isn't my job title."

"Really?" Scot drawled. "I didn't realize you counseled people. That must be a very gratifying line of work. Did you go to school for that?"

"Who cares about her job?" Joe cut in, deftly saving me from yet another uncomfortable moment and the murder of his big brother. I pretty much adored Joe by this point. "I'd rather hear about how you two lovebirds met."

"At Magical Matchups," Verda said. "I matched them up! And they're perfect for each other. They're going to have beautiful children some day. Three boys."

Joe's spoon clanked against his bowl. Alice choked on her

water. Ethan rubbed her back while Elizabeth handed her a napkin.

Isobel narrowed her gaze at Verda. "You can't know that, Mother. Don't start in on your mystical mumbo-jumbo stuff again. Not now."

Verda pumped her head up and down. "It isn't mumbo jumbo, Isobel, and I do know it! Three boys. They're going to be very important boys, too."

"Julia, can you help me bring the rest of the dishes out?" Alice interrupted in a high-pitched voice. She surprised everyone, not just me, as the noise level in the room dropped instantly. "I think everyone is done with their soup."

I nodded, happy to stop this conversation in its tracks. Three boys? Yeah, right. I'd be lucky if I had one child someday, and three was pushing the limits. Think about it: I was currently thirty-three. Even if I met the man I'd eventually marry tomorrow, there would be a minimum of two years from first date to walking down the aisle, likely more.

One year to date. One year to plan the huge shindig of a wedding my parents would insist on. Possibly eighteen months, depending on the season and the venues that were available for the ceremony and reception. Add in a year of marriage before conceiving—assuming neither of us had any fertility issues—and I'd be around thirty-seven before my first child was born. And that all hinged on meeting the "right" guy within twenty-fours of now. So not likely.

I followed Alice to the kitchen, but right before stepping through the swinging door I heard Isobel say, "I like her. Don't you dare scare her off, Mother."

"I'm only telling the truth, Isobel. Why can't you accept this? You've met Miranda . . ."

Unfortunately, the door swung shut before I heard the rest of Verda's statement. Again I wondered who Miranda was. A friend of Verda's? But what did she have to do with anything? I shook off the questions and smiled at Alice. "What needs to go out?"

Tucking her long, dark hair behind one ear, she frowned. "Let's just give my mother and grandmother a few minutes to chill out, okay?"

"Sure. If you think that's best."

Alice busied herself with putting the finishing touches on her dinner. She'd prepared beef brisket with cabbage, another potato dish—not soup, though, so I'd be able to eat it—and a few other side dishes that seemed to be a mix of different vegetables.

"You've gone to a lot of work," I said, hoping to ease the suffocating silence.

"Last time we were in Ireland, Ethan's grandmother prepared this same meal. It made him happy, so I wanted to try to re-create it." Again, Alice spoke in a low, calm manner, but that same chilly undercurrent remained from earlier.

Normally, I don't really care if random people like me, but Alice's behavior was an irritant. I pressed my lips together, smothering the question burning to be asked, and gave myself a minute to consider the reasons I was so bothered. Her family impressed me. I was quickly coming to admire Verda. And Rose . . . well, that little girl had carved herself right into my heart. But none of that should explain why Alice's like or dislike of me meant a damn.

Finally, deciding that the past two days were to blame—and yes, I blamed pretty much everything on that—I said, "Okay. You don't like me. How come?"

In a Verda-like move, she settled her hands on her hips. "It isn't you. I promise this has nothing to do with you or with who you are as a person." Exhaling a noisy sigh, she shrugged. "I'm sure you're a very nice woman . . ."

"But?"

"I shouldn't say anything." Again I heard the *but* she didn't say. I didn't fill it in for her though.

Alice turned to pull a few large serving spoons out of a drawer. Then, as if making her decision, she faced me again. "My grandmother believes that if she doesn't set Scot up with the right woman—"

"Everyone is getting antsy out there," Chloe said, stepping into the kitchen. "We should get the food out before Isobel and Grandma Verda start brawling. Wine, too. We definitely need wine. Lots of it."

"We'll only be a second." I prayed that Chloe would take the hint, so Alice and I could finish our conversation. "Alice was just telling me—"

"That it's time to serve the food," Alice said, effectively cutting me off. Damn, damn, and damn again. "Everyone take a dish and let's go feed the masses."

Impatience reared its ugly head, but I couldn't really argue, so I nodded and grabbed a large bowl filled with spinach and tomatoes. Maybe I'd have a chance to get Alice alone again before the evening was over.

Or maybe I'd force Scot to fill in some of the blanks.

"Three glasses of wine," Scot said after we were buckled into his SUV. Verda was going home with Vinny, so we were alone. "You drank three large glasses of wine with Elizabeth and Chloe?"

"Something like that. Maybe four. Or five? I don't have an actual count because Chloe kept filling the glass before it was empty." I knew my limits, and I'd gone over them. "I cannot drive my car. So you get to drive me home or I get to call a taxi. I don't really care which."

"You're drunk," Scot said. "I take you to meet my family and you get drunk."

"'Drunk' is a little harsh. Tipsy is more like it." I pointed out the window to Nate and Elizabeth, who had just exited Alice's house. "Your brother-in-law is carrying your sister. And Ben had to propel Chloe to the car. They did this to me. Can't blame me."

Besides which, I'd enjoyed myself. A lot. I liked Elizabeth and Chloe. They were charming, and while they'd shot a few odd glances at each other I couldn't identify, they hadn't once made me feel uncomfortable. I liked Joe, too. And I was pretty much a goner for Rose. Hell, I liked everyone—even Alice, though the jury was out on her feelings for me. She'd flat-out avoided me the rest of the evening. But still . . . so what if I'd had some wine?

Scot's lips—very fine lips, I might add—trembled in the makings of a grin. "Okay, Miss Lush. I'll drive you home. But I'm not coming back in the morning to take you to your car."

"No reason to. Kara or Leslie will. Or if they can't, you can drop me off there tomorrow night instead of at home. You know, after our *date.* I won't put out at all."

"But baby," Scot teased in a husky tenor. "I'll buy you a nice dinner. Show you a good time. If you don't put out, why should I bother?"

"Huh? Oh!" A balmy flush stole over me. Yep. Too much wine. I tried to laugh off my embarrassment, but I'm sure I failed. "Put *you* out. Not put out. But if I were to put out, you'd have to show me more than a good time, buster. A simple dinner won't cut it. No siree Bob."

"You're trouble," Scot murmured. He turned the ignition on and backed out of the driveway. "Crazy amounts of trouble."

"Yeah, and you're a walk in the park," I fired back.

He laughed. "You surprise me, Julia. Look, I pushed you into this arrangement, and I know you don't understand why.

Let's call a truce and just get through this the best we can. What do you say?"

"I say you're still an ass hat . . . but I like your family. So fine, a truce." Besides, getting along with Scot would make this situation that much easier. It should, anyway.

"Good."

Maybe it was our truce, maybe it was the wine, maybe it was the whole getting-to-know-his-family bit, or maybe it was the gentle purr of the engine, or possibly it was a combination of all four, but I had a relaxed, comfortable, and—for better or for worse—loose-lipped hum taking control. "You looked at me funny earlier."

"Define *funny*."

"When I was holding Rose. You looked like a man who . . . ah . . . liked me."

"My opinion hasn't changed." The words were tough, but the tone lacked believability. To my tipsy ears, anyway. "I love my niece. What you saw were my feelings for her. They had nothing to do with you."

"Hm. Well, that's good. Because I'm dating someone else. I'd hate for you to fall in love with me. That would kind of screw everything up." Okay, well, I was *about* to be dating someone. Jameson. Not really a lie, even if it was only Sunday lunch. "And you should really think about giving Leslie another chance. She's nothing like me. Doesn't share my philosophies about love at all." What else had Leslie said to say? Oh, yeah. "She's *changed*, Scot."

"I told you last night, Leslie and I are over. We have been for a while."

"Because she cheated on you."

"I'd say that's a damn good reason." He slowed the SUV at a light. His thumb started tapping again. Nervous? About what? "I hope you're right. I hope Leslie"—Scot's voice cracked the tiniest amount—"doesn't throw something potentially good away again."

"That's it? That's all you have to say about her?" I realized belatedly that bringing this specific topic up under the influence of alcohol wasn't the greatest idea. My brain didn't want to cooperate. Otherwise, why would I be relieved by his response instead of dismayed? I tried for one more push, anyway. "Why not take her out once more? Just to see?"

"Because what's done is done. Relationships aren't a chalkboard. I can't erase what happened, or how she threw it—" Breaking off, he cursed. "Never mind. I don't want to discuss my relationships with any of the women I've dated, including Leslie."

I'd have to give more thought to the Leslie and Scot thing. I didn't press any further, just stared out the window. Scot was also quiet. Before too long, we turned into my parking lot.

"So, thanks. For tonight. I enjoyed meeting everyone. You have a nice family." I shoved my door open. Then, remembering the scene that had touched me so profoundly, I said, "Really nice. They care about each other. They care a lot about you."

"I care a lot about them." Scot nodded toward my building. "Think you can get to your place on your own, or do you need some help?"

"Tipsy is not drunk, and I can walk just fine when I'm tipsy."

"Alrighty then, Julia. Have a good night and I'll see you tomorrow. Seven."

"Yep. Casual. I remember." He didn't drive away until I'd entered the building, which proved he wasn't a total ass hat. But damn if I hadn't wanted him to come up with me.

Stupidity. With a sigh that began at my toes, I unlocked my front door and let myself in. After the hours I'd spent in noise and bedlam, my apartment seemed way too quiet—absurdly quiet—so I flipped on the TV on my way to the bedroom. And then I saw the journal.

It was still on the floor. I literally hadn't touched the dang thing after dropping it. Verda's words tickled my senses, and almost as if she were standing right in front of me, I heard her again. "Magic, Julia. You experienced magic."

For whatever reason, that statement didn't seem as ridiculous now. I can't explain the why of that or what I did next. Not in detail, anyway. Hard to put into words an action that doesn't follow any rhyme or reason. But I grabbed the pen with one hand and the journal with the other and curled up on my sofa. My muscles buzzed with the memory of the energy, the fire that had roared through them earlier.

Verda's handwritten message and her question about wishes merged with everything else, and before I knew what I was doing, my hand flew across the first page of the journal. I didn't think about what I was writing, because I wouldn't have written it if I had. For one, I wouldn't have had the courage. For two, I surely would've talked myself out of it. But the quiet moments with Scot, the softening in his gaze when I held Rose, and the effects of the wine created a nice, happy fuzz that allowed me to push past my mental barriers. I wrote,

Scot drives halfway down the road before remembering he left his jacket here. He turns his SUV around and comes back, knocks on my door, and when I open it . . . he drags me into his arms, holds me tight, and then . . . then he kisses me.

A slow, deep, engulfing warmth encased my fingers and spread over my skin. The air thickened with the arid stillness that occurs right before a summer storm rolls in, with its flashes of lightning, knives of rain, and shouts of thunder. I gripped the pen tighter and the writing in the journal blurred enough that my wish—fantasy?—became an illegible mess of blue ink.

I inhaled weighted air though my nose, exhaled through my mouth. I did this over and over until the constricting pressure surrounding me evened off and then finally lightened. Dizzy, I dropped the pen and the book and struggled to stand.

Wine. That's all it was. Too much wine.

I stumbled toward the bedroom on wobbly legs, but only made it a few steps when a reverberating knock echoed through my apartment. *No.* It couldn't be. But I knew. I knew in a way I'd never known any other thing at any other time ever.

Still, I pretended that I didn't. Because acknowledging that would have been too damn much. I told myself that my visitor was Kara or Leslie. Or both. I told myself that someone in my building had ordered food and the delivery guy was at the wrong place. I told myself that the neighbor down the hall had locked himself out and needed to use my phone to call the landlord or the maintenance guy. And I kept telling myself these things as I approached the door, as I unlocked the door, and yep, even as I swung it open.

"Sorry, Julia," Scot said. "I remembered you had my jacket and—"

I grabbed his sweater and pulled him inside. His arms came around me and he yanked me against him tight. Hard. The second before his lips touched mine, he whispered, "Yeah. Crazy amounts of trouble."

Chapter Nine

I dumped two Extra Strength Tylenol capsules into my palm, swallowed them with a glass of water, and then, without a flicker of hesitation, followed those up with two more.

After the kiss, which could also be described as the stupidest moment of my life, Scot and I had jumped apart as if the fires of hell and damnation were licking at our ankles. Well, okay. That was how *I* felt. Scot's polite but quick-footed departure didn't necessarily mean his thoughts were on a par with mine.

He'd kissed me in such a way that my toes curled, and the flower of attraction—probably a damn rose—finished unfurling its stupid, fluttery petals, and the icicle that had begun to melt in Scot's car last night became a messy, watery puddle. He might have left because our kiss had given him a stomachache and he hadn't wanted to toss his cookies in front of me. Perhaps he'd recalled Verda's dinner-table pronouncement of our someday three boys and had escaped before we went on to create number one. Or, I supposed, there was always the chance he'd become filled with so much desire for a wine-saturated woman that he had to get away before he acted on his lust.

I doubted it was the last one. My guess was on one, two, or the fires of hell and damnation. Or all three, for that matter.

Whatever the case, we'd kissed, he'd left, and I spent the remainder of the night trapped in the repetitive motions of staring at the journal, gazing off into space, and touching my lips in disbelief and surprised pleasure. That is, until the swift and heavy hand of guilt squeezed my insides to such a degree that I was fairly sure I'd be the one tossing her cookies. At some point, alcohol and the conflicting tide of emotions forced me to get in a few hours of sleep.

Waking up in yesterday's clothes with a headache and that rumble of uneasiness that brought about a shot of nausea was not something I'd experienced often, and up until the other day hadn't happened since college. I took a scalding hot shower, scrubbed myself with gobs of cherry-blossom-scented body wash, used my ultraexpensive, so-thick-it-was-like-butter conditioner on my hair—hair that Scot had decreed beautiful—and meticulously shaved my legs and underarms. I toweled off and rubbed moisturizer—also cherry blossom scented—into every inch of my skin. It wasn't until I'd wrapped an oversized towel around me and had taken tweezers to my eyebrows that I realized what I was doing.

I was *primping*.

Beautifying myself in the way a woman does when she expects a man will see her buck naked. When she expects a man's hands—and, uh, other parts—to be on her body.

"Holy hell," I muttered. The tweezers fell into the sink with a soft clank. I glared at my reflection in the mirror as if it—*I*—weren't any better than a wanton whore. This was wrong on so many levels. Scot was taken. Oh, okay, he wasn't *taken* taken. But to Leslie, he was hers. And that meant he was hands-off. Completely, irrevocably, until-the-end-of-time hands-off. Even if nothing ever occurred between Scot and Leslie again, he was untouchable.

But God, I so wanted to touch him.

Especially those smiley-face freckles. They were begging to be touched. Caressed. Tickled. Licked.

"Stop," I told my reflection in a firm, no-nonsense tone. "Even if Leslie weren't an issue—but she is!—the most you can ever have with Scot is meaningless sex. Steaming-hot, make-your-toes-curl sex, probably, but . . . No! He's not right for you. You are not right for him. So stop!"

Unfortunately, my strict chiding didn't halt the sudden image of my legs wrapped around Scot's naked torso with the bedsheets tangled between us. It didn't detract from the very real fact that sex—meaningless or otherwise—sounded pretty damn great. And it also didn't stop me from noticing that I had one perfectly plucked eyebrow and one that resembled a curled-up caterpillar. Okay, a baby caterpillar, and there certainly wasn't any unibrow stuff happening, but in direct comparison with the other brow? Not attractive.

"Okay." I picked up the tweezers and waved them in front of the mirror. "You can pluck. But no more primping!"

"You *like* Scot?" Kara's startled voice hit from the side of me, from the hallway outside the open bathroom door. "Are you serious?"

I dropped the tweezers again, my heart in my mouth. "Shit, Kara. How long have you been standing there?" Maybe I was going to have to rethink this whole sharing-keys-with-my-friends thing.

"I was in the living room and heard you talking. I thought you knew I was here . . . and yeah, Julia, 'shit' about sums it up. What's going on?"

Pulling my towel tighter, I turned. "Is Leslie here?"

Kara crossed her arms over her chest. "No. She's working today. Some big case they just got."

"Oh." I wheezed. "Okay. That's good."

"Doesn't mean I'm not going to fill her in." Confusion streamed into Kara's green eyes. "Damn, Julia. This is huge. You seriously like Scot?"

"I—I don't know. Maybe?" This was all so new. Hell, less than three days since bizarro world started. I was still trying to catch up. "I haven't actually . . . um . . . decided that for sure."

"Oh-kay. Why don't you give it some more thought while you get dressed? I'll be in the living room." Kara didn't say anything more, just left me alone.

Fuck, right? I backed up to the edge of the tub and sat down. I gave myself a couple of minutes to pull my ragged emotions together. Maybe this was for the best. Maybe once Kara told Leslie—because she would—Leslie would let me out of this agreement. And yeah, she'd be ticked. No doubt about that. But as long as the impossible didn't happen—like falling head over heels for Scot—she'd get over it. At least I hoped she would.

Then I'd just have to go through the motions for the next couple of weeks until Scot decided our pretend relationship had run its course. It wouldn't be that bad. Then I'd be able to carry on as normal. Focus on my real life again: trying to keep Introductions afloat, meeting my parents once a week for dinner, hanging out with my friends here and there. Reasonable. Logical. Sound. The *proper* way to proceed.

But the quick burst of disappointment that sank in was not reasonable. The craving to kiss Scot again couldn't be described as logical. And the sudden wish that Verda was right, that Scot and I were somehow meant to be together, wasn't sound in the least. For many, many reasons.

I sidled out of the bathroom without looking into the living room. Safely in my bedroom, I closed the door for privacy and threw on a pair of jeans and a T-shirt. My gaze landed on the journal, which I'd brought in this morning. It sat on my nightstand. I'd pretty much decided that last night's hastily scrawled entry and Scot's abrupt arrival at my door were nothing more than weird coincidences. Because thinking it was *magic* that had propelled him to return wasn't only idiotic, it was . . . well, nuts. He'd left his jacket here. He came back to get it. I was tipsy and threw myself at him, we kissed. That simple. But a tiny, infuriating voice in my head reminded me of the numerous things I'd written off to coincidence over the last few days. Maybe too many?

"Let's prove it once and for all." I rifled through my nightstand's top drawer to find a pen, picked up the journal, and without any hesitation at all, flipped to a clean page. What should I wish for?

"I wish Kara hadn't let herself in and heard what she heard," I whispered. Yeah. Perfect. I wrote the words and waited. Nothing happened, so I underlined the sentence and thought the wish again. Still nothing. Hm. Maybe the eerie stuff only happened with the first wish.

I eased my bedroom door open a crack and peered out. Nope. I could just make out the edge of Kara's shoulder. So she was still here, last night *had* been a coincidence, and that was that. The barest twinge of regret settled inside.

Unless . . . I chewed on the end of the pen. *If* the journal really had the power to grant wishes, maybe changing events that had already occurred was impossible. So focusing on the future, on events that hadn't yet happened, might be the best way to go. Excitement replaced the regret. This made sense. Otherwise—wow—think of the havoc I could create with history.

I bit my lip and wrote.

Kara agrees to keep everything she heard about Scot to herself until I work it out on my own and either tell Leslie myself or give Kara the go-ahead.

Light-headedness hit the instant my pen stopped moving. The writing—*my* writing—glowed in shimmering sparkles for several seconds before returning to normal. Had that happened last night? Ugh. I couldn't recall. Again, though, the air grew in weight and volume, shifting and pulsating against me, drawing painful attention to every breath I drew in and out of my lungs.

No wine today. Inebriation wasn't to blame for the warmth suffusing my body or for the rapid goose bumps coursing along my skin. I was wide-awake, alert, and more than a little awestruck. I swallowed, gripped my hands into fists, and used the same breathing technique that had gotten me through before.

When the effects subsided, I closed the journal and tucked it into my nightstand drawer. Standing, I slicked my damp palms down my pants. I ignored the twisting in my stomach. I ignored the way my hands trembled. Kara was waiting. I'd flip out later. "This is it, Verda," I said. "Let's see if you know what you're talking about."

I found Kara on the sofa. She had one leg crossed over the other and was bobbing it up and down as if she were a battery-operated mechanism set on high speed. She planted her gaze on me and kept it there while I slid into the chair across from her.

"I've been trying to decide if I should cheer and congratulate you or be pissed and scream at you." Her tone was soft, tense, and bewildered all at once. "You're Leslie's friend. Why'd you agree to help her with Scot if you like him?"

"Because she *is* my friend. And I never said that I like Scot," I pointed out, grasping on to the truth, even if it hung on a technicality. A slim one at that. "I said *maybe*. Maybe I like him. I don't know how I feel, Kara."

"You expect me to buy that? You either like a guy *that way* or you don't."

"I'm stupid, then." I joined her in the leg-bobbing tournament. "And it isn't as if I have a ton of experience in this area."

Her mouth formed an O. "That's right. You've dated, but you haven't actually fallen for a guy since Ricky Luca, have you?"

"I was twelve. I don't think that counts."

She snickered. "It counts, all right. But—" My glare made her rethink her words. "Okay, then. You don't have much one-on-one practice with guys that make you . . . um . . . get all hot and bothered. Wow, Julia. You're probably megaconfused, huh?"

"Exactly. Yes!" I nearly shouted, pleased she understood. Not that being clueless about men at the age of thirty-three was something to cheer about, especially when the clueless woman owned a dating service. Er . . . a failing dating service. Sheesh. "Have you gone through this?"

Kara sucked in her cheeks. Probably to keep from laughing. "Of course I have. The first time was when I was thirteen. Maybe fourteen? A wicked long time ago."

"Can we drop teenage love from the conversation? I'm an adult, not some gooey-eyed girl with a crush on the football captain."

"Oh, sweetie. The feelings are the same, no matter how old you are. The way we deal with the feelings might change with experience, but—"

"Do you have any advice?" I interjected. "Because I'm drowning fast."

Her eyelashes dipped in a slow, puzzled blink. In the length of our friendship, I'd always served in the counselor role. "You're asking *me* for guidance?"

"Yes." My request was sincere. Whether the journal proved to be magical or not didn't alter the fact that I was sinking in emotional quicksand. "Please."

Kara's leg ceased bobbing. "When you look at him, do your knees turn to Jell-O?"

"Jell-O?"

"Uh-huh. You know, 'Watch it wiggle, see it jiggle, Jell-O brand gelatin,'" she sang in an upbeat voice. "Do your knees wiggle and jiggle?"

"I know what Jell-O is," I said. "And isn't it 'watch it jiggle, see it wiggle'?" Okay, and that mattered why? "Never mind. To answer your question, yes. Sort of. Maybe more like jelly. Not quite as wiggly as Jell-O."

Her lips twitched, but she nodded. "And when you're near him—like smelling distance near him—does your heart go all shaky and fast?"

Fuck. "Sort of. Maybe. Fluttery?"

More mouth twitching ensued. "Do you find certain parts of his body utterly irresistible?"

"Sexual attraction doesn't mean I *like* him!"

"Answer the question, Julia."

"Do freckles count? Smiley-face freckles, in particular?" I winced as soon as the ridiculous question left my mouth. "Don't answer that."

"Oh, honey. Freckles?" Kara gave me a look filled with amused pity.

"All those questions prove is that I think Scot is sexy. I thought the same thing when he and Leslie dated. Nothing new there," I admitted in a rush. "So that doesn't help me at all."

"This so blows." Kara sighed. "I'd be ecstatic if it weren't for Leslie. I've waited for this to happen to you. You deserve to have a crazy, heart-pumping, *fairy-tale* relationship once in your life. Every woman does."

"This isn't a relationship! And I said nothing about fairy tales or . . . or . . ."

"But it *could* be. Look, the reason I popped in this morning was to talk to you about this. Leslie gave me the entire scoop last night." Kara hesitated and gnawed on her lip. "Convincing Scot to give them another go-around is such a bad idea. Do you know what it was like when she was dating Scot?"

"She liked him. A lot. But couldn't deal with his blue-collar trade." Scot worked in construction. That was about all I knew. "So you two went out one night and she hooked up with someone else."

"Yeah, but even before that—" Kara shook her head, interrupting herself. "She was always saying how things weren't going to go anywhere with them. That he was looking for a certain type of woman and she wasn't it. But she *wanted* to be that woman, so she tried. She wasn't herself with him."

This was a front-page bulletin. "In what way?"

"He wants kids. You know Leslie doesn't, but she told him she did. He's a major Cubs fan and Leslie hates baseball, but she pretended she loves the sport. Literally, everything he likes that she doesn't, she said she did."

Oh, dear God. "But Leslie despises fake people."

"I know! Don't you see? She shouldn't be with any guy she can't be herself with, and she isn't herself with Scot." Kara frowned. "And sorry, but the cheating thing isn't cool. And if she really fell for a guy, I don't believe she'd cheat. So I wanted you to talk her out of this. She listens to you more than she does me. But if you like Scot, then you can't. Because she'll think that's why, and it will turn into a huge thing."

"I don't know if I—" I breathed in deeply. "Doesn't matter. Nothing is going to come of whatever is going on with Scot, so quit worrying about that. I can handle Leslie. I can handle Scot." Well, I hoped so, anyway.

"She has the right to have this information. If you don't tell her, everything will be worse later." Kara's shoulders slumped forward. "I don't see her with Scot, but she's my friend."

I understood. Kara believed in the sisterhood of friendship:

total honesty, total trust, total acceptance. Usually, we were on the same page. "I will if there's anything to tell. But for now, I need you to keep this between us. Let me work this out, Kara. Please?"

Her face scrunched up. "Don't ask me to do that."

"Just for a little while. Until . . . well, until I have the chance to get a grip."

"I can't." She stared at her toes. "If it were you, I'd feel the same."

Huh. Not magical, then. A new surge of disappointment gathered in my gut, which was dumb. In a brisk voice, I said, "Fine, Kara. I get it. I do. I'll figure out how to tell her tonight."

Relief erased Kara's frown. "Good. It will be hard, but it's better if it comes from you. And maybe she'll react okay. Maybe she'll give you her blessing."

"I don't need her blessing," I said, suddenly exhausted. "Scot is cute, yes. Sexy, yes. But honey, he and I are very different types of people. He's not my winning lottery ticket."

But man, he was a jackpot for some lucky woman.

Kara's eyes clouded, grew darker, as if she were lost in thought. It was odd. Not to be rude, but Kara isn't exactly a heavy thinker. Not that she isn't smart, because she is. She's just the lighthearted, bubbly, live-in-the-moment type. Fuzzy tingles swept down the back of my neck. Was this it? Magic?

"Kara? Are you okay?"

"Maybe I was too hasty," she murmured. "You're sure you can handle this—Scot and Leslie and whatever's going on for you?" Her voice sounded hollow and faraway.

"Yes! I promise that I'll deal with this." And then I took a leap of faith of the magical variety. "But . . . um . . . if you could just keep this quiet until I'm ready to talk to Leslie myself, even if it takes a few weeks, I would so appreciate it."

Kara smiled. "Yeah, Julia. That's fine. I won't say a word."

Whoa. Just freaking whoa.

Magic. A freaking magical journal. My rational brain continued to scream *Coincidence! Only a coincidence!* as I—trying to expend my jumpy energy—cleaned my entire apartment, did a week's worth of laundry, and reorganized my kitchen cupboards. Well, only one of the cupboards. Jangled nerves and my preoccupation with Scot, Leslie, Kara, and *wishes* wouldn't allow me to move on to the next.

So I chickened out and decided to cancel my date with Scot. I pretended to myself that my decision was the *smart* choice, that I needed more time to consider how to proceed before seeing him again. But the down and dirty truth was that being in his presence so soon after locking lips turned my knees into—as Kara suggested earlier—Jell-O.

But I didn't have his phone number, and he either wasn't listed or he wasn't listed in a way that I could find him. Of course, Elizabeth's bakery *was* listed, so I called there, hoping she'd be around on a late Saturday afternoon. She was, and while she found my request odd, she gave me both of Scot's numbers. Now I just had to work up the courage to call him.

I checked the time. Three hours to go before he arrived. I was already pushing the boundaries of proper protocol. Canceling this late was rude. But, come on, if dialing the phone brought about a sweat of cold fear, what would the evening be like? I'd try his home number first.

It rang once, twice. "Scot Raymond," he said. "Oh, hey Julia."

"How'd you know it was me?" I asked, taken aback.

"Caller ID. It's been around for a while now." His words were teasing, but his tone was strained.

"Yeah. Right." I aimed a cough into the earpiece. "Elizabeth gave me your number. I can't go tonight. I have a . . . cold. Came on all of a sudden. Better if I stay home and rest."

"How about I bring you a bowl of chicken soup and a DVD?" he fired back. "I'm cool with staying in."

Aw. No guy had ever offered to bring me chicken soup before. But having Scot here with my queen-size bed a mere wall away was a bad idea. Of epic proportions. I quashed the *yes* quivering on my tongue and went with, "No! You don't want to catch this. Sore throat," I croaked. "Runny nose. Phlegm!"

Had I actually said the word *phlegm* to a hot, sexy guy? Yeah, I had. Brilliant. Just friggin' brilliant. I smothered a groan.

"Julia," he said in a husky, deep-throated way that forced a shiver. "We kissed. Chances are if I'm going to catch your cold, the damage has already been done. Might as well suffer together."

Desire rumbled deep in my belly. "You might not! Catch it, that is . . . and I won't be good company." I tried to fake a sneeze. It came out sounding like a snort-whistle. As if I'd gurgled water up my nose and spurted it back out. "I'm going to swill some NyQuil and sleep. So thanks. Really. But I'll be comatose within the hour."

"'The nighttime, sniffling, sneezing, sore-throat, coughing, aching, stuffy-head, fever, so-you-can-rest medicine'?" he recited without missing a beat.

"Um. Yeah. That one." I felt myself grinning. "Is there a reason why you know the NyQuil slogan by heart?"

"Nope. I hear a jingle or a slogan and it's implanted in my memory forever." I knew he was smiling. It made me tingle, a warm, toasty sensation. "Used to drive my mom nuts."

That made me grin wider. "What's the Jell-O jingle?"

"'Watch it wiggle, see it jiggle. Jell-O brand gelatin.' Why?"

I imagined saying *Because that's what my knees turn into when I think about you*, but instead said, "Curious. What about AT&T, smarty pants?"

"'Reach out and touch someone.' Gotta give me a harder one than that."

"Hm." I racked my brain. Everything I thought of were major brands with well-known slogans. "Timex?"

"'Takes a licking and keeps on ticking.'"

I thought of and tossed away Maxwell House's "Good to the last drop," Nike's "Just do it," and Alka-Seltzer's "Plop, plop, fizz, fizz, oh what a relief it is!" before coming up with "Motel 6!"

"'We'll leave the light on for you,'" Scot said. "I'm telling you, you can't get me on this game. If I've heard it, I know it."

My tingles increased. This . . . talking to him was nice. "Oh! I got it. L'Oreal?"

"'Because I'm worth it,'" he said in a feminine soprano.

"Bush's beans?"

"'Roll that beautiful bean footage.'"

I plopped down on a kitchen chair and laughed. "Okay, you win. I'll have to give this a lot more thought."

"I'll tell you what. If you find a business that I don't know the slogan or jingle to, I'll answer any one question."

Oooh. "Anything? Doesn't matter what I ask?"

"Anything, Julia." I heard a dog whine in the background.

"What kind of a dog do you have?"

"Heinz 57. No clue what she is. Your cold suddenly seems much better. Sure you want to swill that NyQuil?"

Oh, shit. I'd forgotten I was supposed to be sick. And no. I wasn't sure. Now I wanted to see Scot. But my earlier reasons for canceling remained valid. "I'm sure. But I've enjoyed talking with you."

Silence descended. I filled the empty space with a round of hacking coughs.

"What's his name?" Scot asked, suddenly all serious. "The guy you're dating."

"Jameson. He's an attorney. And . . . ah . . . I've known for him for years." Not one lie there, thank you very much. "Our dads work together."

"And where is Jameson tonight?" Scot asked quietly. "While you're home sick?"

"He . . . um . . . ah . . ." The abrupt change in his voice threw me. "Not sure. We didn't have plans for this evening. But you know that. Since I was supposed to be—"

"Jameson and Julia, eh? Has a nice ring to it." I heard the distinctive tapping of a finger—or more likely, a thumb—come through the line. "Get some rest, Julia. I'll call you in a few days."

Victory! Whew, right? Except, I didn't feel victorious. I felt lonely, kind of sad, and incredibly out of sorts. "Thanks, Scot. You have my number now?"

"I've had your number for a while. 'Night." He hung up before I could respond.

I scowled at the phone. Somehow, I didn't think that last statement referred to my phone number. Argh! And how had we'd gone from slogans to Jameson so fast? And why did Scot even care? The silly, girlish side of me—a side I'd never been properly introduced to, by the way—wanted jealousy to be the inspiration for Scot's curiosity. But that was doubtful. In general, people are pretty much glued to their initial opinions of someone else. It takes a lot to change a mind once it's been set. So while Scot and I shared a few minutes of niceness— okay, and a scorching-hot kiss—the odds were low those had altered his base opinion of me. Which was basically that of a bottom-feeder.

Whatever. I very purposely shoved Scot, Jell-O, and my soppy state of emotions into another hemisphere of my brain. With a free evening stretching out in front of me, I decided to learn more about the journal. Okay, it was less of a decision than a compulsion that refused to be ignored.

In Verda's assessment, I had a slow-to-adapt personality. It was an assessment I agreed with, and before I could 100 percent delve into a belief system opposing what I'd followed for most of my thirty-three years, I had a few more tests to run. Thickheaded? Yep. Stubborn? Maybe. Yet beneath all of that was a little girl who remembered her daddy reading her fairy tales about princes and princesses, pumpkins turning into carriages, and worlds filled with enchantments—worlds where anything was possible. That little girl *had* believed. I found I wanted to believe again.

I settled myself in the kitchen with the journal, a notebook, my trusty pen, and a large glass of water. Wine, beer, and other assorted alcoholic beverages were off the menu for the time being. In the notebook, I wrote, "Possible Wishes," and began to think of possibilities that would be near impossible for me to pass off as flukes. I needed to determine, as scientifically as something so unscientific would allow, if what I thought was happening really was.

Not any wish would do. Verda's message clearly stated that whatever I wrote had to be "truest of heart, purest of soul." What that meant, exactly, escaped me. But I didn't think the *size* of the wish mattered. Only that I truly wanted it and that no harm would come from it.

Off the top of my head, I listed ten maybe-wishes in the notebook. I narrowed that list down to five, and then again to three. I studied them a bit longer, trying to decide if these were the right three to start my experiment. But heck, how was I supposed to know until I tried?

I'd purposely chosen three wishes that varied in levels of importance and had zilch to do with Scot or Leslie. Deciding to begin with the easiest, most trivial of the three, I scrawled, "I wish for pizza for dinner tonight, but not pizza that I've ordered, purchased, or asked anyone else to bring me."

Yes. Lame as far as wishes go, but I had my reasons. Simple. Somewhat immediate. Something I'd know before I went to bed that evening. Plus I was hungry, so I figured the wish would be true of heart, and how would a pizza showing up hurt anyone?

Ignoring the zip in my bloodstream and the suddenly glowing words, I wrote the next wish. "I wish for my parents, Gregory and Susanna Collins, to be able to relax and worry less about their social standing." My reasoning for this wish was twofold: one, I'd love it if my parents chilled out a bit, and two, if they did, maybe we'd become closer and our family gatherings would stop resembling a board meeting. Yeah. I'd like that a lot.

Energy vibrated through my muscles, sending a spasm through my fingers, but I wrote the last wish before giving in to the buzz. "I wish for an influx of new clients at my business, so that Introductions becomes stable again."

The power swelled and bobbed, turning the air into a thick, heavy blanket. I closed my eyes, breathed in and out, and thought about each of the wishes I'd just written, one at a time. Probably unnecessary, but doing so gave me a measure of control, a feeling that I was in charge. Ha.

Slowly, almost too slowly, the sensations flooding my body faded until everything returned to normal. I downed half of my glass of water in one, long, satisfying gulp. I picked up the notebook and used it as a fan to cool my heated skin.

It startled me to realize how much I wanted this wish-granting situation to be true. It scared me a little, too. Because

I'd always known who I was, what I believed in, and truthfully, existing in a logical world was fairly easy. One plus one equals two. A square has four sides. One mile is precisely 5,280 feet long. A year is 365 days. Magic is not real.

But . . . what if magic was? My entire modus operandi for life would change.

"Julia? I'm calling out this time so you know I'm here!" Kara hollered. "I have some awesome news!"

Soul mates. If Verda was right about magic, then who's to say she wasn't also correct about Scot? About *us*?

"Julia?" Kara's voice now came from the living room. "Come out, come out, wherever you are. Verda just called me! She says she's found my perfect match!"

I grabbed the journal and slid it under my leg. "In here," I said.

Kara entered the kitchen and plopped a box on the table. A four-sided, white cardboard, medium-size pizza box. "Want some dinner? Leslie isn't home yet and I'm so excited! Verda said his name is Brett, and he's . . ."

The rest of my friend's words melted away. Pizza. For dinner. I said a silent good-bye to my nice, orderly, logical world and accepted that I, Julia Collins, knew jack about . . . well, basically everything.

Chapter Ten

I wasn't able to eat the pizza, and it seemed lunch the next day with Jameson was going to turn out just as bad, at least as far as my appetite was concerned. I pushed the piece of balsamic-glazed chicken I'd just speared into my mouth and chewed. Jameson ate his lobster and scallop risotto with a gusto I envied.

This restaurant was one of my favorites, and I loved this chicken. But not today. Today, I could've been chewing on an eraser. I sighed and set my fork down.

Jameson's eyes narrowed quizzically. "Is that not to your liking?"

I attempted a smile. "Oh, no. It's fine."

"You aren't one of those girls who doesn't like to eat in front of a man, are you?"

Ha. Not hardly. "I guess I'm not all that hungry." Probably, I should've canceled this date, too. But getting out of my apartment and away from the journal seemed a good plan. "I had a big breakfast," I lied. "Because I skipped dinner last night." Not a lie.

He considered my statement for a second. Then, with a quick flash in his green eyes, he gestured for the waiter.

"What are you doing? Please, finish your lunch." Wow. A little over an hour in Jameson's company, and I'd struck out. Not that I was aiming for a home run, but still, a girl has her pride, you know?

The waiter stopped at the table. Jameson nodded toward

our plates. "We'd like these to go, and you can bring the bill as well."

Once we were alone again, I said, "You could've finished. I didn't mean to make you uncomfortable."

Jameson wiped his mouth with his napkin before saying "You're not enjoying yourself, Julia. Why force you to sit here while I eat, when you're miserable?"

"I'm not miserable! I swear. I'm just going through a few . . . peculiar . . . changes."

One eyebrow wiggled. "Aren't you a bit young for menopause?"

I blinked. "Not those kinds of changes."

"Hm. Well, you see, I have this rule when I'm on a date. No one is allowed to be disappointed." Both of his eyebrows bobbed up and down, belying the serious edge to his tone. "And I am very disappointed. If you weren't such an important woman for me to impress, I'd take you home right this instant."

"Is that so?" I played along, curious and oddly charmed. Quite a coup for Jameson, considering the circumstances.

"Indeed. So you've left me with no choice but to go to drastic measures to correct this sad state of affairs."

"And what do you have in mind?"

"An outing." Jameson winked. "Are you up for it?"

Was I up for a little distraction and some distance? Hell yeah. "Sure. An outing sounds fun."

I didn't bother asking where we were going, and he didn't offer the information. The waiter returned with our boxed meals and handed Jameson the bill. A scant few minutes later, we were headed out of the city in Jameson's car.

Okay, calling his panther of an automobile a "car" was a sacrilege. Jameson drove a shiny black BMW Z4 with leather seats, every gadget known to man, and a get-up-and-go engine that went from purring to growling in no time flat. I'd never been a girl who went gaga over anything on four tires, but I had to admit that Jameson's ride was smooth, sweet, and sexy. Well, if a car can be sexy, that is.

Jameson, reading my thoughts, vroomed the engine, proving that yes, his car hit the sexy mark. My gaze settled on his profile. He wore narrow, black-framed sunglasses to combat the glare of the midday November sun. His clothes were Ralph Lauren: khaki chinos teamed with a pale-yellow-and-blue-striped slim-fitting oxford that fit his lean body well. He smiled easily and often, with a hint of quirkiness that I appreciated. Somehow, he reminded me more of a little boy dressed up in his daddy's clothes, driving his daddy's car, than he did a grown man. But Jameson worked a serious job, and from what my father said, was good at it. An interesting mix of characteristics.

Verda's paperwork and the many questions I'd answered came to mind. "Tell me about the type of women you're interested in dating, Jameson. Maybe we can get a head start on Monday."

He gave me a sidelong glance and chuckled. "You are so much like your father."

"Why? Does he also ask you about the women you'd like to date?"

"You're both business-minded individuals," he explained. "Always considering what move to make next on the company chessboard. What needs to be done at work. How you can take whatever situation you're in and apply it to the job."

"It's a hard habit to break. But really, I just thought it would be something we could talk about. It can wait until tomorrow, though." I shivered a little. Not from a chill, but from Jameson's description. Was I that much like my father?

"Nah, it's fine. What am I looking for in a woman?" Jameson mused as he merged his car into the most left-hand lane. "I suppose someone who is independent. I don't like clingy. Smart. Has her own career." He glanced my way again. "And not to come off as a jerk, but a real career. I'm not interested in dating a cashier or a waitress or a beautician."

I coughed to hide my surprise. Not at his statement, but at my gut reaction. His words turned me off—but why? I'd always subscribed to the same philosophy, though I'd never expressed it so baldly. Similar backgrounds and similar goals made it easier for a couple to forge a future, right? I'd always thought so.

"That sounded elitist, didn't it?" Jameson sighed. "I don't mean to be that way. But my life—the way you and I were both raised, Julia—"

"It's okay, Jameson. I get what you're saying." I interrupted him because I didn't want to hear the rest of that particular thought process. "So, a woman with a career." My thoughts instantly centered on Leslie. Wow . . . Jameson hit every one of her five qualifications. Huh. It was a good idea, possibly a great match. If Leslie weren't so hot on Scot, I might even hook her up with Jameson. "Go on," I prodded.

"Someone who can take care of herself."

"So . . . ah . . . no damsels in distress or women who need the big, strong prince of a man to make everything right for them?" And there I went down Fairy Tale Lane again. "Got it. A strong, self-assured, career-focused woman who is looking for an equal partnership."

"Exactly. So, can we continue with *our* date now?"

Oh. I'd almost forgotten this was a date. Warmth trickled into my cheeks, so I faced the window. "Of course. Sorry!"

Jameson took the next exit. "From here on out, you're not Julia Collins, the owner of Introductions. For the rest of the day," he said, slowing and then stopping at a traffic light, "you are Princess Julia, being escorted by—"

I laughed. I couldn't help it. References to fairy tales seemed to be shadowing my every move. "A prince?"

"Close, but no . . . not a prince. Not yet." His tone was easy, bantering. But the tiniest hint of seriousness lurked beneath. "I'm like the frog, perpetually waiting for the one kiss from the right woman who will forever remove his amphibious shackles."

"You're not a frog," I said lightly, trying to match his tone. "And I gotta say, more women than not would view you as pretty dang perfect just the way you are."

I twisted so I could see him again. The faintest flush of pink stole over his complexion and he cleared his throat. "Hm. Well I don't know about that, but thank you for the compliment."

"You're welcome. So . . . ah . . . where are you taking me?"

"The Brookfield Zoo." He turned the car and nodded out the front window. "And we're here. A day spent outside will lift anyone's spirits."

Well, he had a point. And I loved the zoo. I was even a card-carrying member. But, "It's November and there aren't any special events or exhibits happening." Not to mention my lack of sensible clothing or footwear. I had on a skirt and heels. "It's kind of cold out. My legs are going to freeze."

Jameson parked the car and removed his sunglasses. Mischief and boyish fun sparkled in his too-green-to-be-real eyes. "We'll hit a gift store right off and I'll buy you whatever. They sell sweatshirts, sweatpants, anything you need. I'll happily buy you three of each in increasingly large sizes so you can layer up."

"And my shoes?"

His forehead wrinkled in thought. "Didn't think about . . . Well, perhaps this wasn't such a great idea for an outing."

Suddenly, I wanted nothing more than to spend the day at

the zoo. "I'm sure there's some type of a store up the road. Feel like buying me a pair of sneakers?"

The disappointment fled Jameson's features. He stared at me, his gaze as steady as a surgeon's hand. "Add that to the list."

"Yes. Sneakers, sweatshirt, and sweatpants. Got it."

"Not that list. The other one." Jameson pivoted and started the engine. "A woman who can live in the moment. Add that to the list of what I'm looking for."

"Oh. That list. Will do."

I pressed my lips together to stop a question I *shouldn't* ask from tumbling out. I had to be wrong. Jameson didn't *like* me, like me. I couldn't be a contender for the one woman with the one kiss he'd referred to earlier. After all, our going out was instigated by our parents. Sunday dates were for current girlfriends, not for would-be girlfriends. When a man wants to impress a woman, especially a man raised in the manner of Jameson, he wined and dined her. That's what was expected.

For me, though, a day at the zoo ranked well above the standard wine and dine. Had Jameson known that and was trying to impress me, as he'd jokingly stated at the restaurant, or was this just a lucky guess and a nice way to spend an afternoon with the daughter of a business associate?

I stifled a groan as Mendelssohn's "Wedding March" swept into my head. Only instead of the graceful sound of a piano or an orchestra or even a freaking guitar, I heard . . .

"Ribbit," I murmured.

"What was that, Julia?" Jameson asked. "Did you say, 'Ribbit'?"

I smothered the swirling sensation in my stomach with a nervous laugh, knowing I was being silly. "Nope. I said . . . ,'Terrific.' As in, the zoo is a terrific idea."

Reaching over with his right hand, he lightly touched my knee. "I'm glad you think so. It'll be fun, I think."

"Mm. Me too."

We weren't the only crazy people who'd decided the zoo was a great way to spend a chilly Sunday afternoon. Couples and families dotted the walkways and exhibits, though not nearly the numbers you'd find during spring or summer, or even during the zoo's special holiday-lights exhibit in December. It was nice. I liked the less hectic atmosphere.

"Warm enough?" Jameson asked for the third time in ninety minutes.

We'd managed to find a small strip mall not too far from the zoo that had several clothing shops and a discount shoe store. I'd tried to purchase the jeans, sweater, socks, and sneakers I now wore, but Jameson insisted on paying. I chose to let him rather than argue.

"Yep. I'm good." We'd entered the zoo from the south gate, and had already visited the baboons, the birds, the reptiles, and the pachyderms. The west side of the zoo boasted several large natural habitats for a variety of animals, but we bypassed that area, focusing instead on the individual houses and smaller areas.

"Ready to go Down Under?" Jameson asked in a fake Australian accent. But the question came out as "Rudy to go Dune Oonder?" As far as impersonations went, not that successful. But he made me laugh.

"Yeah. But then we're going on the carousel."

We stopped at the field-research station and poked around a little, reading up on the ecosystem in Australia and the various animals represented here. I'd read and seen it all before, naturally, but that didn't lessen my enjoyment. Jameson had been right. My spirits were lifting. Funny, really, how sweet a drop of normalcy tastes when you've been choking down gallons of the abnormal for days.

"Look." Jameson weighted his arm on my shoulders and pointed toward several megasized black and white birds that were clumped together in twos. "Emus."

"Uh-huh. Do you know they travel in pairs?" His fingers wove into my hair, startling me. "Sometimes . . . well, um, sometimes they'll group together in la-larger flocks. But normally"—my neck stiffened as his thumb grazed my jawline—"they pair up. They like to pair up."

Babble City, USA, here I come.

"You sound like a romantic." His arm tightened around me, and he twisted a few strands of my hair in his fingers. "Are you a romantic at heart, Julia? I wouldn't have guessed that of you."

I laughed. Cackled, really. A nervous, strangled, I-don't-know-how-I-feel-about-this cackle. "Me, a romantic? Surely, you jest."

The wind picked up and blew a lock of my hair into my eyes. Jameson stepped around so that he faced me, and he pulled me close. With his free hand, he gently smoothed my hair back. "I'm not jesting at all. You do run a dating service," he said in a warm, low voice.

"I . . . ah . . . yes. But that's about people and logic and . . . and . . ." I inhaled a breath. "Not a romantic. Not me," I said loudly. "The birds . . . I just think they're, you know, really beautiful. And that they pair up is interesting. Good bird trivia."

"Hm. I suppose I can see that. But I think birds in general are a bit on the scary side." He shuddered, but there was a teasing glint in his gaze. "They have beady eyes that bore into you. You haven't noticed that?"

I swallowed. He meant the birds. I knew that. But with the concentrated, focused way he stared at me, as if he was going to kiss me . . . "Yes. Very scary. You're right. I've never noticed that before. Thanks for . . . pointing that out."

He grinned and dipped his head. "Julia," he said. "I think— "

I blinked, craned my neck back, and stepped out of his embrace. Glancing toward the overlook platform, I attempted to speak in a controlled voice. "Hey! Let's go over there and check out the kangaroos. They're like big bunny rabbits, and their eyes are anything but beady. Nothing scary at all about kangaroos. Think there will be any joeys? I love looking at joeys. They're really cute."

Humor darted over him but he refrained from laughing at my babble. "There's only one way to find out. Lead on, Princess Julia."

So I did. We watched the kangaroos for a while, but weren't able to see a baby one anywhere. The entire time we stood there, though, I tried to work out why Jameson's touch bothered me so much. It was more than my anti-touchy-feely tendencies. And what I'd experienced wasn't so much an uncomfortable sensation as an unfamiliar one. Different than Scot. But hell, that wasn't a surprise.

Also just different. Period.

Ugh. Deciding the best way to get over my weirdness was to touch Jameson before he touched me again, I angled my arm through his and tugged. "Let's go ride the carousel."

On our way, we passed the aardvarks and then the camels. Fewer and fewer people milled about, and it sort of felt as if we had the zoo to ourselves. I kept my arm securely tucked into Jameson's as we walked, stopped, looked, and chatted. For some reason, it was important to prove to myself that normal human contact with a nice guy, a guy I rather liked, didn't turn me into a spaz. I did okay, and was a lot more at ease when we reached the carousel.

Of course, that all changed when he kissed me.

We were nearing the end of our second carousel ride. The music was lively, the wind blew in my hair, and an invigorated, happy rush of being alive and having fun swept through me. I'd focused so hard and for so long on my business, I'd sort of forgotten the simplicity, the pure joy, of doing something for no other reason than to have fun.

I looked over at Jameson, who was seated on a zebra next to my tiger, and I smiled. He smiled back and tipped his imaginary hat. Laughing, I said, "Thank you for bringing me here! This is wonderful, and exactly what I needed."

In a moment that can only be described as a scene from an incredibly romantic movie, probably a chick flick, Jameson half slid, half leaped off of his zebra—which, yes, is against the rules when the ride hasn't ended—and came to my side. My hands clenched the pole tighter, and my legs squeezed around the tiger for balance. Nervous trembles cascaded down my spine in a wash of awareness.

Jameson smiled again. "You're most welcome."

He waited until the tiger was moving downward before cradling my cheeks in his hands. And then, he kissed me. A slow, searching, yearning type of a kiss that answered all of my earlier questions regarding Jameson's intent. Yes, it seemed that Jameson liked me. As in *liked* me, liked me. Or if he didn't, he sure knew how to pretend.

The kiss itself was nice and caused a warm little somersault in my belly. Not a flash of searing, blood-pumping heat like with Scot. But nice. Nicer than I'd have thought. Nicer than I expected.

We separated when the music ended, when the ride came to a stop. Jameson clasped my hand and in a gallant—dare I say, princely?—move, helped me off the tiger. It was all very sweet, very enjoyable, and in all honesty was probably the most romantic gesture any man had ever offered me. But as we walked away, I couldn't help continuing my comparison of Jameson to Scot.

And I couldn't help but notice that my knees didn't wiggle or jiggle at all.

When I arrived home that evening after Jameson dropped me off at my still-parked-at-Magical-Matchups car, I heated up my uneaten lunch and camped out on my couch. We'd only spent another thirty minutes or so at the zoo, having already gone through most of what the park offered. He hadn't kissed me again, though.

I was okay with that. I still didn't know what to make of the first kiss. Especially because I couldn't get my mind off Scot. Or the journal. Or Verda. Or Leslie. But I knew this: if I'd had that date with Jameson before any of this madness with Scot, soul mates, and magic had occurred, I'd have been pleased. Very, very pleased.

Jameson and I were cut from the same cloth. Our parents were friends, gathered at the same social events, and our fathers were business associates. Our life experiences were eerily similar, as were our goals for the future. Yes, we were a good match. Hell, we were a *great* match. A match like this between any of my clients would have me grinning and jumping up and down with joy for days. Instead of brimming, I was somewhat deflated.

The chicken still tasted bland. I threw it away. I stood in the kitchen, not knowing what to do with myself. I stared at the phone, and the desire to hear Scot's voice hit strong and heavy. What the hell was wrong with me? I'd had a nice date with a nice man and we'd shared a nice kiss. Now I wanted to call a different man. A man who was my complete opposite. A man who infuriated me and turned me on all in the same breath. A man who, other than an acknowledgment of his sex appeal, had barely been a blip on my radar four days ago. And finally, a man I didn't—couldn't—belong with.

Frustrated and lonely and both angry and proud for not giving in and calling Scot, I did something completely nonsensical: I made a batch of Jell-O. My rationale for preparing strawberry-flavored gelatin escaped me, but wow, I focused on this task with the precision and single-mindedness of a chef cooking for royalty. I made the Jell-O the quick-set way and then poured the glop into individual bowls so it would firm up even faster.

A cherry-blossom-scented bubble bath took up the better part of the next hour, me flipping through the latest issues of *Money* and *Bon Appétit* magazines, not finding much of interest in either. Then I poured myself a glass of wine, grabbed one of the bowls of Jell-O, and retreated to my bedroom, where I situated myself against a pile of pillows. My chest felt heavy. Like a moose or a bear or some other large animal had curled up between my breasts. My throat had this scratchy, tight thing going on. My eyes were achy, tired, and hot. And my temples throbbed with the beginnings of a headache.

Miserable. That's what I was. Probably a cold coming on. Or the flu. Ha. That would serve me right. Catching a cold after lying about having one.

I sipped my wine and ate a few bites of my gelatin. I stared at the walls and picked lint off of my pajama bottoms. I dug out an old bottle of nail polish and painted my toes a fiery red. Another hour passed with more inane tasks, such as reciting the fifty states in alphabetical order, the alphabet itself backward, and then in a last desperate attempt to not think about Scot, I counted to one hundred in French. This, sadly, was all I remembered from four years of high-school instruction.

When I ran out of ways to occupy myself, I pulled the journal from its hidey-hole and reread Verda's message. I slid my finger over the ink, waiting for the heat, the pull, that had happened before. Nada. That didn't mean anything. The magic was still there, still alive, just waiting for me to take pen to paper.

Oh, wow. I could. You know, if I wanted. Right now, *if* I wanted, I could wish for Scot to call or come over. Heck, I might even be able to dictate every word of our conversation, every action and reaction. I mean, I hadn't tested that theory yet, so I couldn't be sure. But what if I could?

What if . . . ? Oh, God, a million and one possibilities flooded me all at once. My hand trembled with the need to try. Just to see, of course. Another experiment, another test. Verda had given me this journal with this power for me to use. So, why not?

I was tempted. So. Very. Tempted. I even went so far as to find a pen before lucid thought won out. While I believed to the core of my being that Verda had somehow instilled magic into the journal, and while I believed that my other two wishes were going to come true, I also didn't know how, I didn't know when, and possibly most important of all, I didn't know what, if any, the side effects would be.

Belief is one thing. And believing in magic had been a difficult enough barrier to cross. But I remained Julia Collins: rational, practical, focused on facts. I was still the same woman who planned out every step before taking it.

"You're just chicken," I said to the empty bedroom.

Yeah, well. That too.

With a sigh, I closed the journal and put it away. I got a second bowl of Jell-O and more wine, and then powered up my laptop. Googling "well-known slogans and jingles" brought up a host of sites with lists and lists of examples. I studied these lists as if I were prepping for a final exam, memorizing a handful that might stump Scot.

Returning to Google, I typed in, "Scot Raymond, Chicago IL." Oh! He owned a business? I clicked on the link and a Web site opened.

"'Raymond Construction & Carpentry,'" I mused, reading the header. The site was simple but clean and easy to navigate, consisting of a mere four pages: Home, About, Services, and Contact. He worked with a larger construction crew in the summer, but off-season he specialized in home improvements, odd handyman jobs, and carpentry.

Yep. A blue-collar guy. But also, a man who was good with his hands.

My melancholy mood lifted and I yawned, suddenly beyond tired. I shut everything down, locked up—including engaging the chain on my door for once—and crawled into bed with a contented sigh.

The image of Scot stepped to the front of my mind, and I sighed again. "Mmm," I said, snuggling into my pillows. Verda had said three boys. Whom would they look most like? I hoped Scot. Brown eyes are dominant over blue, so chances were—

"Oh. Oh, hell!" I sat up in bed and turned the lamp on. "Damn, Julia! Damn, damn, damn, and damn!"

God help me. I *liked* Scot Raymond. *Liked* liked him. Thinking-what-our-children-might-look-like liked him.

"Three days! One kiss! How?" I don't know whom I was asking. Myself . . . fate . . . God? All three, perhaps. Grabbing a pillow, I squeezed it tight to my chest. In a lower voice, one of confusion and a solid dose of teenage-girl-type angst, I said, "Why? Why him and why now?"

Being alone and all, I didn't expect a response. But the air stirred, and the faintest brush of a rose-scented breeze kissed my cheek.

My blood chilled. In the space of a heartbeat, I thought I knew what that scent and that breeze meant. Heck, Alice and Ethan had named their daughter after that flower. It was significant. Very much so.

"Who are you?" I whispered. "And why are you here?"

The aroma grew in strength, saturating the room, chilling my blood even more. I was right. I was sure of it. Let's face it. If magic was real, then why not ghosts?

Chapter Eleven

"Verda? This is Julia Collins." I said into the phone. "I need to talk to you as soon as possible. It's about . . . um . . . the roses. Can you please call me back? Thanks." I rattled off my cell number, clicked the "end" button, and dropped the phone on my desk.

Three freaking times I'd tried to call her already. Though this was the first message I'd left. I mean, come on, how was I supposed to leave a message about a rose-perfumed ghost without coming off as a lunatic? Exactly. I couldn't.

I swallowed a groan. It was early Monday afternoon and I'd accomplished less than nothing. Between obsessing over the journal, Scot, ghosts, Scot, Jameson, and yeah, Scot, I'd been lucky to remember to brush my hair this morning.

The business line rang. Diane was already gone for the day, so I grabbed it. "Introductions, this is Julia."

"Hi, Julia. It's Jameson." His voice was clipped. "I need to cancel our appointment this afternoon."

A tingling sense of relief eased over me. "Oh. Is everything okay?"

"Just busy. A development with a client requires my immediate attention." His voice dropped to a low rumble. "But I was thinking it might be best to hold off on becoming a client. I'd like to see you again."

"Yes. Of course. We have your family's—"

"Party," Jameson filled in with a laugh. "But I want to see you before that. I really enjoyed the time we spent together yesterday."

"Yes. Right! The zoo was lovely," I managed to say. "Too bad we didn't see any joeys!" Oh, dear God. I instructed myself to pull it together. *Now.* "I enjoyed myself too, Jameson."

"How about dinner this week? Seeing how our lunch didn't pan out all that well."

Crap. I grabbed a paper clip and started untwisting.

"Dinner?" I coughed the word. Not on purpose, but I went with it. "I might be getting a cold. I'll . . . ah . . . give you a call in a few days. Let you know how I'm feeling."

"I'm sorry to hear that." I heard a bunch of noise in the background. "I have to go. Take care of yourself, Julia. We'll talk soon?"

I agreed and we hung up.

I continued twisting and untwisting my paper clip. He had not offered to bring me chicken soup. "Stop," I hissed. "Stop comparing them. Just stop."

Hell. I'd eventually say yes to another date. There wasn't any reason not to. We were about as compatible as two people could be. But I hadn't worked out how I felt about Jameson, and the weird sensation of being pulled along with the tide hadn't disappeared. I felt as if our outcome was somehow a done deal. Marriage. Kids. Many uncomfortable functions with his family and mine—years and years and years of them. Piling up on one another until they meshed into a lifetime of . . .

Pressure tightened my throat, encased my chest. I breathed evenly to loosen everything up. Scot. Three boys. Relaxed family gatherings that were filled with humor and ease. A lifetime of . . . love?

"Stop!" I said again. But the image refused to leave, and that irritated me. "You don't like him. You *can't* like him. Even more to the point, *he* doesn't like *you.*" I sighed and closed my eyes. I'd repeated the same assurances pretty much all of last night and today. Why weren't they sticking?

Because I was an idiot, that's why.

And where were all of my new clients? I'd had Diane make a slew of new client files this morning in preparation for the influx I'd wished for, but so far, nada. Even worse, I'd gotten Diane's hopes up enough that she'd asked about full-time employment. If I couldn't increase her hours and give her some benefits soon, she was going to leave. Or worse, I'd have to let her go.

Ugh. I needed to get off my sorry ass and get to work. I pulled up my client calendar. Mondays were check-in day for clients who'd had first dates over the weekend. It used to take several hours to handle this task. Lately, I was done in thirty minutes or less. I sighed again as I looked at more proof of my failure. Only three couples to phone.

I'd learned to contact the men first to find out if they were interested in another date. More often than not, women forgave perceived faults more easily. Oh, not all the time, for sure. But usually, a woman was more apt to give a second date a shot if the first date fell flat. Men mostly weren't.

I skimmed through my choices. Good news would be nice. Out of the three couples, there was only one I felt sure was a great match. Darryl Ogden it was.

I punched in his number. When he answered, I said, "Hi, Darryl. This is Julia Collins from Introductions, just checking in to see how your date with"—I glanced at my monitor—"Zita Hildebrandt went on Saturday night. Is this a bad time?"

Darryl earned his living as a pediatrician. Zita was a social worker. Their compatibility score was in the low nineties. All of this gave me hope. Heck, all things considered, they might even be a better match than Jameson and I.

"You caught me at a great time," Darryl said. "Done with patients for the day. And yes, to answer your question, Zita's terrific."

Yay! Maybe the day wouldn't be a total bust, after all. "That's wonderful news! How was the conversation? Did you two have plenty to talk about?"

"Absolutely," Darryl enthused. "She listened to every word I said. She barely ate her dinner, she was so focused on our conversation."

Years of experience tempered my excitement. Sure, this could be excellent. If Darryl's interpretations of Zita's behavior were correct. But Darryl's opinion might not be Zita's. Just because something looks and quacks like a duck doesn't necessarily mean it's a duck.

"Well, that certainly seems promising. Did you two do anything after dinner?"

"I took her to a play. I'm not a fan of stage performances, but Zita noted in her profile that she loves them," Darryl said. "Before I drove her back to her car, we stopped for coffee."

Easily a five-to-six-hour span of time. Good news. If Zita had been willing to do dinner, a play, and coffee, then everything looked excellent. I mentally patted myself on the back. "That all sounds lovely, Darryl. Can I assume you're interested in seeing Zita again?"

"Yes," he replied instantly. "Have you spoken with her yet?"

"I wanted to talk with you first." I typed in Darryl's comments about the date. "I'll give her a call now, though, and will get back to you."

We hung up and I dialed Zita's number. When she answered, I went through my introductory spiel and then asked, "How are you feeling about Darryl?"

"Well . . . he's a nice guy," Zita said slowly. "Definitely nice."

Uh-oh. My good vibe started to fade. "But?"

A loud sigh spilled through the phone line. "He . . .

uh . . . There's zero spark. It was completely flat between us. And he chews with his mouth open. It was uncomfortable to watch, but I couldn't *not* watch. So I ended up staring at him all through dinner."

Ugh. Her attentiveness wasn't based on interest but on the gross-out factor. Lovely, right? Not ready to give up, I tried for a positive spin. "Hm. Maybe we can work on that. Darryl said he took you to a play? You love plays, don't you? That was sweet of him!"

She sniffed. "The play was an adaptation of *Gone with the Wind*, except it wasn't about the North and the South. Uh-uh. It was about aliens and vampires. And it was a musical. An alien vampire musical version of *Gone with the Wind*."

"That might be interesting," I said, spinning the positivity wheel harder. "If done properly."

"You think? Because it wasn't. And about halfway through there was full-body nudity. I didn't know whether to laugh or cry. And Darryl watched the damn thing like it was Shakespeare or something." I could just about visualize Zita shaking her head. "It was . . . odd. All very odd."

"But you must have liked him a little? I mean, you went out for coffee—"

"He insisted. I'm not sure I could've said no. It was more like an order." She lowered her tone to a deep growl. "'Buckle up. We're going for coffee now, Zita.'" In her normal voice, she said, "And he didn't seem to hear me when I told him I was tired. That it had been a long day and that I'd like to get home. Just drove us to this diner with single-minded determination."

Oh, geez. So. Not. A. Duck.

"Did you feel threatened? Like, if you didn't go for coffee—"

"Nothing like that. He isn't a creep. It was more like he

didn't know how to behave on a date and was trying really hard. Like he had to call the shots, you know?" She sighed again. "I mean, the eating thing was unattractive, okay? But the rest of it . . . I felt like he was so focused on proving we were having a good date, he forgot to check with me."

"Well, he *hasn't* dated much. And I know he was nervous." These two appeared to be such a great match. On paper, anyway. "Did he do anything right, Zita?"

She was silent for a few seconds, and then, "He brought me flowers. At first, on the way to the restaurant, he asked me about my job and my family. It wasn't until we were sitting across from each other that the date started to go south."

Yep, Darryl had let his nerves get the better of him. So, should I try to smooth things over or just move on? I made a snap decision. "Even with everything else, you think he's nice?"

"He *is* nice. He needs to relax, though."

Inappropriate humor bubbled up. Poor Darryl. Most doctors I knew suffered from too much confidence, not too little. "If I were to talk to him about your perceptions—in a nice way, of course—would you be willing to go out again?"

"Oh, gee, Julia. I don't know. I don't think there's anything here."

"Your compatibility numbers are solid. Maybe he won't be as nervous next time. Maybe it will be different." Okay, I shouldn't have pushed so hard. But something told me that Zita should give Darryl another chance. Recalling a discussion I'd had with Darryl early on, I said, "The first time you and I met, I asked you to name the one trait in a man that was most important to you. Do you remember what you told me?"

"Family. I said I wanted to date men who valued their family over and beyond anything else."

"Right. Did Darryl mention he had a successful practice in

Atlanta, but returned to Chicago when his mother died? It was important to him to be here for his father." Probably, I should have mentioned this to Zita from the very beginning, but I'd gotten too caught up in their compatibility numbers.

"Wow. No, he didn't." She was quiet for a minute. "People don't always make the best first impressions, do they?"

"Nope." Scot's first impression of me winged into mind. "Definitely not. But this is completely up to you."

"Yeah. I . . . I think I'd like to give this another chance. Do you think you can talk to him without hurting his feelings?"

"I don't know," I said honestly. "But I'm willing to try."

"My mom would love it if I brought a doctor home. And he *is* cute. Oh, all right. I suppose. What can one more date hurt?" Zita said. "But this time, I'm planning it. Make sure he knows that."

I chuckled. Partly in humor, but also in relief. "You got it."

One fifteen-minute phone call to Darryl later, and he—while horribly embarrassed about Zita's assessment of his eating—agreed to hand over the reins for the next date. Maybe because that seemed easier than restarting the process with someone new.

I finished my phone calls. The second couple was equally unsure about each other, but for different reasons. He disliked her chattiness, and she—for whatever reason—disliked the color of his hands; they were too red and he had messy cuticles. The final couple hated each other from minute one. Not a surprise. Their compatibility score was in the fifties, but they'd found each other's profiles, liked each other's looks, and had pushed for a meeting.

With that work done, I went home and huddled by the phone. Surely Scot would call. He'd said a couple of days, right? Well, this was a couple of days. But the hours dragged by without the phone ringing. I checked the dial tone a few times—oh, okay, six times—so Scot's silence wasn't because the phone was out of order. He just didn't call.

I finished my Jell-O, drank more wine, and because I had the same sluggish, yucko symptoms from last night, swallowed several vitamin C tablets to ward off the cold I was sure I was catching. Then I slept with my covers pulled over my head. Oh, and with the bedside lamp turned on.

Tuesday was more of the same. No Scot. No new clients. I spent hours running the numbers, trying to find new ways to cut costs to hold Introductions steady until the wish came true, but I'd already cut everything that could be cut and still stay in business.

Verda returned my call late Tuesday afternoon. I was on my way home, and like an idiot had the radio turned up loud enough that it drowned out the ring. I didn't notice her message until later. She said she'd try me again.

On the good-news front: I hadn't smelled roses since Sunday night. Thank God.

By Wednesday, I was in a rotten frame of mind. I was almost back to my belief that coincidence was to blame for everything. I so wanted to believe. I was ready to believe. Hell, I think a part of me *needed* to believe. Why that was, I didn't have a clue.

I left work early for once, determined to arrive at my parents' place for dinner right on time. I stopped on my way to pick up a the-maid-only-lasted-three-weeks present for Mom, and on a hunch also grabbed a one-week-and-the-maid-is-gone gift. Normally, the simple act of shopping for these items was enough to make me smile. Today, I sort of just went through the motions.

When I arrived, I rang the doorbell like normal. Waited. Waited for longer than normal. Rang the bell again. I dragged my key out to let myself in—something, by the way, my folks frowned upon. I didn't live here, so I should be greeted at the door like any other guest. The only reason I still had a key was so I could stop in when they were traveling. Otherwise, I'm sure it would have been confiscated after I'd moved out.

I shoved the heavy door open and walked in. Went to turn off the security alarm, except it wasn't on. Huh. It was *always* on. The lights in the foyer were set low, like they were at night when the house slept. Odd.

I checked the living room first, to find it empty. So was the parlor. Unexpected apprehension coiled inside, tight, sharp, and fast. My parents never, ever, weren't here for a Wednesday dinner unless they were out of town or had another social engagement. Had I forgotten something? No. Nothing was said last week about canceling tonight, and they hadn't called. My worry climbed higher, so I went to the kitchen in search of Rosalie.

Empty kitchen. Nothing in or on the stove.

Panic iced my gut and liquid quivers slid down my spine. I carefully and methodically walked through the entire house, even rooms that weren't in use any longer, calling out as I did.

No dice. My mother didn't use a cell phone, but Dad did, so I dialed him. Voice mail. I left a message and then stared at the phone in confusion. Where were they? My parents did not behave this way. Hell, they were about as spontaneous as glue. And they weren't old, but they weren't young either. What if my dad had a heart attack or a stroke? What if my mother was in a car accident? What if . . . what if . . .

I returned to the living room, poured myself a drink, and collapsed on the sofa. They were fine. Of course they were. Gregory and Susanna were indestructible. They'd probably just forgotten to mention they had other plans. Sure, forgetting something wasn't their normal behavior, but that didn't mean it wasn't possible.

My wish—the one about my parents relaxing and worrying less about their social standing—flitted into my mind. Yeah, I'd been excited to see if anything had changed. Hopeful, even. But their absence couldn't be magic related. If it was, if my wish worked, then that meant they considered our dinners another one of their social functions. And that sucked.

I sipped my drink. Tears grew behind my eyes. I blinked and took another sip. No. Just no. Sure, these dinners drove me nuts, but I loved my parents. They loved me. No matter how stiff and uncomfortable Wednesdays were, we were family. I couldn't stand the thought of something bad happening to either one of them, but the thought that they'd forgotten me was somehow just as awful. They had never forgotten me before.

One tear and then another crept down my cheek. I drained the rest of my drink and wiped my face. I should get up. My mother kept a social calendar in her office. I should check that. I should see if their cars were here. I should find Rosalie's number and call her. But I couldn't seem to find the energy to stand.

The irony didn't escape me. If my wish had caused this, then whoa, how it had backfired. My goal was to lessen the gap between me and my folks, not increase it. *Get up,* I told myself. *Do something.* So I reached into my purse, found my cell phone, flipped through my saved numbers, found the two I'd entered the other day, and selected one.

It rang twice, and then, "Hello, Julia. Feeling better?"

"Stouffer's," I said in just above a whisper.

"'Nothing comes closer to home,'" Scot said. "You okay?"

I wiped another tear off my cheek. "Reebok?"

"Julia? What's going on?"

"Reebok," I repeated, swallowing the stupid bubble of emotion in my throat.

"'Because life is not a spectator sport.'" The thumb tapping started. "Where are you?"

More tears fell. I swiped those away, too. "Wind Song. Do you know that one?"

He was silent. His breaths were slow and deep, and I could almost see those sexy, dark eyes of his crinkled in thought. "I can't"—he coughed—"I can't seem . . . I can't seem to think of it. You got me, Julia."

"One question?" Now, I whispered. "I get one question?"

"That was the deal. One question."

"Do you—" Fuck these tears! I wiped them away again. "Do you really think there isn't a man alive who's right for me?"

His intake of breath was swift and harsh. I huddled, pulling every ounce of strength I had together, and waited for the response that would surely do me in. Why'd I ask that? All the questions in the world, all the things I wanted to know, and I wasted it on something I already knew the freaking answer to? Stupid. So, so stupid.

"No, I don't think that." The tapping got louder. "I should never have said that. I was angry . . . I'm sorry. I'm sorry for hurting your feelings."

"You didn't! I'm cold and heartless and have no feelings." A sob burst out from a raw place deep within. I tried to cover it with a round of coughs. "Sorry! Guess I'm not better yet. You . . . ah . . . you really think there's someone out there for me?"

You, Scot? Could it be you? my heart asked. At the same time, my mind screamed, *Jameson. You belong with Jameson. Or someone like Jameson.*

"Of course I do. You're smart, beaut—pretty, easy to talk to. Of course there is."

"Okay. Well." *Tell me it's you. Tell me it could be you.* "I should . . . um . . . probably go. I . . . Thanks for playing!" I said in an overly bright voice.

"Julia," Scot said, his tone rough and perhaps concerned. Nah. No way. "What's wrong? Are you okay? Has something happened?"

The yearning to open up, to tell him where I was and how lost and unsure and afraid and stupidly lonely I was came over me. I wanted to lean on him. How dumb was that? I had *never* needed anyone to lean on, to kiss my boo-boos and make them all better. "A bad day. That's all. I'm fine, Scot. I'm always fine."

"Why was it a bad day? Talk to me. I'm right here."

He sounded like he cared. Obviously, my one drink had been one too many. Even so, the calmness of his voice pushed me forward. I pressed the fingers of my free hand to my temples.

"My—"

"There you are, Julia! We're so sorry we're late, darling," my mother said, dashing into the living room. "We got caught up at the dealership. Why everything always takes so long is beyond me. I swear they do it on purpose."

My tears disappeared in a rush of relief. Shock came next. My jaw dropped open. Susanna Marie Kaiser-Collins was dressed in . . . jeans? And a T-shirt—one of my gag gifts—that depicted a fifties-era housewife holding a vacuum cleaner. Written in hot pink letters in a lipstick type slash across the front was the message THIS REALLY SUCKS!

"Scot?" I sort of gasped into the phone. "I . . . ah . . . I need to go. Something's come up."

"Are you all right?" he demanded.

I tried to respond, but my mouth refused to work. What with my fixation on seeing my mother in jeans. Jeans! Sneakers, too. When had she gotten those? Noticing my appraisal, she waggled her fingers at me and did a little hip swish.

"Julia?" Scot said, louder this time. "Are. You. All. Right? Do you need me to come get you? Just tell me where you are."

"No. I'm . . . yeah, Scot, I'm okay. Just need to go."

"Call me later." Again, a demand. It should've ticked me off, but a warm glow suffused me. "And just so you know, you didn't get me. The Wind Song slogan is 'I can't seem to forget you, your Wind Song stays on my mind.'"

With that bit of surprising information, delivered in more of a growl than anything else, he hung up. And I was left staring at the alien who'd taken over my mother's body.

I replaced the phone in my purse and kept my focus on my mother. Her blue eyes shone with excitement and her cheeks were apple-blossom pink. "Hi, Mom," I said carefully. "You seem . . . happy?"

"Oh, I am! Your father is bringing dinner in." She saw the gifts I'd deposited on the coffee table. "Are these for me?"

"Yeah. Well, one is. The other . . ." I squinted my eyes. "Is Helen still employed here?"

"Yes! She's working out marvelously!"

Wow. Kudos to Helen. I reached for the second gift I'd purchased. "This one is for a . . . friend. But the other is yours."

"Wonderful! I love your gifts. They show what a great sense of humor you have." Mom settled herself on the chair. "You weren't waiting long, were you, darling?"

Darling. Twice in the same conversation. And since when did my mother offer me a compliment? "Not too long. But I was worried."

"Whatever for?" Surprise glimmered in her eyes. I couldn't tell if she was honestly confused or if she was faking me out. Believe it or not, I kind of hoped for the latter.

"You weren't here. You're always here. And where are Rosalie and Helen?"

"I gave them the rest of the week off." My mother the alien picked up my gift and shook it. "I'm going to take this with us. It'll be nice to have something from you to open at such a special moment."

"Take it where?" Was it me, or was she not making a heck of a lot of sense?

"Your father and I are going to Las Vegas tomorrow morning. We haven't been in years."

I didn't know they'd ever been. "And why are you going?"

"We're celebrating our anniversary," she explained, as if that made perfect sense. It didn't. Their anniversary wasn't for three months. "We're going to exchange our vows again!"

"You did that five years ago," I pointed out. "Remember? At the country club? I was your maid of honor. You made me wear that hideous peach dress."

My mother's lips turned downward in a scowl. Ha. She was still in there. Somewhere. "Of course I remember. What a tedious affair that was. This ceremony will be intimate." A weird, gushy sigh floated out of her. "Just like the first time."

I propelled myself to the drink cart and poured another drink. I was pretty sure I was going to need fortification. "What first time, Mother?" I asked when I returned.

"We were married in Las Vegas three months before our formal ceremony. It was one of those wonderful spur-of-the-moment decisions, after we found out about you." My mother winked. "We were going to invite you to join us this time, since you were there then, but we assumed this would be too last-minute."

Oh! Oh. My. God. "You had a shotgun wedding? Because you were pregnant with me? How have I never heard of this before?"

"Have you told her, Susanna?" My father walked in with an armful of stapled brown paper bags. "And do we want to eat here or in the dining room?"

"Let's eat here! And yes, Gregory, Julia knows we're renewing our vows."

"Good. But I meant the RV." Dad deposited the bags on the coffee table. I was pleased to see he wore his normal suit and tie. "I hope you still like Chinese, sweetheart. We were in a hurry to get back here."

Darling. Sweetheart. I started to down my drink but had second thoughts. Probably best to stay clearheaded. Had my—Verda's, I mean—magic done this? Of course it had. What else could it be? "Guys? You're sort of scaring me here."

"Why don't you fill her in on the RV, Gregory, and I'll get us some plates and silverware." Mom stood and took a couple of steps toward the kitchen.

"No!" Whoa. Too loud. I lowered my volume a notch, and said, "Mom. Please tell me about your first wedding."

"Haven't I ever told you this story?"

"No, Mom, you haven't. I'd love to hear it now, though."

She shrugged and returned to her chair. "My parents wanted me to marry Skippy Peterson." A shudder rolled through her, shaking her slim shoulders. "Skippy! A ridiculous name for a squirmy little man who couldn't keep his hands where they belonged. But I was in love with Gregory, so when we discovered I was pregnant, we went to Vegas and tied the knot. It was the most romantic week of my life."

My dad strode over to her, leaned down, and kissed her. On her mouth. Not on her forehead, on her mouth. Standing straight, he said, "Me too, cupcake. I'll grab the plates."

Cupcake? My eyes stung. My brain hurt. The only time I'd ever seen them lip to lip was during their second—er, third, I guess—wedding. And they did not call each other by terms of endearment. Ever.

I had second thoughts again and swallowed a large portion of my drink. This metamorphosis was, perhaps, more than I'd planned on. "I take it Grandma and Granddad weren't too happy with your . . . er . . . running off to Vegas?"

"Not at all. They so disliked Gregory, you see." Mom started opening the bags. "But once they found out about you, they gave up on the idea of an annulment, and Gregory and I were married properly posthaste."

I wasn't completely stupid. I'd done the math. I'd already assumed the honeymoon had happened before the wedding. But wow. My parents . . . running away to be married to ensure they would be together? Wow.

Dad returned and handed me a plate. "Dig in. You used to love almond chicken when you were little. I hope you still do."

"Yeah. Fine." Then, what he'd said earlier sifted into the fog. "You mentioned an RV?"

My mother clapped her hands. "Oh, do tell her, Gregory!"

"Yes. Do."

"We just bought a gorgeous, state-of-the-art RV. Ordered it, actually. We won't take possession until spring." He spooned rice on his plate. "You're going to take over the business, I'm retiring, and your mother and I are going to travel the country."

"We're going to be vagabonds, darling!" My mother enthused. "This place is going on the market right after Christmas, and come June, we're off!"

My ears buzzed with the words *You're going to take over the business*, pretty much overriding everything else. My spell had worked, all right. Too well. And it had bitten me in the ass. Talk about a side effect.

"I expect great things from you, Julia," my dad said. "We'll need to get together soon so we can decide when you can come on officially. Lots to do to get you up to speed. We'll make it as smooth a transition as possible."

"Wait. Just wait." I lifted my gaze to his. "What about Introductions?"

"It takes a strong person to admit failure. You've worked hard, but your business is not going to recover. You'd need a miracle." Dad's blue eyes darkened with emotion. I could tell he really felt bad. "This is a hard lesson to learn, and I'm sorry you've had to learn it. But our agreement was, if Introductions failed—"

"Mom said I had a month or so to pull things together! Last week!" No. No way. I didn't need a miracle. I had magic. *This* spell worked. That one would too. Eventually. Wouldn't it? "That was a verbal agreement and is just as binding."

"She's right, Gregory." Mom patted his knee. "Give her another month."

He nodded—a tight, small movement that expressed his complete faith that another month wasn't going to make a bit of a difference. "An agreement is an agreement. Thirty more days, then, Julia, and we'll begin the transition."

It was enough time. It had to be. After all, the kiss and the pizza happened almost immediately after the wishes were cast. Granted, I didn't have a timeline for the changes in my parents, but at most, three days. So really, there was no reason to believe that the influx of new business wouldn't start soon. "Thanks, Dad. I think a month will be all I need."

Another nod, but a bewildered haze clouded his features. Confused by the level of confidence in my voice, I'd wager. Of course, it was fake bravado. "I wish you success," he said in a soft, firm tone. "I've always wished you success."

Wow. One newsflash after another. "That means a lot to

me," I said. And it did. But I wondered if his statement was true or if it was just another magical side effect.

Probably a side effect. But I wanted it to be real. More than I can say.

Chapter Twelve

I drove home, fretting the entire way. I passed the bank of elevators in my building, hitting the stairs instead, and fretted some more. All of this—my parents' magically enhanced behavior, the cutsie names, the doe-eyed looks, their all-of-a-sudden trip to Vegas—had me feeling like I'd eaten an extra-large wand of cotton candy on an empty stomach and then hopped onto a roller-coaster.

I didn't hate the image of my folks being so in love that they ran off and tied the knot; it just didn't add up. It wasn't *them*. I huffed out a breath and stopped at the top of the second flight of stairs and admitted, well, it was them—thirty plus years ago. But it wasn't them now.

And what the hell was up with the vagabond thing? I started up the stairs again, going slower now, trying to imagine my mom living out of an RV. I couldn't. It was incomprehensible on every level. My father only slightly less so. He, at least, enjoyed the outdoors. And they were going to *sell* the mausoleum? Mind-boggling. All of it.

Apprehension slowed my steps further. I should have been excited. My wish had come true. Magic was real. But it hadn't altered my parents' focus on the role they thought I should take in my father's company. If anything, that aspect was worse. My father was a major workaholic, and I was fairly sure he hadn't planned on retiring for years. Now, thanks to me and that journal, he'd relaxed enough that he wanted to travel the country in a freaking RV.

I stopped again and dropped to a sit. My muscles were itchy

and tight and my breaths came short and fast. Myriad emotions clogged my throat. This was not the time to let emotion rule. I needed to be my old self: practical, rational, play-by-the-rules Julia Collins. She would be able to figure this out.

Okay, then. I had the journal. I had magic. I had power at my fingertips. My job was figuring out the best way to use it. What were my choices? Well, there was the obvious: do nothing and wait for the Introductions wish to come true. Once it did, the business side of my problems would disappear in a snap.

But what about my parents? It was cool, sort of, seeing this other side of Gregory and Susanna. I just didn't know if that side was real. Were the changes in their behavior their true selves coming to the surface because of magic, or had I magically altered who they were? The former, while perplexing, I could live with. The latter brought a shiver.

I hated not knowing the rules. Could I wish away my wish? Could I wish for Dad to let me out of my bargain? Could I reverse the first wish so that my folks returned to normal, and did I even want that? Would they want that? A new round of tears popped into my eyes. More stupid emotion. Instead of being excited or enchanted or even happy, I felt defeated and deflated. Lost, even.

The same engulfing loneliness from earlier sank in. At that moment, all I wanted was to return to my old life. To go to bed and wake up tomorrow as the Julia I was before the madness started. No more magic. No more unexplainable rose-scented breezes. No more nutty old ladies—okay, one nutty old lady— filling my head with the idea of soul mates and the vision of three someday sons and . . . and . . . Oh, God.

No more Scot. Loss pinged through me, quick and sharp.

Jameson! I'd still have him. I was sure to appreciate him a hell of a lot more without the ongoing commentary of comparisons running through my brain. And Leslie. I wouldn't have to deal with the Leslie and Scot dilemma, because if I worded the wish right, assuming success, I wouldn't have this foolish longing for him. Or the ridiculous desire to see if Verda was right, to discover if Scot and I were meant to be together.

Did the journal have that power? Somehow, I doubted it. I probably couldn't erase the past week. That whole changing-history thing. But I might be able to . . . Pain shattered through me at the idea that flooded in. My eyes filled with more tears. My heart grew heavier, thudding against my breastbone like a fist. Yeah. That wish might work. And if so, it would solve the personal side of my problems. Kind of, anyway.

I gave myself another minute to regain my balance. For now, I'd let the Mom and Dad wish stand—mostly because I was afraid of worsening the situation, but also because I wanted more time to get to know the new, hopefully improved versions. So much so, I decided to go to Vegas. Not only would that give me the ability to see how my spell was affecting them, but the days away would offer some much-wanted distance.

I also put Introductions into the wait-and-see category. I had a month, so plenty of time to cast another wish if I needed to. But the rest of it required action. The sooner, the better.

Now. I should do it now.

I pulled myself upright and trudged up the remaining steps, my legs weak and unsubstantial. My heart even more so. *Focus,* I told myself. *Focus on why this is the smart, the only, way to go.* By the time I reached my floor, hot tears gushed down the sides of my face. I, having learned something, didn't bother brushing them away. They'd just keep coming back. Even if I didn't understand why.

Before I turned the key in my lock, I heard Kara and Leslie's door open behind me. My spine straightened in defense. I so didn't need company tonight. Especially in my current sappy condition.

I unlocked my door and pushed it open. "Hey!" I said without turning around, in as chipper a tone as I could pull off. "I'm exhausted. Going to take a hot bath and go to bed."

Hands landed on my shoulders. Large hands. Heavy hands. Not Leslie's or Kara's. The very weight of them offered a strange sort of comfort. My throat squeezed tight and a raspy, wheezy breath emerged. Scot's scent—that earthy, wholesome, male fragrance—filled the air. I shivered again as relief and awe and happiness shuddered through me.

Happiness? But he'd come from Leslie's. He was *at* Leslie's. Maybe they didn't need magic to set things right, after all.

"What are you doing here?"

"You sounded funny on the phone. I was worried about you. I needed to be sure you were really okay." He applied a small amount of pressure to my shoulders. "Are you?"

I couldn't seem to locate my voice, so I nodded.

"You're lying. Why?" I didn't answer. Scot tightened his hold on my shoulders. "Come on. Let's go inside."

A zillion urges kicked to life. *Yes!* I thought. *Come in and hold me. Kiss me. Touch me.* But I had to stay strong. "Um . . . not tonight. I have to pack. I'm going out of town tomorrow. Or Friday. It depends when I can get a flight." My voice held my tears. I tried again, going instead for cool, calm, and collected. "My parents are renewing their wedding vows in Las Vegas. I . . . I think I'd like to be there."

"I won't stay long." He bent over, so his breath teased my neck. In a whisper, he said, "Besides, we're supposed to be dating. Remember?"

He spun me toward him before his meaning became clear. Strong arms folded around me. He pulled me close. So close I forgot how to breathe. His lips found mine in a hot, melting kiss that turned my Jell-O knees into butter.

My blood heated up and sizzled through my veins in a rush

of flat-out want. Need and desire ignited deep in my belly, and I pushed myself closer to Scot. Coherent thinking disappeared, and all that existed was this man kissing me, holding me, tantalizing me.

Someone cleared their throat, but I was so lost in the moment that the sound barely registered. A tiny moan of regret gurgled out as Scot pulled away. I started to reach for him, to bring him back, when reality intruded. We were still in the hallway. I'd heard someone . . . Leslie! Oh, God. Oh, no. I stepped to the side and whirled around.

Yep. There she was. Not in front of her door, but farther down the hallway. As if she'd just gotten off the elevator. Her coat was on, so that seemed likely.

Outright shock and condemnation gleamed in her eyes. Her mouth was pinched in a tight pucker. She held her briefcase to her chest, the whiteness of her knuckles another sign of her distress—and I was a horrible friend. Because my first reaction was relief. Relief that Scot had been hanging out with Kara, not Leslie, while waiting for me.

On the heels of that came a tide of sickening guilt. I lurched toward her. "Leslie! I . . . this . . . It isn't what—"

"Isn't what?" She tilted her head to the side, looked at Scot and then back to me. "I have to say that you two make a perfectly dashing couple. I'm tired. We'll talk later, 'kay?" She walked the few remaining feet to her door and let herself in without saying another word.

Shame and anger collided with my guilt. I rotated and faced Scot. "Did you see her there before you kissed me?"

"No." His eyes narrowed. "I'm not that cruel. I know she thinks she still has feelings for me. I wouldn't have . . ." He shook his head. "No," he repeated. "I did not see her."

"Okay." I tried to work out what I should do. My stomach

somersaulted and nausea climbed my throat. "I need to talk to her, Scot."

He looked as if he was going to argue, but he didn't. "Want me to come with you?"

I thought about it for a minute, because having him there would shore me up. But it would make things worse for Leslie, so it wasn't a good idea. "No. I should do this on my own."

His left hand came to my chin and he tipped it upward. His other hand came to my cheek and he brushed away the remnants of my tears. "Are you sure?"

Words escaped me, so I nodded.

"Listen," he said softly. "Whatever chance Leslie and I had disappeared a long time ago. There isn't any reason to feel guilty over this. Do you hear me, Julia?"

"Yes. And you and I aren't really together. This is just pretend." I stared into his chocolate brown eyes, somehow wishing things were different. "But you kissed me, so . . . is this still pretend, Scot? Or has something changed?"

He returned my stare for what felt like forever, though it was probably only a few seconds. I longed to run my finger over the line of his jaw but kept my hands at my side.

"I don't know why I kissed you," he finally said. "I was worried. I was glad you were okay. I . . ." He gave his head a brisk shake. "But yes. Still pretend."

A burning sensation flared in my chest, probably indigestion from the Chinese food. "Good to know," I murmured. "Now I need to talk to Leslie, so thanks for checking in. But as you can see, I'm fine."

"Go. But I'm not leaving yet. I'll wait in your apartment."

And because I didn't have the strength to argue, I nodded again and went to face the music. I wasn't sure, exactly, what

I was going to say to Leslie. But putting this conversation off was out of the question.

I waited until I heard my door close before knocking on Leslie's. It was Kara who opened up. "How is she?" I asked.

"I have no idea. What happened, Julia? She stormed in, didn't say a word, and closed herself in her bedroom." Kara stepped to the side so I could enter.

"Scot kissed me just as she came off the elevator. Bad timing."

"Maybe not. Maybe it was good timing." Kara darted a glance toward the hallway that led to the bedrooms. "This gives you an opening. Use it."

"Are you working tonight?" I asked, mostly to change the subject. Kara, while she had a degree in art history, worked as a bartender at a local hot spot. She'd yet to decide what she really wanted to be when she grew up.

"Uh-uh. I'm meeting Brett for a drink, though. He's wonderful," Kara gushed. "Oh! Before I left for work this afternoon, though, you had a delivery from a bakery. Chocolate-fudge brownies. From someone named Elizabeth? She was really nice and said she hoped you were feeling better." Kara regarded me quizzically. "I didn't know you were sick. Anyway, they're in your kitchen. I put them in one of your plastic containers so they wouldn't get stale."

Nice of Elizabeth, but right now, my concern was for Leslie. "Thanks. If I'd known, I'd have brought one as a peace offering." As much as Leslie focused on healthy food, she was a major chocoholic. I almost ran across the hall to grab a brownie, but with Scot over there, decided it was smarter to stay put. "I'm going in. Wish me luck."

"You don't need luck. Just be honest with her."

I sucked in a large mouthful of air and went to Leslie's

room. I rapped on the door once and walked in, not waiting for her to call out. She was seated at her desk, typing away on her laptop, her back to me. "Hey, Les," I said. "Can we talk?"

Her hands paused for a millisecond, hovering over her keyboard, before she started typing again. "I have a lot of work to do. Can't this wait?" Her voice was low and even. This worried me right off. Leslie didn't shriek or scream when she was really upset, she stayed quiet and calm.

"No." I approached her and put my hands on her shoulders. They tensed instantly. "I'm sorry you saw that. I'm sorry it even happened. He . . . shouldn't have kissed me."

"Really?" she drawled. "Then why did you look as if you enjoyed it?"

"Scot's . . . um . . . a good kisser. So yeah, it wasn't the worst kiss I've ever had." More like the best. But saying that might result in bloodshed. "I'm sorry," I repeated.

"I don't believe you are." She inhaled a shaky breath. "I asked you on Friday if you liked him. You told me no. So what is it, Julia? Did you lie to me then, or have your feelings miraculously changed?" Her nails clicked as she continued to type. "I'd appreciate the truth."

"We're not a good match."

"That isn't what I asked." Leslie's hands stilled as she waited for my response.

"He and I have nothing in common."

"Still not what I asked."

I swore under my breath and retreated to her bed, taking a seat on the edge. "I don't know. No. That's not true. I didn't know on Friday, but I know now. Yes, Leslie, I like him. But nothing's changed. My beliefs about love haven't changed. So it doesn't matter if I like him."

She swiveled in her chair. Emotion brightened her tawny

eyes to a burnished copper. "It does matter. He kissed you, Julia. I want him in *my* life. Seeing you two together like that hurt."

"I know. I'm sorry." I nearly pointed out that she was the one who'd ruined things with Scot to begin with. Not me. But doing so would be cruel and useless to this conversation. "I was upset earlier tonight. He was worried and came over to make sure I was okay. He didn't mean to kiss me, Les. It sort of just happened."

Her left eyebrow arched and her jaw twitched. "You don't know Scot very well if you believe that. He's a very methodical man. That's actually something you two have in common."

Scot, methodical? I tried to see it but couldn't. Shaking my head, I said, "He's pigheaded, opinionated, and believes he is always right."

"Exactly. And the man who thinks he's always right kissed *you.*" Leslie closed her eyes for two beats. "How much do you like him?"

"I have no idea how to quantify something like that. Come on, Les. It was a mistake. I'm not planning on anything else happening with Scot." Wishing it was possible, maybe. Fantasizing about it, definitely.

In a prim and proper move, she folded her hands on her lap. My stomach clenched. She was too composed, even for her. "I would think, after hearing what your *friend* Celeste did, that you would know how this feels." Temper colored her cheeks red. "You are supposed to be convincing Scot to give me another chance. Not swooping in and stealing him for yourself."

"That's not what I'm doing!" Not on purpose. Oh, God. "Les, he isn't—" I gulped. "I've tried talking to him about you. He brushes me off. You really hurt him and . . . But I think . . . I might be able to fix it. You just have to trust me.

I need a little more time to figure it all out completely, but I have an idea."

"You want me to trust you?" She leveled her gaze with mine. "Forget it. I don't want your help. I don't want you to see him anymore. I don't want you to talk to him anymore. I want you to walk away."

Walk away from Scot? Not talk to him, not see him. Well, yeah, I understood that. Hell, a part of me even agreed with her. But the rest of me rallied up in defense. *I* hadn't cheated on Scot. *I* hadn't pretended to be someone I wasn't. And he didn't want to be with her. Well, he didn't want be with me, either.

"That's not really fair. What about—?"

"Your business and the ad that Scot threatened to run? I don't care. If you're my friend, you'll walk away." The sharp iciness in her voice, in her gaze, chilled me to the bone. But her actual words, her *assumption*, ticked me off.

"I was going to say, 'What about the promise I made to Scot?' but it's nice to know you think I'm more concerned about Introductions than I am about you or my word." I stood. "I'm leaving now. I'm sorry I hurt you, Les. Really, really sorry. But what are you really blaming me for? That kiss or the fact that you cheated on a man and wish you hadn't? Or that you screwed things up right when he was about to introduce you to his family? You might want to think about that."

Her chin gave a slight tremble but she didn't look away. Anger and remorse and stubbornness had me halfway across the room before she asked, "What are you going to do?"

I paused but didn't turn around. "I'm going out of town for a few days. I'll figure the rest out when I get home. I guess you can wait and see," I snapped.

Okay, that was rude. She was upset. But damn it, so was I. Besides, I didn't think she was being fair. Or maybe, just maybe, the thought of walking away from Scot was too much to bear. Maybe I wasn't ready for such a final action, even if it was the right thing to do. Even if it was stupid to feel that way.

Kara wasn't around when I emerged, so I let myself out, locking the door behind me. I found Scot pacing in my living room, his cell phone to his ear. He caught sight of me, grinned, and held up a finger, signaling he'd be a minute. Pleased I had a moment to refocus, to let the conflicting tide of emotions ease from my discussion with Leslie, I removed my coat and deposited my purse, not paying attention to Scot's conversation.

I joined him in the living room. We did a shimmy-tango kind of shuffle so I could get around him to the couch. Our hips brushed and a tingling sense of déjà vu swept over me. As if we were used to making room for each other, as if we'd done it a zillion times before. Almost more bewildering was that his being here felt right. Natural. How had that happened so fast?

Scot continued to pace as he talked on the phone, so I curled my legs beneath me on the sofa. A half-filled glass of milk and a plate scattered with brownie crumbs sat on the coffee table. He felt comfortable enough to raid my kitchen? That, too, felt natural. Right.

I leaned my head against the cushion and closed my eyes. Leslie's face popped into my consciousness and my stomach sloshed with acid. My resentment at her and her demands surpassed my guilt over my feelings for Scot, over the kiss. And that scared me. Maybe I was a cold, heartless bitch after all? Shouldn't I care more about her feelings than mine? Of course I should. She was my friend.

But Scot . . . He elicited all of these strange and wonderful and confusing and crazy emotions. He, more than magic, more than anything else I'd ever experienced, made me believe in the potential of love—the romantic, fairy-tale, head-over-heels type of love. The love I'd argued against so vehemently with Kara and Leslie a mere week ago.

How in the hell was I supposed to reconcile that with my friendship for Leslie? The burning in my chest increased. In the stairwell, I'd decided to use the journal for Leslie. To give her that chance she so thought she wanted. But now, God help me, I wanted that chance for myself.

Feeling this way was wrong. It made zero sense, and it went against everything I believed to be true. So yeah. I guess ice did flow through my veins. Because as much as I wanted Leslie to be happy, I—

The rumble of Scot's voice suddenly stopped, and while I'd totally tuned out his conversation, the abrupt emptiness of sound in the room startled me out of my thoughts. I opened my eyes to see him sliding his credit card into his wallet.

"We're all set," he said. "I have us on the five-thirty flight tomorrow night out of O'Hare. We'll get in around seven thirty Vegas time. We come home on Sunday."

Blood filled my ears with a roar. "We? You're going to Las Vegas with me? You *bought* our tickets?"

He scooted into position next to me. Reaching over, he removed my hairclip and shrugged, as if making this decision and following through without discussing it with me was natural and right.

"You mentioned Vegas, and I—" Confusion darted over him. "I don't know, Julia. I had the idea and I went with it."

I think I nodded. The prickle of déjà vu returned, along with a solid measure of apprehension. How was I supposed to find my balance if Scot was at my elbow for the next several days? I opened my mouth to do the right thing, to tell him that he couldn't go to Vegas. Because despite what my heart said, despite what I craved, my loyalties *had* to stay with Leslie. To do otherwise would prove I was a person I refused to be.

"Scot," I said. "I don't—"

"Shh, Julia." His hand cradled the back of my head. I tilted my chin and looked into those dangerously sexy eyes, and I was lost all over again. His lips found mine and I sighed in defeated pleasure as every part of me opened up to his kiss, to him. My body responded instantly. My nipples hardened against his chest, a flash of heady warmth erupted, and my fingers wove into the softness of his hair.

God, this felt so good.

My mouth parted, and his tongue flicked lightly over my lips and then plunged inside, tasting me, branding me, as if nothing in the world could possibly be more important than this moment. Fire licked through my blood, through me, and a moan slipped out. I didn't care. I pushed his head closer to mine and deepened the kiss. I reveled in the kiss. In *Scot's* kiss.

We expelled ragged sighs when we separated. I missed him immediately. "That didn't feel pretend," I whispered. "That felt like you meant it."

Scot cursed and pushed himself farther away from me, every muscle in his body tense. My heart dropped into my toes. "It has to be pretend. You're in a relationship. Damn it, Julia! What about Jameson? I can't be the other man. I *won't.*"

Hope and understanding flared. "You think . . . Of course you do. I . . . I've dated him once, Scot. Only once. It isn't anything serious." It *could* be. Jameson wanted it to be. But it wasn't. Not yet, anyway. "I was upset about what you said. About there not being a guy alive who was right for me, and I was trying to make myself feel better, and I was tipsy, and . . ."

Oh, shit. I'd let my *feelings* take control.

Comprehension dawned. "You exaggerated the truth?"

"Yes. I'm sorry." I expected him to be upset that I'd lied. Because really, that's what I'd done. Instead, relief eased the hard line of his jaw.

"So you're not in a relationship?"

"I'm not," I said firmly. My brain hollered for me to shut up, to find a way to save the lie, but my heart—my stupid emotions—fueled my words. "My parents would love it if I were, but as of this minute, I'm single and unattached."

He blinked those long, luscious lashes and my stomach went all topsy-turvy. "That's good. But we're not soul mates. My grandmother cannot be right about this," he said slowly, but with conviction. "You're—no offense, Julia—you're not the type of woman I see myself with."

A little piece of my heart withered and died. But I nodded and smiled. "I know. You're not the type of man I see myself with, either."

"But there's something . . ."

"Yes," I agreed, going for matter-of-fact. "There's something. So, what is this? What . . . um . . . what do you want, Scot? What's going on here?" I purposely pushed Leslie, Jameson, magic, and all thoughts of soul mates out of my head and waited. Hoped a little, too.

His answer, when it came, was a low and determined growl. "That's a massive question. Do you know what *you* want? Do you know what's going on with us?"

I swallowed and shook my head. "No, but—" I bit my lips together. I couldn't say this. I wouldn't say this.

"But what?" His entire body angled forward, every ounce of his attention on me. "Tell me."

And just that quickly, I surrendered. "I like kissing you."

Scot ran his thumb over my lips and desire sprang to life. "I like kissing you, too." He exhaled in exasperation. "Hell, Julia. I don't know. You're like no one I've ever known."

Somehow, I didn't think he meant that as a compliment. "Right back at you, buddy," I said.

"So, about Vegas. I shouldn't go." He spoke in a serious, decisive tone. If I hadn't been gazing into his eyes like a love-struck teenager, I would've bought it too. And I would've been crushed.

But his eyes didn't mirror his words. They showed his conflicting emotions, his internal battle. They very much reflected mine. So I took a chance.

"I want you to go. Maybe a weekend away will give us some answers about . . . about whatever this is."

"You're sure? I should've checked in with you before making that decision." He shook his head in confusion. "I don't know why I didn't. But I don't want you to feel pressured."

"I'm sure." Whether it made sense or not, the thought of having Scot to myself in a different place, a faraway place, suddenly seemed way too good an opportunity to pass up. Maybe that's all it would take to put my head and heart back on the straight and narrow. "You took care of the flights, so I'll handle the hotel reservations. In the morning."

His gaze sharpened. I readied myself for rejection, or at least an argument.

"Two rooms, Scot," I clarified. "One for each of us."

Still, his nod of agreement surprised me enough that my breath locked in my chest. Then, everything stopped. I swear, the very air around us paused. Almost as if waiting for me to breathe again.

Scot settled his hands on my waist, his touch electrifying and stabilizing. In agonizing slow motion, he kissed me again. The air moved when I exhaled, and the soft scent of roses trickled in when I inhaled. But I was too busy melting to care.

When he left an hour later, I was even more wound up than earlier. So I packed. I almost didn't bring the journal, but in the end tucked it into my suitcase with my clothes.

You know, just in case I needed a bit of magic.

Chapter Thirteen

I hate flying—something I probably should've mentioned to Scot before we boarded the plane. I didn't, because while being thousands of feet up in the air, helpless, sitting in a metal tube, freaked me out beyond belief, I'd learned methods that helped me manage my fear.

Fortunately, I'd flown dozens of flights without losing myself to panic by using these methods. Somewhat stupidly, as it turned out, I assumed this flight wouldn't be any different. Unfortunately, none of those flights were as turbulent as *this* flight. So while Scot sat next to me relaxed and reading and fending off our flirty flight attendant, I was staring straight ahead at my focal point—the bald head of the man two seats up—and attempting to breathe correctly. Deep, slow breaths that were supposed to reduce my panic.

I had the air from the valve above my head set on high and aimed at my face. I reminded myself that it was safer to fly than drive. I even went through the mental recitation of what turbulence is, because facts center me. Basically, I was doing everything right, everything that had worked before—but it wasn't enough.

Partially, this was because we weren't seated in the middle of the airplane. I prefer the middle. I always chose seats that were in the middle, my obsession forcing me to forego first class, which drove my parents crazy whenever we traveled together. But the middle seems more stable. Like the center of a teeter-totter. So sitting in the middle was always my first line of defense. But I hadn't purchased these seats. Scot had. And we were way in the back.

The biggest reason for my panic, though, was the fact that we were going to crash and die. Soon. Very, very soon.

"I'm on a bus. We're driving over potholes. Potholes. I'm on the ground. Not in the air." I spoke in a barely audible voice. When that didn't help, I broke into song. In an attempt to keep my mind off of the horror of crashing to the ground and my body parts scattering in the wind, keeping my voice low, I sang, "The wheels on the bus go round and round, round and round, round and round, all through the day."

"You're doing it wrong!" A little boy's freckled face peeked over the seat in front of me. "It's all through the *town.*" Then, in a rather loud voice, he sang the song for me. All nine verses. When he finished, he offered a dismissive look that seemed to say he was way smarter than the dumb lady behind him, and faced front again.

His seat belt should have been on. Didn't his mother know we were going to crash? I leaned forward to tell her to securely fasten the boy's seat belt, but the plane bucked against another air bubble. I shoved myself against my seat, tightened my hands into fists, and breathed. Well, I tried. What I did was more like a series of ineffectual gasps.

"He told you," Scot said lightly. His light tone didn't fool me. Curiosity and concern also lurked. Nice of him, really. Sweet, even. But I preferred to keep my paranoia to myself. It was less embarrassing that way. Besides which, trying to hold up my side of a conversation greatly reduced my ability to stay calm.

"Yes. He did. Smart little guy. Why don't you go back to your reading?" I offered. I continued to stare at the bald-headed man. His scalp was shiny. I wondered if he polished it or if his skin was naturally that glossy. "I'm trying to concentrate. About work. And a new client I have."

Scot's book snapped shut. Out of the corner of my eye, I saw him tuck the paperback into the seat pocket in front of him. "Look at me, Julia."

He pried open my right fist and wrapped his hand around mine, the dampness of my palm against the cool dryness of his creating a suctionlike grip.

"Can't. I'm . . . ah . . . practicing meditation. My focal point is up there."

"I thought you were thinking about a client."

We hit another pocket of air and I made a noise that greatly resembled a squealing pig. My muscles stiffened and I pushed my legs together. I also clenched Scot's hand in a death grip. Which was fitting, since death was right around the corner. "I am! I'm meditating about my client. Please go back to your book. I'm f-fine."

"I don't think you are," Scot said softly. "Why don't you want me to know that you're afraid? Maybe I can help."

The bald-headed man's seat tilted back, and he must have scrunched down, because all of a sudden I couldn't see much more than the very top of his head. He wasn't supposed to do that! Not with this much turbulence! We were in the "keep your seats in their upright position and seat belts securely fastened" time. "Not afraid. I just need to stay focused on my focal point," I added. My voice was thin and wobbly.

"I can be your focal point. Look at me, sweetheart."

"I can't. I'm trying very hard not to lose it. You don't want me to lose it, Scot."

"Look at me, Julia."

He didn't ask so much as command. A submissive part of my brain clicked in, and almost without realizing, I shifted my vision to Scot. Warm, intense brown eyes met mine, and the effect was something along the lines of a cozy blanket on a frigid night. A tiny amount of my fear lightened immediately. Just by looking into Scot's eyes.

"There you go." He used his free hand—the one I wasn't squeezing with every bit of my strength—to stroke soaked strands of hair off of my cheek. "What can I do?"

The plane shuddered over—through?—another series of bumps, and perspiration dotted my forehead and dripped down the back of my neck. I hadn't handled air travel this badly in years. "If y-you talk, maybe. Focusing on something else helps a lot."

"I can do that. Just keep looking at me. Try to relax."

I nodded and buried myself in the depths of Scot's eyes. He stared right back, and while that should have been uncomfortable because of the nakedness of eye-to-eye contact, it wasn't.

Another ounce of tension evaporated when he began to talk. He kept his voice low and intimate, almost seductive, as if he were whispering sweet-nothings to his lover. Which, you know, he wasn't. But that, along with his grip and his sturdy gaze, worked as well as an anchor steadying a ship in stormy waters. I opened myself completely, accepting this as another type of magic, and bit by bit began to relax.

He shared funny little stories from his childhood. Like the time he tried to "hard-boil" an egg in the microwave without pricking or cracking the shell, or without the use of water, and the forthcoming explosion that had sent him running to the house next door for help from a neighbor, his barking dog and screeching siblings in pursuit.

He related when his sister Elizabeth, at the age of six, "borrowed" money from their father's wallet to buy an ice cream from the ice-cream man without asking. Elizabeth would have missed a school friend's birthday party as punishment, so Scot stepped in to take the blame.

He went on to talk about Alice, about how she'd fawned on him from the moment she could crawl, and how he'd pretended he hated it but actually loved her attention. I learned how Joe sneaked out of the house and drove the family car around the neighborhood before he had his license, just to prove he could. But he couldn't. He took out a few street-side mailboxes before giving in and walking home to get Scot, who'd had to help Joe fix—and in one case, replace—every single one.

It all sounded wonderful. I'd never given much consideration to what it would be like to have a brother or a sister, but now I kind of thought I'd missed out on something spectacular.

"You take care of them. Your sisters and brother," I said. "They're lucky to have you."

A deep laugh barreled out of Scot's chest. "I don't know if they'd agree with you. I gave them hell a lot, too. Still do. Depends on the day."

"But when it counts, you're there for them. That's special, Scot."

He fidgeted, apparently uncomfortable with my praise. "I told you that my family means everything to me. I'm sure your family is the same. Tell me about them."

Ha. I hadn't warned him about Gregory and Susanna—mostly because I had no idea what to expect from them at this point. "I don't have any siblings. It's just me and my parents."

"What was that like, growing up as an only child?"

"Sometimes lonely, sometimes too much. Everything . . ." I tried to find words to express what it had been like. What it was still like. "When you're the only child, everything rests on your shoulders. I can't disappoint my parents. I can't make a mistake. There isn't anyone else to pick up the slack, so I have to be perfect. Always perfect."

Compassion and understanding flickered over Scot's face. "That has to be difficult. But I'm sure your parents don't expect you to be perfect. I'm sure they love you and want what you want. It's okay to make a mistake, Julia. It's okay to be human."

I tried to laugh. "I am human! I have a job and friends, and . . . Kara and Leslie are good for me. I can relax around them. Kara's been my best friend forever."

"Really? How did you two meet?"

If it hadn't been for Kara, I'd have spent most of my childhood with my head buried in a book. I shared that. "And then she met Leslie in college, and the three of us are a family now. I guess they're the sisters I never had."

Scot stayed quiet for a minute. "You're not who I thought you were." He tweaked my chin with his free hand. "You should show the world who you really are."

Pleasure soaked me. "So you no longer think—" The plane shook and vibrated, and I gasped. "Aren't we there yet? Talk to me, Scot. Please."

"Sure," he said easily, but his gaze remained watchful. "Any particular topic?"

"Your family's ghost." Oops. I hadn't exactly meant to say that. But now that it was out . . . why not? "Tell me about the ghost."

He schooled his features into a mask of nonexpression. "What ghost, Julia?" he asked lightly. "I think the altitude might be getting to you. How about if *you* talk for a while? Tell me why you decided to open a dating service."

If I hadn't sat and listened to Scot's cadence for the past thirty minutes, I might have missed the nuance in his voice. But I had, and I didn't, and his raised pitch was more than simple shock at being asked such an out-there question. He knew what I was referring to. And I was fairly sure that his surprise wasn't at the question itself, but that I knew enough to ask.

"Your family's ghost," I repeated. "You know, Scot. The one who smells like roses. I'd like to hear more about her. Well, I think she's a she, because I don't know any guys who smell like roses. Unless that's an afterlife thing? Do all ghosts smell like roses?"

He blinked and shifted in his seat. He even dropped my hand to flex his fingers. Though perhaps that was simply because of that death-grip thing. For half a second I doubted my sanity, because Scot kept staring at me in the oddest way. You know, as if I had the word *crazy* stamped on my forehead in flashing neon lights.

Then he let out a noisy sigh. "Did my grandmother tell you about Miranda?"

Miranda. A whole bunch of stuff slid into place: Verda's "message from Miranda" when I was stuck at Magical Matchups, not to mention everything that happened while I was there. The way she'd laughed when I asked her if I could call Miranda. The fact that Isobel "should believe" in Verda's mystical mumbo jumbo because she'd "seen Miranda." And yes, even the name that Ethan and Alice had given their daughter—Rose.

Huh. A family ghost. And magic. Soul mates?

"No. I've sensed her. Smelled her. So tell me, Scot . . . Who is Miranda?"

"This is a conversation you—no, *we*—should have with my grandmother and sisters. They know a lot more about Miranda than I do." His eyes and his voice held all the right notes. He was being 100 percent honest.

Still, he had to know something. Excitement that some of

my questions might be answered buzzed away a large chunk of my remaining fear. "Just share what you know."

Scot's Adam's apple bobbed with a heavy swallow. "She was—is, I guess—my great-great-great-grandmother. I've never seen her, but others in my family have. Well, the women. I don't think Joe or Dad have."

"Do you know why she's hanging around? I mean, I never believed in ghosts before, but assuming all of this is true, there has to be a reason she's here, right?"

"I don't know if any of us know her reason," he said carefully. "But if I were to guess, based on certain recent events, I'd have to say . . ." He snapped his jaw shut, and his face paled a full shade. "When you say you've sensed Miranda, what do you mean?"

His sudden intensity combined with my nerves weighted the air between us. My mouth went dry. "The roses. I mentioned that I can smell the roses. That made your grandmother very happy, by the way. But there have been other things, too."

"Such as?"

"Breezes when there shouldn't be. That . . . um . . . feeling you get when someone else is with you. You know, like when you're out somewhere, and you're sure someone is staring at you, so you turn around to see—and there usually is. An old friend or a cousin, or even a stranger, but in these cases, I was completely alone, Scot. There wasn't anyone else with me. So . . . I'm assuming I sensed Miranda." I shivered. "Who is, apparently, an actual ghost. At least I know I'm not losing my mind!"

I tried to sound relieved, but in reality, I was reeling. It's one thing to decide that a ghost might be haunting you. It's another to discover that a ghost truly *is* haunting you.

Scot's shoulders and jaw hardened. A shield dropped over his eyes, effectively hiding his emotions. "Miranda is real. But anything else I might say is only conjecture."

He didn't appear angry, but tension reminiscent of the night he'd barged into my place thickened his voice and tightened his mouth. Huh. I wanted answers. I wanted to know what he was thinking. But I wanted the other Scot back, the one who held my hand and calmed my fears. The one who'd talked to me in that intimate, seductive voice. So it wasn't that hard to fake a smile and say, "It's good enough to know that I wasn't imagining things. You asked about my family. Guess what I just found out? My parents are going to sell their house and travel the country in an RV."

The severe edge of his shoulders softened. Slowly, his mouth stretched into a grin. "Is that so?"

I nodded. Now it was my turn to talk and watch. So I did.

By the time we landed at McCarran, the shroud of stress surrounding Scot seemed to be gone. His color was back to normal, too. Both good things. But I had the feeling he was pretending, and that if I brought the Miranda topic up again, our weekend would end before it started. So, fine. I'd hold my tongue and wait for our return to Chicago. But if I had to corner all of the women in Scot's family to get my answers, then I would. Because yeah, it was obvious that someone outside of Scot's family sensing Miranda was not the normal state of affairs.

No way was I going to hazard a guess as to what that might mean.

Scot and I caught a cab outside of the airport, neither of us much in the mood for further conversation. I stifled a yawn. Air travel always tires me out. Add in the two-hour time difference between Chicago and Las Vegas, and my body was in rapid wind-down. Luckily, the evening's agenda was up to me and Scot.

My parents were doing their own thing tonight, but had

suggested—via a voice mail from my mother in response to the message I'd left saying we'd come—getting together for breakfast in the morning. I had a sneaking suspicion that my mother assumed the friend I'd brought with me was either Kara or Leslie, because she specifically said, "We'd love to have breakfast with you girls." This probably should have worried me. I mean, my parents generally don't handle surprises well. But I found my curiosity outweighed my worry. After all, there was no guessing how the relaxed version of my parents would react.

The cab stopped and Scot paid the driver. I'd reserved our rooms at the Luxor casino and hotel because my parents were staying at Mandalay Bay. Separate hotels had seemed smarter. This way, Scot and I would have a little distance from them, they from us, and the indoor walkway made it easy to go back and forth. Besides, I'd always wanted to stay at the pyramid.

I'd visited Vegas once before, but the volume of the casino still shocked me when we entered. The jangle of the slot machines, piped-in music, and the grumbling roar of voices from a whole bunch of people created a cacophony of noise that was at once exhilarating and too much to take in.

And just like that, excitement replaced fatigue. I said as much to Scot after we checked in and were headed toward the wall of elevators—or as the check-in agent called them, inclinators—that would take us to our floor.

Scot shot me one of his sexy grins and my knees did their wiggle-jiggle thing. My God, would that ever stop? "Not tired at all, eh? Maybe we should get some dinner and hit the casino for a few games?"

We stepped into the elevator, and Scot pressed the button for the twenty-second floor. "Sure," I said, fighting disappointment. We were in Las Vegas. Of course he'd want to do something more than stay in and get room service. But that's what I wanted. A quiet, calm night alone with Scot. "But give me an hour or so. I'm feeling a little dirty."

Oh. Wow. That hadn't come out quite right, had it?

His grin widened, but he didn't use the opening to tease me. Which was also disappointing. The Scot from the other night would've in a heartbeat. Instead, he said, "A shower sounds good."

"Yeah. That's what I meant," I mumbled.

Silence descended and neither of us broke it until we stopped outside of my room. His was a couple of doors down, so at least we were close to each other. He leaned against the wall and watched as I used my card key.

"I'll be back," he said in a very good Arnold imitation. "In an hour."

"Yep!" I gave a little wave and almost fell into my room. As soon as the door closed behind me, I crumpled to my knees. Tonight was going to be a disaster. I knew it, but couldn't put my finger on why.

Well, it had something to do with Miranda. Everything had been fine between us until I'd brought her up. So he either disliked that I knew about her, or he disliked why I knew about her. Or, I supposed, both. Ugh. Why had I even mentioned the ghost? I should've waited until after I'd spoken with Verda. Now, I'd likely ruined the entire damn weekend. A weekend that was going to be my one chance to spend time with Scot without Leslie lurking across the hall, or me thinking about Jameson, or worrying about Introductions or soul mates or anything else. Yes, I was here for my parents, but I was also here, by no design of my own, to enjoy myself with Scot.

I shoved my limp body off the floor, unpacked, and then took a quick shower. Thirty minutes later, I gave myself a narrow-eyed once-over in the mirror. My hair was loose and long, because Scot liked it that way, and I wanted to please him. For clothes, I stuck with the simple: loose black cotton slacks and a gauzy blue blouse that matched my eye color. A thin silver necklace, slender hoop earrings, sensible black flats, and a watch completed my ensemble.

I looked, at best, okay. In the humdrum, nothing-special sense. But it wasn't as if I had a wardrobe of sexy, slinky outfits to slip into. Everything about me screamed basic, including the clothes I wore. Which was my own fault. Even with my mother's influence—or maybe, *because* of her influence—I'd never cared all that much about fashion.

"Well, it will have to be good enough, won't it?" I said. But it wasn't. Not by a long shot.

I mentally ran through what I'd packed, and scowled. I had what I wore, an outfit that was almost an exact replica, except in different colors, a few pairs of jeans, a few tops, and a dress meant for my parents' ceremony. Why couldn't I be more like Leslie? She was always beautiful. Always sexy. She could walk into a bar wearing anything and have half the men there begging to buy her drinks. One flippy, flirty toss of her hair and a smile would draw the attention of every male in the room. It was easy for Leslie. She channeled sexy. I, on the other hand, channeled schoolmarm.

Maybe it was a mental thing. I dug deep, in search of my inner vixen. Mimicking Leslie, I batted my eyelashes at my reflection, smiled, and gave it a go with her flippy hair toss. My hair slapped against my right cheek, several strands twisted in my earring, my still-damp-from-mascara lashes left a sticky blob of black beneath my eyes, and my front teeth were now smeared with raspberry-blush lip gloss. Lovely. Rather than bringing my inner vixen to the surface, I'd summoned a seizure victim.

I repaired the damage, all the while doing everything I could to ignore the insane desire to be someone else. I'd always liked who I was. But now, practical and rational didn't seem so hot. It felt boring and nondescript. Flat and unappealing. The compulsion grew as I stared at my reflection, as my self-confidence plummeted. Damn it! Why couldn't I be someone else? You know, just for the weekend.

Two distinct voices sounded off in my head. Sort of like the devil on one shoulder and an angel on the other. The devil voice insisted I *could* be someone else, that all I had to do was use the power of the journal. The angel's voice was softer but no less insistent. It stated loud and clear that magically altering anything with Scot would only result in unhappiness. That at the end of everything, nothing that might happen, nothing he said or did, would be real. And yeah, the angel—damn her—was right.

Strangely, I found I didn't care. I was in Las Vegas with a beautiful man. A man who melted every bone in my body with the barest of touches, the smallest of glances. Hell, even when he was angry, my attraction for him sizzled. The simple scent of his damn jacket had almost put me over the edge, so yeah, regardless of what might happen after this weekend, I wanted—no, I needed—to be more than myself, to experience more than I ever had. Every woman deserves one magical weekend in her life, right? One weekend of craziness. So what if mine took some real magic to accomplish that?

I glanced at my watch, saw I only had a few minutes before my hour was up, and raced to the journal so fast I nearly tripped. I grabbed one of the pens the hotel supplied, whipped open the journal, and wrote instinctively, tossing every iota of rationality to the wind.

Between now and my return to Chicago, I will feel sexy, beautiful, desirable, and seductive.
From the second I open the door tonight until the minute

I step off of the plane at home, everything about this weekend will be—

Three firm raps sounded, waking me from my haze. I started and my pen skidded along the page. Crap! Scot was here. But I hadn't finished. I *needed* to finish.

"Just a second!" I called out.

My skin tingled as if I stood at the edge of the ocean and the spray of waves was misting over me. Energy rippled from my fingertips, heating my skin and the air. I tasted the sharp tang of magic on my tongue, felt the power with every breath I took. My hand trembled, my fingers tightened around the pen. I tried to focus, tried to remember the enchantment I was going to cast.

But couldn't. "Everything about this weekend will be . . . ," I whispered. Wonderful? Amazing? Well, yeah, but those words weren't enough. They were too vague. I needed to be specific. Otherwise, I could have an amazing weekend with a friend.

"You okay in there?" Scot called from the other side of the door. I recognized his anxiety, but didn't understand why. It had only been a minute. Two at most.

The energy swirled and bobbed and stole my breath. But then, as if someone pushed the pause button, the momentum ceased, waiting . . . waiting for me to finish the wish. It was an odd feeling, this absence of movement. It left me off balance and uncomfortable, because while the pressure, the vitality of the power remained, it existed without flow.

What did I want from this weekend? My soul answered instantly. *Passion.* I wanted to experience passion, and I wanted to experience that with Scot. True, unadulterated, blood-pumping, sweaty, all-consuming passion. And then, when I got home, I'd do whatever needed to be done. Once I had more information and could make a decision based on facts.

But that . . . Well, I didn't have to think about that now. Right now, all I needed to do was complete my wish.

Scot knocked on the door again, harder and more insistent. "Julia? I'm getting worried out here. What's going on?"

"One more minute, Scot. Sorry! I'm . . . ah . . . putting my shirt on."

The energy grew hotter, teasing over my skin like a lover's caress, reminding me to get on with it. I bit my lip and scrawled one word: *passionate*. Which finished my wish, so it read, "From the second I open the door tonight until the minute I step off of the plane at home, everything about this weekend will be passionate."

The pause button released and movement returned. Magic, potent and electric, pushed against my skin, raising the hairs on my neck, my arms, my entire body. A numb, knotted-up ball unraveled from somewhere in the center of me, and tiny explosions of sensation erupted all at once. I pressed my lips together, muffling the moan of pleasure that escaped. This— dear God, this wasn't like any of the other wishes.

I dropped the journal and the pen and gripped the bedspread with both hands, squeezing tight, hanging on while my body vibrated. My head tilted back and another moan came to my lips, begging to be released. I felt *everything*. My blood flowing through my veins, my heart beating in my chest, my breaths panting in and out of my lungs, the sensual glide of the air along my hot skin. It was a level of awareness I'd never before had, and it was exquisite. It was terrifying. It was something dormant coming to life: the power of *me*. Of being a woman. A sexy, alluring, desirable woman. A woman who craved to be touched.

I kicked the journal under the bed and bolted to my feet. I ran to the bathroom and stood in front of the mirror. My cheeks were flushed, my eyes bright. I flipped my hair and smiled, and this time . . . this time, the result was definitely that of a vixen wanting to play.

This time, what I wore had nothing to do with my sex appeal. I had never, in my entire life, seen myself as beautiful, as sexy, as desirable, as I did at that second. I wanted to stare at myself, dissect the reasons why, because truthfully . . . I didn't look all that different. Same hair, same clothes, same body, same girl.

But I *was* different. And there was absolutely nothing to dissect. It was magic, and I had three days to enjoy *this* woman before the other woman, the boring one, returned. I lifted my chin and smiled again. Oh, yes. This was going to be so much fun.

Scot pounded on the door again, and I remembered why I'd cast this wish in the first place. I was at the door as fast as my legs could carry me. I opened up and did the flippy toss, and I gave him the smile and said, "Why don't we stay in and order room service?"

He blinked. His gaze sought my face and eased down my body all the way to my toes, and then back up. Those firm, straight lips I loved kissing slid into a slow, lazy smile. My spell worked! Desire burned low in my belly, and images of all the delicious things we might do to each other whisked into my mind. I opened the door wider, making room for him to enter.

And then he laughed. Laughed! "We're in Vegas, Julia! You seriously want to stay in our first night here? Come on . . . let's go get dinner. I'm starving."

Well, shit.

Chapter Fourteen

The magic from the spell laced around me in an intricate weave, like millions of invisible spiderwebs gathering on my skin, tightening with every step, every breath, as Scot and I made our way through the casino. Instead of feeling restrictive, the sensation added to the energy zipping through my blood. It was powerful. Almost addictively so.

The signs of my spell's success were everywhere. People removed themselves from our path, giving us room to pass without our having to alter direction. Interested gazes followed our movements in the type of awe usually reserved for celebrity sightings. One man tripped over his feet, another dropped his drink before it reached his lips, and yet another received a well-aimed punch in his arm from the woman standing beside him. Probably his wife or girlfriend.

It was liberating. And I would've enjoyed the process a hell of a lot more if it weren't for one thing. Or, rather, one *man*: Scot. He appeared to be completely unaffected by the magic.

He walked next to me, but he wasn't really *with* me. He didn't offer any sidelong glances or smiles. He didn't rest his hand on the small of my back, and other than asking if Mexican food sounded good, he hadn't said a word. Not one. It was frustrating to the nth degree. Especially because I wanted to drag him to my room and rip every article of clothing off of him. Or his room. Either would do. Not only were my hormones out of control, but Scot looked freaking amazing.

He didn't require magic to ooze sex appeal. His black slacks hung on his rock-solid frame as if they were professionally tailored, but they were off-the-rack. He'd teamed the slacks with a white button-down shirt worn beneath a cobalt blue V-neck sweater, the top several buttons of the shirt left undone. The clothes, along with his rough-shaven jaw, dark eyes, and the air of cool confidence he carried, created a hot and sexy *GQ* vibe. Simply speaking, I was on fire and melting fast.

We entered the restaurant and were seated immediately. Good thing, too, because I didn't think my legs were going to hold me upright for much longer. Scot opened his menu, so I did the same. But being all hot and bothered, I couldn't settle.

The Mexican-themed restaurant was all brushed aluminum, dark wood, leather, and glass. These design elements, along with a huge bullfighting mural on the back wall, gave the establishment a fun and funky aura. "This place is fantastic," I murmured.

"Yes, it is," Scot said without looking up.

I rolled my bottom lip between my teeth, wondering if my spell had somehow managed to have the opposite effect on him. Perhaps he now found me revolting. Which, I guess, wouldn't be that far off from how he'd originally seen me. But I thought we'd moved on from that.

I hoped so, anyway.

Our waiter stopped at our table. His gaze landed on Scot first. "My name is Chet. And it will be my pleasure to . . ." Chet's narrow jaw clenched when he switched his attention to me. His body straightened. He blinked several times and a cloudy haze dripped into his eyes. In a higher, almost squeaky, pitch, he continued, "Chet. My name is Chet. And it will be my *utmost* pleasure to serve you tonight. Would you like something from the bar?"

"I . . . uh . . . I think I'll try this raspberry tequila drink," I said. Chet nodded without dropping his eyes. It was flattering. It was also slightly disconcerting. "Oh, and a water. Please."

"It will be my pleasure to bring you those drinks," Chet replied earnestly. His blond, shoulder-length hair was tied back in a tight ponytail, accentuating the sharp angles of his cheekbones. "My *utmost* pleasure."

"It's my pleasure to be served by you," I quipped, trying to make light of his studied appraisal. Chet didn't crack a smile but continued to stare. The flattery became uncomfortable. "Shouldn't you write my order down?"

"Yes! I will do that!" Chet flipped to a new page of his order pad, but his hand jerked so hard the pad flew out of his grip. He nearly stumbled in his haste to retrieve it. "Okay. Write it down," he said, his pen poised above the pad. "Write your order down."

But he didn't. He kept staring at me with bunched-together eyebrows and a blank, vacant expression that clearly stated he'd already forgotten my order.

Scot coughed to draw the waiter's attention. "The lady would like the raspberry tequila drink and a water. I'll have a Dos Equis Amber. And bring us an order of nachos." Scot spoke in an authoritative manner, but he wasn't unkind. Just firm. "Can you do that for us, Chet?"

"Y-Yes. Of course." Chet scrawled the order and then offered a faint, bewildered smile. "Sorry. I'll put this right in."

As soon as he disappeared, I breathed a sigh of relief. Be careful what you wish for, right? "That was odd," I said. "Maybe it's his first night on the job or something."

I mean, I knew the deal, but Scot didn't. For some reason, it seemed important to rationalize Chet's behavior for Scot's benefit.

Scot chuckled. "Our waiter is besotted with you, Julia. You made him nervous."

I fluttered my eyelashes. "And what about you, Scot? Are you besotted with me? Do I make you nervous?" Oh, hell, no. I hadn't just said that, had I?

"Not nervous," he replied. "But you confuse me. I think I have you figured out, and then—" A sigh pushed out of his lungs. "What was going on in your room tonight?"

"What do you mean? I'm sorry I kept you waiting, but it wasn't that long. Just a few minutes, right?"

"There was something . . . Lights flashed under your door. Your voice sounded off. I thought that maybe—" Scot lifted his shoulders in a barely discernable shrug, and the muscle in his arm pulsed. "Never mind. It doesn't matter."

"It does matter. What did you think?" Flashing lights? I hadn't noticed. Though I'd been a bit preoccupied with the unexpected surge of passion rippling through my body.

"That maybe Miranda followed us to Vegas and was in your room. I don't know that much about her, and I'm sure she's harmless. But I was worried."

"Nope. If Miranda is here, I haven't sensed her." Which, you know, made me rather happy. What with the plans I had in mind for me and Scot, I didn't need an invisible spectator. "I was running late. That's all."

Scot eyed me with a mix of doubt and relief. I readied myself for more questions, but Chet arrived with our drinks. He set four glasses in front of me. Three of the raspberry/tequila concoction and one of water. "The nachos will be out in a few minutes," he said without so much as a glance.

This probably had to do with the tension emanating off of Scot. "Thank you, but I didn't order all of these," I said to Chet. "And it is probably a bad idea for me to drink so much."

"The extra two are from the gentlemen at the bar." Chet angled his head in the general direction. A dark-haired man sat on one end, and an older man at the other. Both smiled when I looked over. Chet passed me a couple of napkins. "Here. They wanted you to have these."

Wow. Guys buying me drinks. I read the napkins. Each one had a hastily written name (Robert on one, Mike on the other) and a phone number. I didn't recognize the area codes of either. Again, the pleasure of being noticed sifted in.

I glanced at Scot, took in the taut line of his mouth, and cleared my throat. "Tell them I said thanks for the drinks, but I'm here with someone." I returned the napkins to Chet. "And please return these."

Chet still refused to look directly at me. "Are you two ready to order?"

"I'll have the mahimahi." I named the one and only dish I remembered from my quick perusal of the menu.

"Excellent choice." Chet jotted it down. And then, out of reflex, his gaze flipped to me and the fog came back. "It will be my—"

"Utmost pleasure to serve her. Yeah, we know," Scot interjected. "I'll have the carne asada, and you might as well bring me another beer with the meal. Please." When we were alone again, Scot said, "You're a popular girl tonight."

"I'm not really used to this type of attention." Complete honesty, there. "But you must be. I'm sure you've had plenty of women buying you drinks over the years."

"Why would you think that?"

I laughed. "Oh, come on! You're a very good-looking guy, Scot. You have to know that. One walk through this place and you'd have women handing you their numbers in droves." I leaned forward slightly. "You're a hot specimen. As the owner of a dating service, I am professionally entitled to give you that designation."

Scot grinned. "I have never been called a 'hot specimen.'"

"Yes, you have. Just not to your face." I reached over and ran my finger across the top of his hand. Wow. Kind of a bold move, but I didn't pull back. His skin radiated warmth into my fingertips. I stroked my finger along the curve between his thumb and index finger. "Leslie called you that. So did Kara."

"They called me a hot specimen?" Ruddy color bled over his cheeks. Did he really not know how other women saw him? "I can't see that."

Apparently not. "Actually, Kara's exact words were 'Scot's a hunk of grade A prime beefcake,' and Leslie's were more along the lines of 'the sexiest man I have ever known.' But basically the same thing." Now, I rubbed my finger across the top of his knuckles, dipping into the depressions between each.

"Leslie said that?" Pulling his hand away, Scot grasped his beer bottle.

"She did. I swear." My voice came out breathy. "How did you guys meet?"

Something I couldn't identify crossed over him. "You don't know?"

"Uh-uh. Leslie talked a lot about you, but she's never mentioned how you met." Actually, that was kind of weird. Why hadn't she?

Scot's eyes narrowed. The muscle in his jaw flinched. He was quiet for so long, I thought he wasn't going to answer, but finally he said, "The standard bar thing. I sent a drink to her table. She really didn't tell you any of this?"

"No, but why would she? Men buy her drinks all of the time. So . . . uh . . . you two hit it off right away?" Why was I talking about Leslie? Morbid curiosity. I *had* to know.

"Leslie is a beautiful, intelligent, charismatic woman. But

no. We didn't hit it off right away." He downed a gulp of his beer. "We did eventually or we wouldn't have continued to see each other."

"Right. Obviously." It was on the tip of my tongue to ask more. I knew where I wanted to take this, but I wasn't sure of the proper route. A reprieve arrived in the form of Chet and our nachos. Oh, and another drink from another admirer. Scot frowned, so I sent the drink away. Not that I needed it, anyway. I was still on my first.

We dug into the food and silence settled around us. After a few minutes, Scot asked, "Why are you so interested in my relationship with Leslie?"

"She's my friend." Well, I hoped she was still my friend. "And we're supposed to be figuring out what's going on between us." I chomped on a nacho to hide my embarrassment.

"Your cheeks are pink. You do that a lot, you know. Blush when you're uncomfortable."

"I'm not uncomfortable!"

His left eyebrow rose in humor. "Okay. You're not uncomfortable. Maybe you're coming down with the flu? Are you feverish, Julia?"

"No. I'm . . . Dang it, Scot. Yes, I'm uncomfortable. You make me nervous." I sat straighter in my chair and pulled my sagging confidence together. "You're mean to me one minute, nice the next, cold and distant the next, and scattered in in-between moments, you kiss me. You're confusing. I don't know what's going on between us. I don't know what you really think of me."

"I'm attracted to you. You're attracted to me. It's simple chemistry." Scot's response was so immediate that it should have bothered me. It didn't, though, because as quick as his reply was, it also felt practiced. As if he was trying to convince himself as much as he was trying to convince me.

Besides, it wasn't as if his statement was incorrect.

"Mmm. Right." I winked at him, going for light, breezy, and flirty. "And attraction is good. Is that how it was with Leslie?"

Scot sighed. A frustrated sound if I've ever heard one. "It took a few dates before I thought we might be good together."

"Elaborate." I whisked my fingers through my hair, as I'd seen Leslie do a hundred-plus times. "I'd really like to know."

"Elaborate on what? We went out. I liked her. I liked her more when I learned how similar we were. We both want kids. We both want to get out of the city at some point. We're both into sports, and we read the same types of books. Watch the same types of movies."

I squelched the devil on my shoulder who wanted me to spill the beans that Kara had shared, that Leslie had been faking. "Do you love her?"

"No." Another immediate answer.

"*Did* you love her? Before . . . before she . . ." I couldn't say it. Not again. Every time I did, I felt like I was rubbing Scot's nose in Leslie's infidelity.

The rest of our meal was served, and the relief on Scot's face was palpable. But I wasn't about to let him off the hook. I needed this information. I waited until we'd eaten about half of our dinners before asking again, "Did you love her?"

"No."

"That's it? Just 'no'?"

"If I answer this, can we move on to something else?" He wiped his mouth with a napkin. "I'm here with you. Not Leslie. She's my past."

Well, I liked the sound of that, even if it was disloyal to Leslie. "Yes. If you answer this, we can talk about anything you want."

"I'm holding you to that." Scot exhaled a quick breath. "You asked if I loved Leslie. No, I didn't. I cared about her and I think I could have loved her, if given enough time. We were headed in the right direction and I was ready." He pushed his plate away. "But she wasn't ready, was she?"

"No, I guess not." *He could've loved her. They could've made it.* Well, maybe. How much would've changed when the real Leslie presented herself? The one who didn't want children, disliked sports, would never live anywhere but the city, and rarely cracked open a book that wasn't filled with legal text? "But what if she's ready now?"

Scot was shaking his head before I finished speaking. "Nope. We're done talking about this."

Fine with me. I'd learned enough. If Leslie hadn't gotten cold feet and cheated, she'd probably still be with Scot. And I wouldn't be sitting here now. "No more Leslie talk for the entire weekend," I promised. "But thank you for sharing."

"You're welcome." Scot leaned forward and captured my hand with his. My libido, which I'd mostly silenced, roared to life. "I'm curious about something," he said in a slow, soft, mesmerizing way that brought about a shiver of awareness.

"Oh, yeah? Curious about what?" I held my breath in anticipation.

"Why did you decide to open a dating service?"

Aargh. Business talk. Really? I'd rather focus on other topics. Like escaping to my room and getting naked.

Unfortunately, my boldness only extended so far. "Because I believed that a dating service could be successful," I said, slipping into my all-about-business persona. "At the time, there weren't any true local dating services in Chicago. We had the national chains, and there were a few independent matchmakers, but I felt sure that a niche dating service would thrive. So I chose my niche—upwardly mobile professionals— and marketed to them."

"Smart. But why a dating service instead of another type of business? There had to be a reason you chose this field," he pushed. "Do you like matching people?"

Jeez. No one had ever asked me either of those questions. Not even my parents. "I like it well enough. As for why, I guess because I have a talent for sizing people up, so I searched for possibilities where I'd be able to use that skill and be successful."

"So your decision to open Introductions was based solely on your chance of success? You didn't have a burning desire to help couples find each other?" Now, why did that sound like negative criticism?

"Why else would anyone open a business? Of course I'd choose something I thought I could be successful at."

"There is more than one kind of success, Julia." Scot let go of my hand and started tapping his thumb against his empty beer bottle. "Do you love what you do?"

This question, for whatever reason, raised all of my defensive hackles. "You don't need to love your job to be successful! It's work, Scot. It's how you pay the bills, you know? You just need to be a high-ranking performer. Know the job and do it well."

Scot held his hands up in mock defeat. "I didn't mean to upset you. My grandmother loves matchmaking. She gets a major kick out of the entire process. I think that's a large reason why Magical Matchups has done so well, so quickly. I was curious if you felt the same about Introductions."

Huh. "No, I don't." The admission surprised me. "I care about doing well, and I care about my clients. But I can't say I get all jazzed over the process. It's just a job to me."

"That's too bad."

"So you love your job? Every single day, you're excited to pound nails, raise walls, and do whatever else you do?" Ouch.

Too snarky. "I'm sorry. Introductions is struggling right now, so it's a tender subject."

"Of course not every job is wonderful, and of course I have bad days," Scot replied with an edge to his voice. "But I like working with my hands, building something concrete. Something that will last. I wouldn't be in construction if I didn't love it."

"That's nice. Really nice."

"Perhaps Introductions is struggling because your heart isn't involved." He shrugged. "Something to think about."

Could that be my issue? It seemed so nonsensical. Such a little thing, loving your job. I sighed. Honestly, it didn't compute in my analytical brain. But even so, the idea intrigued me. Enough to do as Scot said and give it further thought. At some point, anyway.

"Did you always know you wanted to work in construction?" I asked.

"Nope. I have a BSEE." At my blank look, he said, "Bachelor of science in electrical engineering. But five summers of working construction changed my mind."

"Wow. How did you decide—?"

"What are you passionate about?" Scot asked. "What excites you beyond anything else?"

You, I thought. What I said, though, was "Nothing."

"I don't believe that. There has to be something."

"No, Scot. There isn't. Unless you want to count success. I'm passionate about being successful." But even that wasn't completely true. I wanted success so I wouldn't be forced into running a business I had no desire to run. But that didn't make sense, either.

If I wasn't passionate about what I did now, then what did it matter if I ran Introductions or my father's firm? Wasn't one just as good as the other? Probably. But it didn't feel that way. "I'm happy enough. Come on, I'm ready to get out of here."

So we did. I let Scot talk me into playing a couple of rounds of blackjack. After those, he tried to teach me the basics of craps, but most of what he said went in one ear and out the other. I couldn't concentrate. There were simply too many things clogging up my mind.

And the men! My God, they were everywhere. And many of them stopped whatever they were doing to stare at me when we got near. A few even approached but backed off quickly under the weight of Scot's glare.

Why oh why hadn't I been more specific in the writing of the spell? I should've focused the magic on me and Scot. Because I gotta say, by the time we gave up gambling for the night and headed to our rooms, I was exhausted by all the attention from strangers. I wanted Scot to pay attention. Only him.

We stopped outside my room and I fished my card key out. "Thank you for dinner. I had a nice time tonight." I unlocked my door and pushed it open. "We're supposed to meet my parents in the morning. You don't have to come if you don't want."

Scot brushed his fingers along the plane of my cheek. "Why wouldn't I? You've met my family. I'd love to meet yours."

"My family is nothing like yours. It might be odd." Desire from his touch slurred my words. "They're in this . . . um . . . midlife-crisis thing now." Hey, how else was I supposed to explain their magically enhanced behavior? "But they can also be unrelenting in their opinions. It's really okay if you'd rather skip breakfast."

"But I don't want to skip breakfast." His fingers spread into my hair, the heat of his touch easing my tension. "I came here to spend time with you."

"Oh. Okay. If you want—"

"Julia?"

"Yes?" I whispered.

"I've been wanting to kiss you all evening. I'm going to do so now."

Before I could process his statement, before I could even blink, he shifted his head and his lips touched mine. I wrapped my arms around his neck, pushed my body closer to his, and let the tide of sensations, of emotions, take control. All of my concerns about ghosts, soul mates, my parents, my business, and yes, even Leslie, drifted away. The only thing I cared about was this kiss with this man and the way both made me feel.

Scot's tongue teased at my lips. I opened my mouth wider and moaned in pleasure. Twisty heat in the center of my belly forced another groan. I brought my hands to his chest and pressed, breaking our contact long enough to say, "Come inside, Scot."

"Are you sure?" His eyes locked onto mine. They were darker than I'd ever seen them—pools of inky brown, just this side of black. And they were filled with desire for me. They also begged for confirmation . . . which I gladly gave.

I grasped his hand and tugged, pulling him into the room with me. The door shut behind us and we tumbled onto the bed. Our movements were frantic. He yanked his sweater over his head and then took off his shirt. I did the same with my blouse. Every muscle, every nerve in my body, trembled with need. With want. Together, as if we'd done this dance a thousand times before, we settled into position. My back against the pillows, his body straddling mine.

I reached for him. "Kiss me again," I whispered. "Please."

"Please?" The husky, need-drenched quality of his voice about did me in. "Are you begging me, Julia?"

"Just being polite. You're always supposed to be polite, no

matter the situation," I teased. "Something my mother taught me."

He laughed. "Remind me to thank her." His lips came back to mine in a searing, engulfing kiss that ripped every other thought out of my head. This man . . . dear God, this man was perfection with a capital *P*.

He brought his mouth to my neck, leaving a trail of hot kisses down to my collarbone. I arched my back and whimpered. The desire our earlier kisses had unleashed was nothing compared to this. Not nearly as powerful or consuming. Not nearly as deep.

I lightly ran my hands down his well-muscled back, his skin hot and soft to the touch, bringing forth another whimper. And then I thought of those freckles. The smiley-faced grouping on his flat abs that had filled me with such lust.

"W-Wait," I groaned. "I need to do something."

Scot paused and lifted his head. "Whatever you want. Just say the word."

I pushed him off me. "On your back, buddy," I commanded. "Please."

His eyebrow arched in amusement, but he did as I asked. "Now what?"

I knelt next to him and traced the freckles with one finger. "I've been wanting to kiss these ever since I saw them. I don't know why." I bent forward and lightly kissed Scot's abdomen. "Hm. Not enough. I want to lick them, too." So I did. My tongue slid over his skin, tasting him in a sensual, heated glide. Scot's stomach clenched tight and he groaned. My muscles quivered at the sign of his pleasure. I liked bringing him pleasure.

He gripped my shoulders in a gentle but firm hold, and he pulled me to him. We rolled until he was once again straddling me. One hand went to my back, and he fiddled with my bra strap. The other hand rested flat against my stomach, his fingers brushing at the waistband of my pants. Apparently, Scot was ambidextrous, because he managed to unhook my bra and unbutton my pants at the same time.

"What talent," I murmured, my mouth against his neck. "You continually surprise me."

It was his turn to taste, and he started at my breasts. A sigh whispered out of me when his tongue brushed over each nipple, when they hardened beneath his mouth. I closed my eyes when his kisses tickled their way down to my stomach. Heat and desire and want and need coursed through my blood in a wash of unbelievable bliss.

The hot flash of his tongue moved lower, pausing only long enough for Scot to tug my pants down and off my legs. My panties followed.

"No fair. I'm naked. You're not." I sat up and fumbled with his slacks, but my hands trembled from the overwhelming necessity of removing his pants so that I couldn't seem to unbutton and unzip no matter how hard I tried. "Help me," I finally said.

He did. We sat on the bed, facing each other, me in his lap with my legs wrapped around him and his hands on my back. We were skin to skin, and the feelings, the arousal of such intimacy, burned the fire hotter.

We kissed again, a slow, searching, soul-baring kiss that knocked me senseless. Scot grasped my hips and pushed me closer, and a throaty groan spilled from his lips. "I don't have a condom with me. Please tell me you do."

"I . . . oh. No, I don't." Disappointment that this night was not going to be what I wanted crashed in, but the passion—the need—remained just as hot, just as heavy. Scot's hands stilled and our breaths came out ragged and uneven.

Scot shifted and my body slid down enough that his

erection throbbed against my inner thigh. I rested my cheek on his chest, the beat of his heart echoing beneath my ear. "We don't have to completely stop, you know," he said softly.

"We don't? Without a condom—"

"Think about it, sweetheart. There are plenty of things we can do without a condom. And I know exactly where I want to start." He stroked one finger along the inside of my thigh. "Want me to show you?"

"Yes, please. I'd like that very much."

That was all he needed to hear. He eased me down, so I was lying flat on my back, and then bent my knees and pushed my legs apart. Pressing his lips to my belly button, he kissed me softly. A tingle began there, where his mouth touched my skin, and skimmed along with each kiss, each lick. My nipples ached, begging for his touch, but he had something else in mind.

I gasped when his mouth brushed against the curls between my legs. He anchored himself by holding my thighs and he eased my legs farther apart. His tongue pushed in, pleasuring me in a way that was at once unexpected and tantalizing. I buried my hands in his hair, and with another gasp, raised my hips. He stopped and slowly lifted his head, his eyes meeting mine, and I saw so many things in his gaze.

Desire, yes. Passion, yes. But I also saw a teasing glint. He returned to kissing my thigh, licking skin that was now so sensitive, almost too sensitive. Tendrils of heat crawled through me at a breakneck pace as his kisses burned down my leg all the way to my ankle. There, he switched to my other leg and made his way slowly, excruciatingly, back up to my stomach.

I closed my eyes and let myself go, succumbing to the vibrations pulsating through my body with such ferocity. When his lips finally returned to the place I most wanted them, I thrust my hips against his tongue, matching his rhythm, and moaned again. "I . . . Please, Scot. Please."

He could've continued to tease me, but he didn't. His tongue tasted and pressed, swirled and pushed at my pulsing core over and over and over. My pleasure and need continued to build until I thought I couldn't handle it for another second. My body tensed. My hips drove against Scot's mouth in an increasing, desperate tempo. And then, finally, the release I needed came in a burst of all-consuming sensation and pleasure that left me limp and drained in the aftermath.

I squeezed my eyes shut and panted, waiting for my body to reconnect. When I opened my eyes again, it was to find Scot next to me, watching me, his expression intent. "Wow. Just wow. That was incredible. Thank you," I said.

He chuckled, a warm, rolling sound that filled me with happiness. "So polite. But you're welcome. Very welcome."

My eyes drifted down his beautiful, naked, sexy physique and just that fast, my blood spiked in temperature, and desire returned. "Don't get too comfortable," I murmured. "It's your turn."

And then I proceeded to show him exactly what I meant.

Later, much later, we fell asleep with our arms and legs wrapped around each other. It was, in a word, incredible. And far more than I'd ever expected.

Chapter Fifteen

Blinking against the morning sunlight, I woke with the languid contentedness of a cat who's lapped up an entire bowlful of cream. I yawned and nuzzled deeper into Scot's embrace, reveling in the weight of his arms, the firmness of his body, and the warmth of his breath on my neck. I'd spent an incredible night with a sexy man.

It boggled my mind how natural this felt. How right. So much so, that mornings upon mornings of waking up just like this stretched out in front of me. Maybe the idea of Scot and I being soul mates wasn't such a whacked-out thought. Maybe it was time to seriously consider if Verda—who I'd decided must be a witch—knew something that I didn't.

The devil voice whispered in my ear then. Reminding me that the more likely truth rested in the power of the journal and the very real possibility that my passionate night with Scot was due to my spell. To magic. I silenced the voice. For now, my goal was simply to enjoy.

He stirred beside me, as if awakened by my thoughts. His hand flattened on my stomach, warmth unfurled inside, and he hooked one of his legs over both of mine, drawing me in even closer. "Morning, beautiful," he murmured. "Sleep well?"

"Mmm," I purred. "Very well. And you?"

"Better than I have in months." A soft kiss landed on my shoulder.

I shivered in delight. "I could stay like this all day. Lying here with you."

"Feeling lazy, are you?"

"Exquisitely so." His arousal pushed against my bottom, and that—the proof of his desire—made me shiver again. "Of course, we still don't have any condoms. So we might have to get out of bed after all. At some point."

His breathing paused and he rested his forehead against my shoulder. When he spoke, it was with muffled hesitance. Anxiety whisked from him to me. "I think . . . I think there's something you should know. Something I should have told you last night."

Every part of me tensed and went on alert. If this was the morning-after, we-should-just-be-friends speech, I wasn't ready to hear it. Not yet. Not until we got home and our weekend together was over. Hell, probably not even then. But definitely not now. I forced my muscles to relax again, and I settled my weight against Scot. "Listen to you, sounding so serious. Can't we leave serious behind for a few days and just enjoy ourselves?"

Now it was his body that tensed. "I'm sorry, sweetheart, but this is important." Scot tightened his hold on me. "This is about Leslie. I know she's your friend, but—"

"Nice, Scot," I interjected before he could say more. My heart raced in panic and fear. I disentangled myself and sat up, pulling the covers around me. Going for lightness in tone to soften my actual words, I said, "Are you seriously going to bring up your ex-girlfriend before we're even out of bed?"

He huffed out a sigh. "Not that tactful, I guess. But I've never been great at keeping my mouth shut. And this is something you should hear."

Emotion gathered in my chest, behind my eyes. Refusing to look at him for worry I'd burst into tears, I pivoted so my back faced him, and swung my legs over the edge of the bed.

"If you're sorry about last night, just say that. I'm a big girl. I can take it."

"No, Julia. I'm not sorry. Not at all." He trailed my spine with his finger, starting at my neck and moving down to the small of my back. Even in my distress, I relished his touch. Ached for it, even. "I . . . You know what? Maybe you're right. This conversation can wait for a few more days."

Pure, sweet relief smoothed my panic. Yes, whatever he had to say could wait. The real world loomed around the corner, a world filled with issues and heartache and choices I didn't want to make. But all of those could wait, too. "Okay. Good."

"Come here. Spoon with me." I recognized his attempt at teasing, but it came off flat. Still, I would've complied, because if Scot held me, the rest of my nerves would ease for a little while. But I caught sight of the clock.

"We have breakfast in forty-five minutes!" Adrenaline rushed through me. I jumped off the bed, my nudity less of a concern than arriving late. Far less. I was at the bathroom door before I thought to say, "Meet me back here in thirty minutes. Can you be ready in thirty?"

"Thirty it is. But if we're a few minutes late, I'm sure they'll understand."

Ha. Not likely. I was beyond positive that no amount of magic had the ability to alter my mother's penchant for punctuality. Plus, regardless of what Scot wanted to tell me, and regardless of what happened once Scot and I returned home, I wanted my parents to like him. In fact, I wanted them to approve of him.

So, no. We absolutely couldn't be a few minutes late.

We actually arrived at the restaurant with ten minutes to spare, getting there two minutes before my parents. It was, in all likelihood, the first time I'd ever beaten my parents to any gathering, ever. Mom and Dad were both dressed in what I call classy casual. They looked like what they were: a well-to-do older couple on vacation.

I saw them and whispered to Scot, "Here they come. Put on your game face."

He flashed me a grin. "Quit worrying. Parents always like me."

Oh, God. My stomach cramped with nerves. "They can be very opinionated," I hissed under my breath. "Don't take anything they say to heart. Promise?"

My mother's blue eyes gleamed with curiosity, my father's with silent appraisal. Yeah, he'd already begun the process of determining Scot's worth. Before breakfast was over, Dad's opinion of Scot would be set in immoveable, impenetrable stone.

I mentally crossed my fingers, hoping for the best but expecting the worst, and wasted no time in making the introductions. "Scot, these are my parents, Gregory and Susanna Collins. Mom, Dad, this is Scot Raymond."

Scot shook my father's hand and lightly kissed my mother's. I think I was as surprised as she by the old-fashioned gesture. From her smile, I'd say it also pleased her.

We took our seats. Dad sat across from Scot, which wasn't a shocker. One of the first lessons I'd learned from my father is to always look at a person straight on when determining their worth. Mom sat on the other side of me. I tried to breathe evenly. When that didn't work, I instructed myself to relax. That didn't prove successful, either. But the waitress came by with coffees and menus, and the distraction helped settle my uneasiness.

"How was your flight yesterday?" I asked as a way of taking

control of the conversation. It seemed to do the trick. For a few minutes, anyway. But once the hassles of air travel were covered, my father focused in on Scot.

"Tell me, Scot, how do you earn your living?" Ah. Dad's favorite opening question. Career talk was straightforward, and tended to put people more at ease than personal questions. From here, though, he'd spiral into other topics, all of which he'd base on Scot's responses. Within fifteen minutes, my father would likely know more about Scot than I did.

My mother tugged my sleeve.

"Construction," Scot answered easily, already falling into the trap. I should've warned him to respond to all questions with a new question. That was Dad's trick.

"Really? Isn't that interesting. And how did you decide to go into construction as a profession?" Dad angled his body slightly forward, his complete attention on his mark.

Mom tugged at my sleeve again. I patted her hand absently, but kept my concentration centered on Scot and Dad's conversation.

Scot smiled and humor darted into his gorgeous chocolate eyes. "Funny you should ask that, Mr. Collins. Julia and I had this same discussion last night." Scot added several teaspoons of sugar to his coffee and stirred. "Specifically about how important it is to choose the right profession."

Oh, no. Scot delving into his theory of how loving your job increased your chances of success was not a good idea. My headhunter, bottom-line, all-about-success father would see Scot as flighty and emotional. Which he wasn't. But once Dad formed that opinion, it would never change.

I jumped in. "That's right, Scot. It is important. And we ate at an amazing Mexican restaurant last night, Dad. You and Mom should check it out before you leave."

Mom tapped my shoulder. "Julia," she said in a low, insistent voice. "You should have told me you were bringing a man with you."

"Yes. Right. I should have," I said in the same low tone. "Sorry about that."

"I agree with you one hundred percent," Dad said to Scot. "So many kids today choose a career with about as much thought as ordering fast food." He frowned and took a small sip of his coffee. "In my business, I come across this often. People who have settled into the wrong professions and find themselves struggling with failure without understanding why. How did you choose construction as your career, Scot?"

"Nachos!" I screeched. "This restaurant had the best nachos. Don't you think so, Scot?"

"Um . . . sure, Julia." Scot's grin held equal amounts of humor and confusion. "Anyway, Mr. Collins, to answer your question—"

"None of that," Dad said. "Call me Gregory."

"Gregory, then. I chose construction because it makes me happy." Scot tapped his thumb against his coffee mug. So he *was* nervous, even if he hid it well. "I was explaining to Julia that I believe if a person does something they love, it's easier to create success."

Oh, the poor, poor man. My dad was about to eat him alive.

"Julia, darling," Mom said with another tug on my sleeve. "Can I have your attention, please?"

"Is that so? You raise a good point, Scot." Dad's eyes squinted in either annoyance or consideration. Hell if I knew which. "But don't you think there's more to it? Loving what you do is one element, but not the whole enchilada."

"They had enchiladas, too! I bet they're as good as the

nachos," I said desperately. "Maybe we should go there for lunch today. What do you think?"

"Your mother and I have plans, Julia," Dad said before returning his focus once again to Scot. "If the only key to success is to love your job, then we'd have a lot more millionaires in our world."

"That's only if you consider millions of dollars the only definition of success," Scot said. "Take me, for instance. I have a degree in electrical engineering, and I could have made an excellent living if I'd continued along that path, but . . ."

"Julia! Stop ignoring me," my mother said, her tone exasperated. "The men are fine."

"This is a difficult time for construction," Dad said. "How has the current climate . . . ?"

My mother, apparently tired of my rude behavior—and who could blame her?—pulled on a lock of my hair. Hard enough that it stung. "Ow!" I yelped. "Okay, okay. You have my attention. What?"

"Darling," she said, all sweetness and light. "I thought you and Jameson were becoming serious. I'm quite perplexed why you'd bring another man as your guest if that's the case."

Oh, dear Lord. I did not want to talk about Jameson. "One date. Not nearly enough to be described as serious." Hm. Not quite true. I had serious feelings, attraction, whatever, for Scot, and they'd been there almost from the start.

"But see, Gregory, that's exactly why I think it's smarter to select a profession based first on something you feel passionate about. Then find ways to turn that passion into success. That's where these other elements come into play," Scot said. "But I know a lot of people don't believe . . ."

"Are you and Scot dating?" Mom asked. "Or is he just a friend?"

Oh. My. God. Way too much going on for my brain to take in. Scot seemed to be holding his own for now, so I tuned him out and focused on Mom. "Yes, we're dating." For a few more days, anyway.

"You and Scot or you and Jameson?"

"Scot. Me and Scot." Wasn't that what she'd asked?

"So you're not dating Jameson?"

"Mom! Why is this so important to you? No . . . yes . . . sort of." I counted to three. "I don't know. Jameson and I haven't established anything yet."

She twisted her napkin between her fingers. "I do wish I had known that. Your father made it sound as if you two had hit it off splendidly. So, dear, we thought it would be nice—"

"We did. Hit it off, I mean. And I like him well enough. But—"

"Gregory! Susanna! How are you two lovebirds doing?" A masculine voice came from the side of me, just out of my line of vision.

My mother paled. "I'm sorry, Julia," she whispered.

Huh? Frustration merged with curiosity. I craned my neck and turned my upper body, and saw . . . oh, dear God, no. I had to be hallucinating. I closed my eyes for a millisecond, hoping that this was some sort of a mental breakdown. But it wasn't. I opened my eyes to see Jameson taking the chair next to my father.

Fuck, right? Jameson was here. In Las Vegas. With me, my parents, and *Scot*.

I groaned. Yes, an audible groan slipped from my mouth.

"Please accept my apologies for being late," Jameson said as he unfolded his napkin and put it on his lap. "My flight was a tad behind schedule."

Maybe if I prayed hard enough, the floor would crack open

and swallow me whole? I squeezed my eyes shut again and prayed as hard as I knew how. Nothing. God, apparently, wasn't listening.

Okay, then. I'd have to make the best of the situation. I glared at my mother before smiling at Jameson. "Wow, Jameson! This is a surprise," I somehow managed to say. "I had no idea you were coming. How . . . uh . . . how did this happen?"

"Julia, it's so nice to see you. And wow is right. You look magnificent," Jameson said as he gestured for the waitress. "Gregory phoned me yesterday afternoon with an invitation. Once I learned you would be here without an escort, I naturally agreed to join in the festivities."

What the hell was my father up to? First a bet and now this? We were going to have a long-overdue talk once we were all in Chicago again. "I see. Well, it's nice you're here. But I—"

Scot cleared his throat. "I think what Julia is trying to say is that she already has an escort. Me."

Jameson looked from Scot to me with uncertainty. I was at a loss. Here, sitting across from me, was the perfect-for-me-on-paper man, and next to me the heart-wants-what-the-heart-wants man. I liked them both. I just liked one way more than the other, and on very different levels. And that wasn't Jameson's fault.

My father broke the agonizing silence first. "Jameson Parkington, meet Scot Raymond. Jameson is an attorney, and the son of a friend and client. Scot owns a small construction company, and is a . . . friend of Julia's. We've been having quite the illuminating conversation. Maybe you can add some insight, if we bring you up to speed, Jameson."

God, no. Scot would be double-teamed. I sent my mother a pleading look, hoping she'd understand and take my side. Just this once. Surprisingly, she did.

"Gregory," she chided. "This is supposed to be a work-free weekend. Can we please eschew all talk of business for the remainder of this meal?"

My father nodded, but I could tell he wasn't wholly pleased. I was, though. For about thirty seconds flat. Because that was when the posturing started.

Jameson threw the first blow. Oh, not in the physical sense, but he still packed quite a punch. "Julia and I spent a terrific day at the zoo last weekend," he said. "I hadn't been there in years, but we had a wonderful time for our first date. Didn't we, Julia?"

"Yes." I gulped some coffee, hoping the caffeine would startle my numb brain cells awake. So, you know, I could speak in more than one-word sentences. "Wonderful."

"Last weekend?" Scot touched my arm. "You canceled our date because you were ill, and then spent the day at the zoo with him? Is this true?"

"Oh, were you ill, Julia?" Jameson's ridiculously green eyes brightened. "You were the picture of health on Sunday. I'm glad you recovered so quickly."

"My date with Scot was on Saturday. I . . . um . . . felt a lot better by Sunday." I reached under the table and put my hand on Scot's knee. Just so he remembered whom I'd come to Vegas with. "It was the NyQuil. You know, the nighttime—"

Scot's lips twitched. "Sniffling, sneezing, sore throat, coughing, aching, stuffy head, fever, so-you-can-rest medicine." He looked at Jameson. "My hat's off to you, Jameson. It takes a lot of confidence to plan a first date on a Sunday afternoon. Good for you."

Jameson's nose flared the slightest bit, but that was the only sign of his frustration. "Ah, but Julia is an animal lover. The zoo is less crowded on Sundays, which made the day the perfect choice for our first date."

"It was nice! I also enjoyed our first date, Scot," I said. "Dinner with your family was very . . . um . . . enjoyable."

Jameson laughed. "Now, that's confident! Planning a family dinner for a first date."

Oh. God. I needed to derail this. Now.

"Mom," I said loudly. "Tell us about the renewal ceremony. That's the reason we're all here. When is it?"

My mother, bless her magically softened heart, understood exactly what I needed and went with it. "The service is right here, in one of Mandalay Bay's chapels. Do you know they have three? It's at seven o'clock sharp, so please don't be late. They have us booked in between two other couples." Her eyes filled with emotion. I wished I had a camera, because she glowed with beauty. Nothing intangible about that, thank you very much. "And I meant to ask you right off, darling, but with all the excitement forgot. Will you be my maid of honor again? I won't make you wear anything peach."

"Oh! Of course, I will." Tears misted in my eyes, screwing with my vision. "I would love that. Thank you for wanting me."

"Who else would I want?" Mom said softly. "You're my only daughter."

Jameson leaned across the table and grasped my hand. Scot's leg jerked beneath my other hand. "Gregory asked me to stand as his best man, and I was honored to say yes. We'll stand together for your parents, Julia."

I looked at my father in shock. "W-Why?"

"Well, Julia, when your mother shared that she was going to ask you to stand for her, I felt it appropriate to ask Jameson to stand for me. We've grown quite close recently. Besides, with you two kids dating—"

"What? No . . . that's—"

Scot placed his hand on top of mine and squeezed. I

stopped, breathed, and remembered that this was about my parents. Not about Jameson and me. Or Scot and me. Just my parents. If Dad wanted Jameson as his best man, for whatever reason, then who was I to create an issue over it? "Isn't that nice," I said as sweetly as I could.

Somehow, I managed to keep the peace through the rest of the meal. This was easier once we were served food and Jameson and Scot were busier chewing than posturing. Mom and Dad, believe it or not, did their best to fill in the gaps with discussion about their upcoming vagabond lifestyle.

After we finished eating, Mom pulled out my gift from her handbag. You know, the gag gift. The maid-only-lasted-three-weeks gift. Not—and I repeat with great emphasis, *not*—a wedding gift.

"Tonight after the ceremony, your father and I have special plans. For just the two of us." She pushed her plate aside and set the wrapped present in front of her. "Do you mind if I open this now, darling?"

"Maybe you should wait and open it in private," I suggested firmly. "I bought that before I knew you guys were doing this. It isn't meant as a wedding gift, Mom."

I shouldn't have bothered. She was already ripping into the wrapping paper with all the glee of a kid on her birthday. I bit my bottom lip. This wasn't going to be pretty. Well, pretty embarrassing, maybe.

A zillion apologies gathered on my tongue, waiting to be said the second she realized what the presents were. Maybe, in private, she'd see the humor in them. But here in public, I didn't think so. Crumpling the wrapping paper into a ball, she set it aside and then pried off the tape that held the plain white box closed.

"Remember what you said, Mom . . . about how my presents

show my terrific sense of humor." My cheeks heated. "Just something to keep in mind."

I tried to console myself with the very gratifying fact that I hadn't purchased her the edible underwear or body chocolate I'd considered. I mean, yeah, those would have been hilarious choices, but not under these circumstances.

My dad, Jameson, and Scot watched with polite interest, because that's what you do when someone is opening a present. The lid came off, and Mom unfolded the tissue paper I'd wrapped around the items. I held my breath.

Her eyes narrowed. She tilted her head to the side. It took her a minute to figure out what she was looking at. But when she did, she gasped in surprise. "Tattoo hosiery? When would I ever wear such a thing, Julia?" she asked in her coolly modulated tone. "And where?"

Yep, there she was: the mother I knew and loved.

I swallowed. "They're sexy, Mom! They have a seam up the back, and black butterflies swirling around the calf. I thought you might find them . . . um . . . fun."

My dad fished his glasses out of his pocket. "Let me see those, Susanna."

She removed the offending package of tights and passed them to my father. Her gaze returned to the box and she inhaled a sharp-sounding breath. Yep, she'd seen gift number two. "Handcuffs! You bought me *handcuffs* . . ."

Fuzzy pink handcuffs, to be exact. And they were a steal at their sale price of ten dollars. "I . . . uh . . . thought they went well with the tights," I offered. And then, because I was trying so hard to find a way of making these gifts acceptable, when they were only meant to be jokes, I burst out with, "You can role-play! You and Dad. He can be the cop and you can be . . . um . . . a . . . a dancer."

Jameson looked at me as if he'd never seen me before, and Scot gave a sort of gasp/chuckle. Out of humor or shock, I couldn't say, but I hoped for the former.

Mom arched an eyebrow. "Role-playing? You mean . . . Oh! My goodness, what a thought." Now her cheeks turned pink.

"Actually, Susanna, these—" Dad turned the package over in his hands and looked at the woman modeling the tights on the back. He cleared his throat with a little cough. "Julia's right, cupcake, they are sexy. And you have great legs. I can't wait to see you in them."

My breakfast climbed up my throat a little.

Mom batted her eyelashes at Dad. "Really, Gregory?"

He coughed again. "Tonight *is* our honeymoon."

The pink in her cheeks deepened to scalding red. "Well. Yes, it is, isn't it. No promises, but I'll think about it." Facing me again, she said, "You have such *unique* tastes in gifts, Julia. I never know what to expect. But thank you, darling, for the . . . thought."

Finally, breakfast came to an end. Mom and Dad left for a day of pampering at the hotel spa, leaving me with two not very happy men. Disappointment churned that I wouldn't be alone with Scot, but I couldn't ignore that Jameson was here.

"So, how should we spend the day?" I asked, glancing at Scot. His jaw was set in that hard line. The egg-cracking one. "We can gamble or check out the strip or see if there's a show this afternoon or . . ."

"I have a full day of work to deal with before seven," Jameson said in a tight voice. "I'll have to pass on any excursions for now. But I'll see you tonight at the ceremony." He nodded at Scot. "It was a . . . pleasure to meet you."

Scot nodded back. "You too. Sorry you have to work. It can't wait until Monday?"

"Unfortunately, no." Jameson stood and came around to my side of the table. He gave me a quick smooch on my cheek before whispering, "We'll talk later, Julia. But you should know that I'm keeping my hat in the ring."

Of course he was. He'd sort of made that clear. Crystal.

With that, he strode away with the sure steps of a man who was used to getting what he wanted.

I exhaled a long and noisy sigh. "I'm so sorry, Scot. I had no idea he'd be here."

"I noticed." Scot twisted in his seat toward me. "Does Jameson know that you two aren't committed?"

"Yes. Well, he should. But my parents—"

"Would like it if you were," he filled in. "I get it. Families have a way of thinking they know what's best for us. Even if they don't."

"Exactly." I sighed again. "Anyway, I totally understand if this is too much for you to deal with. You don't have to come tonight, Scot. I know this is weird."

"Quit trying to dissuade me from family events. I like your parents, and I'd like to be there. If you still want me there."

"I do! I just don't know how Jameson is going to act. Or my parents, for that matter. The last thing I want is for you to feel uncomfortable." Well, I didn't really want Jameson to feel uncomfortable, either. Dang my father!

"This is an odd circumstance, but we're all adults. It will be fine." Scot winked. "Besides, if I don't show, Jameson will think he's won. I can't have that."

A swirl of warmth began at my toes and drifted upward. I laughed. I couldn't help it. "Okay. That's settled."

We left the restaurant and headed outside, deciding to walk off breakfast by checking out the strip. For the most part, we laughed and talked easily. We talked about everything. It was nice, getting to know more about Scot and sharing pieces of my life with him. But every now and then a mask of distance slipped over his features and he would grow silent.

I didn't know what he was thinking about during these times. Probably, it was better that way. But they, along with Jameson's unexpected appearance, put a damper on what should have been an incredible day. It made me wish that I had the power to turn back time. If I did, I'd return to this morning, to the minute when I first woke, lying in bed naked with Scot's arms wrapped around me. When everything felt natural and right.

Yeah. That was a moment to remember.

Chapter Sixteen

A thick ball of emotion gathered in my throat as I watched my parents exchange their vows. Susanna Marie Kaiser-Collins was dressed in a simple, antique white, vintage-style gown that skimmed just below her knees. She held a small, brightly colored, cascading bouquet of yellow dahlias, white orchids, and orangey-red mini calla lilies. Her grandmother's pearls adorned her neck, and tiny diamonds glittered in her ears. She exuded beauty and grace.

My austere father stood tall and proud beside her in a black suit and yellow bow tie. He had a mini calla lily pinned to his suit jacket, and he radiated old-world charm and elegance. The pride and love on his face when my mother stepped into the aisle had taken my breath away.

Jameson stood to the right of my father, I stood to the left of Mom, and Scot sat behind us as the only guest. I hated that. But he swore he was fine.

The standard wedding vows, altered slightly due to this being a renewal ceremony, were used, but my parents spoke the words with such tenderness, such depth, that it seemed as if I had never truly heard or understood them before. This, too, took my breath away.

Mom passed me her bouquet, and my parents clasped hands.

My mother's soft voice filled the chapel. "Gregory, I have always loved you. I will always love you. You are the best part of me, and I can't express how joyful I am to be standing here with you today. Together, we have laughed and cried. We have celebrated and mourned. My life is better with you in it. I am stronger with you beside me." Her voice caught. When she spoke again, I heard her tears. "I don't know what the future will bring us, but I am positive that with my hand in yours, the best is yet to come."

I clamped my lips shut to stop myself from sobbing.

"Ah, Susanna," my father said, his voice shaky and thick. "You have always been the master of words in our marriage. I tried to write my feelings down for today. I tried to find the words to express exactly what you mean to me. But it seems I am still the tongue-tied man you married thirty-four years ago."

With a little cough, he pulled a slip of paper out of his pocket. "So please forgive me, but I am using another man's words today. This verse comes from the poem 'Beauty That Is Never Old,' written by James Weldon Johnson. And this is what I would write for you if I could. 'The world for me, and all the world can hold is circled in your arms; for me there lies, within the lights and shadows of your eyes, the only beauty that is never old.'" He coughed again and returned the paper to his pocket. "I love you, my darling."

"Oh, Gregory," my mother whispered. "I love you, too."

My parents kissed, and the tears I'd been fighting to contain came free, silently spilling down my cheeks. How had I never seen the love my parents shared? How could I ever have believed that their marriage was simply a "good match"? *This* couldn't be false, couldn't be from the journal, from my spell. Their feelings were too vibrant, too alive, to be anything but true.

But how could I have remained so blind for so long? What had happened to change them from the young couple who'd believed so vehemently in their love that they defied everyone in order to be together to the parents I'd grown up knowing?

A thousand little moments crashed into my awareness, startling me with their vividness. The way my parents always stayed near each other, no matter the event or who was in attendance. I'd always believed they did this to show a united front, but now . . . now I saw how my father's eyes followed my mother, even when he was embroiled in business talk, and how she would look up, catch his gaze, and smile.

A united front, yes. But also a loving union.

I remembered how my dad had always phoned her every night when he was away on business, and how Mom would steal away to another room to talk. My mother's tireless focus in helping him in any way she could, from planning those god-awful dinner parties with clients she despised, to befriending wives of those same clients, to insisting on downtime to get him—them—away from the stress of his job and their never-ending social calendar. Not just them, I realized, but us. Our family. They never left me at home with a nanny or a babysitter. I was always a part of the quick weekend trips and the longer yearly vacations.

Years upon years of small, barely seen smiles, soft touches, and words of encouragement floated into my memory. No, we were not a sentimental, sappy family. They always expected the best from each other and from me. And yes, they pushed hard. Sometimes, perhaps, too hard. But now . . . now I saw what brought them together, what propelled their actions, and yes, what kept them together: love. True, romantic, heart-pounding, starry-eyed love. It was real. And it could last for a lifetime.

My heart and brain, so often at odds with each other, connected in a blaze of comprehension. I nearly staggered under the weight, the power of this understanding. The last bit of stony resolve melted away, and a burden I'd been carrying around evaporated. Maybe my spell had allowed my parents to show the world their love for each other, but it hadn't created that love. It hadn't fed that love. They had done that. Even if I hadn't seen it until today.

I still had questions about their metamorphosis. Questions I intended to ask at some point, but one answer was clear to me: I wanted what my parents had. I wanted to fall head over heels. I wanted to love a man as deeply as my mother loved my father, and I wanted a man who loved me the way my father loved my mother. I wanted the fairy tale.

My gaze found Jameson, and almost without thought, I shook my head in a silent admission that he was not the man for me. He sort of reeled back, but he nodded, as if he could read my thoughts. A tiny smile of defeat passed over his features. He bent down at the knees, as if he were picking something up from the ground, brushed imaginary dust off of the imaginary something, and placed it on his head.

My tears fell a little harder. He'd just removed his hat from the ring. And while we hadn't spent much time together, a bubble of sadness exploded inside. If it weren't for Scot, I might have been happy with Jameson. He was a good man. He was everything I'd thought I wanted, and he deserved to find that one woman whose kiss would, in his words, help him shed his amphibious shackles. But no, that woman wasn't me. A million more dates wouldn't change that.

A different man called to me. I turned around to look at him, to look at Scot. And there he was, all handsome and strong and sexy. Oh, how I wanted him. Craved him, really. A burning that had started deep inside the second we met months before, when Leslie introduced us. This man would likely drive me ten ways of crazy every single day. If I were lucky enough to see him, to have him in my life, every single day. Did I love him? Had I fallen so fast? My heart and my soul screamed yes, but that damn rational brain of mine begged for more time. Just to be sure. And hey, more time was fine. I wanted to really know Scot, what made him tick, what made him laugh, what made him scowl. I wanted to know what his dreams were, what his favorite food was, and so much more. So yes, more time was fine.

Finally, at the age of thirty-three, I believed in the fairy tale.

Hours later, after hugs and kisses and congratulations to my parents, after a strange dinner and then drinks with Jameson and Scot, I finally had the chance to talk to Jameson alone. We were winding down for the evening, and Scot had just excused himself from the table.

"I'm sorry," I said to him. "Scot came into my life—again—the same day you pretended to be Chicago's biggest pervert. Everything has happened so quickly, and I . . . I didn't see this coming. I didn't expect to feel this way."

"What way is that, Julia? Do you love him?" Jameson swirled the melted ice around in his almost empty glass. "It isn't my concern, but I'm curious."

I shrugged, but instead of answering said, "I had every intention of our continuing to date. But my parents . . . they're so much in love, Jameson. I want that for me. And I guess I realized—"

"I want that, as well. It was a beautiful ceremony, wasn't it?" Jameson regarded me silently for a minute. Then, "Quit looking at me as if you've broken my heart. I'm not a little boy who's lost his puppy dog. I like you. I enjoy spending time with you, but I think—" He set his glass down. "My dad and yours liked the idea of us being together. I'm not going to lie . . . I liked the idea, too. The reasoning is sound. Our fathers are retiring soon. I'll be taking over Dad's firm, and Gregory hopes you'll do the same with his."

"Ah. A good business match. I see." Something I'd expected from my father, but Jameson? I tried to laugh off my bruised ego. "Well. Thank you for telling me."

"You're an attractive woman. Intelligent, socially adept, and proper. We have the same background, similar families. We *are* well suited. But Julia," he said in his oh-so-charming way, "it wasn't all business to me. As I said, I like you. But never fear, my heart remains intact. As *you* said, it was only one date."

Everything about him, from the tone of his voice to his direct eye contact to his body language, told me he was being open and honest. "Okay, then. Friends?" I asked. "Because I have a feeling we'll make terrific friends."

His mouth spread into a full, real smile. "I feel the same. And as your friend, I'm going to let you off the hook for our next date."

"Next date?" Oh . . . his family's preholiday party. "Are you sure? I don't want to leave you in the lurch."

"I'm positive." Jameson twisted his wrist to check his watch. "It's late. I want to call the airline and try to switch to an earlier flight."

"Scot and I are here until Sunday morning. You're welcome to spend tomorrow with us." My upbringing and good manners forced me to extend the offer, but I wasn't disappointed when Jameson shook his head no.

"It was tough to get away. Honestly, I'd have worked a good chunk of tomorrow anyway. Might as well do that on the plane. If I can move my flight up."

He stood and I followed suit. We hugged, and this time, wonder of all wonders, his touch didn't freak me out. Because it was the hug of a friend and not a would-be suitor.

We separated. "Okay. Well . . . good luck."

"You too. If you happen to find a woman looking for a frog prince, let me know." Again, I thought of Leslie. Before I could broach the idea, he put a little distance between us and gave me a long, considering once-over. "You and I would have been good, Julia."

"Maybe," I agreed. "But we wouldn't have been epic."

His jaw fell open in surprise. A loud laugh burst from his lungs. "No, probably not," he conceded. "But sometimes, good is all we need."

I thought about that for a second. "I don't think so. I think we settle for good. Either because we don't believe we can get more, or we're afraid to try. I'm still afraid." I swallowed past the lump in my throat. "Petrified, actually. But I am not going to settle. And you shouldn't, either."

He didn't respond verbally. Just winked one of those emerald peepers, gave me a wave, and walked away.

I dropped into my seat, drained from the emotions of the day. Excited, though, too. I'd followed my heart, had made a decision—one that ignored every rational belief I'd ever had—and yeah, I was scared out of my mind. Of what the fallout would be. But I also felt more alive. As if I hadn't truly started breathing until today. Not only that, but I had two more nights alone with Scot, and I planned to use them to my advantage. Hopefully, to *our* advantage.

I leaned back, closed my eyes, and let out a sigh. So many things to deal with when I returned home. My business. Leslie. Verda and the ghost. Ha. Now that I believed in fairy tales, it almost seemed as if I'd been dropped into one. I just hoped at the end of it, I'd be Cinderella and not one of her unhappy stepsisters.

The stroke of a finger along my arm pulled me from my thoughts. I opened my eyes to see Scot sitting next to me. "There you are," I said. "You just missed Jameson."

"I'm sure I'll see plenty of him tomorrow." Scot's shoulders went rigid. "I can hardly wait."

"Actually, no. He plans on heading home tomorrow."

"Why the sudden change of plans?" It was a nonchalant tone, but I heard an undercurrent of relief that made me grin. Hugely.

"Work. Oh, and the fact that we decided we're better suited as friends than as a couple." I tried for a flirty toss of my hair. "You, on the other hand . . . well, I'm feeling very, *very* friendly toward you right now."

"You know," Scot said in all seriousness, "I'm tired of sharing you today. I'm afraid if I leave you alone, you'll walk off with one of the men who bought you all of these drinks."

Yes, the spell was still going strong. In front of me were six cocktails. After that, I'd told the waiter to quit bringing them. And I have to say, if I weren't afraid of screwing something up, I'd have tried to reverse the spell. Or at least to cast a new one.

But Scot was paying attention to me. He seemed interested in me. Really interested. So I didn't want to take a chance. Besides, the spell would disappear the second we returned home. And then . . . well, then I'd see what was left.

"You're the only man I'm thinking about tonight, Scot." I leaned over close and whispered in his ear, "In fact, I'm ready to call it a night. Are you?"

His eyes darkened in desire. In longing. For me. "I am."

We stood together. With his arm around my waist, we walked as one through the casino, across the walkway, and to the inclinators at our hotel. This time, I didn't notice people moving out of our way or the gazes of other men. I didn't even notice how much my feet hurt in my heels. Every part of me was focused only on one man.

The instant my door shut behind us, Scot's lips were on mine. This kiss, the one I'd waited all day for, was slow, intoxicating, and it drove me wild. I pulled Scot close, as close as I could, savoring the taste, the feel, the reality of his body against my body. His mouth left mine and I moaned in complaint. A wicked smile and a sexy gleam in his eyes forced another moan, this one of pure anticipation.

He bent his head and nibbled my ear, lifted my hair out of the way, and whispered soft kisses of fire down my neck. A sweet, delicious heat fluttered between my legs, expanding inch by glorious inch, until every part of me was left flushed and wanting. Oh, dear Lord. This was torment. Exquisite, yes. But torment nonetheless. And Scot . . . well, he seemed to know exactly what I wanted, what I craved. And he strove to please.

He dropped my hair and fumbled at the back of my dress, searching for my zipper, which he found in about three seconds flat. One quick zip, the dress floated to my ankles, and I stood there, back pressed against the door, in nothing but my bra, panties, thigh-high tights, and two-inch heels.

A gasp, rich with need, pushed out of his lungs. "My God, Julia. You are so beautiful," he whispered, his husky voice bringing me to a new level of desire. "So sexy."

Curls of pleasure, of longing, trickled over me in another rush. "You're not so bad yourself, you hot specimen, you."

Gripping my arms, Scot drew me to him in a tight, intimate hold. I wrapped my arms around his neck and pulled his head down so we could kiss again. This time, I took control, and slipped my tongue inside his mouth. His hands found my bottom, and he squeezed, and then he lifted me up into his arms, capturing me in his embrace. I kicked my heels off and circled his waist with my legs.

I kissed his neck, his jaw, his cheek, his ear, as he carried me to the bed. With one hand bracing my back, he carefully, as if I were the most valuable object on earth, set me down. Kneeling on the bed in front of me, his thumbs grazed my nipples, still covered by the thin fabric of my bra. They hardened and ached in blissful agony, and I gasped.

I tugged off his jacket and loosened his tie, and when those were off and on the ground, began unbuttoning his shirt. The masculine beauty of his solid, muscular chest stole my breath and made my hand tremble as I stroked the taut, firm lines of his stomach. I moved to his pants and unbuttoned, unzipped, and pushed them down his hips, his legs, until they too were off. Beautiful didn't begin to describe him.

He dipped his finger into the waistband of my panties, and down, his thumb pushed inside of me, feeling my wetness— the proof of what he did to me, the need I had for him—and he groaned. "You're a vixen, Julia."

"Am I?" I asked in a throaty whisper. I thrust my hips, so his finger went deeper, so deep, and I whimpered as pleasure thrummed through me. "Well, this vixen wants to play with you. You did buy condoms tonight, didn't you?"

"I did. Jacket pocket." Rolling to the side, he fumbled with his jacket. Then he fumbled with the box. I slipped my bra and panties off, so when he was ready, I would be, too. And oh, was I ready. Never had I wanted a man with such intensity.

He ripped the packaging open, and I yanked at his boxer briefs, not able to wait another second to feel him inside of me. I ached with the want of it.

"Patience, grasshopper," Scot teased—but his eyes, they weren't teasing. They were serious and dark and filled with the same intrinsic yearning that pounded through me.

With one hand, he unrolled the condom on his cock. With the other, he tickled the line of my hip to my belly button to my other hip and back again, leaving me breathless and hungry for more. Hungry for him. Hungry for everything.

Undeniable desire washed over his features. Centering himself between my legs, he slowly peeled off my right stocking, stopping to kiss and suckle my thigh, my knee, my calf, and my ankle until the flimsy piece of fabric fell to the floor. And then he did the same with the other leg. It just about did me in.

"You're killing me, Scot," I breathed. "Enough foreplay."

This, for whatever reason, brought a grin. "Fancy that. A woman telling me too much foreplay. Well, sweetie, I aim to please. Tell me what you want."

"I want you inside of me. Now."

Scot's body trembled with those words, and in a heartbeat, I knew that he'd been fighting for control, fighting his desire, in order to do as he said: please me. And that made me want him all the more, which shouldn't have been possible. But oh, it was.

He shifted so that he once again straddled me. His cock throbbed against my belly, teasing me, and I shuddered in delight. Bracing his hands on either side of me, he leaned over and took my mouth with his in a hard, hot, hungry kiss. I threaded my fingers into his hair as my body rocked beneath him.

Reaching down, he spread my legs open and settled himself between them. Right there, right where I wanted—no, *needed*—him. I wrapped my legs around his waist and wiggled my bottom, tempting him . . . taunting him . . . tantalizing him. He looked up, his eyes locked onto mine, and it was as if he could see straight into my soul.

The intimacy, the power of that, shattered every bit of control I had left, and I put my hands on his butt and pushed. He entered me in a slow, sliding thrust, and I gasped in surrender. Shivers cascaded over my skin. Heat pumped through my blood. I thrust my hips against his harder, wanting more of him, wanting to feel all of him inside of me.

Scot groaned in pleasure, a deep, throaty sound that filled

me with satisfaction. My breath came faster. I tightened my legs around him and stroked his butt, his back, his arms. His skin was hot, so hot to the touch. He kissed me again as we moved together, our bodies in perfect rhythm. I met his hips thrust for thrust, and the driving need turned into a building pressure of sensitivity that wouldn't let up.

Lightning-fast tingles shot through me. I brought my legs down, planting my feet on the bed, and shoved my hips up, hard. A million tiny fireworks erupted one after another, growing in strength, until finally, I reached the highest crest and a blast of mind-numbing pleasure exploded from the core of me.

I focused on Scot's eyes as the tide of sensations overtook me. He thrust again, the muscles on his back clenched beneath my hands. A shudder rippled through him, and then another. I tightened my legs and arched my back, brought him into me as deep as I could, and watched in delicious rapture when his body shivered and shuddered again.

A minute, maybe two, passed, where we stayed frozen, our limbs entwined and our bodies combined. He pushed out a long, slow breath. "That was incredible," Scot murmured. "*You* are incredible."

"Right back at you," I said, suddenly feeling shy. Silly, maybe, especially after our sexual escapades last night. But it had been a day of revelations, and this . . . well, this was one more.

He rolled to the side and opened his arms. I curled myself into them and rested my head against his chest. The beat of his heart, the feel of his body, and the touch of his hands on my skin should have relaxed me. But they didn't. I couldn't help but worry that in Scot's mind, all of this was still just pretend. And in my mind, in my *heart*, nothing had ever been so real.

Chapter Seventeen

We slept in late on Saturday, ate a leisurely breakfast in bed—gotta love room service—and then hopped into the extra-large shower. Together. We stayed there for a while, a very long while, enjoying each other's wet, naked, soapy bodies. It was luscious. I'd never showered with a man before, and I'd never had sex anywhere but on a bed.

Definitely worth every water-soaked wrinkle. If I could start every day the same way, I'd happily walk around looking like a prune.

That evening, Scot took me to a dinner show at the Excalibur Hotel and Casino. It was medieval themed, complete with jousting knights, fair maidens, swords, horses, and fireworks. We gambled a little before turning in for the night. I won close to eight hundred dollars on a very lucky slot machine, and he won just over a thousand at blackjack. Then we tumbled into bed for another night of make-my-toes-curl sex. I was pretty sure his toes curled a little, too.

It was, in nearly all ways, the perfect weekend. But the second we stepped off of the plane in Chicago on Sunday afternoon, everything seemed to change. Now we were driving to my place in Scot's SUV, both of us quiet, each of us lost in our own thoughts. Mine were a weird conglomeration of the good—dreams, hopes, and wishes—and the bad—questions, worries, and fears. I had no idea what his thoughts were. I didn't ask, and he didn't share.

But I was tired of the silence, so I said, "Who watched your dog while you were gone?"

"My brother." Scot rolled to a stop and flipped the left-turn blinker on. "Joe keeps saying he doesn't want a dog, but he loves Frisbee. He's always thrilled when I need him to dog-sit."

"That's nice. At least you don't have to put him in a kennel when you travel." Scot swung the SUV onto my street. "How . . . ah . . . how did you come up with the name Frisbee?"

"Easy. He showed up at a job last summer with a Frisbee in his mouth and no tags. I put up signs, ran a few ads, but no one claimed him. So he's mine now, and Frisbee seemed as fitting a name as any."

"Lucky dog," I murmured, somehow jealous of the four-footed, furry animal. Maybe if I showed up at one of Scot's job sites with a Frisbee in my mouth, he'd claim me, too.

We pulled into my parking lot. This was it. I was home and my weekend with Scot was officially over. Scot put the SUV in park and kept the engine running. I waited for him to say something—anything—but he was quiet, tapping his thumb against the steering wheel. This time, I didn't see the action as a reflection of his nerves. This time, I saw it as impatience.

Probably, he wanted to get Frisbee and go home. It probably had nothing to do with me. But it felt as if it did. My heart squeezed in sadness.

"Thank you for coming with me. It was great. All of it was great." I opened the door. "Pop open the back so I can get my luggage, okay?"

Scot's thumb paused. The cords in his neck tightened. In a quick, decisive move, he turned off the ignition. "I'm hungry. Feel like ordering a pizza?"

"Pizza . . . yes. Uh-huh . . . sounds good," I babbled in surprise and relief. He wanted to stay. The spell was over, and he wanted to stay. "I'm starving."

Grabbing his keys from the ignition, he tossed them to his other hand and tucked them into the front pocket of his jeans. His gaze met mine. A spark passed between us, and hope blew up inside like a gigantic helium balloon. "I had a great time, too, Julia—"

"Good!" I interrupted. "I'm glad."

His unsaid *but* hung in the air between us, weighing everything down. I leaned toward him and brushed my lips along his jaw. A trail of small kisses led me to his mouth, and I gave him a soft, lingering kiss. His hand came to the side of my neck, his thumb grazed along my cheek. Funny, how one kiss can silence the demons. Funny, how one kiss could make me feel safe. At least for a little while.

"Mmm," I whispered when we separated. I rested my forehead against Scot's chin. "I do enjoy kissing you."

I wanted him to say "I enjoy kissing you, too," but what I got was a pat on the back of my head. He cleared his throat. "Ready for that pizza?"

"Sure." Fighting disappointment, I shifted away. Images of Scot sitting me down whipped into my consciousness: all nice and private in my apartment, reminding me that our relationship was only supposed to be pretend, and that as much fun as our weekend was, nothing had changed. "Hey, how about if we go out, instead? Maybe catch a movie?"

"If you'd rather go out, that's fine," Scot said carefully. "But I'll probably fall asleep in a dark theater." His grin didn't quite reach his eyes. "I'm a little worn out."

I held back a sigh. Was I really going to drag Scot to dinner and a movie on the heels of a busy weekend just because I was afraid he might say something I didn't want to hear? I could be wrong. Maybe tonight would be a beginning and not an end.

And even if I was right, why put it off? I told myself to grow a spine, and said, "Of course we can stay in. I wasn't thinking."

We gathered my luggage and went upstairs. I half expected to see Leslie lurking in the hallway, waiting for us. But that was a silly, stupid thought. And she wasn't. Still, I couldn't deny my relief when I closed my door and latched the chain lock.

But I needed a minute to be alone, to stabilize my emotions and pull together my courage, so I smiled at Scot. "I'm going to unpack really fast and freshen up."

He shrugged off his leather coat and hung it in my closet. Ridiculous, maybe, but that one tiny action increased my hopes for the evening. If he was planning on breaking my heart and taking off after we ate, why hang up his coat when he could just toss it on a chair?

Yeah, I know. I was looking for signs everywhere. Which meant I'd find them. Everywhere.

"Mind ordering the pizza for us?" I asked.

"Not at all," he said without looking in my direction. "How does Vito's sound?"

Even in my distress, I smiled at the memory of the first time we'd shared a Vito's pizza. Everything about that night felt far away. "Sounds perfect. Vito's is my favorite."

"I know." He faced me and returned the smile. "Where's your phone book?"

I told him and made my escape. Once in my room, I collapsed on the edge of the bed. I rehashed every second, every word, every action since we'd left the airport, trying to read his body language, his thoughts, and therefore, his intent. But I came up blank. He'd been quiet, a little distant, but so had I.

The logical explanation was also the simplest: he was tired from a long weekend and hours on a plane, probably even more than I was, because he'd been thrust into an uncomfortable situation with Jameson at the same time he met my parents. After all, meeting new people can be draining. So logically, his reticence and distance weren't any reason for alarm.

Okay, then. I wouldn't worry. I wouldn't panic. Not outwardly, anyway. Because while fatigue might be the simplest explanation, it didn't take magic into account. Or my spell.

It only took a few minutes to unpack, and the activity helped calm my nerves. That is, until I picked up the journal. I'd come this close to accidentally leaving it in Vegas. That first night, I'd kicked the book under the bed at the tail end of my spell, and in my hurry this morning, had nearly forgotten it was there. Thank goodness I'd remembered.

I turned the journal over in my hands, as I had the very first time I held it. The leather was soft, supple, solid. Real.

I stared at the book. A long, hard tremble hit. Why not cast one more wish? Just for tonight? So I could relax and enjoy the evening with Scot. So he could relax and enjoy his time with me. What would that hurt? My fingers tingled with the need to guarantee one more night of bliss, to save myself from one more night of possible heartache.

The compulsion swirled around me, pressing in, potent and powerful. I reeled back and dropped the journal. "No," I whispered, my voice shaking. "Don't be that person."

I paced back and forth, breathing in and out, fighting against the nearly overwhelming desire to cast "just one more wish." Not only because I'd already had my weekend, and not only because it wasn't right to continue to use this power in that way, but because I knew if I succumbed, it wouldn't be just one more. I'd use the magic again and again and again, losing myself in the process. And that . . . well, that scared me more than anything Scot might say.

When the desperate edge of the compulsion eased, I picked up the journal by its corner and shoved it into my nightstand. It was there if I needed the magic for something else, but I refused to cast another spell that might cloud what was really happening—or not happening—with Scot.

I brushed my hair and washed my face. I changed into fresh clothes. I looked at the nightstand a dozen more times, but the crazy compulsion didn't return. Thank God for that.

When I exited the safety of my bedroom, it was to find Scot lying on the couch. His eyes were closed, his face relaxed in sleep. My heart softened as I took in the sight of him. See? My rational brain screamed, *He's tired. There's nothing to worry about.*

Feeling a little more upbeat, I silently grabbed a notebook from my desk and went to the kitchen. There was no reason to wake him until the pizza arrived, and maybe I could figure out a few other things while I waited.

I poured myself a glass of red wine and started a pot of coffee. Elizabeth's brownies were still in the large round plastic container Kara had stored them in. As long as they weren't stale, and they shouldn't have been, they'd do for dessert. Well, unless Scot had other ideas for dessert. I shivered, in both longing and hope.

Sitting down at the table, I sipped my wine. Ever since I'd heard Scot's "love your job" theory, I hadn't been able to get it out of my head. Now, after my epiphany at my parents' ceremony, the concept didn't sound as far-fetched. Think about it: if a person chooses a profession they truly love, and then combines that love with a solid business plan, marketing data, and of course, the proper skills, they might have an advantage. They'd likely focus harder, work longer hours, do whatever needed doing, to create success.

Well, not necessarily. But the idea had merit.

Of course, there was also more to lose. If I loved Introductions with the passion Scot described, losing my business might cripple me beyond the pain of failure I already felt. Because once your heart is involved, it's involved. End of story.

It was sort of like walking away from a relationship. I chewed on the end of my pen, thinking. I mean, I already knew that losing Scot would hurt buckets worse than any of my other relationships. Even the breakup of my two-year relationship with Paul, a financial planner, hadn't caused me much more than a flicker of regret. I'd liked him. We'd had fun together. But then came the "where is this headed?" conversation, and neither of us had an answer. So we went our separate ways, and I'd barely thought about Paul since. Because, yeah, my heart wasn't involved then. But now—with Scot—it was.

Oh. That was why my wish for Introductions hadn't come true. Why it wasn't *going* to come true. *Truest of heart. Purest of soul.* Yeah. That wish was dead in the water; I knew it to the core of my being. I might still be able to save Introductions, but could I do so in a month? Probably not.

My father wasn't a tyrant. If I went to him and told him that this was my passion, he'd let me out of our deal. I knew this with a surety that defied reason. I think on some level, I'd always known that. But I'd never used those words with him. So the bigger question to answer was, why not?

The answer kicked me in the gut. Because if I didn't have Introductions, and if I didn't work at my father's firm, I had no idea what I would do—what I *wanted* to do. My entire life had been focused on success. First in education, and then in work. I excelled. I made my parents proud. I'd followed the path I thought they wanted me to take.

Well, not completely. Dad had offered me a job directly after graduation, but instead I'd accepted a position somewhere else until I was ready to open Introductions. But I had never given any true thought to the path I wanted to take.

That was about to change. I opened the notebook and wrote at the top of the page, "What are my passions?" I stared at the question blankly. What did I love? There had to be something, and *Seinfeld* wasn't going to cut it.

Animals! I loved animals. I wrote that down. I tapped my pen against the table, trying to think of something else. Sheesh, was I really this boring? I had to have other interests, because as much as I liked animals, going into veterinary science or opening a pet store held zero appeal.

The knock of the pizza-delivery man saved me from further torment. I put away the notebook with the promise I'd go at it again later. I paid for the pizza and got everything set up in the kitchen; then I woke Scot by kissing him gently on his cheek. "The food is here. Do you want to eat or keep sleeping?"

He blinked sleepy, warm brown eyes at me and looped an arm over my shoulders. "Sorry. I didn't mean to drift off."

"It's okay. You had to keep me calm all the way home. You deserved a nap."

I leaned in for another kiss, closed my eyes, and waited to be swept away. His lips landed on my nose for a quick peck, as if I were his sister or a child or a friend, a not-so-subtle reminder that our weekend was over. Or was it just a sweet show of affection and I was reading way too much into it? Probably the latter. Until given other notice, I was going to stay as positive as possible. Even if it killed me.

I pulled myself upright, saying, "The pizza's in the kitchen. Let's eat there."

He went to wash up before meeting me at the table. Over pizza, we talked about anything and everything that had zip to do with us. Some of our fascinating topics included the weather, the holidays, and the recent roadwork on I-90. This, in turns, proved frustrating and comforting. Frustrating because I so wanted to hear that our relationship wasn't pretend, and comforting due to the fact that I was petrified he'd say the opposite. Basically, I was calm one minute and tense the next.

Reading my thoughts, Scot said, "Are you okay? You seem jittery."

"Oh, just tired, I think." I stacked our empty plates. "I made coffee and there are plenty of brownies left. Want some?" *Please don't leave yet. Stay with me. Kiss me. Touch me. Prove that our weekend wasn't because of magic.*

His eyes, dark with concern, centered on me. "Sure. I always have room for dessert. You get the brownies, I'll get the coffee."

We maneuvered around each other easily. Scot's arm lifted over my head to get the coffee mugs, and I turned on instinct, tilting my chin. Our gazes met and an electrifying bolt of energy zapped between us. Dropping his arms, he settled his hands on my waist and in one fast tug, our bodies pressed together. His mouth came closer . . . closer . . . closer. I tilted my chin higher. My heart raced and it felt as if everything I wanted, desired, and craved was going to be decided at this very moment.

Our lips connected and the kiss was scorching in intensity. It was just as hungry and hot as the kisses we'd shared in Vegas, but it was also sweet and searching. Tender and filled with yearning. I opened my mouth wider, pressed myself against him tighter, and every thought process evaporated.

Scot groaned and pulled away. "We . . . we need to talk, Julia." His voice was thick and heavy with emotion, but also with an unknown something that scared me.

I brushed my hair off my cheek with a shaky hand. This was it, the beginning or the end. I slid to the side to grab napkins and paper plates. "Okay," I said in forced calmness. "Let's talk."

We settled at the table again. I chose a brownie—not because I was hungry, but because I needed something to do with my hands—tore a chunk off, and popped it in my mouth. Scot's sister was a fantastic baker. Probably, it was the best brownie I'd ever eaten. It held exactly the right amount of richness versus sweetness, and the chocolate melted on my tongue. I supposed these brownies were my silver lining. Because if this conversation went downhill, I'd have vast amounts of chocolate—excellent chocolate—with which to console myself.

I ate another bite, swallowed a mouthful of coffee, and readied myself for whatever was about to happen. "Go ahead, Scot. Say what you need to say."

His head dipped in a slight nod. In a serious, quiet tone, he said, "I had an incredible weekend, Julia. It was . . . fantastic spending more time with you. Getting to know you better." Grasping my arm, he squeezed. "I learned a lot. Enough to . . . I have to ask. Why were you at Magical Matchups the morning my grandmother phoned me? What led you there?"

Okay. This wasn't wholly unexpected. But I hadn't expected to go down this line of conversation now. And it wasn't a good start, because I couldn't—wouldn't—lie.

"You're not going to like my answer. But you have to promise you'll hear me out completely."

Scot heaved a breath. "I was afraid you'd say that, but yeah, I'll listen."

I twisted my fingers together, wishing for a paper clip, and prayed for the right words. "Introductions is failing, Scot. I told you that. But . . . what I didn't say was that most of my struggles didn't begin until after Magical Matchups opened. I had client after client leaving my company for your grandmother's, and I . . . I couldn't figure out why."

Another nod, but this one was sharp. "Okay. You lost some business."

"Not just *some* business. A lot of business." I sucked in air and put the rest of the story out there. How I'd asked Kara and Leslie to check out Magical Matchups for me, and how they'd agreed but had second thoughts. How I'd known if I didn't do something, I'd lose my company, and how that had driven me to visit Magical Matchups. "It was late," I explained. "The place was closed, but I walked by and peered in the windows."

The tight lines creasing Scot's forehead relaxed. "So you were looking in the window and my grandmother found you?" He shook his head. "No, that isn't right. She said you were asleep on her couch. How did that happen?"

So I told him everything: the open door and my decision to snoop, the feeling of another presence, the roses and the breeze, and the fear that had pushed me to leave. "Except the door wouldn't open. My cell wouldn't get a signal, and Verda's phone didn't have a dial tone. I was stuck." I shrugged. "And when Verda found me in the morning, she decided you and I were soul mates and called you. You know the rest."

Well, most of the rest. Scot didn't know about the journal. And I wasn't going to tell him. Not until I talked to Verda. "But please believe me, I never planned on hurting anyone. I just wanted to understand why I was failing. I wanted to see if"—I swallowed nervously—"Verda had something that I didn't. A secret to her sudden success."

"So those papers I saw here." Scot gripped his coffee cup so hard, his knuckles whitened. "The sign-up papers from Magical Matchups. You stole those?"

"No. It wasn't like that. Verda . . ." I closed my eyes, trying to remember every detail of that morning. "Your grandmother was upset when you left. She realized we knew each other, and I explained about Leslie. I told her that she was wrong about us. So she offered me a free membership to her services as an apology for my being locked in all night."

"I see."

"No. You don't." God, he had to understand. "I said no, Scot. But she insisted. Her exact words were 'I don't take "no" easily. All of this will be much easier on you if nod your head and agree.' So yeah, I agreed." I breathed in deeply. "What you said hurt me. I wanted to be alone. So I took the papers, agreed to return the next night, and got the heck out of there."

Scot's mouth curved into a slight smile. "I know how persuasive my grandmother can be. You probably made the right decision." He sighed. "What were you going to do with that information, though, Julia?"

Ugh. Of course he'd ask that. "I planned on looking through the paperwork. I'm not going to lie about that, but even then I liked Verda. I wouldn't have hurt her. I won't hurt her." I thought of something else. "Oh, and I hadn't even planned on going back. I was going to call her and cancel and wipe my hands of the whole thing."

"But then I showed up at your door." Scot rubbed his hands over his face. "God. Did I really threaten to hurt your business if you didn't date me?"

"Yeah. You were kind of a jerk," I pointed out. "But I get it. I do. With the same information, I might have acted similarly."

"No, you wouldn't have," Scot said with assurance. "You would've gathered all of the facts and then made a decision. I just reacted. But—"

"You thought you had the facts," I rushed to say. Scot cared deeply about his family, about his role as big brother, as protector. He wouldn't be Scot if he hadn't reacted. Though there was still a missing piece. A bit of crucial information I didn't have. "And you saw me as a threat. Like I said, Scot. I get it. I really do. But I'm glad . . . well, I'm glad we've moved beyond that. But I'd like to know—"

Ugh. I wanted to ask about the ghost, about Miranda. But

the last time I brought her up, Scot had shut down, and that wouldn't help either of us. Not when we seemed to be making headway.

"It isn't an excuse." Scot captured my hand with his. Warmth and comfort and hope swarmed my senses. He leveled his eyes with mine. "I'm sorry for what I said to you."

"Well," I admitted in complete honesty, "you weren't totally off base in your thoughts. I . . . I shouldn't have entered Magical Matchups and snooped. I'm sorry about that. Really, I am." Though if I hadn't, maybe Scot and I wouldn't be sitting here now. Fate? Possibly. Deciding it was time to put my cards on the table, regardless of the result, I said, "But this soul-mate thing. Why does your grandmother believe in our . . . um . . . connection so strongly?"

"I wish I knew. I've tried to get it out of her, but she refuses to say anything other than 'It's critical,' and to trust her." Scot swallowed a gulp of coffee. "And pushing my grandmother doesn't do any good. She clams up and does whatever she wants."

"Then we'll have to try to talk to her together. Because, Scot . . ." Beads of perspiration slicked the back of my neck and my heart picked up an extra beat. "I know we started off as pretend. I know that's all this was supposed to be. But it's changed for me. I don't understand how or why—" My words got stuck in my throat. God. Why was this so freaking hard? "My feelings for you aren't pretend. Not anymore. Maybe your grandmother is right? Maybe we are supposed to be together. Is that crazy? I—I—"

"Stop, Julia," Scot cut in, his voice firm, his tension plainly visible. "I can't say . . . There are too many things you don't know." He snapped his jaw shut and shook his head. "There are things you need to know. We can't have this discussion until you do. You might not feel the same once you hear everything."

He continued to hold my gaze, but I couldn't read him. This had to be about Leslie, whatever it was he'd tried to tell me our first morning in Las Vegas.

"This is about Leslie, right? I thought you said you two were over."

Leslie. For the first time, I understood what she'd been going through. She'd dated Scot for longer than I, and if her feelings were anywhere near as strong as mine, then seeing me—one of her best friends—kiss Scot had to have been agonizing. Much worse than Ricky abandoning me for Celeste. Yeah, now I understood. With complete and utter clarity.

Heartsick, I stood. "Then, what?" I gathered our empty plates and napkins, needing to move, needing to do anything but sit still. Opening the cupboard beneath the sink, I dragged the trash can out. He still didn't answer, and my insecurities about Leslie and the guilt I felt because of our friendship hit me hard. "Just tell me, Scot. I'm a big girl, remember? Whatever this is about . . . I need to hear it."

"Damn it, Julia. Sit down and look at me." When I didn't, he jumped out of his seat and came to me, placing his hands on my shoulders. "Look at me, Julia."

"Is this about Leslie or not?" I crumpled the paper plates and shoved them in the trash. I could handle this. Hell, if he had even one iota of feeling left for my friend, they should give it another go. Even if it killed me. After all, she had first dibs.

"Partly, but—" His gaze moved down and his grip on my shoulders tightened. "What is that?" he asked, his tone stiff and disbelieving. "That box . . ." Letting go of me, he reached into the trash and pulled out a squashed white bakery box. "This is from Elizabeth's bakery. What is this doing here?"

Startled by his sudden vehemence, I staggered backward away from him. "That's what it is. A box from her bakery. Why does it matter?"

The brown in his eyes turned almost black. His jaw, shoulders, every part of him, went rigid. Anger pooled over him, but when he spoke, it was with steady control. "Yes, Julia. How did a box from A Taste of Magic end up in your trash?"

Weird, right? Every one of my senses perked up, warning me to tread carefully. Something was wrong. Very, very wrong. This question was important. But why? "The brownies," I whispered. "You must have told Elizabeth that I had a cold? Which, actually, I didn't. I was just nervous about going out with you, after that first kiss. Anyway, she . . . um . . . delivered them on Wednesday. As a get-well thing. I thought it was nice, Scot."

I watched him continue to fight for control, still not comprehending the reason for his distress. And because I didn't understand, I didn't know what to say or how to help.

"Well, isn't this wonderful?" he said. He dropped the box in the trash and shoved his thumbs into his pockets. He stared at me for what felt like forever. My ears roared from the deafening silence, from the distance growing between us. We might have been standing miles, rather than just a few inches, apart.

I touched his arm. "I . . . I want this to be real. You and I. I want to see where this might go, if we give us a real chance."

He expelled a gravelly sigh. Angling away, he glanced at the container of brownies and then back to me. I saw his decision the second he made it, and I almost toppled over from the force of my disappointment and despair.

"This isn't going to work. I won't . . ." Scot's mouth straightened into a firm line. He closed his eyes for a long moment. "I'm sorry, but I have to go."

He was halfway to the front door before I caught up to him. "Stop! What's going on with you? Why do you care if Elizabeth baked me brownies? We were having a conversation, Scot. An important conversation. You need to know that I've never felt this way—"

Scot paused, turned on his heel and looked me straight in the eyes. "Of course you haven't. None of this is real, Julia. You deserve . . . better than this." He combed his hand through his hair. "Look, I'm sorry. I won't be bothering you again, and won't be running an ad, and I'll make damn sure my family leaves you alone from here on out."

"Scot! What—?" I clamped my lips shut. My head hurt with the want to understand, the need to change his mind. But everything I knew told me both things were impossible. I held myself straight and kept my chin up. He would not see me cry. "Are you sure?"

"Positive." For a millisecond, I was sure he was going to say more, but in the end he didn't. He just shook his head, pivoted, and let himself out.

The door closed behind him and a host of nonsensical, stupid, ridiculous, and intangible emotions exploded inside. And every one of them hurt like hell. "Well," I whispered. "I guess what they say about Las Vegas is true: what happens in Vegas, stays in Vegas."

Especially when magic was involved.

I tried to get my bearings. I tried not to cry. I reminded myself that this was ending the way it began, which shouldn't have been a surprise. And while I was curious why the bakery box had upset Scot so much, in the end, what did it matter?

Probably, he didn't want his family getting close to me—a woman he had zero intention of staying with. He didn't introduce women to his family often. It had been like a decade. So yeah, the fact that Elizabeth liked me enough to bake me something, believing I was ill, had probably made him realize we were playing a dangerous game.

I understood. I didn't like it, but I couldn't blame him.

The blame rested on *my* shoulders. On the magic I'd used to become desirable. On the spell I'd cast to ensure a passionate weekend. And as much as I hated this, as much as it hurt, as much as my heart cried out, my brain and the rational side of me knew I'd never be happy with a man who didn't want me for me.

Without conscious thought, I moved to the closet to get Scot's jacket. In his haste to get away from me he'd forgotten it. I put on the coat, hugging the leather around me, pretending that he was holding me.

I blinked and one tear, and then another, fell. I wasn't Cinderella. Scot wasn't my prince. We weren't a fairy tale. But once upon a time, he'd had feelings for Leslie. He'd believed he might love her. He was going to introduce her to his family. And she . . . well, I knew she still had feelings for him. I knew she still wanted a future with him.

Maybe my role in this really was to bring them back together. Maybe Verda had been wrong the entire time, and Leslie and Scot were meant for each other. Damn it! That made sense. So much freaking sense I nearly crumpled to the ground.

Leslie had gone to Magical Matchups before me. Leslie already had feelings for Scot. They had a history. And yes, she'd made a mistake. A horrible mistake. But she regretted her actions. The only reason Verda focused on me was because I'd gotten stuck at her place, and the only reason I was there at all was because Leslie and Kara had backed out of our agreement. All of it started with Leslie. *She* should have received the journal and the magic. Not me. And all I'd done was muck everything up.

Tears sped down my cheeks. My eyes burned. My throat was raw with emotion, with the sobbing that wouldn't stop. I pulled my spine straight, thought everything through, and made a decision. Maybe the hardest decision of my life. I could fix this. I could set things straight. *I* could give them another chance, if I was strong enough. If I put my own selfish wants and desires on the back burner.

I ran to my bedroom before I could change my mind. With Scot's scent around me, with the feel of his jacket on my body, I retrieved the journal and grabbed a pen. This wish was important. I had to do it right. I didn't want to force anyone to be with anyone—I'd learned my lesson there. I just wanted to open the door of opportunity, so if Scot and Leslie chose to step through they might have a chance for that happy ending. For a love like my parents'. That was the greatest gift I could give.

I wiped the wetness from my cheeks and wrote,

If there is any chance at all for Scot and Leslie to find happiness with each other, then my wish is for them to erase the past so they can forge a new future—but only with honesty, and only if this is what they both desire.

The magic came alive instantly. It whirled around me, through me, heating my skin and the air with the weight, the electrifying sizzle, of power. I closed my eyes, my breathing rapid, as my body rippled from the energy of my spell. It was stronger than ever before. More intense. More vibrant and vivid. More everything. And every second hurt like nothing I'd experienced.

When the magic finally ebbed away, I curled into a ball, knees to chest, and cried. Sobbed, really. I didn't try to stop my tears, and I didn't try to rationalize them away. I simply let myself feel.

Chapter Eighteen

I stayed home on Monday and ate Elizabeth's brownies, watched *Seinfeld*, and cried. I thought about calling Verda to get some of my questions answered but couldn't face the reality of actually picking up the phone, dialing her number, and delving into magic, ghosts, soul mates, and anything else she might say.

Missing Scot was a physical ache. After spending three nights with him, it seemed incomprehensible that he wasn't with me. I also recognized how foolish—maudlin, even—I was behaving. I'd always laughed at those sappy heroines in movies and books who climbed into their beds for days, stuffing their faces with junk food over a broken heart. Over some guy. When the bruised woman was Kara, I'd pat her back and offer her comfort, but inside I'd shake my head in disbelief. Now, I understood. A part of me hated that.

That didn't stop me from eating another brownie. It didn't halt my tears or ease the hollow ache deep inside. And it sure as hell didn't stop me from missing Scot. Or from hoping he'd stop by, even if it was only to pick up his jacket. I yearned to see him, to talk to him.

Tuesday was much the same. Kara came over twice, but I told her I was ill. It didn't feel like a lie. I attempted going to work on Wednesday but made it as far as my closet before giving up and crawling back to the couch to call Diane. She'd already worked two full days due to my absences, and this would be the third. My winnings from Vegas would pay for her extra hours, though, so I didn't care. I even canceled dinner with my parents so I could stay home and mope.

I fell into a chocolate-induced coma late in the day. I woke up with hair sweat-plastered to the side of my face, and a stomachache from my nutrition-absent, sweets-heavy menu. My mouth was dry, my throat hurt, and pain pounded at my temples.

I stumbled to the bathroom to swallow a few Tylenol and, in the process, caught sight of my reflection in the mirror. My wrinkled T-shirt had two coffee stains and one I didn't recognize. Orange juice, maybe. The pale skin below my puffy eyes was bruised with purple shadows. My cheeks were devoid of color. Seriously. My skin resembled the shade of a bottle of Wite-Out, only whiter. And my hair . . . my God, what a mess. I looked a little—okay, a lot—like the bride of Frankenstein, only worse. So. Much. Worse.

Laughter bubbled up and out as I stared in shock. Who the hell was this person? How had I allowed myself to drop to this level? Screw this! I didn't need it. I hadn't asked for it. I hadn't gone looking for magic, ghosts, or Scot. I hadn't even believed it possible to fall in love, so I certainly hadn't gone looking for *that*. But the damn universe, destiny, fate—whatever—decided to give me a wake-up call and had swooped in and changed every last freaking thing. In two weeks my view of the world turned upside down, shifted focus, and I'd gone and fallen in love. Any rational person would say that was impossible. But I was living proof that it wasn't.

My laughter subsided. Anger rolled in. I wanted to scream at someone, kick something, demand answers. Why me? Why now? And why Scot? I could have learned the exact same lesson by falling for . . . for Jameson. Now, not only did I love a man I couldn't have, but I knew what I was missing. Oh, and let's not forget Introductions. Not only did I want a fairy-tale relationship, but I wanted a damn job that I loved.

"Thank you, Universe," I muttered as I stripped off my

clothes. In two weeks, I'd gained a world of knowledge and had come up empty-handed. I had nothing that I wanted. "Thanks for showing me how little I knew about everything, teasing me with what could be, and then ripping it all away."

I turned the shower on full blast. I was done moping. I was done with self-pity. Maybe I couldn't have Scot, but I could sure as hell get some questions answered, and I could sure as hell do something with my life that gave me pleasure. And it wasn't Introductions, and it wasn't working at my father's firm. Of course, I didn't have a clue as to what this mystery profession might be, but I'd figure it out. And someday, if I were absurdly lucky, I'd meet another man who would turn my knees to Jell-O. A man I would love, who would love me, and Scot would become nothing but a distant memory.

Tears ran down my cheeks, mingling with the hot spray of the shower. I'd spoken strong words, but who was I trying to fool? No one could replace Scot. He'd never be a distant memory, and if my wish worked, and if Leslie and I somehow managed to remain friends, he'd still be in my life . . . as *her* man. And I'd have no choice but to learn to live with that.

I went to work two hours early on Thursday. Ignoring work for three days because of heartache was stupid and self-indulgent. It didn't matter that I'd made a decision about Introductions; I still had responsibilities there. Diane deserved a little notice before she was out of a job. I also had clients to inform, plans to make, and an office to empty.

I began the day by drafting a letter to my clients, explaining that Introductions would be closing its doors within thirty days. Within the letter, I included my apologies, the offer of a full refund for anyone who'd joined Introductions in the past two months, and a glowing recommendation for Magical

Matchups. This, sadly, took a lot less time than it should have. I simply didn't have that many active clients left.

I posted a similar letter to the company Web site, added date limitations to the current client profiles, and disabled the new-client section altogether. The lease for my office didn't expire for several months; I jotted a note to call the building's management company to see if we could work something out. I made a list of other accounts I needed to cancel, whom I owed money, and who still owed me money.

All of these steps should have been difficult. But other than a twinge of regret at saying good-bye to something I'd worked so hard at, it was strangely easy. Of course, almost anything would have seemed easy in comparison to saying good-bye to Scot.

Finally, I wrote a letter of reference for Diane. This was hard. She had stuck by me, had put her trust in me, and now she was going to be out of a job. I called her into my office as soon as she arrived and gave her the news. She took it better than I expected. We agreed she'd stick around for at least two weeks, but if she didn't find something else in that time frame, she'd stay until the end. I added two weeks of severance to the money I owed her. It wasn't enough, but it was all I could manage.

By the end of the day, I was exhausted but motivated. Now I just had to come up with a plan for after Introductions closed. Preferably something that didn't include moving in with my parents. Or traveling the country with them in their RV. Something to do with food, I was thinking. I hadn't decided exactly what, but I figured that would come to me sooner or later.

That night, worn out from my up and down emotions and the day's activities, I dropped into sleep easily. Almost instantly. I dreamed of a woman with long, luxurious dark hair. She had ruby red lips, pale white skin, and deep brown eyes. Colors and light rippled around her, reminding me of a crystal prism hanging in a window, turning the sunlight into a rainbow. In my dream she hovered beside my bed, her mouth moving frantically as if she were talking to me, telling me something of extreme importance, but no matter how hard I tried, I couldn't hear her voice or make out her words.

I woke with a gasp. Clammy sweat coated my skin, and the scent of roses lingered in the air. I sat up, turned on the bedside lamp, and searched the room. No one was with me. Or at least no one I could see when awake. I rubbed my arms, trying to chase away the chill, trying to calm the crazy beat of my heart. Both were impossible.

Under the cover of sleep, in the guise of a dream, I'd come face-to-face with Miranda, Scot's great-great-great-grandmother's ghost. I was as sure of that as I was of the power of the journal. But what had she wanted? What had she tried to tell me?

"Miranda," I said in a loud and clear voice. "I'm not afraid. You're welcome to be here. If there is something you want me to know, please come back. Please try again."

I waited and watched, wondered and hoped. But she didn't miraculously appear before me, and after a while the scent of roses disappeared. I was alone again.

With a sigh, I hugged a pillow to my chest, breathed slowly in and out, and concentrated on relaxing every muscle in my body. Maybe Miranda needed me to be asleep to show herself. Maybe our connection was stronger then. I didn't know, but it was worth a shot. I desperately wanted to hear what she had to say.

The next day, I yawned and rubbed my eyes while staring at nothing out my office window. Miranda hadn't delivered an encore performance. Though maybe that was because I hadn't fallen into a deep sleep again. Or maybe my dream had been just that—a dream. I probably hadn't really seen Miranda. In all likelihood, I was looking so hard for signs that my subconscious gave me one.

Especially since the woman in my dream resembled Elizabeth and Alice. She had the same dark hair and eyes as both women, though her willowy frame reminded me more of Alice than Elizabeth. Still, if my brain wanted to conjure Miranda, then who else would she look like than her great-great-great-granddaughters?

But even if Miranda hadn't tried to connect with me through my dream, she had been in my room. The roses were not figments of my imagination. I was sure of that.

I pushed away the hope of what a visit from Miranda might mean. The facts hadn't changed. Scot and I weren't real—on his end of the equation, anyway. On some level, he'd recognized that, and I had no choice but to respect his decision.

Swiveling in my chair, I returned my attention to my computer monitor. I was still trying to narrow down what I would do when Introductions closed. So far, besides the vague decision of finding a food-related career, the only thing I knew was that I had no desire to run a business. I wanted to go to work, do something I enjoyed, and clock out at the end of the day and come home.

The business line rang. Diane was at the post office, mailing my end-of-the-company letters, so I picked up. "Introductions," I said. "This is Julia."

"Julia! This is Zita Hildebrandt."

Ack. I'd never checked in with Zita or Darryl about their second date. "I was just about to call you," I lied. "To see how your date with Darryl went."

"Well, that's why I'm calling," Zita said, her tone hesitant.

"It's okay, Zita," I said, thinking of Jameson. "Sometimes

what looks good on paper is anything but good in real life. I shouldn't have pushed you to go out with Darryl again. If it isn't right, it isn't right."

"That's just it. I'm glad you pushed. We . . . ah . . . had a terrific time. Just not with each other. I like Darryl, and he was definitely more relaxed, but we don't zing, you know?" Zita rushed on to explain that she'd set up a double date, hoping that another couple would help Darryl relax. She'd brought a friend of hers, and Darryl had brought a friend of his. "We were totally with the wrong people."

I blinked in confusion and tried to keep up. "Wait a minute, Zita. You're telling me that you and Darryl's friend hit it off, and Darryl and your friend—"

"Yes! Through Darryl, who you matched me with, I found a guy I really like. We have a ton in common, too. He's a single father, completely devoted to his daughter, and I . . . I looked into his eyes and something clicked. So I wanted to thank you for setting me up with Darryl."

I laughed at the absurdity of the situation. My matchmaking skills—for the past year, at least—were crap, but somehow two of my clients were walking away happy. I'd take it. "I'm glad for you, but no thanks are necessary. This was your doing."

"It *is* because of you! Fate led me to Introductions. You led me to Darryl. And Darryl led me to Adam," Zita said. "But I think I'm done with Introductions for now. I want to see what happens with Adam before going out with anyone else."

"It's funny you say that." I explained that Introductions was closing its doors. We talked for a few minutes before I wished Zita luck and disconnected the call.

Fate again. Only for Zita, it had worked in her favor. I went through my chain of fate once more and came up with the same answer, the one that had led me to cast the wish for Leslie and Scot. But if that were the case, then why would I have fallen so hard and fast? I looked at all the pieces and parts again, trying to find a loophole that would give credence to my hope, to the love I felt for Scot.

Introductions failing led me to Kara and Leslie for help. That led me to Magical Matchups, which brought me to Verda, who led me to Scot, which then led me back to Leslie and her feelings for him. So yeah, this, as much as I wished otherwise, seemed to be about Scot and Leslie. The trail was solid.

"That's that. Stop obsessing." Easier said than done, but I tried. Really, I did. But something sat there on the edge of my consciousness, distracting me from everything else I needed to do.

Shortly after two o'clock, I gave up all pretenses of work, told Diane we were closing for the day, and took off. I drove aimlessly for a while, my brain still attempting to work out the impossible. I knew the answer I wanted to reach, but couldn't get there. Two plus two doesn't equal five, no matter how often you add the numbers. The answer is four. The answer is *always* four.

"But I want it to be five." I gripped the steering wheel tighter. "I need it to be five. Why can't the freaking answer be five?"

I blinked against tears. No more crying. I'd had enough of crying. Instead of giving in to my urge to go home and crawl into bed to sob like a love-struck teenager, I aimed my car toward my parents' house.

I used my key to let myself in. My mother was in her office with a large map spread out on her antique desk. I didn't see Dad, but it was a little early for him to be home.

"This is a surprise, Julia," my mother said, glancing up from the map to see me hovering in her doorway. "Did we have plans I forgot about?"

"No, Mom. I . . . didn't mean to interrupt. Do you have a minute to talk?"

She tilted her head to the side and appraised me. I wondered what she saw, if my misery was written on my face and in my body language. "Of course I do. Would you like some tea? I can have Rosalie—"

I started crying then. Loud, engulfing sobs that shook my body. She froze, shocked by my sudden show of emotion. In two beats of my heart, she was up and to me, urgently patting me down. As if she were a cop searching for a concealed weapon.

"What is it? Are you okay?" Her hands stilled on my arms. "Are you hurt?"

"No . . . yes . . . Not like you mean, but yes." Another sob wrenched out from a raw place deep within. "Yes, I'm hurt. And afraid. And confused." I hiccupped. "And angry. I have just about every emotion going here, Mom."

Understanding and concern coated her expression. "I see. Well then, darling, let's get you calm so you can tell me what's going on."

I let her lead me to the small sofa in her office. We sat down and she patted my knee, a small, uncomfortable action meant to offer me comfort. I laughed through my sobs. The magic hadn't changed her so much after all. She raised her eyebrow in question.

"I'm in love," I said, as if that explained everything. Maybe it did. "With a man I can't be with. With a man I shouldn't even love."

"Scot?" she guessed, handing me a tissue. I nodded and blew my nose. "Why can't you be with him? He isn't married, is he?"

"No, nothing like that."

"Then tell me what it is like." She tucked a loose strand of hair behind my ear. "Why can't you and Scot be together?"

In a halting voice, I told her as much of the story as I could. Meaning, everything except for magic and ghosts. I even admitted how I'd entered Magical Matchups in my desperation to find a fix for Introductions. By the time I was done, I felt calmer than I had for days. I shrugged. "So you can see how impossible this is. I probably don't love him, right? I mean, you're the one who told me never to trust my heart."

A startled expression flitted over her. "When did I tell you that?"

"When I was twelve and Ricky Luca broke mine." God, it was so long ago, she probably didn't even remember.

She surprised me.

"Oh, that? Honey, you were just a baby. I wanted you to focus on your schoolwork, on being a girl and enjoying your friends. Love is such a sticky thing." She shook her head. "I hated seeing you so upset when you had your entire life in front of you. And I guess I wasn't ready to see you grow up. Falling for a boy was a sure sign you weren't my little girl anymore."

Confusion welled inside. "So I *should* trust my heart?"

"There isn't a yes or no answer, my dear."

"Great. That helps a lot," I said in a semisarcastic tone. "How do I know if I love him or not? And why did it take me so long to feel this way about someone?"

"Oh, you love him all right. You're a perfectionist, Julia. It doesn't surprise me at all that you waited for the right man to sweep you off your feet." Mom squeezed my hand in both of hers. "The question is, what are you going to do about it now?"

"Leave him alone. There is nothing else I can do." She snorted in a very unladylike way. "Scot walked away from me, Mom."

"Then you need to find out why. He has feelings for you. Your father and I both saw that clear as day. We were quite impressed by him."

Well, yeah. That was when my spell had been going strong. "I don't think he does. I think he . . . got carried away by spending the weekend together."

"Men do not work so hard to impress a girl's father unless there are serious emotions involved." Mom offered me another tissue. "Blow your nose, darling. Why can't you see what we saw? Why, your father even admitted he was wrong about you and Jameson."

And that reminded me of the bet. "Did you know Dad made a bet with Jameson to come into Introductions pretending to be someone else? Just to see if I could figure it out?"

"I did, and I scolded him for it. But he wants you to be happy. We both do." My mother's blue eyes softened in emotion. "You've always been so focused. We wanted to see you loosen up and have a little fun. Jameson seemed like a—"

"Good match," I said, finishing her sentence. "And I agree. It would've been a heck of a lot easier if I could've fallen for him."

"Love isn't about easy." Mom sat back and crossed her legs. "Your dad and I had to conquer serious opposition from our families to be together."

"Did Grandma and Granddad really dislike Dad that much?"

"Yes, but his parents weren't that fond of me, either. You see, they both had ideas of whom their children should be with, and our fathers were often on opposite sides in business. Your father felt the weight of my father's dislike, so Gregory worked himself to the bone to prove that he was a good provider."

Emotion made my mother's voice waver. She coughed to clear her throat. "And I . . . Well, let's just say that Mother Collins never believed I was good enough for her son."

"That sucks." Ineloquent, but true. "How did you and Dad manage?"

"It wasn't easy, and for a lot of our years, we became so bogged down in doing everything we were supposed to do that we forgot to enjoy our life together. We forgot to enjoy you."

Okay. Well, that explained a lot. "Do you ever regret following your heart? I mean, with all the problems and—"

"Not even for a second. After thirty-plus years of marriage, I can tell you that every minute of difficulty has paid off in spades."

"But wouldn't it have been easier if you'd followed your parents' wishes and—?"

She cut me off with a wave of her hand. "Easier, maybe. I have regrets, but none of them have anything to do with marrying your father." She was silent for a minute, and then asked, "You love this young man, correct?"

"Yes," I answered instantly. "But—"

"That's all you need to know to move forward. Maybe I'm wrong and Scot doesn't have feelings for you, but what if he does?"

Well, she had a point there. Partially, anyway. "You're right. But there's more to this."

"There always is, but that doesn't matter. Even if it's all complicated and messy, you'll never forgive yourself if you don't try." Mom opened her arms. I scooted into them for one of her rare hugs. It was nice. Maybe I wasn't the touchy-feely-phobe I thought.

"Thank you," I said when we separated. "I don't know what I'm going to do, but just talking about it helped."

"You're welcome. I'm always here if you need me." She

twisted her fingers together nervously. "You're such a contained, capable young lady. You always have been. I'm sorry you're going through this, but I am . . . pleased you came to me."

Tears sprang to life again, albeit for a different reason. "I thought you wanted me to be contained and capable. Perfect. I didn't think I *could* come to you."

"And I thought you didn't need me. I looked for ways to insert myself into your life." She shook her head in disbelief, and humor danced into her eyes. "God forgive me, but I became my mother."

I started laughing. "Lamb, Mom. You do know I hate lamb, right?"

She blinked several times, but then she laughed, too. "Well, I never had Rosalie prepare lamb for the sole purpose of upsetting you, but . . . yes, I am well aware of your dislike."

"I knew it!" I wiped away tears of laughter. "There's something else I need to tell you. Two things, actually."

"Are you pregnant?"

"Nope," I said lightly. But Verda's proclamation of three boys whisked into my mind. I glanced at my mother's desk, at the spread-out map, to center me. "When did you and Dad decide to do the RV thing?"

"What a strange question. Traveling the country has always been our plan. I began to doubt if it would ever happen, what with your father's love for his work."

"Okay. But when did you make the decision to go ahead with that?" It was imperative that I find out how much of my parents' behavior was natural, and how much was magical.

"Several months ago. Your father came home one night and said he was ready." Curiosity edged into her voice. "Why is this important?"

"I . . . um . . . just wondered. You never mentioned it before." Several months meant their vagabond decision had zip to do with my spell. Huge relief, there. "How have you been this last week or so? Feeling any different? Better or worse?"

"Better, I suppose. Less tense." She tipped her head to the side, watching me. "Now that I think about it, there was a change in your father and me. We seem to have found our rhythm again . . . something we've both tried to recapture for years. But somehow, it suddenly became effortless." She shrugged. "We're both happier, less inclined to fill our days with silly social functions. Is that what you wanted to know?"

"Yes. And you still feel like yourself?" I asked.

"Who else would I feel like?"

"No one. I . . . well, I've been worried about you and Dad. He's doing okay, too? You haven't noticed anything weird with him, have you?"

"Nothing weird. We're both looking forward to retirement."

Whew. So my spell *had* helped them. How cool was that? "Good. I'm glad. So . . . ah . . . if given the choice, would you change anything about the past couple of weeks?"

"Absolutely not." Then, obviously deciding she'd had enough of my odd questions, she returned to her desk. "I've already started mapping out our journey. We plan on traveling through the summer and fall. We'll return here for the winter, and head back out in the spring."

"I thought you were selling the house."

"We are, but we'll buy a smaller home. Maybe a condominium. We always want our home base to be near you."

"What if I don't stay in Chicago?" Not that I'd given any thought to moving.

"Why wouldn't you?" She highlighted a section of the map. "Your father's firm is here. I expect you'll find it easier to continue living in or near Chicago."

"That's the other thing we need to discuss." I steeled myself the best I could. "I have no intentions of taking over Dad's firm. I don't mind helping out for a while. I can even stay on long enough to look for and train someone, if that's necessary. But I—"

This snagged her attention. "So, you've found a way to save Introductions?"

"No. I'll be shutting down in the next month."

"Introductions is closing and you're not going to work in Gregory's company, even though that was the agreement you made?" she clarified.

I pulled myself straight. "Yes, Mother. That's right."

"Well," she said calmly. We could've been talking about the weather. "That is good news, darling. It's about time you came to your senses. Your father will be pleased. Stay for dinner so we can tell him together."

"What? I thought you said . . . He said . . ."

"Yes, we did. But we had to do something to push you out of your comfort zone." Mom tipped her chin, and I saw so many things in her gaze: pride, concern, love . . . relief? "You haven't been happy for a long while. Your father believed if we pressured you, if we made you think we were going to hold you to our agreement, you might push back. And now you have." She tossed me a smile of satisfaction. "Yes, this is very good news."

Well, hell. That was unexpected.

Chapter Nineteen

My eyes whipped open to the early light of dawn. Urgency flooded me. I had to do something. I had to . . . to . . . what?

A soft, lilting voice whispered in my mind. The fragrant, almost overpowering scent of roses filled the air, tickling my nose. Dark, fathomless eyes seared my consciousness. Ruby red lips. Colors—so many colors. I gasped.

Miranda. I dreamed of her. She spoke to me, and this time I'd heard her.

Oh, God. What had she said? I jumped from the bed and raced to the other room for my notebook and a pen. I scrawled the words as they came to me, my hand stuttering to a stop when my memory blanked out. I tried to remember more, tried to remember everything, but couldn't. It was gone. I read the partial message—if that's what it was—slowly.

"Silly girl," I said, hearing Miranda's voice instead of mine. "You fought so hard for what you don't love but cast away what you do. Have you learned nothing? Trust in your heart. Believe . . ."

Believe what? I blinked and read the words again. *Trust in my heart. Fight for what I love.* "Well, yeah. Makes perfect sense, when you say it like this."

I sat on the couch for a while, reading Miranda's words over and over, considering everything I knew and wondering about all I didn't. Then I retrieved the journal and read the wish I'd written for Leslie and Scot. Relief sank in, along with a good amount of hope. As upset as I'd been when casting this wish, as sure as I'd been that my role was to bring them together, I'd left the outcome wide open. Even more importantly, I'd left the outcome up to them. Not to magic.

I thought about the night in my kitchen. About the brownies and Scot's reaction. About my belief that our weekend in Vegas was caused solely by magic. *My* magic. Or rather, Verda's magic. Pieces of knowledge wove together to create a bigger picture, one that filled in some of the blanks.

My rational brain urged me to connect the dots. That first night with Scot, he'd said something about his family—Verda, Chloe, Elizabeth, and Alice—and how I didn't want them combining their wills to turn us into a couple. And then, at Alice's house, Elizabeth said that they were all "harmless," and everyone had laughed. Well, everyone except for me and Isobel—the same Isobel who didn't believe in Verda's mystical mumbo jumbo.

"None of this is real, Julia," Scot had said. And then, "I'll make damn sure my family leaves you alone from here on out."

Oh, dear Lord. Scot hadn't really meant their *wills*. He'd meant their *magic*. They were all magical, not only Verda. So . . . what? He thought the reasons I wanted to stay with him, the reasons for my feelings, were because of magic? His family's magic. And based on his reaction to the bakery box, he thought it had something to do with the brownies. Brownies from Elizabeth's bakery, A Taste of *Magic*, that she had baked and personally delivered.

Yes. This was it. *This* was the reason he'd walked away. Or at least an important part of the reason. But he was wrong. My feelings for Scot hadn't happened in the time it takes to eat a freaking brownie. They'd been there all along, growing stronger with every look, every touch, every conversation. Hell, every time I smelled him. My feelings were real.

Could his feelings be real as well? Would our weekend have happened even without my spell? I flipped through the pages of the journal to read the exact words I'd written in Vegas. *Desirable. Beautiful. Seductive. Passionate.*

But I hadn't wished for Scot to fall for me. I hadn't altered his feelings with magic. I hadn't even named him specifically. That spell had been all about me. About how I wanted to feel. And it had worked. I *had* felt more beautiful, more desirable, and more seductive than ever before.

Okay, this was good. This gave me hope. Though I had also wished for a passionate weekend. So was our lovemaking a result of that, or would we have tumbled into bed together anyway? There was no way to know. Not for sure. But he'd raced here, to my place, to make sure I was okay the night I was worried about my parents. He'd kissed me in the hallway, and again on the couch. And he'd held my hand and talked me through my fears on the airplane.

Well, I couldn't know for sure if our intimacy last weekend was the result of magic, but I didn't think it was. Not entirely, anyway. Hell, I didn't even know if any of my thoughts were correct. Because, come on, all of this certainly did not equal the simplest explanation. Instead, it was convoluted, crazy, perhaps even bordering on desperation, but I didn't care. In a rational world, two plus two never equals five. But maybe, just maybe, in an irrational world, one filled with ghosts and magic and fairy tales, it did.

I had to find out. Even if I was wrong. My mother was right: I'd never forgive myself if I didn't.

A light breeze wafted through the room, ruffling my hair and brushing my cheeks with a rose-perfumed kiss. In approval? Maybe. Hopefully.

An idea came to me, and I smiled. "Hey, Miranda? Do me a favor and have Verda, Elizabeth, and Chloe meet me at Alice's house. Say, around ten or so? It's time we all talked."

In the snap of a finger, the breeze and the fragrance

disappeared. I took their absence as a sign of Miranda's agreement to my request. And yes, I could've used the phone, but it seemed fitting to use the family ghost to pass on my message.

You know, when in Rome, do as the Romans do.

"You all have a lot of explaining to do," I said to Scot's sisters, grandmother, and cousin. We were in Alice's living room, and even with everything I'd seen, I was somehow still surprised to find them all here. On time, even. Miranda sure knew how to get a message across.

Verda shifted in her seat. Elizabeth and Alice exchanged a look I couldn't identify. Chloe broke the silence. "That will be difficult. Scot made us promise we'd keep certain things to ourselves. So maybe you should start, Julia."

Verda's blue eyes twinkled. "Yes, dear. Why don't you tell us why you brought us here. Once we know that, I'm sure we girls can figure out a way to give you the information you need without breaking our promise to my mule-headed grandson."

Scot had made them all promise? No wonder I hadn't heard anything from Verda. I looked at her. "First, I need to apologize to you. I lied to you from the beginning, Verda. I'm sorry about that, and I hope you'll forgive me. But you see . . . Well, I own a dating service, and—"

"Yes, yes. Introductions." Verda winked. "I know how to use Google. And people don't keep secrets from me for long. You're forgiven, dear. Let's move on, please."

"Okay. Well, thank you. That certainly makes things easier." Now what? Should I simply tell them everything I knew, everything I thought I knew, and go from there? Deciding that was the best avenue, I started with the journal, which I pulled from my purse. "Scot doesn't know about this, does he?"

Verda shook her head. "But I don't see why we need to discuss that now."

"What is that, Grandma?" Elizabeth and Alice asked at the same time.

"Oh, nothing really. I've found it . . . ah . . . helps my clients if they write their thoughts down." Verda narrowed her eyes at me. "Julia, dear, that is for your private use. We discussed that, didn't we?"

Chloe gasped. Her eyes rounded. "You didn't . . . Oh, you did." She reached a hand out. "Can I see the journal?"

My cheeks grew warm, but I passed it over. "Please don't read beyond the inscription from Verda. The rest is . . . personal."

After reading the inscription, Chloe gave the book to Alice, who then gave it to Elizabeth. "You gave Julia the ability to use your magic?" Elizabeth asked. "That was a risky move, Grandma. I didn't even know that was possible."

"I did, and yes, it is. But that's of no concern right now." Verda straightened her frail shoulders in a defensive line. "She needed the magic. And it brought her here, so there's no harm done." Verda's lips twitched. "You did need the magic, Julia. You can see that, can't you?"

"Yes," I answered. "Finding out that magic is real was my first step in believing in . . . well, in love. In ghosts. In . . . in soul mates."

"But magic can be dangerous. Unpredictable." Alice reclaimed the journal and gave it back to me. "Anything could have happened, Grandma."

Verda huffed out an exasperated breath. "I took the proper precautions." Focusing on me, she said, "Did anything bad happen as a result of your wishes?"

"No. Not at all." But I'd used the magic sparingly and with great caution. Well, except for the passion spell. Still, maybe *rational* and *practical* weren't such bad adjectives, after all.

I stood and crossed the room. "But Verda, as much as I appreciate this gift, I don't want it anymore. I don't need it anymore, either." I put the journal in her hands. "I need you to take this back."

She accepted the book with a nod, and I returned to my seat.

"Do all of you have powers of some sort? Magic . . . whatever?" I asked.

Uneasiness drifted through the room, but no one spoke. Apparently, I'd stepped solidly into one of the no-no topics.

"Fine. I'll take that as a yes. Can you somehow tell me more? Because Scot became really upset when he realized I had brownies from Elizabeth's bakery."

"Why do you think that is?" Elizabeth asked. "If you say something first, I'll tell you whatever you want to know on that topic."

"Your magic is through your baking," I guessed. "Scot thinks you cast a wish in regard to my feelings for him, and that's why he was upset." If I weren't so keyed-up, I might have laughed at the look on Elizabeth's face. "How am I doing?"

"Quite well, actually. And you know who Miranda is?" Elizabeth prodded.

"A ghost. Your great-great-great-grandmother."

"Yes. Have you given any thought to who she was in life?" This came from Alice.

"No. But . . . Oh! The magic comes from her," I guessed. Alice's nod told me I was right. "And that would have to mean she was a . . . a witch?"

Verda laughed. "Not quite, but close enough to hear the rest. Her name is Miranda Ayres, and she was a Gypsy with great power."

"She almost cursed the man who broke her heart, but instead created a gift to be passed from one daughter to another," Chloe jumped in. "And that gift is—"

"Magic," Elizabeth said. "But it manifests itself differently in each of her daughters. You already know that Grandma Verda's power is in her writing."

"And yours is in your baking," I said, glancing at Alice and then Chloe. "What about you two?"

"Mine is gone. Well, kind of. For the most part." Chloe shrugged as if the admission weren't a big deal, but I kind of thought there was a story behind that. She didn't look eager to share it at the moment, though. "And Alice can use her artwork to create pictures of the past and the future. Drawings and paintings."

I thought of the beautiful painting in Verda's office at Magical Matchups. Now I understood how Alice re-created a scene from so long ago without a photograph. With magic. Wow. An entire family of Gypsies.

At some point I hoped to hear more, but today I was on a mission. Returning my attention to Elizabeth, I asked, "So, did you cast a wish on those brownies?"

"I did, but not the wish Scot thought. I know better than to alter anyone's feelings." Elizabeth squirmed, and guilt flashed over her features. "Because of the . . . of things that Grandma has shared with me, I also believe that it's important for Scot to find his soul mate."

"So you think Verda's right, and Scot and I are . . . supposed to be together?" As soon as I asked, I wished I hadn't. Never ask a question to which you might not like the answer.

Elizabeth bit her lip and glanced at Alice. "I don't know. But Grandma is sure. I wanted to give you both a chance, in case she was right."

Fair enough. "So, what was your wish?"

"That you and Scot would relax your defenses a little, so you might be able to really get to know each other. That was it. I'm careful in how I use the magic, Julia. I know you have no reason to believe me, but—"

"I do believe you." I mean, why would she lie? "Does Scot know this?" Because if he did, if he knew magic wasn't to blame for my feelings, then why hadn't he contacted me?

"He does. But he . . . well, he's stubborn. Once he heard everything, he . . ." Elizabeth sighed. "I can't say anything else on this topic. Not without breaking my promise."

"Please, Elizabeth. I came here because of a ghost. Your great-great-great-grandmother. Doesn't that mean anything?"

"It does. It means a lot, but I can't. I'm sorry, Julia," Elizabeth said. And she was. I could hear it in her voice. "But Scot has his reasons. He's my brother. I have to stand behind him."

"Right. Of course." I tried to work out what my next step should be but came up blank. I mean, yeah, I planned on talking with Scot, but it would help hugely if I knew more. My rational brain demanded as many facts as possible before putting my heart on the firing line again. "Did . . . did he say how he feels about me?"

Heavy silence drenched the room. My heart cracked.

"Not in so many words," Chloe said carefully. "He was just very adamant in us leaving you alone."

"Well, yeah. If he's worried you're all going to magically coerce me . . ." I tried to make a joke out of it, but no one laughed. The atmosphere in the room reminded me of the calm before a storm. "Why does he want you to leave me alone?"

No one answered. There was something else they weren't sharing. "Verda? Why is it so important that Scot find his soul mate?"

She shifted her gaze away from me. "I can't say."

Tension swirled in the air, thick and heavy. "Well, what *can* you say?"

Verda didn't respond. It was obvious she wanted to. Her entire body angled forward, and in her eyes, I saw that if I pushed, she'd give in and tell me everything. It was on the tip of my tongue to do just that, but then I thought of Scot. Of how much he loved his family. I couldn't—wouldn't—be the reason any of these women broke a promise. That could hurt their relationship with Scot, and mine too, if we ever got that far.

Fine. I'd pull up my big-girl pants, shield my heart the best I could, and go directly to the source. Probably what I should've done in the first place.

"This was a mistake. I'm so sorry I put you all in this position. Please forgive me." I looked at Elizabeth, then Alice, then Chloe, and finally, Verda. "I truly hope I see you all again. Thank you for doing what you could."

"I have faith," Chloe said with a smile. "Go get him, Julia. I'm rooting for you."

"Thanks," I said again.

Somehow, I managed to make a graceful exit. And hey, not one tear. I was making progress. I crawled into my car and laid my forehead on the steering wheel. God, that conversation was out-of-the-ballpark odd.

A sharp rap sounded off next to my ear. I looked up and saw Alice. She gestured to roll the window down. I did that one better and opened the door.

"Actually, can I slide in the other side? Just for a minute?" she asked with a quick look over her shoulder. "It won't take long."

"Sure. Hop in."

She did, and when both doors were closed she turned toward me. Her wide brown eyes held worry but also warmth. Huge surprise. "The other night, when you were here for dinner, I wasn't very welcoming. I owe you an apology, Julia. My rudeness really wasn't about you—which isn't an excuse, but it is the truth."

I took her words at face value and nodded. "It's cool, Alice. I appreciate the apology."

"Thank you . . . but I'd like to explain. Grandma came to us a while back, before she opened Magical Matchups, and told us that she had to find Scot's soul mate. That it was imperative," Alice said, her voice quavering. "She didn't tell us why, but she . . . she believed that she had to do this quickly. Before she dies."

"Oh! Oh, God, Alice. That had to have been difficult to hear." Especially in a family where magic and ghosts were fact and not fiction.

"Exactly. I love her. I don't want to lose her, even though I know I'll have to face that eventually, whether Scot falls in love or not. But this belief of hers—"

"Programmed you not to like me the second Verda said I'm Scot's soul mate." Whoa. Yep, that would account for Alice's chilly attitude. I couldn't even blame her. But I didn't know what to say, other than "I'm sorry."

Tears sparkled in Alice's eyes. "But that's not why I wanted to talk to you in private."

"I really would prefer you not break a promise to Scot, Alice. I—"

"I'm not. He doesn't know about this." Reaching into her coat, Alice pulled out a folded piece of paper. A shiver of anticipation mixed with apprehension trickled over me. "I drew this the other night, after everyone left."

"Is this one of your"—I gulped—"magical drawings?"

"It is. Before you look at it, though, there's something you need to understand about the way my magic works." She paused, considered her words, and then said, "I recently learned that my drawings of the future are not always absolute. With Chloe, I actually drew four different pictures depicting four different futures."

"Oh." I sifted this information and realized that even magic can be rational. Who knew? "That sounds right, Alice. Our actions and decisions can shift our future from one minute to the next, right? So whatever you drew the night I had dinner here might already have changed."

"Maybe. I don't know." She offered me the paper. "But I think it's worthwhile for you to look at this."

I accepted the drawing but didn't open it immediately. I believed what I'd just said, so no matter what future this drawing depicted, that didn't mean I hadn't already altered my course. But my want to know was strong. How could I not look? Besides, I'd come here today to get all of the facts. This was another to add to the pile.

"Okay. I'm going to open it." I inhaled a deep breath. "Now. I'm going to open it now."

I unfolded the paper quickly, before doubt could set in. When the drawing was open fully, I stared, trying to make sense of what I saw. "This looks like a family portrait."

"Yes," Alice said. She leaned in closer and pointed. "I'm here with Ethan and Rose. Look how beautiful she is! Elizabeth and Nate are over here, with a toddler on his lap." I didn't have to see Alice's face to know she was grinning. "Chloe and Ben . . . and look, they have *two* babies. Joe is standing in the back, with his arm around a woman I haven't met yet. This . . . this is Sheridan, Chloe's sister. I don't know who the teenage girl with her is, but she kind of looks like Chloe, doesn't she?"

I'd stopped listening. I found what I wanted to see. "Not necessarily absolute, huh?"

"Not necessarily. No. But you're here, Julia. With Scot and a son, just like Grandma said. He looks to be about three, wouldn't you say? It's so hard to tell." Alice's finger ran across the page to the other side. "My parents are over here, and

Mom is holding another baby. Maybe mine and Ethan's. Maybe yours and Scot's. I don't know. But you're here." She laughed. "And so are a whole lot of children. I can't wait to meet them all."

"I don't see Verda," I said softly. "She's not here."

"No, she isn't." Alice's voice caught. "But this is what? At least four years from now, maybe five. I guess it isn't a surprise, but I would've liked to see her here. We look happy, though. All of us."

"Yeah, we do." Ridiculously happy, even. "Thank you for sharing this with me." Tears clouded my vision. I sat up straight and turned my head, away from Alice. "Can I keep this? Even if only to make a copy?"

That way, if I'd already changed this future, if this day was now out of my reach, I'd have a visual reminder of what could have been.

"Of course you can. I already have a copy. This one is for you." Alice's hand brushed across my shoulders. "I'm going to go inside now, before they all wonder what I'm doing out here. But in case you want to go in search of my brother, I wrote his address on the back. It's actually my old place, and before that, it was Grandma's. I wasn't sure if you'd been there or not."

I hadn't, but I didn't say so. Instead, I thanked her again. When she was out of the car, I drove up the road a bit before pulling over. So I could stare at Alice's sketch of me, my son, and—I had to assume—my husband.

I punched Scot's address into my GPS. I wanted this future, and I wasn't going to sit around and wait for it happen. After hearing me out, if Scot didn't want the same future, I'd deal with it. But damn me if I wasn't going to try.

Chapter Twenty

I found Scot's condo easily enough, but unfortunately he wasn't home. I had all of this pent-up energy building inside, and the thought of leaving without seeing him, without talking to him, seemed impossible.

So I didn't leave. Instead, I sat in my car and waited. I stared at Alice's drawing for a while and then stared at Scot's door for a while. I did this repeatedly, my emotions fluctuating from happiness and hope to the crazy need to do something. Anything.

I picked up my cell phone and considered my options. I could call him, tell him I was here, that we needed to talk, and that I'd wait until he got home. But that felt a little stalkerish. I was also afraid that given the option, he'd find a reason not to see me. So, no. I'd wait for a while longer. If he didn't show, I'd visit again. He had to return home at some point.

Another hour passed without any sign of Scot, and I was beginning to draw furtive glances from the woman who lived next door. Probably it was best to leave before the police arrived.

With nowhere else to go, I headed for home. I told myself the entire way that everything would work out fine. That trusting my heart meant all good things. That Scot and I would realize the future Alice's magic had shown her. But I'd be lying if I said I wasn't worried. As far as I knew, at this very second, Scot and Leslie were talking about their future. I wasn't being overdramatic, either. I was being realistic. My action—my wish for Leslie and Scot—might have been enough to change the fates of us all.

Sadness struck. I let the possibility sink in for just a minute. Any longer would have been too much to bear. If such a thing happened, I'd wish them well and go about seeking whatever else the universe had in store. I didn't regret anything. I couldn't. Without Verda, I might never have seen the love my parents shared. I might never have experienced that type of love for myself. I might never have understood. And that made everything—no matter the outcome—worthwhile.

"No regrets," I whispered as I parked my car. "No matter what. No regrets."

I stopped outside of my apartment and looked at Kara and Leslie's door. I hadn't seen or talked with Leslie since the horrible conversation we'd had in her bedroom, mostly because I'd been caught between fear of what she might say about Scot and worry that I'd lost a friend. I missed her. I also owed her an apology.

Rather than letting myself in, I knocked. You know, just in case she was curled up with Scot. Or, um, doing other things. That was something I most definitely did not need to walk in on.

Less than a minute later, the door opened. Leslie's eyes were red. From crying or lack of sleep, I couldn't tell.

"Hey, Les. Are you okay?"

She sneezed, and her gaze darted across the hall to my apartment. "What are you doing here, Julia?"

Ah. She had a cold. "I miss you," I said, hoping that being simple and direct would put us on the right path. "And I wanted to tell you how sorry I am. You didn't deserve to see . . . well, what you saw."

Something unknown glittered in the tawny depths of her

eyes. Anger? I didn't think so. Worry? Maybe. She sighed. "I'm sorry, too. I was a bitch. And our friendship is important to me. I . . . Did you just get home?"

"Yeah. Can I come in?" She hesitated for a millisecond but stepped to the side so I could pass. "Is Kara here? I haven't seen her around the past few days."

Leslie shuffled to the couch and pulled her blanket up and around her. A box of tissues sat on the end table, along with a gigantic bottle of water and a bag of throat lozenges. She grabbed a tissue and blew her nose before answering. "Kara's hardly ever here. She's with Brett all of the time."

I took the chair across from her. "So that's going well?"

"Exceedingly well. I bet they'll be living together within the year."

Wow. Good for Kara. Somehow, I wasn't surprised. "Is he a pomegranate?"

Leslie grinned. "No clue. But he's nice and he treats her well." She gave me a long, searching look. "Scot's a pomegranate."

I blinked. Okay, ready or not, we were having this conversation. "Yes. I think so, anyway. He's . . . um . . . pretty incredible."

Leslie unwrapped a throat lozenge and popped it in her mouth. She offered me one, but I shook my head. Today I wasn't pretending to have a cold.

"I screwed up," she said, her gaze sliding to the side of me. "I . . . I did something I'm not proud of, and—"

"Are you talking about your one-night stand?" I interjected. "Because if so, that's . . . well, it isn't my business."

"No, that's not what I'm talking about. Yes, that was a huge screwup. Classic Leslie, right?" She twisted the lozenge wrapper in her fingers. She released a slow breath. "He liked you first, Julia."

"Wh-what?" I heard her but didn't understand.

Now she lifted her chin so our eyes could meet. "Scot. He liked you first. I never told you that. But . . . um . . . Scot thought you knew."

I reminded myself to take in air. Then I reminded myself to stay calm. "Explain. I'm . . . You've lost me. I didn't even meet Scot until you introduced us. So how could he have liked me first?"

She answered my question with one of her own. "How did *I* meet Scot?"

"He said he sent a drink to your table."

"Yes. But the drink was for you, not me," Leslie said. "We were all at O'Halloran's together. You, Kara, and me. You left before us. Scot sent the drink to you, but you'd already left by the time the waiter brought it over. I took the drink to Scot, told him you said thanks but no thanks, and we started talking." The admission poured out of her, as if she were afraid that if she didn't come clean fast, she wouldn't at all. "So you see, Julia, I wasn't *that* surprised to see you two kiss."

Oh. Oh, wow. Men *never* bought me drinks. Well, men who weren't clouded by an enchantment. But Scot had? Without a spell. "Why didn't you tell me?"

She swallowed heavily. "It was wrong. But I really liked him. And you didn't seem interested in dating at all. So I figured it wouldn't matter to you."

So many pieces clicked into place. *This* is what Scot wanted me to know, what he'd tried to share with me in Las Vegas. And oh, God. He thought I'd rebuffed him. But I hadn't. Would I have? I didn't know, but I'd have liked the opportunity to find out.

Something else came to me. "Did you purposely tell him things about me that you knew he wouldn't like?"

"Not on purpose, no. But Kara's right. I lied to him about me." Leslie angled her arms over her chest. "Scot and I only worked because I lied. He . . . he's not right for me. I don't know why I fixated on him so hard."

"I see. When did you figure this out, Leslie?"

"I don't know. Over the weekend, I guess. I felt horrible about what I said to you. And Kara and I had a long heart-to-heart, and that cleared things up more," Leslie said. "Scot and I talked, too. You should know that."

"When?" I demanded. "When did you guys talk?"

"Today. This morning, actually. We're on the same page, in case you're wondering." She blinked several times. "So . . . um . . . how angry are you?"

"I'm not angry that you and Scot talked. As to the rest . . . I haven't decided yet." Wait. Maybe I had. "That was a really crappy thing to do, Leslie. We're *friends*. I've been walking around with all of this guilt inside because of how I feel for Scot. I tried to ignore my feelings out of respect for you." Um. Well. "That didn't work so well, though," I admitted in a rush.

"Be angry. You have the right. But eventually, I hope you'll forgive me."

I sighed in frustration. "Of course I will. We both made mistakes." Then what she said hit me. "Wait . . . you said both of you are on the same page? Meaning . . ."

"Well, I should say I'm finally on his page." Her face split into a wide smile as she realized my confusion. "The *friendship* page, Julia."

"Oh. Okay. Well, that's really great news. I have to go." I stood. "We'll talk more about this later, but we're still friends. No, Leslie. We're family."

My hand was on the doorknob when she said, "Where are you going?"

"To Scot's. I hope he's home by now."

"Uh-uh. He isn't," she said quickly. "He, uh, told me had a ton of errands to run. He didn't expect to be home until later tonight. So going there now is a waste of time. Go home, Julia. Try him tomorrow."

Ugh. Well, hell. I'd waited this long, what were a few more hours? "I could stay here with you. Maybe watch a movie?"

"I'm going to sleep." In a firm voice, she said, "Go home."

"All right. I hope you feel better. And . . . when you're ready to date again, let me know. There's someone I'd like you to meet." Yes, I still thought Jameson and Leslie might be good together.

This perked her up. "Really? Tell me more."

"He's an attorney, Les. His name is Jameson Parkington, and he's a really great guy." I told her about him, hitting on every one of her five qualifications. The longer I spoke, the less ill she appeared. I finished by sharing the story of how he almost put one over on me with his Harold Johnson prank.

"He likes practical jokes, huh?" I saw the wheels turning in her head. "Feel like getting a little revenge?" she asked.

"What do you have in mind?"

"Maybe I could . . . ah . . . dress rather provocatively and knock on his door one night." Leslie winked. "Tell him that I'm a friend of an associate who is aware of his propensity for household objects and sent me over as a gift."

I laughed in a mixture of shock and delight. "And then, at the right moment, you could drop Harold's name. Is that what you're thinking?"

A mischievous smile curved Leslie's lips. "With your permission. It might be fun, and you definitely have to get him back. Besides, I owe you."

I gave it another three seconds of thought and nodded. "I'll get his address from my folks and pass it along. I can probably even find out his schedule, so you can plan it out better." I laughed again. "God, I'd love to see the look on his face when you show up."

Leslie yawned, but the twinkle in her eyes remained. "We'll go over all the details later. But right now . . ." She nodded toward the door.

"Yeah, yeah, I know. You need to sleep." I gave her a little wave and let myself out.

Leslie, Jameson, and the upcoming practical joke disappeared from my mind the second I entered my apartment. Anxiety pooled in my gut. How in the hell was I going to get through the next several hours? I wanted to talk to Scot now. Not later. I took off my coat and deposited it, along with my purse, on the dining-room table. My stomach grumbled with hunger, which was sort of a shocker. How could I be hungry at a time like this? But I was, so I went to the kitchen . . . where I stopped. Every muscle in my body froze. My jaw dropped open. A million little shivers cascaded over me.

"H-How?"

"Hey, beautiful," Scot said in his low, husky voice. He was in the kitchen. *My* kitchen. "Leslie let me in. I hope you don't mind."

"I don't. Mind, that is." Okay, now that he was here with me, my tongue refused to function properly. And wow, he looked so good. Tall, strong, handsome. Too good to be real. Like an oasis in the middle of a desert. "You're not a mirage, are you?"

"I am definitely not a mirage." Three steps carried him to me. He brought his hands to my face, one on either side, and brushed his thumbs beneath my eyes. A ragged-sounding sigh pushed from his lungs. "You look bruised here. Did I do this to you?"

"I haven't slept well." My body swayed from his touch, from the reality of his presence. All the words I wanted—needed—to say gathered on my tongue, but voicing them seemed impossible. He might stop touching me if I did. Instead, I said, "I'm surprised you're here."

"Good surprised or bad?" he asked.

"Depends on why you're here."

"That depends on if you'll forgive me." His fingers spread into my hair. Warmth suffused my body inch by delicious inch.

"I probably will," I assured him. "But you hurt me."

"I know." And in those two tiny words, I heard his pain at causing mine. "But I was trying to protect you. I thought—"

"I know. Part of it, anyway." I cupped his cheek with my hand. "I paid a visit to Alice today. Well, not just her. Verda, Elizabeth, and Chloe were there, too."

The muscle in his cheek flinched against my palm. "They promised to stay out of this."

"Oh, they were very careful in keeping their promises. I had to guess most of what I know. But Scot, those brownies didn't do anything to me. I hadn't even eaten one until after we got home from the airport." I breathed in his scent, and somehow, that gave me courage. "I dabbled a bit in magic, myself." In as concise a manner as I could, I explained about the journal, the wishes I'd cast, and how I'd worried that his desire for me had been because of a spell. "I hope that's not true, but you need to know it's possible."

He stared at me, into my soul, with his rich, dark chocolate eyes. I tried to read the emotions I saw there, tried to discern his expression, but both escaped me.

"No, Julia. I thought you were beautiful from the second I saw you."

Relief eased some of the suffocating pressure sitting on my chest. So far, so good. "Leslie told me how you two really met, so I hoped that was the case."

"I'm glad that came from her." A quick flash of humor darted over him. "So, my grandmother gave you a magical journal. That shouldn't surprise me, but it does. You know about Miranda and you know about the magic. What else?"

"Nothing, really." Okay, that wasn't completely true, but I wanted to hear the rest before showing him Alice's drawing. And it didn't feel right—in any way whatsoever—mentioning what Alice had said about Verda. "But I'd like to know all of it, Scot."

"That's why I'm here." He stepped away from me and dropped his hands, and I missed him immediately. "Come on. Let's sit down for this."

I didn't argue, just followed him to the living room. Once we were settled on the sofa, I said, "You're kind of scaring me here. Is this so bad, I have to be sitting to hear it?"

"Not bad." Scot's shoulders stiffened. "But I'm not sure how you'll react. Hell, I didn't react well when I first heard the story." He swore under his breath. "There isn't an easy way to say this, so I'm just going to say it. My grandmother believes that you are my soul mate. She also believes that you and I are going to have three sons."

"I know all of this, Scot."

"Supposedly, there are going to be more daughters born into the family."

I thought of the picture and nodded. "And Miranda's magic is a gift, passed from daughter to daughter. Not to the sons. Correct?"

"Yup." Scot ran his hand over his jaw. "But my grandmother is positive that the magic is growing and changing with each new generation. And she believes that the future women in our family will struggle with the power, and that some of them could lose their way."

"Okay . . ."

"She dreamed of a . . . well, a prophecy, I guess. For lack of a better word. And that prophecy showed her that our sons will create some type of a stabilizing balance for the magic. A grounding for the power." He swore again, shaking his head. "I'm not explaining this well. But this is why my grandmother has been so focused on finding my soul mate."

Okay. The right woman with Scot. Three sons who would somehow keep the growing magic in check. It was a lot to take in, but after the last couple of weeks, it was remarkably easy to go with the flow. "That's startling, I'll give you that. Do you believe this . . . uh . . . prophecy to be true?"

"If you'd asked me that question a couple of years ago, I could've said no. But that was before I learned about Miranda. That was before I'd seen what my sisters can do with their magic. And my grandmother is right far more often than she's wrong." Scot shrugged, but his tension came through loud and clear. "Yeah, I believe everything she has said about the prophecy."

"But why walk away from me?" That's the part I couldn't wrap my head around. I mean, Scot would do *anything* for his family. He protected his family. So if I were somehow the one woman he had to be with in order to protect his family, his actions were the opposite of what they should've been. Unless . . . oh, God. All of my hopes swirled down the drain. Tears flooded my eyes instantly. "You don't think I'm the right woman, do you? You care about me, but—"

"That's not it. I *know* you are that woman."

"Then I don't understand." I mentally went through

everything he'd said, every action he'd taken, again. Scot sat next to me, quiet and still. And then all at once, I got it. Oh, wow. Just freaking wow. Two plus two *can* equal five.

"You chose me. When you thought your family was using magic to coerce me to fall for you, even knowing what you know about this prophecy, you . . . you chose to walk away. To protect me over your family." God, what a horribly difficult decision that must have been.

"I love you. Of course I chose to protect you from a life that wasn't real."

"Then—" I had to swallow a sob. "What brought you here today? What changed your mind?"

"The same reason, Julia. I love you." He touched my chin, my cheek, my hair, and I melted. It was at once that simple and that complex. "I knew I'd hurt you, and that was unacceptable. I had to make sure you were okay. I also missed you. If there was any chance that your feelings were true, I had to find out."

"They are true, Scot. I know that without question. But you put me through hell," I whispered. Here it was: the beginning. Our beginning. "I love you, too. And if you ever try to make a decision for me again, I'll . . . I'll . . ."

"You'll what?"

"I don't know," I said through my tears. "But it won't be pretty."

"I'll keep that in mind." He wiped my tears away. "I will do everything in my power to never hurt you again. I promise."

"So, Scot, I have a question for you," I said, purposely lightening the moment. "Is this real, or is this still pretend?"

"This is real. No more pretend." His voice was soft, his eyes intense. "That work for you?"

"Uh-huh. But we better start thinking of names. I saw our eldest son today. He's quite the looker."

An eyebrow shot up in surprise, and Scot's lips quirked into a grin. "Alice?"

"Yeah. Remind me to show you the picture later." His arms came around me, tight, secure, and wow, it felt so right. So natural. "One more thing," I murmured. "I'm out of a job in a month, and could use a little help deciding what I'm going to do next."

"We'll figure it out. My advice is to follow your—"

"Heart," I said, just as his mouth met mine. The entire world dissolved into nothingness. I sank into the kiss, reveled in the heat and hunger that roared to life, in the way our bodies fit together so well. As if we were made for each other.

Up until now, I'd lived my life in a secure bubble of rules, rational thought, and practical decisions. I hadn't gone looking for this. I hadn't believed in the fairy tale. Fake magic had once pulled me away from a boy I had a crush on, but real magic had brought me to Scot . . . to love . . . to everything I needed. Everything I would *ever* need. I'd follow my heart wherever it might lead. And with Scot by my side, the journey would be nothing short of magical.

CPSIA information can be obtained at www.ICGtesting.com

259968BV00001B/2/P